PENGUIN BOOKS

MARTHA PEAKE

Patrick McGrath was born in London. He has lived in various parts of North America and spent several years on a remote island in the north Pacific. He moved to New York City in 1981. He is the author of *Blood and Water and Other Tales, The Grotesque, Spider, Dr Haggard's Disease* and *Asylum*, all of which are available in Penguin. He lives with his wife, Maria Aitken, in New York and London.

Martha Peake

A Novel of the Revolution

PATRICK McGRATH

PENGUIN BOOKS

PENGUIN BOOKS

Published by the Penguin Group
Penguin Books Ltd, 27 Wrights Lane, London w8 5tz, England
Penguin Putnam Inc., 375 Hudson Street, New York, New York 10014, USA
Penguin Books Australia Ltd, Ringwood, Victoria, Australia
Penguin Books Canada Ltd, 10 Alcorn Avenue, Toronto, Ontario, Canada m4v 3b2
Penguin Books India (P) Ltd, 11 Community Centre, Panchsheel Park,
New Delhi – 110 017, India
Penguin Books (NZ) Ltd, Cnr Rosedale and Airborne Roads,
Albany, Auckland, New Zealand
Penguin Books (South Africa) (Pty) Ltd, 5 Watkins Street, Denver Ext 4,
Johannesburg 2094, South Africa

Penguin Books Ltd, Registered Offices: Harmondsworth, Middlesex, England

First published by Viking 2000
Published in Penguin Books 2001
1

Copyright © Patrick McGrath, 2000
All rights reserved

The moral right of the author has been asserted

Printed in England by Clays Ltd, St Ives plc

For Maria

Contents

CROOKED TIMBER

In the beginning, all the world was America.

JOHN LOCKE

I

It is a black art, the writing of a history, is it not? – to resurrect the dead, and animate their bones, as historians do? I think historians must be melancholy creatures, rather like poets, perhaps, or doctors; but then, what does it matter what I think? This is not my story. This is the story of a father and his daughter, and of the strange and terrible events that tore them apart, so it is to those two unhappy souls that I would direct your gaze. As for me, I shall soon sink from sight, and you will forget me altogether. No, I am merely the one who *happened upon* the story, as you might happen upon, say, a cache of letters in the attic of an ancient uncle's country house; and blowing away the dust of decades, and untying the ribbon that binds them, finding within those crumbling pages a tale of passion so tragic, yet so sublime – as to transform, in that instant, the doddering relict in the bath-chair below to a spirited youth with a fiery heart and the blood of a hero racing in his veins!

Now in those days, as it happens, I did indeed have an ancient uncle, and for some time I had been aware that his health was failing; and being his only surviving relation, I had speculated that his property would come to me when he passed on. The old man had been living a life of seclusion ever since the death of his benefactor, the great anatomist Lord Drogo, so when I received his letter, asking me to come to him at once, I wasted no time. I need not describe to you the journey I took across the Lambeth Marsh, nor the house itself, for both Drogo Hall and its drear landscape will emerge strongly in what follows. Suffice to say that I rode across the marsh alone, and carried a loaded pistol with me; and upon arriving at dusk, I was admitted by a little bent man called Percy, who took me up the great staircase to my uncle's study and then vanished without a word.

I found the old doctor seated close to a blazing coal fire in a small gloomy room with a heavy Turkey carpet on the floor and thick dark curtains on the windows. He had a blanket on his knees, a tome in his lap, and a jorum of Hollands-and-water close to hand. As he turned toward the door I saw at once that he could not be long for this world, so frail did he appear, his skin in the firelight as white and brittle as paper. But on recognizing me a light came up in those dim and milky eyes, he fixed me with a gimlet stare and cried to me to come in – come in, for the love of God! – for the draught was a chill one; and he pointed with a trembling finger to the aged leather armchair on the other side of the fireplace.

But still I stood there in the open door, rooted to the spot. I was transfixed by the painting hanging over the mantelpiece. I had never seen it before. It was the portrait of a robust, broad-shouldered man of between thirty and forty years. He stood against a wild moorland scene, a pine flattening in the gale on the brow of a distant hill, and rags of black cloud flying across the sky. He wore neither hat nor wig, and his long hair was tied at the back with a blue ribbon, a few strands torn free by the wind. His shirt was open at the throat, his skin was pale, and his eyes were like great dark pools, full of life and full of pain but hooded, somehow, lost in shadow as they gazed off into some unknown horizon. It was not a handsome face, it was carved too rough for that, but it was a strong, complicated face, hatched and knotted with sorrow and passion, a big stubborn chin uplifted – the whole head uplifted! – lips unsmiling and slightly parted, and the expression one of defiance, yes, and purpose. I felt at once that the artist, for all that he had caught some fleeting expression of this fierce, romantic spirit, could not have done him justice, nobody could have done justice to this man. My uncle William nodded at me with a pursed smile as I closed the door behind me and moved to the chair by the fire, my gaze still fixed on the painting, and slowly sat down.

'You know who he is, eh?'
'No, sir,' I said, 'I do not.'
'No? Then shall I tell you?'
It was Harry Peake.

*

4

The name clawed at the skirts of memory as I sat down by the fire and warmed my jaded heart on the image of that proud rough man. America – for some reason as I gazed at him I thought of America – I thought of the Revolutionary War, and of all that I had learned of that great conflict from my mother, herself an American who pined in exile for her country every day of my childhood. An incident by the sea – a burning village filled with women and children – a red-haired girl with a musket at her shoulder – these ideas tentatively emerged from out of the mind's mist, but all else remained shrouded and obscure. I found myself sitting forward in my chair and staring into the fire as I tried to remember. At last I looked up, and told my uncle I saw a village in flames somewhere on the coast of North America, but no more than that. For some moments there was little sound in the room but the hiss of the coal in the hearth, and the wind rising in the trees outside.

'Come, Ambrose, sit closer to the fire,' he murmured at last, turning away from me, seizing up the bottle of Hollands at his elbow. 'Here, fill your glass. You shall hear it all. I have held it in my heart too long. It has blighted me. I am withered by it. He never got to America. God knows he wanted to.'

My uncle put his fingertips together beneath his chin and closed his eyes. Silence.

'Many a man,' I murmured, 'has never got to America.'

A sort of sigh, at this, and then silence again. I waited. When next he spoke it was with a clipped asperity that belied the desperate pathos of what he told me. To know Harry Peake, he said, you must first know what he suffered. Then you will understand why he fell. Why he turned into a monster.

'A monster –!'

' "Even brutes do not devour their young, nor savages make war upon their families" – eh?'

He was quoting an author, but I missed the allusion.

'He devoured his young –?'

Then I had it. Tom Paine.

'Lost his mind. What a waste. What a mind.'

'But who was he?'

Here my uncle turned to me, and again fixed me with that gimlet eye. 'One of those cursed few,' he said, 'to whom Nature in her folly gave the soul of a smuggler, and the tongue of a poet.'

And so it began. Much of the detail I have had to supply from my own imagination, that is, from the ardent sympathetic understanding of the tragic events my uncle William described. His recall was patchy, for time had worn his memory through as though it were an old coat. The seams had split open, there were fragments of alien fabric, rudely stitched, and everywhere the pattern was obscured by foreign substances, such as those that were liberally splattered about the papers I later received from him, blood, soil, gin, etc. So I was forced to expand upon the materials he gave me. But when it was over I felt that I *understood*, I understood the extraordinary life not only of Harry Peake, but of his daughter also, of Martha Peake, who died at the hands of her own countrymen, and who, by her sacrifice, helped to create the republic to which my mother swore allegiance, and whose spirit I have come to love.

Later that evening the wind came up, it started to rain, and I was glad indeed of the shelter of Drogo Hall, for I had no desire to be out on the Lambeth Marsh in such conditions. We supped in the grand dining room downstairs, and a strange meal it was, the two of us up at the end of the table, a single branch of candles to light us, the wind howling about the house and that peculiar little man Percy, now wearing a ratty scratch wig, presumably on account of the formality of the occasion, serving us with silent swiftness, appearing suddenly out of the darkness with tureen or decanter and just as suddenly vanishing again. From the high, dark-panelled walls of the dining room the portraits of the earls of Drogo of centuries past peered down at us through the gloom, and our conversation seemed at times to struggle forward as though burdened by the span of years that separated us from the events of which we spoke, indeed that separates me now from that dismal stormy night so long ago.

My uncle sat in the great chair at the head of the table, a tiny slumped figure against the vast gloom behind him, and picked at his food with sharp little jabs like a bird. We ate cold mutton and boiled potatoes. He had frequent recourse to the decanter, which was filled with a sweet Rhenish wine, and with every glass his speech grew more fluting, more rapid, and more inflected with the fancies of a failing mind, such that I had constantly to steer him away from the wild places where he seemed inclined to wander, and back to the track of his narrative. And all the while the silent Percy flickered in and out of the candlelight like a moth, again and again refilling my uncle's tall crystal goblet with that undrinkable sweet white wine.

Oh, we talked on long after the last dish had been removed, and the candles had burned down to guttering stubs, and still the wind could be heard out on the marsh, and the boughs of the trees slapped against the high windows of the house. Later I made my way upstairs with a candle, to a cold room with a damp bed where I lay sleepless for many hours as the storm exhausted itself and I attempted to digest not only my uncle's mutton but his story as well.

2

We know only a little, said William, of the circumstances of Harry Peake's early life, but that little is enough, certainly, to point the way forward. It all began in the west of England, in Port Jethro, a remote fishing village on the north coast of Cornwall, where sometime in the 1730s Harry was born the bastard child of a wild and lonely woman called Maggie Peake. This poor ragged soul lived on the seashore near the harbour, in a shack built of fishing net and ship's planking. She scraped a living cutting seaweed on the beaches thereabouts, which she sold for a few pence the cartload to a farmer inland, to spread on his fields. Maggie Peake, in her pitiful dwelling, reared her child with a fierce protective devotion, and Harry grew into a robust and healthy boy. Hearing this, I remarked to my uncle that it did not surprise me, for there is often more love to be had in a hovel than a palace.

Quite so, he said shortly, eager, clearly, to get on; I think it was not a truth he cared to dwell upon.

By the age of five young Harry was often to be seen out on the beach with his mother, in the early morning when the tide was low, the pair of them barefoot, bent over their work with rake and pitchfork, filling their baskets with good fresh stinking seaweed swept in on the tide overnight. They emptied their baskets into a rickety cart harnessed to a donkey. Later they set off along the beach, and what a picturesque spectacle they made, I imagined, on that vast stretch of damp sand, beneath the high cliffs, the little boy and his workworn mother walking beside their old cart, which groaned with its load of shining seawrack, the gulls all flapping and screaming about them –!

At the age of seven Harry was put to work on the boats, and their lives at once changed for the better. I should have liked to tell you, said my uncle – and here he cast upon me a long lugubrious gaze, the meaning of which escaped me – that even at this tender age the poetry rose in Harry like a clear fresh spring, and that he could no more hold back the flood of it than he could stop the beating of his heart – but alas, he murmured, it was not so. No, he showed no marks of genius, young Harry, he was distinguished, if by anything, only by his wickedness.

Wickedness! – what kind of wickedness?

But it was merely the wickedness of a boy. Harry was a scoundrel, said my uncle, he was a thief and a liar, he recognized no authority, and he would fight with anyone in the village who crossed him, or tried to block him, for he was a wilful child who was accustomed to getting his own way. Hardly remarkable, said my uncle, given that his mother was a whore and a drunkard, and probably mad. Here he sniffed, and I detected in that sniff of his a moral opprobrium, which was distasteful to me, and I would have challenged him had I not been avid to hear more. So I asked him to go on, and he told me that Harry was soon popular on the boats, for he was strong, he was a natural sailor, he understood the fishing, and he amused the men.

How did he amuse the men?

He told them the stories his mother told him, said William, for Maggie Peake had a great trove of old tales and legends which she passed on to Harry by the fire on the long winter evenings. Ah, but Harry told his mother's stories with embellishments all his own, and wove into them the boats and men he knew in Port Jethro, the cliffs and coves thereabouts, the fish and the birds and the changing seasons, and it amused them to recognize their own world in his stories. How Harry acquired such powers of invention nobody knew, but in later years, when he recited, say, a passage of his 'Ballad of Joseph Tresilian', he could seize the imagination of an entire London pot-house, hold a company of seventy or eighty men and women in a rapt silence, not a cough to be heard, nor the scrape of a chair-leg, for many minutes together, until he had finished; whereupon the whole house would erupt with a great shout of applause –

But all that, said my uncle, was still many years in the future. So there we have him, he said, a tall strong boy with a shock of wild black hair, always panting from his exertions, his eyes afire, his spirit hungry for life, and he could have gone any way, any way at all. Oh, he could have had his own boat in a year or two, had he wanted it, or he could have lit out for London, as he sometimes talked of doing – or he could have gone to the bad. And after his mother died – he would have been twelve years old then, and he had loved old Maggie Peake, loved her despite her drinking, and all the fishermen she brought back to that squalid hovel – after she died it looked as though he would go to the bad. One night at around that time a sinister incident occurred in Padstow, an affray in a yard behind a tavern that left one man badly injured and another blind in one eye. A small sum of money was stolen, not so small however that the thief would not have gone to the gallows for it; and although nothing came of it, it was rumoured darkly that Harry Peake had been involved.

Curious, I murmured, and his mother just gone, but my uncle was not listening. His eyes were closed, his mind was already far away. A minute passed, and then another –

But then the boy was saved!

All at once the old man came to life once more, and spoke now with some animation. It seemed that Harry was to have a guardian, for the vicar of the parish, the Reverend Edward Penwarden, a cleric and scholar, a man of good sense and few illusions about the character of his congregation, had long recognized that here was a boy of singular intelligence, and he chose this moment, just when Harry looked set to ruin himself, to intervene. He brought him up to the vicarage and gave him a room in the house. He set about teaching him to read and write, and opened his library to the boy; and soon, said my uncle, whenever the weather prevented the boats going out, Harry was to be found poring over an old volume of Milton, or a traveller's journal, or some such, in the vicar's library; and within a few months he was much altered. So it was, that as the last years of Harry's childhood passed, and he stayed safe under the wing of his new friend and protector, his imagination ripened, and began to stray from the wild north Cornish coast into regions of the earth he had encountered only in books.

*

By the age of seventeen Harry had yet to cross the Tamar, and to the idle glance of the stranger he would have seemed no more than a big handsome strapping lad who smelled of the harbour and the alehouse, a boisterous, good-natured boy with a tough body and a strong will and a quick eager mind. But to those who knew him – and by this, said my uncle, turning toward me, I mean the few educated men in those parts – he was an unusual, even an exceptional youth, whom some believed to be destined for great things.

I interrupted him at this point. For several minutes I had been aware of his growing warmth as he spoke of the young Harry Peake, that warmth now rising to a pitch almost of rhapsody as he described Harry's attainments and possibilities. I had no wish to puncture the old man's enthusiasm, but as yet I did not altogether share it, and so I asked him, how had he learned of the precocious talents of this barely literate Cornish fisherman?

I need not have worried that I would deflate him. His mood shifted like quicksilver. Gone, the warbling fustian, again he turned to me, this time with eyes that glinted coldly in the candlelight, and asked me briskly, did I doubt it?

I lifted my hands and said nothing.

Very well then, he said, I ask you to imagine this –

But I imagined nothing, for at that moment Percy entered the room to refill our glasses and poke the fire into fresh life, and to report to my uncle on the severity of the rainstorm now howling about the house, and the status of various leaks in various of the upper rooms. When he had left us I discovered that my uncle's mood had changed once more, and that he wore now an expression of some despondency. I begged him to continue. Another sigh, and after a moment or two he resumed, and told me that despite his wild ways – or perhaps, he said, because of them – Harry Peake won the heart of a fine young woman from a remote farm on the Bodmin Moor. Her name was Grace Foy, and after a brief tempestuous courtship they were married. Harry was then eighteen years old, Grace a year younger.

Grace brought with her a small dowry, and that, along with the money Harry had saved from his work on the boats, and his other endeavours – a glance here from my uncle, did I take his meaning? – they acquired a house made of stone with a steep slate-hung roof halfway up the hill behind the harbour. They moved in at once, and six months later Grace bore Harry a daughter. They called her Martha. About Martha Peake, said my uncle, we know a great deal, but about her mother much less, beyond that she came from a family of sisters, that she was a tall proud laughing woman with broad shoulders and a loud voice, that she had a head of flaming red hair, and that her temper was as fierce as Harry's own. With two such passionate natures, said my uncle, peering at me now like an owl, it will not surprise you to learn that their marriage was a turbulent one.

Some sad nodding here.

The sad nodding was followed by head shaking, glances were cast at the painting over the fireplace, and a deep frown appeared in the parchment skin of my uncle's forehead. Ah, but there was a flaw in Harry's nature, he said, it had announced itself during his childhood, and then more dramatically when his mother died. Perhaps it arose in reaction to the teeming energies of his imagination, perhaps the seeds of madness were already in him at birth, passed on by Maggie Peake; we will never know. But as he entered upon his manhood a sort of fevered restlessness was observed in him, a wildness in his words and actions that had not been there before, and at such times it seemed to those who knew him that his very spirit was on fire. By this time he owned a pair of horses, and would spend his days galloping along the cliffs, so close to the edge that his life was despaired of; or he drank himself into oblivion, after talking in the Admiral Byng for hours to anyone who would listen to him; or he stripped his clothes off and flung himself into a heavy sea, for the sheer pleasure of getting out safe again.

But after some days of this there would come a sudden precipitous collapse into the blackest melancholy, and for a period he would be morose, silent, smouldering, dangerous. Harry's dirty weather, they called it in Port Jethro, and it was first evident, said my uncle, his tone low and rapid now, and inflected with the darkness that permeated the matter of his narrative, to his companions in the Admiral Byng during a severe winter when the gales howled about the village day and night, and great seas dashed themselves against the cliffs, and no boat went out for weeks on end. There were many nights, that winter, when Harry showed more interest in his drink than he did in the sport of his roistering friends, and it became apparent that he was drinking harder than the others, that he did not want to go home when the landlord called time, and that his mood darkened the more he drank. He lost his temper one night and flung himself on a man who he believed had insulted him, and the two were only with difficulty separated. There were other fights that winter, and there were nights when Harry sat off by himself, staring into the fire, sullen and muttering, brooding on matters he would speak of to nobody. It was said that he often quarrelled with his wife, and that he was not settling well to the responsibilities of marriage and fatherhood, indeed voices raised in anger were heard that winter from the slate-roofed house up behind the harbour, where Grace had given him another child, a son called Jonathan.

Come the spring, and the return of warmer weather, and longer hours of daylight, Harry's spirits lifted and he was something like his old self again. But a certain gladness, a certain lightness of spirit had gone from him for ever, and he now showed signs in his face of anxiety, of conflict, and pain. Often he drank to excess, and his friends left him to himself at such times. He would sit in the shadows at the back of the inn, and the drink gave him no release from his demons, whoever or whatever they were.

Seven years passed, and Grace Foy bore Harry three more children. His temper improved, and in time he came to believe that he had shaken it off, the black mood that had dogged his spirit through that terrible winter. He prospered, bought his own boat, and came in time to be regarded as one of the first men of Port Jethro. For Grace and her children these were happy years, and there were times in Martha's early life that she would never forget. Often she went out with her father on his boat, Harry being that unusual creature, a fisherman who took pleasure in sailing, and the stronger the wind the better he liked it.

He took her up on his horse with him, when he had business in Bodmin, and together they galloped across the moor, the big laughing man and the little girl gripped between his knees and hanging on to the saddle for dear life – her face to the wind like her father's, and no more fear in her than he had in him. They tramped the cliffs together, and told endless stories, each one wilder than the one before. Harry loved his wife with a strong and jealous intensity, and if they fought and stormed it was because their passions were at root the passions of attachment; but he loved his Martha no less passionately, for she took after her mother, she had her bones, she had her spirit, she had her flaming red hair.

Then late one night, said my uncle – and here his narration grew dramatic indeed, up came his hand, his fingers seeming to mould the figure of the poet in the glow of the fire – late one night Harry came home from a landing – a ship from the West Indies on her way up to Bristol – with a dozen casks of rum stowed in the back of his wagon –

Again I interrupted him, but even as I began to ask the question I glimpsed the answer, and my uncle paused to remind me that in those days there was not a man, not a *family* in Cornwall which was not involved in the free trade, and Harry Peake was no exception; indeed, said my uncle, Harry was the leader of a loose association of men who worked that stretch of the coast, which was known for its many sheltered bays and inlets, its caves, its hidden beaches, its myriad natural harbours where on a moonless night a small coasting vessel, or even a merchantman could offload hundreds of gallons of spirits – not to say tobacco, lace, glass, tea, silk, satin, and china – and every local man was ready to help bring the cargo ashore, to carry it up the shingle, to load it into carts and wagons, and see it safely cached inland, all before dawn.

But that night everything had gone wrong, they had been sur-prised by a cutter from the Excise, the landing had been abandoned in confusion, and Harry had been lucky to escape unobserved with his wagon. The night was dark, no moon at all, and he had come away up the track from the beach as though the very devil himself were after him, standing astride the buckboard and flailing with the whip, the terrified horses rearing and stumbling on the slope, but once on the high ground galloping wildly across the cliffs. Behind him, in a narrow shingled cove, a man lay dead, all the rest were scattered, and several hundred casks of rum and sugar were in the hands of the damned Excise.

He brought the wagon in off the road that ran down to the harbour, he wheeled the horses into the yard at the back of the house, he pulled them up to a clattering halt, and sweating and cursing he jumped down off the wagon and stamped in through his own back door and hauled up the trapdoor to his cellar. Down he went with a cask of liquor on his shoulder, breathing hard, the sweat still streaming down his face, and set it on the straw-covered stones of the cellar floor. He did not rest. One after another the casks were lifted from the wagon and hefted on to his shoulder, each one eight gallons of liquor, and stowed in the cellar. At last he was done, he let down the trapdoor, and he knelt on the floor, panting, to secure the bolts. Grace Foy, awoken by his noise, and with an infant in her arms, unlatched the kitchen door and found him there on the floor. Still kneeling, wiping his forehead, he told her that the Excise had disturbed them, the merchantman had had to cut her cables and make a run for it.

'We came away with nothing,' he shouted, careless of his sleeping children – 'Nothing!' – and in his rage, for he had been drinking earlier that night, he hammered his fist on the floorboards.

'Nothing at all?' murmured Grace. She was still half-asleep. She sat down on a chair and her head sank forward as she gave the infant her breast.

'Some bloody rum is all.'

'Where is it now?' Grace yawned.

'Here below,' said Harry.

That woke her up.

'You brought it here?' she cried, rising to her feet, as the infant began to wail. 'You brought it here? They will come here, Harry, what were you thinking of?'

Harry shoved home the last bolt but still he knelt there on the trapdoor, his hands flat on the floor, staring at the wooden boards. A single branch of candles sputtered and flared on the sideboard at the back wall. He muttered that he would move them in the morning, the Excise men were all over the countryside. He did not say there was a man dead on the beach.

'Why did you not leave it there?'

But Harry in his temper was careless of all risk. Nor did he have any patience for Grace's fears, he had seen how childbirth tamed a woman. He stamped out through the back door to look to the horses and she followed him out, a shawl about her shoulders and the infant screaming in her arms. She told him he must get the liquor out of the house, for if the Excise were about they would surely come looking for him in Port Jethro. She did not care where he put it but it must be moved.

'They have no search warrant,' he shouted.

'They will come in without it –'

'Over my dead body!'

'Over your dead body!'

Only Grace Foy attempted to tell Harry Peake what to do, and often she had her way. But not when he had drink in him, and he had a good deal of drink in him that night. Harry uncoupled the steaming horses from the wagon and ignored what his wife was saying to him.

An hour later, and still the rum was in the cellar. Grace had argued loudly with Harry for some minutes, until prudence dictated she keep quiet, but Harry was adamant, that if he moved the rum he would lose it, and he was damned if the night's work was to go for nothing. Grace had gone back to bed, Harry had taken the branch of candles into the cellar and breached one of the casks. He sat on the floor with his back to the wall, an elbow on his knee, his hand clamped to his head, in the other hand a cup of rum, and a pipe of tobacco between his teeth. But for all he drank he could not dispel his foreboding as to the consequences of the night's botched landing. His eyes closed, and with his head still in his hand he fell asleep. The pipe slipped out of his mouth and broke into pieces on the stones, spilling out burning tobacco. He did not awaken. A few moments later, said my uncle, the straw began to smoulder.

Silence as we contemplated Harry in his stupor, and the embers of his pipe catching on the dry straw.

When Harry became aware of the flames, whispered my uncle, they had spread across the floor, already they were licking at the walls! Harry rose to his feet and flung at the fire the contents of his cup, and the flames at once leapt up and caught on a basket of wool. In an instant the cellar was full of oily black smoke. He came charging up the stairs and pushed open the trapdoor, and the flames leaped up beneath him. He flung it shut behind him and began shouting, and Grace came running into the kitchen. A few seconds later she was outside the house with the infant in her arms and the other children clustered about her. Only Martha wanted to go down into the cellar and see the fire.

Outside in the night air Harry stumbled to the stable and let the horses out. He slapped them hard and they cantered off down toward the harbour. After that it all became confusing, and he could never be certain as to what happened next, though he remembered at one point picking up a barrel of rainwater at the back of the house, and staggering into the kitchen with it, and overturning it at the top of the cellar steps. There was a great hissing and sputtering as the water poured down the steps and spilled across the cellar floor below, but the smoke from the burning wool was so thick he could not see if the flames were doused, and back out he came, and set off up the hill to get help.

Grace and the children were meanwhile going down toward the harbour. Then all at once Grace was crying out for Jonathan, where was Jonathan? Lights began to show, people came out into the street, Grace was screaming for Jonathan now, and running this way and that with growing panic. Then all at once Harry saw her start back up the hill, and he shouted to her to stop. To no avail; he saw her go running into the house, and barely had he started back down the hill than there came a muffled explosion, and then another, and another, and all at once flames could be seen leaping and licking in the windows –

Harry reached the back door, in he plunged through the smoke and flames, his arms before his face – he saw Grace go darting through the burning house, her nightgown ablaze, crying for her lost child – he had almost reached her when another explosion rocked the house, another – he staggered backwards –

And then a ceiling beam fell, it swung down like a pendulum, with immense force it smashed into Harry's back and flung him hard on to the floor; then it hung there, over him, blackened and smoking.

For a second or two Harry lay still. Then he was coughing, gasping for air, struggling to rise, but he could not stand, so he crawled toward the door, crawled through the smoke and heat for what seemed an eternity, and then he was lying in the yard behind the house, and he could hear Grace screaming inside. Again he passed out, and this time, when he came to, said my uncle – here he paused – he could hear her screams no more.

3

It was late, I was tired, but I could not withdraw now. I begged my uncle to continue. It was with a sort of grim relish that he described how the falling beam had broken Harry's back in several places, and how very fortunate he was not to have been paralysed at once. I suppose I should not have been surprised at the morbid gusto with which the old man retailed all this. He had been a surgeon much of his life, and for years had worked closely with one of the most eminent anatomists of his time. The treatment for such a fracture, he said, his tone now briskly impersonal, and far removed from the histrionic excess of a moment before, was the same as it is today. Reduce the fracture by bringing the broken parts back to their normal position. Once the bone is set, hold it in place with a splint, having first bound the part with bandages, preferably linen. A splint to secure a damaged spine must enclose the patient's entire upper body, so it will be a boxlike engine, its pressure adjustable by a screw, and into this engine he must be strapped with stout canvas belts. Nature will do the rest.

So a box-splint was built for Harry, and for several months he lay in it on a long table in a room off the kitchen at the back of the Admiral Byng. I was appalled at the idea of Harry being screwed into such a machine of torture, and I said to the old man that surely the months he spent in that hideous box – coffin, more like, I cried! – must have been sheer and utter hell – what had he suffered, knowing that his wife and son were dead, and himself crippled?

Oh, his son was not dead, said the old man, with some surprise; he forgot that I did not know the story. Jonathan had run off down an alley, and did not emerge until the fire had been put out, and nothing was left of the Peake house but its walls of blackened Bodmin granite. I pondered this for some moments, and curiously it made it all seem so much worse, for it meant Grace Foy had died for nothing. Nor was this lost on Harry; and in some dark place in his soul, I believe, a seed of hatred of his son was sowed that tragic night. His own guilt was profound, and he went to terrible lengths to expiate it, but Jonathan's survival was to mark him for ever in his father's heart. At the time of the fire the boy was seven years old.

None of this would come out for many years. In the aftermath of the fire Harry was entirely absorbed in his own suffering. His spirit was as badly damaged as his body, perhaps more so. He now had ample opportunity to reflect on his life and what it had brought him to, and he reached certain conclusions. He recognized that the shame of Grace's death would not leave him for the rest of his days, and he realized, too, that he could no longer stay on this wild coast where they had been happy, for he would forever hear her voice in the wind as he tramped over the cliffs, he would glimpse her face in the sunlight on the sea.

When they unbuckled the straps and released him from the box-splint, and helped him off the table and up on to his feet, Harry Peake could barely lift his head above his chest; he could barely *breathe*! His hair and beard had grown long while he lay there, and he seemed a wild man now, a large bent hairy creature with furious burning eyes. There he stood, said my uncle, in no little pain, snorting loudly, and supported by several of his neighbours, as the doctor examined the damaged spine then asked him to straighten himself up. Every inch cost him infinite torment. Every inch, and the cracking of his spine rang out like gunshots in the back of the silent inn. The sweat poured off him and he cried out so loudly that all Port Jethro heard him, but when they offered him brandy he would not take it. After an hour he had regained as much of his old stature as the doctor believed he ever would.

He was not the man he had been before the fire. His backbone was found to have mended crooked, steeply ridged at each of the several points of breakage, and skewed from the true – bent, in a word – the effect of this being to disturb his gait and to throw his shoulders oddly athwart. He could walk, albeit with a limp, but from any angle, and in any light, he carried now a large flared superstructure of bony matter on his back, and while this rendered him stooped and twisted, it seemed not to diminish his height but rather to exaggerate it, by making him monstrous.

For some weeks he hobbled about the village, and gradually regained the use of his broken body. He did not lift his head; he would meet no man's eye; he drank only a little water, ate but a crust or two a day, and spent much time in the chapel on his knees. He cut his beard off but not his hair, and on good days, in dry weather, he was able to straighten himself a further inch or two, though it cost him much painful effort to do so. His old friends and neighbours avoided him now, the man they had once loved, for he seemed to them and to himself an accursed being. Edward Penwarden came to see him, but Harry had no appetite for another man's religion, and he sent the vicar away. As for his children, after the fire they were taken by one of Grace's sisters to live with her family in Bodmin, where there was great grieving for the lost woman, the Foy sisters having gathered for the funeral, all but Maddy Foy, who some years before had gone to America to work in the household of a Massachusetts merchant called Silas Rind.

One day the children came over the moor in a coach to visit their father in Port Jethro. They were brought into the parlour of the Admiral Byng with their aunt, Mary Carter. A father they barely recognized, dressed in dusty black and leaning on a stick, sat humped on a wooden chair, and gazed at them unsmiling from wracked and harrowed features. His infant son began to whimper, little Jonathan stared at his father with barely concealed terror, the others clustered about their aunt's skirts, and only Martha showed no fear – showed no fear, cried my uncle, she ran to her father, she flung her arms about his neck, she kissed his sunken cheek; and the large strong hands of the smuggler lifted uncertainly, then clasped the child to his breast. Mary Carter seated herself opposite Harry, with the children huddled about her. Harry faced her square, gazed from his haunted eyes into the eyes of the woman whose sister had died because he had been drunk and careless in a cellar filled with spirits. Martha in her dark smock stood by her father and she too gazed squarely at Mary Carter.

The conversation was not easy; nor was it long. Harry agreed that his children should live with the Carter family in Bodmin, and said that he would establish credit for their board and lodging and all other expenses incurred on their behalf. His offer was at once accepted. That done, Mary Carter rose to her feet, bade Harry farewell, and called the children to her. Martha refused to go. She stood by her father and told her aunt that she would not live in Bodmin, and if she were taken back there she would escape as soon as she could and walk to Port Jethro across the moor.

There was, I imagine, a charged silence at this point in the interview, as Mary Carter and Harry Peake questioned one another with their eyes. And out of that silent conversation it emerged that Mary Carter was prepared to leave Martha with her father, if he was prepared to take her; and he was. The comfort he had found in his daughter's kiss – Oh, to a man dying of thirst in a desert of remorse, Martha's love was life itself! In that moment the thing was decided, and when some minutes later the coach rumbled out of the yard at the back of the Admiral Byng, Martha was not in it.

Came the day they left Port Jethro for ever. Only a few of Harry's old companions turned out to see them go. It was early in the morning, a light rain was falling, a mist coming in off the sea, and Harry sat humped in the back of a wagon with Martha beside him. She held her head high, even if he could not. Their few possessions were stowed in an old cabin trunk. Harry bade a silent farewell to the place where he had tasted happiness, only to have the cup dashed from his lips by his own wicked folly, and the wagon lurched off up the street. A minute later it passed the ruins of the burned house, and Harry turned his face aside.

4

And that is where I left them, that night. It was late, and all was quiet in Drogo Hall. I was flagging. More than once my eyes had closed, my head had fallen forward on to my chest, and my uncle had had to awaken me. I should have gone to bed hours before, but I confess that in my desire to hear the story I did not. So all this I had from him before I retired that night, though in a form far more sporadic, more fractured and patchy than the orderly account I have rendered here; and much of it formed the stuff of my dreams.

I awoke shivering early the next morning to find that the storm had blown itself out and the sky was clear; but it was arctic in that bedroom, which had not known a fire, I would guess, for decades, and what little warmth I had found beneath the dank blankets had long since dissipated. I struggled at once into my greatcoat and stamped out on to the landing and down the stairs, determined through the vigorous motion of my limbs to get my blood moving once more.

A strange few hours I had of it, wandering the deserted passages of Drogo Hall, and everywhere I felt there were ghosts present, the spirits of those who had been drawn into the influence of the house, and never escaped. Ghosts and secrets: I encountered locked corridors, sealed rooms, doors that opened on to walls. But I did not encounter Percy, nor any other living soul, although I was aware at times of movement within the house, of low voices murmuring in nearby passages, but whoever they were – my uncle's servants, I presumed, people from the village who worked in Drogo Hall – they kept apart from me. So I settled myself in my uncle's study with a volume of Scott and whiled away the daylight hours in pleasant dreams of antiquity.

My uncle did not emerge from his room until late in the afternoon, just as the light was beginning to thicken over the marsh, and we at once retired to his study, where we found a cheerful fire blazing in the hearth, and Percy on hand with the gin and the brandy. Again I gazed at the portrait of Harry Peake that hung over the fireplace. The fate of that flawed man, of whose existence I had been barely aware just twenty-four hours before, had aroused my most sympathetic concern, and I begged my uncle that he not delay, but resume his narrative at once.

He watched me with a thin smile in which I detected a distinct suggestion of scorn. He saw that he had me hooked, and it amused him. He put his fingertips together, in that familiar way of his, and upon them he lightly rested his chin. It is, he said, an extraordinary story – eh? This poet – this as yet unrealized genius – he lifted his fingers, waved vaguely at the painting – and this brave little daughter of his – eh? Clearly the old man did not intend to resume the story without a preamble of some sort, and so I asked him the question that had occurred to me when I reached my room the previous night. What had it all to do with Drogo Hall?

But on this he would not be drawn.

'You will hear everything, my dear,' he fluted, 'in its proper order.'

London! Or rather – London. They reached London some weeks later, and this, by my calculation, would be the late summer of 1767 or 1768. They came in on the Oxford Road, and after passing Tyburn Field – no doubt with many a shudder – they made for the river. I have a picture in my mind's eye of a big humped man picking his way through the narrow streets of the town, his old black coat dusty from the high road, and a cocked hat pulled low over his eyes. He is pushing a wheelbarrow in which a red-headed eight-year-old sits atop a battered cabin trunk, gazing about her in wonder at the sheer confusion of it all. An endless stream of carts and carriages and wagons, and so many people! Crowds of people, crowds upon crowds, all in motion, all with something to sell, arguing, shouting, weeping, singing. Begging, gambling, drinking, whoring. Men stripped to the waist, fighting bare-fisted for the amusement of the crowd. Bonfires burning in the streets, effigies strung up on inn-signs, animals everywhere, pigs, dogs, monkeys, sheep, everywhere poverty, vice, squalor, corruption – oh, I am filled with horror at the very thought of London in those days – the place is bad enough now, but by God it was worse then, and these two, fresh from the distant shores of Cornwall, had never seen anything like it.

As they got closer to the river the streets through which they passed became no better than open sewers, running with filth of all horrid varieties. No fresh breeze of air penetrated those wretched courts and alleys, where the great part of the people were crowded together in dark dilapidated tenements under a poisonous haze of sea-coal fumes, and sickness everywhere flourished like the weeds of the graveyard. Typhus. Rickets. Scurvy. Syphilis. Various fevers, scarlet, bilious and putrid. Smallpox, confluent and otherwise. Gin lunacy. Dropsy. Gout and gravel. Asthenic defluctions. Palsy, cholera, the plague. Harry must have thought he had arrived in a suburb of Hell.

But then Hell was where he wanted to be. My uncle confessed he did not know much about those early days in the capital, but we may imagine they were grim. Harry had brought away with him a little money only, they had no friends in the town, but somehow they found their way to the docks, and there Harry took lodgings in the garret of a small dark house close to the Thames. That first night I see them settled in a bare room with warped floorboards and the plaster crumbling off the laths. There is a musty bed in the corner and a small table with a broken leg. The smoky stub of a candle throws out a small pool of dim yellow light. Harry stands at the window, his head bowed, for the ceiling is low, his spine, for once, quiescent, and gazes at the masts of the ships where they rise over the rooftops, and the moon sheds a pale gleam on the river. He is filled with sudden longing for the cliffs and coves of Cornwall, and for his wife. Strange cries reach him from the street below, and in the room the scratching of the rats behind the wainscotting grows so intolerable he flings his shoe at the wall.

He sinks on to a chair and covers his face with his hands. After some minutes he turns to look at Martha where she lies peacefully asleep on the bed. The night is close and sultry and she has kicked off the sheet, which now lies tangled in her legs. No childish snuggling for this little girl, no curling up into a ball with a thumb in her mouth, no, Martha sprawls there in her night-shirt with her arms and legs flung wide! – and all at once Harry thinks of how this child of his met each new situation on the road, how she faced down barking dogs, drunkards, thunderstorms, jittery horses and once, a sad old dancing bear in a rusty muzzle. Several times she was hoisted bodily aloft by some jovial fellow enchanted by her dogged, serious little face, and her great untidy mane of hair, and always she detached herself without panic, and without recourse to her father. Only eight years old, but she displayed all the qualities that Harry had loved in her mother. She was curious, and she was unafraid; and she had her mother's hair, fanned out now across the bolster, long thick tresses the colour of old bricks.

Suddenly Harry Peake's love for his daughter wells up within him with such intensity that he feels the tears starting in his eyes. He heaves a great sigh. It is good, he thinks, as at last he feels the sleep come stealing over him, that she will be beside him for all that lies ahead. She is a wise one, he thinks, an old soul.

Harry Peake was a saintlike figure in those early days, said my uncle. Not a saint, but saintlike. Almost at once he was subject to the cruelty and malice London dispenses to those it does not favour, and I sometimes imagine the only real peace he knew were the hours he spent with Martha by the river. Though even then there would be disturbance and interruption, always there would be those who could not leave the poor man to himself, but must ask him questions about his back. Nor was it unusual, said my uncle, that Harry by his mere presence aroused passions in primitive men, who then found the means to taunt and abuse him, he who had done no harm at all to them.

There was one night, my uncle said – and he peered at me with eyes grown suddenly grave and mournful, and spoke with a catch in his voice, as though grieving for humanity's lost innocence, as indeed in a way he was – there was a night, he whispered – and he told me of the night Harry and Martha were set upon by three or four apprentice boys, all much the worse for drink. They only narrowly escaped serious harm, and that, said my uncle, was in some part due to Martha's boldness.

I was of course agog to know more. So he described to me how, as the drunken apprentices yelped like hounds behind them, they had run through the darkness, through the narrow streets behind the meat market, their old coats flapping about them, Harry all lurch and shamble and Martha hauling at his arm, crying out to him to hurry. Turning into a courtyard they found themselves before a pair of high wooden gates fastened with a chain –

Trapped?

Trapped.

And –?

The outcome, said my uncle, was this. The apprentice boys rushed upon them, and Harry was thrown bodily to the ground. Martha began to seize up stones from the street and hurl them as hard as she could, screaming at the boys to get away. But the boys came forward, laughing now; Martha was, oh, nine years old, but she was tall for her years – her figure was formed – and those boys saw it. They saw it. Harry was struggling to his feet, lifting a hand, crying out that he meant them no harm, that he was a poor man, like themselves, he had nothing they wanted –

But he did have something they wanted, whispered William, and that was Martha. So Harry pulled the child behind him and shielded her with his body, and one of the apprentice boys, enraged now, and blind with lust – and how my uncle's old eyes fired up as he spoke of it! – this apprentice boy suddenly flailed at Harry with a stick, and Harry stepped forward into the blow, and took the force of it full on his shoulder.

The next blow was aimed at his skull, and this one he took on his lifted arm. Again he cried out that he meant them no harm, but they shouted louder for Martha – 'Give us the whore!' – and still Harry made no attempt to strike back, and still the blows rained down on his arms and shoulders, while Martha pelted their tormentors with whatever she could find at her feet, and screamed at them with all manner of violent threats. And still Harry came forward, head down and arms outstretched, crying out for mercy; and it was then, said my uncle – and here he paused again, and flung at me a dark glance from lowered eyes – that he took a savage blow to the ribs, and such was the force of it that at last he was provoked to retaliate.

With a roar Harry rose up to his full height. Seizing the stick, and wresting it forcibly from his assailant, he made as though to attack him; and the boy fell back, shouting at his companions, who rushed at Harry but were thrust aside, not with the stick, no, but with a sweep of Harry's arm; and then he lifted high the stick with both hands, and brought it down hard across his thigh, breaking it in two as though it were kindling wood. He flung the pieces to the ground and stood there, huge and panting, streaming with blood, his eyes wild and his lips pulled back from his teeth – and the apprentice boys lost what courage the drink had given them, and rapidly fell back; and then they were gone.

Harry sank groaning to his haunches and wrapped his arms about his head. Martha knelt before him, clutching his wrists.

'What have they done to you?' she cried.

He muttered something, he shook his head.

'Father –!'

Now his face came up.

'I would have killed them, had they touched you,' he whispered.

'Father, they were animals –'

'They were men. I want no man's blood on my hands, have I not done enough harm?'

A half-hour later Harry sat in the garret, stripped to the waist, while Martha sponged his poor bruised body and wiped the blood from his face and hands. After a while she began to speak angrily about their recent ordeal, but Harry at once silenced her, he would have no more talk of it.

Nor, said my uncle, after we had sat some minutes in silence, was this the only occasion when I Iarry suffered bodily assault. But while he understood that cruelty toward a deformed creature like himself was in the nature of some men, it cost him constantly to step away, to turn the other cheek; there was conflict in him over this, as there will be in any being whose pride urges him one way, but whose reason counsels caution, and reminds him of the likely outcome should he turn and fight. And this was not the only form of self-restraint he practised. He allowed himself none of his accustomed pleasures, those he had once enjoyed in the taverns and bawdy houses of Bodmin and Padstow, for he was intent, now, on demanding of himself the sternest retribution possible. So it seems, said my uncle, that for a considerable period of time Harry avoided almost all human society, other than that which he had to endure when he began to work the street fairs and taprooms of the town.

All human society? I had to interrupt him here. Did he not count Martha? So no, not all human society, for he did have Martha, and but for her, I believe, he would surely have gone mad. But what a curious couple they must have made, I reflected, Harry Peake with his great bent back, and his eyes always shadowed by the brim of his hat, shuffling along with his quarterstaff, more phantom, in those roistering filthy streets, than man; and from somewhere nearby, always the sound of a fiddle, or a song, to remind him of the good times he had forsworn. I said this to my uncle and he replied that more distressing by far to Harry's ears was the constant rattle of the fife and drum. There were always redcoats in the streets in those days, he said, and the sight of them disturbed Harry profoundly.

Why did the sight of soldiers disturb him?

Why do you think? Smuggling had been his livelihood; of course he hated the soldiery. Not only that, but somewhere – a small indignant snort from my uncle here – somewhere Harry had come upon the idea that a standing army was the first tool of the tyrant.

Well, so it is, I began; but he glared at me with such utter astonishment that I did not think it prudent to pursue the question. His heart was not strong.

So yes, the picture of Harry shuffling through those dangerous streets, and Martha beside him with her head up, her quick eyes darting this way and that, missing nothing and alert both to danger and opportunity, like a blind man's minder. And indeed, I reflected, Harry was a sort of blind man, his eyes turned ever inward upon the spectacle of his own guilt. They found friends, of course they did, among castaways and fugitives like themselves, the tramps and beggars and one-legged fiddlers who eked a living from the streets and quays around the London docks. With these unfortunates they would share a crust or two, but Martha saw how her father soon grew restless in any company but her own, and after a short time they would be on their way.

Martha was a talkative child, but living constantly in her father's company she learned to be quiet when he was sunk deep in his own suffering, and unable to escape the idea he had of himself as a flawed and fallen creature with his sin carried incorporate on his spine, that spine the outward manifestation of a spiritual deformity within. But when they sat side by side on the end of a damp wharf, perhaps, as the sun went down over the river, and ate their frugal supper – then she would ask him to talk to her, and the stories would come.

Oh, he told her about the free trade, he told her about ships he had sailed in with double bulkheads and false floors, he talked to her about landing parties, and this he knew well, having commanded such parties on many a moonless night, though he never spoke of the one that went wrong, the last one.

One night he told her the story of Ned Ratcliff, the man who attended his own funeral. Martha's imagination was at once fired by this.

'But father,' she said, in that firm, direct way she had, a small knot gathering between her eyes, her chin coming up and her lips pressed tight together, consternated, 'it is not possible for a man to attend his own funeral.'

Harry sat at the table, bent forward to relieve his spine, one hand flat on the table with the arm arched sharp to support it, and his chin rested in his palm. Such twisted postures were necessary for him now.

'It is possible, and I will tell you how.'

Martha set her own elbow on the table, her own chin in her palm, and sat angled at the table like her father. Harry observed this with silent pleasure.

'Well, go on then,' she said.

'Well, I will then,' he said. And he told her how this Ned Ratcliff had half-a-dozen kegs of good French brandy hidden in his house, which he wanted to move inland to a customer, a wealthy man in those parts, who was growing impatient for it.

'Then why did he not carry them in a wagon?'

'Because an Excise man was living in the village,' said Harry, 'and he was watching him.'

'Oh.'

So Ned put it about that he was ill, indeed that he was dying. The doctor, another one fond of French brandy, said there was no hope. The vicar was seen leaving Ned's cottage, sadly shaking his head.

'But he was not really ill at all,' said Martha.

'He was not.'

'So what happened?'

'The next thing they knew,' said Harry, 'poor Ned was dead.'

Martha gave a shout of laughter. 'But he wasn't!'

'He was not.'

'So they had a funeral,' cried Martha, 'and he came to it!'

Harry nodded. Martha frowned.

'But father,' she said, 'why?'

'What do you think was in his coffin?'

'The brandy!'

Then she had it; and by the time Ned Ratcliff's funeral procession reached the graveyard, with Ned himself bringing up the rear – dressed all in black, his face powdered white, and wailing loud, a ghastly sound! – not only had the Excise man fled in terror, and locked his doors, and pulled his shutters closed, convinced that the wailing figure could only be Ned Ratcliff's ghost – so had the rest of the village, all but Ned's friends, and the vicar of course, and the doctor; and they made sure the six kegs of brandy were on their way to their rightful owner before the first spade of earth landed on Ned's coffin.

Martha was entertained by this tale for many weeks, and when they were out on the streets together, among the crowds that thronged the docks, she liked to find somebody to whom she could tell the story of the man who attended his own funeral. Few could resist her, and those who did not grasp the excellence of the story at first hearing had it repeated and explained. Martha never tired of listening to tales of her father's smuggling days, and I dare say the smuggling was in her blood; and had she stayed in Cornwall I believe she would have been active in the trade herself. One day, after thinking deeply on the question, she asked Harry why the Excise men did not like him landing cargoes. 'Because otherwise,' she said, 'you could do it during the day.'

Now here was a question, but Harry was equal to it. He explained that if the cargo were landed at Bristol, then the customer would have to pay much more for it. And the reason for that was, because the king wanted the extra money.

Why did the king want the extra money?

To fight the French.

Martha pondered this for some minutes. She did not understand why the king wanted to fight the French.

Harry said he did not know either, but that he himself had no argument with the French; indeed, did he not do business with the French? He began quietly to laugh. Martha gazed at him astonished. He had not laughed since the fire. But now it came, like molasses from a barrel, hoarse, low and dirty, a deep rumbling amusement – did he not do business with the French? It was infectious, Martha began shouting with laughter, soon the pair of them were slapping the table.

And that was where they left it; though Martha would return to the question often in the months to come, and as she began to answer it for herself, so a first political idea stirred to life within her; and as you might imagine, in a firebrand like Martha Peake, it was radical. I suggested this to my uncle. Quite possible, he said.

Thus did father and daughter amuse themselves in their lonely garret. Ah, but a man of Harry's temperament could play the holy outcast only for so long, and as time passed, and he became familiar with London and its ways, so his natural sociability gradually asserted itself. He still met with mockery, he met with abuse, but he learned to defuse a situation with his wit, and became an adept of that curious form of discourse known as London banter. And as he was slowly drawn back into the current of life, so he became aware of a need for more substantial intellectual fare than the chatter of Martha and the endless circuits of his own dark thoughts. He began to sit in the coffee houses and read newspapers, and talk with other men about the urgent issues of the day – oh, the food riots, the slave trade, the brotherhood of man – the large issues that inflamed the political temper of those turbulent years. And his old humour stood him in good stead, as he recovered his spirits, for if he was no longer the robust man he had been in his youth, he found he had a sharp eye for folly and corruption, the folly and corruption, in particular, of the milords who lived west of Westminster and came east only for their pleasures. In time he became something of a character, the big, quiet, sardonic man with the strangely humped back, and although he was often asked how he had 'come by' his back, he spoke of the fire to nobody, though he took a perverse pleasure in devising other accounts of his disfigurement.

As for his work, he had known for some time how he would earn their bread in London, when the money he had was gone. He would show off his backbone to paying audiences in the inns and taverns of the poorer parts of the town. This he saw as a spiritual labour, a kind of penance. To humiliate himself before the crowd was to invite the contempt and disgust he felt he deserved. For he wanted to cauterize his soul, he wanted to burn off all that was in him that stank of indulgence and pride, having, as he saw it, a great debt to discharge before he was fit once more to call himself a man.

This then was the life they established during the first hard years in London. Harry was no stranger to the tavern, nor indeed was Martha, she had been with him often in the taproom of the Admiral Byng. But the inns and pot-houses of London were unlike anything they had known in Cornwall – the nightly displays, I mean, of drunken violence in smoky low-ceilinged barns where ale and gin were consumed in vast quantities by a populace worn down and worn out by the sheer misery of their lives. Into those roiling noisy taprooms Harry would go to make a few pennies showing off his backbone. He quickly discovered how best to arouse the interest of the crowd, how to talk to them, how to play them as though they were fish, until their curiosity was keen and impatient, and then, before he removed the final veil – until, that is, his shirt came off – round went the hat, and the coins clinked sweetly.

   This was Martha's job, taking the hat round, and she was no less adept than her father at working the crowd. Who could deny this child a penny? Many could, of course, but others, well along in drink, and beaming with sad rheumy eyes at the red-haired girl stamping about the taproom with her father's cocked hat held out before her – oh, there was usually a farthing to be found in one pocket or another.

Seven years passed, said my uncle William, since first they had arrived in London; and he paused, his eyes grew milky, and he drifted away, as though the very idea of seven years, so short a measure in such a history, yet such a span in a man's life, had overwhelmed him with grim intimations of his own mortality.

Seven years, he said, and in all those years Harry never touched a drop of spirits, nor any wine or beer. No, though he worked the taprooms and pot-houses where the drink flowed like water, he stayed sober; and in time he became a familiar figure all along the river, down past Shadwell Dock and Limehouse Reach to the Isle of Dogs and beyond. But he made his home in Smithfield, hard by St Luke's, where he was known as the Cripplegate Monster.

And what, I said gently, of Martha?

Martha, said my uncle, distractedly, Martha – matured; and curiously, he said – though it was not curious to me – curiously, he said, she was untouched by the vice that flourished everywhere around her, but grew straight and strong, clear and honest, and with all the vigour and appetite her father had possessed in his youth.

Appetite?

The old man lifted his hand, the fingers flickered in the firelight, ah yes, appetite, he murmured, she matured early, she was a ripe girl . . . Again he drifted off, lost in some vapour of vagueness at the thought of Martha's ripeness.

A *ripe* girl?

Now he flared. Ambrose, he snapped, do not make me say it. A ripe girl, yes, a girl with appetite, yes, will you make me speak of the natural functions? The story is not about her!

It was then, at that moment – the hour was late, I had just heard the clock in the hall strike two – that it first occurred to me that what I wanted to hear from my uncle was perhaps not what he wished to tell me. But I let it pass, I said no more of Martha's *ripeness*, of her *appetite*, and could only speculate that he meant she discovered the pleasures of being touched by a man; that she danced, perhaps, in the natural overflow of her abundant animal spirits, and that when her blood was warmed – and I speak of Martha at fourteen or fifteen, *ripe* Martha, I speak of now – she might be minded to loosen her bodice, lift her skirt, perhaps, for a clean young fellow who had pleased her –?

Or perhaps not. Perhaps, living in such close quarters with

her father, she found little opportunity to indulge her dawning 'appetite', perhaps Harry actively discouraged her, and held her to his own standard of chastity. But I wonder, did he not observe, as she washed herself in the corner of the room, or sat in his lap, as she had done since she was small, that she was fast becoming a woman? Did he not anticipate the day when he must relinquish her to a boy with a straight back, and find himself replaced in her affections?

But my uncle's rectitude forbade me to speak with frankness of such things, and I held my tongue.

Harry, meanwhile, had returned to those habits he had first learned in the library of Edward Penwarden, that is, of reading, and writing, and he found now that the work of writing came easy to him, that all he had known in his thirtysome years was as fuel to the fire of an awakened imagination; and that the stories from his boyhood in Port Jethro, when he had sat at the knee of Maggie Peake in that windswept hut of netting and ship's timbers, now came to him charged, as it seemed, with new meanings. It was around this time, I believe, the winter of 1773, that he began work on his 'Ballad of Joseph Tresilian'.

One night he incorporated into his act a few lines he had scribbled the night before; and to his surprise he was wildly applauded. He pondered this later, he discussed it with Martha, he saw that an opportunity presented itself and, old smuggler he was, he could not pass it up. And while he had renounced that greed for profit which he had come to see as the root of the evil whose fruit was the death of his wife, to live better, materially, he felt, could not be wrong, and Martha was wholeheartedly with him on this.

Ah, but when he awoke the next morning he at once dismissed these thoughts with a shudder of disgust; had he not turned his back on all such temptation? And besides, what more did he want? He and Martha had taken lodgings at the top of the Angel, a large public house on Cripplegate Street, close to the Smithfield market, where Harry performed nightly in the taproom. There they had been living for some months in tranquil mutual affection. And thus, no doubt, they would have continued to live, had it not been for the intrusion into their lives of Lord Francis Drogo and his assistant, Dr William Tree; that is, my uncle William.

5

By the summer of 1774 my uncle had been assisting Lord Drogo in his anatomical work for some years, and was certainly familiar with the means by which his lordship secured the bodies he needed to do that work. They came from a slinking, diminutive creature called Clyte. Clyte was a *resurrection man*, by which I mean he was a dealer in fresh cadavers, one who was not scrupulous as to how he came by the cadavers in which he dealt; and it was around this time he acquired one such. Mary Magdalen Smith, an actress, a girl no older than Martha Peake, had gone to the gallows for lifting a snuff-box from a rich man's pocket in Drury Lane. As no friend came forward to claim her body it was cut down from the scaffold at Tyburn Field and purchased from the hangman by Clyte. That night, said my uncle, Clyte brought Mary Magdalen Smith's body out across the Lambeth Marsh to Drogo Hall – yes, to this very house, he said, at my cry of surprise – where he himself took delivery of it. He and Clyte then prepared it for Lord Drogo to dissect before an audience of medical men the following afternoon.

The dissection went off well, and later, when the theatre of anatomy was dark once more, and the sawdust all swept away, in an ill-lit scullery with a guttered slate floor the two surgeons washed the gore from their bodies as Clyte went through the clothing of a girl who – and here my uncle peered at me with an air of jaunty humour – having but the day before lost her life, had since lost her organ tree and much else of her innards besides. In a pocket of her skirt Clyte came upon a folded handbill, and finding that it advertised, of all things, a *poet*, who displayed himself nightly in the Angel at Cripplegate, he began to read aloud; and Lord Drogo paused in his ablutions – the noble head lifted – and he listened close.

The poet was of course Harry Peake; and the description on

the handbill of his twisted spine at once aroused the professional curiosity of the great anatomist.

My uncle William spoke with a kind of wistful fondness of Harry and Martha, as he first knew them. Martha was of an age now to talk to her father about those questions which occur early to young people, that is, those simple, profound questions on the order of why the people they lived among could barely afford the staples of life, while others had so much.

Nor was she alone in this; for she was growing up among free-thinking men and women, many of whom were her father's friends, and all of whom were passionate enemies of the corruption then rife in the government. Some wrote pamphlets, attacking the ministry, or the church, or the king, or all three, the printers of the more intemperate of these screeds being hauled off to gaol. Harry not only shared these men's principles, he intended that one or another of them should publish his ballad when it was done; and indeed, promises to this effect had been made to him. As for Martha, her political sympathies were established early, when as a child she had talked to her father about the free trade; and if the arbitrary power of the king had once been something of an abstraction to her, it was abstract no longer.

For she knew girls like Mary Magdalen Smith, she knew men with children to feed who could not afford bread. She knew why they robbed, and she had observed the savagery with which the society that first had forced them into penury and desperation then punished them for taking the course of last resort; and there were not a few she had known who ended their days at Tyburn, or were languishing deep in the vaults of Newgate, victims of a penal code which honoured one idea and one idea only, and that was not HUMANITY but PROPERTY. Harry provided no sort of brake of moderation to the political opinions his daughter began to voice, if anything the opposite, he encouraged her.

My uncle sniffed with distaste as he told me this last, and I understood that these were not opinions he held himself. On being probed a little, he said curtly that the poor would always be with us, and should be put to work at once lest in idleness they acquired tastes they could never afford to indulge. I lifted an eyebrow at this, but I let it pass, eager, rather, to hear more of Martha's early life. So he sighed, and then described to me the rituals of their day, as he construed them, and after a moment or two a rather soft and silly smile began to twitch at the edges of his thin old lips; I should mention here that my uncle William had never married, and had fathered no children.

In those days, he said, Harry and Martha lived at the top of the Angel in a pair of adjoining rooms with sloping ceilings and small dormer windows with leaded panes that peered out from beneath the mossy eaves on to the stable yard below. Each room contained a few pieces of old heavy furniture, including, in Harry's, a canopied bed with swags of rotting curtain hanging off the frame. Also in Harry's room was a large fireplace, unused during the summer months, whose mantelpiece spilled over with ill-stacked books and papers, as did the table in the middle of the room. By Cripplegate standards these were good lodgings, for which they paid only tuppence a night.

Martha would come into her father's room in the evening, and Harry would lay aside his writing or reading, and make himself ready for his work downstairs. He would seat himself on a low chair, legs splayed sideways as he hunched before a looking-glass propped against a book on his table; then peering at his reflection, with practised fingers he selected what he needed from his various jars of theatrical cosmetics.

As he worked Martha strode about the room and acted out her day for him, becoming now angry, now helpless with laughter as some incident returned to her in the first full passion of its remembering. Those shabby rooms often rang with Martha's laughter, said my uncle William. He then fell silent. A moment later he closed his eyes. Then a faint whistling came from between his parted lips. I wondered was he musing, or sleeping; or perhaps dying.

What, I asked him, was Martha Peake like, when he knew her?

Ah, Martha, he said, opening his eyes, as though I had introduced a new topic into the conversation. He had told me the story was not about her; but now, at the sound of her name, he sat up in his chair, the dim old eyes gleaming, a hand lifted and the spindly fingers trembling as he aroused her in his mind. She was a most unusual creature, he murmured, most unusual. Her father was unusual, and so was she. A robust, broad-shouldered girl, he said, she would sweep into a room like a force of Nature and fling herself on to a chair or a couch as though she had just come back from tramping round the world! She pinned up her hair in a loose bun – glorious shade of red, Martha's hair – and her flesh was of such plump and pearly whiteness, and so warmly touched with a rising flush, that she *glowed*, said my uncle, she glowed. I see a stubborn chin uplifted, he whispered, just like her father's, and a high, white, imperious forehead, large dark shining eyes, the expression one of petulance and challenge, and oh, none of your dimpling coyness there, she was raucous. Loud. Big girl, yes, milky skin, bosom like a pigeon. Flashing eyes. Moody at times, languid and moping, like every young girl. But such heart! Such spirit! She feared no one, you know; not even Drogo.

Here my uncle shook his head for several moments; clearly the idea of anybody not fearing Drogo was an impressive one, even now, with his lordship apparently dead and buried these last fifteen years.

And her temper, I said –?

Oh, she could be formidable, he cried, fierce as a tiger when roused in defence of her father, but then placid in repose; until those last months in London – and here my uncle sank back, a great cloud passing across his mind – when she knew no repose at all. Though this of course I say – he said – in the melancholy knowledge of all that was to come. Martha had no inkling of what was to come, she was aware only that while life might be hard, there were those who had it harder, and who missed what she had, that is, a good father, whom she loved, and a healthy appetite – a cold glance of warning here – for the simple pleasures of life – a posy for her bosom, an orange or two, fresh from the market, a book of verse –

Spoiled, then?

Spoiled? Not at all. No, she had character, Martha, there was in her already – he swung round to me, his fingers clutching the arms of his chair – something of the rock, yes, some adamantine element in her nature that would surely equip her for the trials that lay ahead! He fell back triumphantly.

Harry by now would have gone behind his screen to get dressed. When he emerged, and had donned his hat – a large black tricorn pulled low over his brow, and crowned with glossy black plumage – and his coat of sweeping black velvet, faded at the seams, a shabby thing with silver buttons down the front – and a good deal of crafty padding in the back, to emphasize his deformity – he was no longer the man Martha knew. Black stockings under dark blue velvet breeches, also distressed by long use, so the fabric was shiny and thin, and on his feet black leather shoes with stacked heels and tarnished silver buckles. He would gaze gravely down at her in all his painted strangeness, and strike a pose, one hand tucked into his coat, the other cocked akimbo on his hip, and ask her how he looked, and if the people downstairs – now loudly anticipating the appearance of a monster – would like him.

Martha loved her father with all the passion of which a young girl is capable, and she never saw him as a monster. Oh, she knew how grotesque he could render himself, when he wanted to, for in truth the architecture of his backbone, in the aftermath of its breaking and mending, was of such grandeur, in a certain light, and with padding, that with but the merest touch of theatricality he could make himself quite horrid. But for Martha he was never horrid; and now, harkening, perhaps, to a fiddle below, he extended a tentative foot, made a step or two of a jig – and Martha needed no more invitation than that, for nothing warmed her quicker than a jig. She unpinned her hair and a moment later the pair of them were happily at it, himself all comical gravity as Martha high-stepped it nimbly about his shuffling legs, her skirt lifted in her fingers and her head flung back, her brick-red tresses streaming out behind her! They had only the faint strains of a distant fiddle to drive their jig, but soon the dust was rising, the old boards groaning beneath their feet – until there came that knock at the door, that wheedling voice

– 'Five minutes!' – and they slowed, and stopped, and gazed at each other with shining eyes and deep dismay.

Harry returned to his mirror to repair the damage done by the jig, and Martha drifted to the window, which overlooked the yard and the stables that enclosed it; and as she stood there, idly gazing out, pinning her hair and humming the tune to which she had just been jigging, she saw a small black carriage with a nobleman's coat-of-arms in flaking goldleaf on the door come rattling over the cobbles and into the yard, a spidery creature all in black up on the cab. The sun was setting, shadows were thickening, the air was warm and close and heavy with the smell of malt. This was the evening Lord Drogo came to the Angel.

Lord Drogo was the first to descend from the carriage. I asked my uncle to describe his lordship, and he told me with what seemed circumspection – could it be that *still* he feared the man? – that while Drogo's clothes bore no sign of ostentation, and his tight-curled wig was modest – the ivory cane 'tactful' – in the marble brow, and superb aquilinity of feature, Martha would have read at once the marks of a high birth and an imperial temper, not to say an intellect of some vigour and cultivation. Drogo glanced about him, said my uncle, and his cold blue eye missed nothing.

A moment later William himself emerged from the carriage. He stepped down, he told me, with a wheeze of self-mockery, with a good deal less decorum than his master had, and in his wake the carriage shuddered violently on its springs. He too looked about him, frowning, and rubbing the back of his neck where two small hard lumps beneath the skin – this memory apparently giving him pause for reflection – had for some time caused him anxiety.

Now the Angel Inn was a genuine fragment of mutilated antiquity, largely constructed in the days of the first Henry Tudor. Having somehow escaped the Great Fire, its oak beams had shifted over the centuries and settled to their own comfort rather than the squared elevation of the builder. The slates were shaggy with weeds and moss, and undulated like a body of water agitated by the wind; and so streaked and pocked were the bricks and plaster that the

43

walls had to be constantly caulked, like the hull of a ship, lest they open to the elements and the house sank. The effect, said my uncle, was one of faltering decrepitude, the whole thing like an old man's frame, kept upright and alive only by the animating inward presence of its tenants. But how the tenants did animate that frame! Shouts and laughter and occasional screams, and through the windows indistinct figures in vigorous confusion could be glimpsed within, and even smelt, despite the strong native odours of the house and the rank stench of horse piss, which suggested unwholesome stables at the rear.

In they came through the back door. The taproom was crowded that night, and oh, it was a hellish place, said my uncle William, with a shudder, all heat and smoke and noise, a large, dark, low room with a flagged stone floor and bowed black beams across the ceiling. It stank, he said, of uncleanliness and spoilage. Great mossy barrels with dripping spigots were stacked on trestles along the wall, and two beefy women in aprons, Moll Goat and her daughter Sal, moved among the company with barks and curses, attempting to serve and control the more than seventy customers milling about down there. They had come for the entertainment, they were there to see Harry Peake, whose fame by this time extended well beyond Smithfield, indeed he was almost as famous as Sal Goat, who was known from Ludgate to the Tower as the tin-toothed trollop with the heart of brass.

William remembered pushing open the taproom door and gazing with horror at the scene within, the seething crowd of poets and apprentices, footpads and strumpets, butchers, fops and sailors, all now eager for the appearance of the Cripplegate Monster. There was a considerable number of theatre people present, and up at the counter, and drinking hard, stood several regular soldiers in the faded red coats of an infantry regiment, these men bound for the colonies and expecting any day to take ship for Boston, which even then was under British military occupation. Deep in conspiracy at the back of the room, in a dense fog of tobacco smoke, sat a passel of muttering radicals, including a bold, jovial young fellow called Fred Lour; and at a table nearby three old printers wagered farthings racing lice picked with inky fingers from one another's wigs. A few last dusty beams of sunlight came shafting through the smoke, and a lurid red glow suffused the place and all its patrons.

Lord Drogo, to whom, it was said, nothing human was alien, joined my uncle in the doorway and lifted an eyebrow at the landlord, a tall, thin man of vicious aspect who worked steady and watchful behind a broad wooden counter, and who, alert to the arrival of quality, now came forward wiping his hands on his apron to inquire as to his lordship's pleasure. This was Joseph Goat, and he ruled absolute in the Angel.

Martha no longer attended her father's performances. Soon after her twelfth birthday Harry had told her of the pain it caused him to think of her watching him as he displayed himself to a paying public, and asked her to stay upstairs. She did not understand this, nor did my uncle seem to know what was in Harry's mind; but I think it was connected to what William alluded to as Martha's 'ripeness'. For I think Harry no longer regarded Martha as a child. She may not have been a woman yet, but she was no longer a child, and a sort of modesty, I believe, was aroused in him at the thought of her seeing him exhibit his body to strangers. His shame in his own eyes served to remind him of the great wrong he had done, and indeed went some way to expiating that wrong; but he did not want to find his own shame reflected in his daughter's eyes. And so, to her bewilderment and distress – and after a passionate, tearful entreaty, I would imagine, to which Harry listened with gentle understanding, but no change of heart – he asked her not to watch him perform any more.

But she did sit on the stairs where she could listen. Darkness would have fallen by now, branches of candles burning fitfully from wall-sconces as voices continued to rise, and huge turbulent shadows surged over the walls. At the back of the taproom hung a black curtain that screened off a low platform, and she would hear Fred Lour, who was a good friend to both Harry and herself, as he clambered on to this platform and called for silence. He then made his introduction, saying that it was his honour – derisive cheering here from all who knew him – to bring before the esteemed company of the Angel Inn that friend of the people – that towering genius – that most remarkable of men – Mr Harry Peake; and more in this vein, as the crowd stamped and whistled and shouted.

Martha would then hear the curtain being drawn back to reveal that the platform contained one piece of furniture only, a great chair covered by an ancient cloth of black and red velvet with a tasselled silver fringe trailing on the floor; and in this chair reclined her father, wearing a pair of spectacles, idly perusing a volume of Dryden, and on his face an expression of such comic aristocratic *hauteur* that it brought a howl of recognition from his audience. Oh, this crowd had no affection for the nobility –!

The laughter would die soon after and there would then be a silence, or rather, more than a silence, a distinct inholding of the breath. For Harry's face was powdered to an unnatural chalky whiteness, and his eyes were blacked with kohl, so they seemed in the candle flame terrifying caves of darkness, with the merest pinprick of light blazing deep within. It made a haunting spectacle, said William; he seemed something from a dream, or from the realm of the vampires. Much murmuring now, a yelp or two from the dandies present; and then Harry rose to his feet, and turned, and it was at this point that his audience properly saw the shape of his back.

Harry was right to forbid Martha to watch. My uncle described to me what happened next. Harry, still with his back to the audience, threw off his coat and opened his shirt and pushed it off his shoulders, and they glimpsed in the gloom the strange bony formations, the peaks and ridges that had lifted and skewed his spine, and pushed his shoulders awry, such that his upper torso was a horribly bent and broken thing, it was crooked timber; and the effect upon the company, whispered my uncle, was powerful.

But this, I said, was simply a disfigured man – a man with a twisted spine –?

Ah, but it seems it was more than that. This was a more primitive age than our own, said my uncle, when Nature was celebrated for her botches rather than her glories, and Harry Peake's spine disturbed the people's confidence in the proper shape and form of things, a confidence they had not known they possessed, it was stitched so deep in their sense of the order of the world. There was a collective gasp of horror, and then Harry reclined once more in his chair, lay there in the posture of a weary noble poet before bestirring himself to read a few lines.

But then, said William, the sparks would fly! For Harry's voice had matured like old port wine, it was deep and rich and liquid. It was from his own 'Ballad of Joseph Tresilian' that he took his readings, and such were the passages chosen, and such the manner in which he spoke them – striding about, now whispering, now thundering, now turning his great back on his audience and peering round it like a man behind a wall – that they might as well have been political tracts, so sharply did he bring them to bear upon that other great question of the day, which was, of course, America, and those themes attendant upon the American question, by which I mean liberty, taxation, and Empire.

Its subject was the Sea, the greed, the madness and the savagery of the Sea; its setting the New World; and its hero a fisherman who, drowning, strikes a bargain with the Sea, that if he is allowed to live one more year, he will return to the shore with his wife, and the Sea may have them both. It was a story of tyranny, and of how Joseph Tresilian's wife outwitted the tyrant Sea – already, you see, cried the old man, he was thinking on the grand scale! For by this time, of course, the popular outrage at the assault upon the natural rights of the colonists by a king as mad, savage and greedy as the Sea itself, grew more passionate with every fresh abuse those people suffered. This, at least, he sniffed, growing quiet after his enthusiasm of a moment before, was the popular view of the thing. He frowned at the fireplace for several seconds before resuming.

Imagine the scene, he said. The old man's enthusiasm returned. He was excited now. He wished to convey to me what he had come to understand as the particular power that Harry had when his genius was in full flood. Harry lifts his head (he whispered), he gazes up into the roof, and silence falls. Oh, and then the breast heaves, and the eyes roll, and Harry's voice is at once filling the room, it is ringing out with a deep masculine music, it is as though this weary hunchback has been taken up and possessed by a spirit alien to his own nature! His very back seems to grow straight! Wildly now he chants his verses, and his words arouse before the company's eyes a sea coast they recognize, for it bears resemblance to the familiar shores of England, but it is an English seashore made immense, made terrifying, made to a scale of greatness, like a boy changed into a giant, or a man into a god – a vision of untamed Nature that will inspire Harry Peake to the end of his days, the sea coast of America with its stormswept headlands, its mighty forests, and here the mouth of a great river – as yet it has no name – a river that sweeps through the Wilderness, through the forests and mountains of a distant continent he has never seen, a vast wild land of infinite and awful grandeur, before pouring its waters into the wilful, all-devouring Sea –!

> 'The hour is come but not the man!
> He creeps upon the lumpen land!
> He dare not come with open hand
> To give the Sea his due!'

And so on; and all the while the audience sits spellbound, all but a few, the radicals, who are watching not Harry but the soldiers, who seem however more intent upon their drink, and the whores, than the performance; and they in turn are watched by Francis Drogo, who misses nothing, but who reserves his closest scrutiny for Harry Peake.

6

The hour was late, the old man was distinctly tipsy, and growing more florid with every allusion to Harry Peake, and his poem, and his daughter Martha; and I had no wish to stem his flow, I was desperate to hear more of it, for I had begun to suspect what was afoot here, and I wanted to be sure I was right. For if I was – and I had every confidence that I was – then my own future, my own anticipated tenure of Drogo Hall, would be much affected. So I refilled the old man's glass and poked the fire to life – we were back in his study, and Percy had not appeared for an hour, he must have gone to bed – and asked him if he would go on.

Oh, he had no wish to retire yet, he said, not with a meeting imminent between Harry Peake and Lord Drogo; and Martha was there too, he cried, oh yes she was!

I waited with patience for the resumption of the history, for it took my uncle some minutes to compose himself. After the performance, he said, he and Lord Drogo were brought to the top of the house to meet Harry Peake. Before they got there however Martha ran upstairs and lit the candles, and opened the window to the breeze, so the room glowed and flickered with a warm low light when her father reached it a few moments later.

He came in wearily. He dropped his books on the table and touched his daughter's cheek. Then he sat down before his mirror, tied his hair back and began wiping the paint and powder off his face; and in the wavering candle flame his skin shone with an unwholesome ghostly pallor. A minute later there came a tap at the door. Martha opened it and there was Fred Lour, grinning broadly at her, and winking, with Lord Drogo and my uncle William behind him. In they came. Harry got to his feet. Fred Lour made the introductions with some flamboyance. Chairs were then set before the table, and the guests were invited to sit. My uncle produced two bottles of claret from one of his pockets, and four slender glasses from the other, and set them on the table. Harry Peake turned his glass upside down as William pulled the first cork.

Lord Drogo was at his most urbane, said my uncle. Not a tall man, he nonetheless communicated in his bearing and manner a distinct authority, and the clear expectation that he would be accorded deference, if not outright servility. It was at once clear to my uncle, however, that Harry Peake had never in his life felt the impulse to defer to any man.

Lord Drogo proposed a toast to Harry's performance below, and his lordship and Fred Lour and my uncle William then drank. Then they sat down, Fred moving to the window, where he deftly hoisted his bottom up on to the sill. Martha – whom my uncle had now glimpsed for the first time, and had recognized, he said, for a most rare creature to find in such a house – Martha had meanwhile retired to a chair by the door, and several times, said my uncle, he turned and smiled at her. I was not surprised by this, and could well imagine the young William Tree leering wetly at a handsome girl like Martha Peake; but mostly, he said, he watched her father. The room was not small, but the presence in it of Harry Peake had the effect, by candlelight, of making it feel constricted. William said that he once again experienced the sense of disorder he had felt below, but now with greater intensity: the furniture seemed skewed out of proportion by the large misshaped man seated in shadow at the table before them. Lord Drogo however showed no sign of the confusion William felt, but gazed keenly at Harry and asked him where he came by his education.

Harry nodded gravely. 'I am the bastard son of a seaweed cutter, my lord,' he said, employing, said William, the rich port-wine tones he had used below, 'but from an early age I was given leave to use the library of a gentleman.'

'And who –'

'That experience,' said Harry, 'taught me that if a poor man is given the chance to read, and then to talk of what he has read, there will be little to distinguish him from the man of superior rank.'

Harry lifted his chin and gazed with level eyes at the great man seated before him, and Martha proudly raised her own chin.

'And then we should all be the same,' said Lord Drogo dryly. 'But tell me, sir –'

But again Harry interrupted him, asking his lordship where he came by *his* education – 'for I am aware, my lord' – and his voice grew sombre and intimate – 'that you have not been content merely to indulge the privilege of your nobility.'

Here Harry glanced at Martha, and her eyes shone back at him in the candlelight.

Fred Lour was much amused at this turn in the conversation, and loudly cleared his throat of phlegm. He had recognized that Harry was in the mood for sport. My uncle William saw it too, and was astonished, he said, that a man who had suffered as this man had, and bore such eloquent marks of that suffering, should have preserved in his nature a sense of humour. And not only that. Here was a man close to destitution, as it seemed to my uncle, but so careless was he of his own interest that he was prepared to lose a benefactor by mocking him – and him a lord! Such things did not happen in London.

Lord Drogo murmured shortly that he had studied with Mr Hunter in Leicester Fields. 'But sir,' he then said, 'your own history is of more interest than mine. Tell me, how did you come by your spine?'

William said that Harry here assumed a most tragic expression. He dropped his eyes. He leaned his head upon his hand. He gave out a small moan. A whiff of pathos came off him, delicate as juniper. After a moment he lifted his face, and in the candlelight his eyes were shining damply. He began to speak in a halting whisper, his voice catching, a haunted quality in him now that had them all straining to catch every last sound that dropped from his trembling lip.

'There was a night, my lord,' he whispered, 'when my mother had carried me close to term, and was returning to her hut on the shore through the dark streets of the village.'

A long pause here; William said the poor man was clearly overwhelmed by the thought of his mother; or pretending he was.

'Go on, sir,' murmured Drogo.

'She was descending a narrow set of steps close to the harbour, with but the moon to light her way,' said Harry, becoming dramatic now, lifting a hand, and his voice rising slightly, such that they at once pictured the scene, the hapless weary woman struggling alone down those steep stone steps with the crashing waves loud in her ears, now pausing for breath, one hand on the wall and the other on her belly.

'Suddenly,' said Harry, slapping his hand on the table so they all jumped – 'a man emerged from a doorway above!'

They saw him, and were as startled by his appearance as the woman on the steps.

'This man's shadow,' said Harry, growing warmer still, 'cast upon the wall, was made huge by the lamplight from the open door behind him. And so monstrous, so *unnatural*, did it appear to my mother' – he paused again – nobody breathed – 'she fainted dead away.'

Another long pause. 'And then, sir?'

Harry leaned forward across the table. 'The impression of this monstrous shadow,' he hissed, 'was stamped so deep in her sensorium, that by means of the vital fluids it was carried down to her womb, and there, my lord, it had its influence on the foetus.'

My uncle William said that on hearing this – he recognized it at once as the famous doctrine of the 'forming faculty' – he fully expected his master to express with some vigour his scepticism as to a great shadow being the cause of a man's deformity; to express, indeed, his scepticism toward all such traffic of the imagination, his lordship having often declared that the true relation of the mind and the body must forever remain a mystery. But clearly he had no desire to argue with Harry Peake for a mystery, and so said nothing.

There was another silence. 'Quite extraordinary,' murmured William at last. 'Will you take a glass now, sir?'

Harry shook his head. He awaited Lord Drogo's reaction to this inspired nonsense of his. But Drogo suspected he was being made a fool of, as indeed he was, and merely asked Harry, did he have a wife? Ah, but this time Harry was genuinely affected, though nobody saw it but Martha. Briefly he told Lord Drogo that his wife had died, so he and his daughter had left Cornwall, and come to London – 'and so you find us today.'

At this my uncle William twisted about in his chair and, pointing to the back of the room where Martha sat with her hands folded in her lap, said: 'And this is your daughter, sir?'

'Come forward, Martha,' said Harry, so she did.

She came forward boldly and stood before the gentlemen, who had both now turned in their chairs. William was friendly and him, he said, she liked. But it was at once apparent to her that Lord Drogo was a fish who swam in much colder waters. The great man positioned her before him and then inspected her in a close unsmiling manner. 'Well-made child, by the look of her at least,' he murmured. 'How old are you, child?'

'Fifteen, my lord,' she said. 'How old are you?'

His lordship stiffened visibly at this impertinence. He stood up, took Martha by the shoulders, and turning her about, placed the flat of his hand between her shoulder blades and ran it down her back. He then remarked to William that she showed nothing of her father's peculiar endowment. His fingers lingered on her buttocks and squeezed them for firmness.

For a moment Martha was taken quite aback, but only for a moment. She shook off Lord Drogo's fingers and rounded on him, fiery with outrage, and demanded to know, was he accustomed to handling women like livestock? Fred Lour could not restrain a shout of laughter, at which Martha turned to her father, who lifted his hand and said to Lord Drogo: 'Her back is straight, my lord. My wife's confinement was not unsettled as my mother's was.'

'Indeed,' said Lord Drogo, regarding Martha coldly and tapping his cane smartly on the floor as she stood before him with her hair adrift, her blood up, and her fists clenched tight. He made a small gesture of acquiescence, and turned again to Harry.

'And are you are often in pain, sir?' then said his lordship.

*

Oh, that question! There was a reason Harry Peake's great face was as knobbed and wedged with chunks of fisted muscle as it was, said William, why as harrowed and scoured, pocked and warted as some wild moorscape of the west country – what a thing that face was! But it had been carved thus by pain, when his spine, as it did periodically, threw up howling storms of torment from between its ill-matched plates, and the fine vessels were trapped and crushed between them. Martha had seen her father twisting on the floor, arching his ridged backbone as it tore him apart, she had seen him in Hell, his eyes clamped tight shut and every muscle bulging in his head, every vessel bursting, the sweat breaking from him in torrents as he fought to endure the unendurable. He had shouted for ardent spirits at such times, and Martha had brought him water. He had dashed the jug from her hands – again he had cried out for strong drink – and she had held him, she had held him until the spasms subsided and the poor exhausted man could fall away into sleep, to awaken, please God, in some relief from his agonies. Was he often in pain? Oh, he was.

'At times I suffer it, my lord.'

'No pain bites like that which has its source in the spine – *nec mordat dolor hic spinus spinorum*, eh, William?'

'Indeed, my lord,' said William.

'Can you cure him?' said Martha.

'Dear girl, there are none can "cure" a spine like this. But physic is not altogether derelict here. You are a scholar, sir, you sit late with your books, smoking your pipe in a closed room. Am I right?'

'You are right,' said Harry.

'You eat meat and you take strong drink. Am I right?'

'I eat meat, my lord, but I take no drink.'

'That is wise. Drink milk. Take the air. Live ascetic. Live as a monk. This is all I can tell you.'

'Will it grow worse?'

'You have consulted other surgeons?'

'I have consulted nobody.'

So they talked then of what a surgeon could and could not do; and a little later Lord Drogo and my uncle William took their leave.

But before they did so, Drogo told Harry he would be pleased to see him again, to talk further about his pain, and indicated that he intended to think further on the subject.

Martha watched from the window as Drogo and William emerged from the back door of the Angel and crossed the courtyard to their carriage. The same spidery figure dressed in black – it was Clyte, of course – held the door for them, then scuttled up on to the cab and took the reins in one hand, the whip in the other. But before the carriage moved off, he turned and stared straight up at the window. Martha did not step away, but held the creature's gaze. A most peculiar sensation, I imagine, difficult to describe, precisely, although I believe I can guess the sentiments Clyte aroused in Martha's heart: she felt the same shiver move up her spine that she had known when Lord Drogo touched her earlier. It was not her first glimpse of Clyte, but it was the first time I believe that she sensed the sheer evil rising off him like a gas. A moment later the carriage rumbled out of the courtyard and into the night. Harry resumed wiping his face clean of paint and powder, and soon was laughing quietly, as he remembered Martha's fiery indignation toward Lord Drogo. Then he remembered being asked about Grace Foy, and at once he grew quiet.

7

It was past midnight by this time and my uncle showed no inclination to retire. It occurred to me that over the years of his isolation here in Drogo Hall he had developed the habits of a nocturnal, and that his vitality was aroused only in the small hours when the rest of the world slept. I speculated now that he might be a user of opium. It was an established fact that within the medical profession the practice was a good deal more common even than in the artist class, largely as a function of availability and temperament: your doctor is a melancholy fellow, as a rule.

Now I reviewed what facts I had. The rapid mood changes, the tendency to drift and dream, the coming to life in the hours of darkness – above all, the grandiosity of certain elements of his story and, at the same time, the minute knowledge he seemed to possess of events he had not witnessed at first hand – it all suggested a narcotic influence, and I believe it was at this point in the narrative that it first occurred to me that I could no longer altogether trust him. His story, it is true, had held together well enough, given the generous assistance of a sympathetic imagination like my own; but I had detected certain omissions, certain small inconsistencies, and anomalies, and all at once the old man's cavalier references to the vagaries of a failing memory seemed suspect. For when I pressed him he simply threw his hands in the air, and gazed at me with an expression of almost comic mystification, accompanied by much shrugging of those bony little birdlike shoulders; and I had had no choice but to accept him at his word.

But now the voice of scepticism within me could no longer be ignored, even as the story assumed the most sombre of tones. Over the next hour or so he brought me forward to what he called the 'precipitating accident', and this event convinced me, if I needed further convincing, that information was being withheld from me.

How else to explain the mystery of Harry's changing habits, his sudden desire to *walk by night*?

Now Harry Peake had always loved to walk. In Cornwall he had tramped across the cliffs or over the moors, when he had business to conduct in a distant village, glad of the chance to swing a stout stick and shout at the sky. Since coming to London he had had to abandon these rambles of his, for he could no longer move as he had before his back was broke. But he could still go down to the docks with Martha, and frequently the two were to be seen making their way through the narrow streets of Smithfield, Harry huge and bent in his old black coat, and his hat pulled low, and Martha – who was not bent at all, of course, said my uncle, but seemed rather to *crest* the morning, like a vessel under sail! – Martha striding along beside him, a shawl flung over her shoulders and her hair pinned up in a chaotic bun. They made a striking couple, he said. Harry had become a familiar figure in this part of the town, and he was warmly hailed by many of those they met; and those who did not know him stared and whispered and were then informed by their companions as to the identity of the great bowed poet in black, and the tall red-haired girl walking with him.

Why did they go down to the docks?

They went down to the docks, said my uncle, because the sight of ships gave Harry comfort. To gaze upon the merchant shipping that crowded the Thames in those days, this, he said, somehow, to some degree, satisfied Harry's yearning to discover the world he had described in his ballad, and the life of simplicity in Nature it seemed to promise him. For he had come to regard London as a corrupt place, indeed all England was corrupt in Harry's view, because governed by corrupt men; and he dreamed that he and Martha might one day escape that corruption and find a place where the evil inherent in man's nature – and had he not glimpsed such evil in himself, and worked and suffered these many years to cleanse himself of it? – where human evil withered and fell away, and the natural virtuous man within could stand forth. That place, that great good place, he called America.

My uncle gazed at me with soured features, licking his lips as though he had just bit into a lemon. He had delivered all this in the ironical tones of an old sniffing cynic for whom the idea of man's natural virtue was but a chimerical wisp dreamed up by boys and poets.

The morning was cool and the sky clear as they passed under the slender wooden bridges that connected the great timbered warehouses on either side of the street, and came out on to a broad cobblestoned thoroughfare by the river. Much noise now, cranes creaking and pulleys rattling, men shouting, and the rumble of wheels, as they made their way through the bustle and tumult of the port to a bench in front of the Red Cock tavern. There Harry smoked a pipe, and Martha peeled an apple, while aproned porters pushed barrows of fish, and plump carters rumbled by atop wagons piled with sacks of grain. And ships! A wilderness of ships! A forest of masts and yards, a chaos of rope and rigging, pennants and ensigns fluttering in the breeze, and all manner of cargo, bales and barrels, sheep and cows, rising from their holds and swinging aloft in nets. For this was the giant's stomach, and into it flowed the wealth of the world.

It was the ships they had come to see. Martha knew little enough about ships beyond what she remembered of the fishing boats of Port Jethro, but these towering vessels, these great three-masters tied up at every wharf, and rocking on their cables in the stream, all streaked with salt and bleached by the sun, and sunburnt men with wild faces padding their decks and with strange cries darting about the rigging – they aroused her imagination with ideas of places with names like Surinam and Chandrapoor and Senegal and Trinidad and Philadelphia. Harry knew more of course, he knew the sea, but his were the eyes of a poet and the sea spoke to him now of epic themes, of storms and wrecks, mutiny and piracy, vessels becalmed in alien waters and attended by weird portents. Oh, they could amuse themselves for hours, those two, and they did. But their mood changed later in the morning, for as they lingered on their bench in the sunshine a regiment of infantry passed by, the Duke of Richmond's Foot, on its way to take ship for the colonies.

They had been aware of them for some time. The drums of course, always the drums, and then the dull shuffling thunder of the foot-soldiers of the Empire as they came marching along the river from the direction of Westminster. The troopships were some way off, but Harry and Martha had for more than an hour watched as the last stores and provisions were swung into the vessels' holds, barrels of beer and ship's biscuit and pickled beef; filthy stuff, said Harry, the quartermasters kept the best back for their own profit. Officers had gathered on the quayside, manifests were perused, men in bright uniforms spoke briskly one to another, one pointing his finger in one direction, another in another; and soon a crowd of the idle and the curious had gathered to watch the redcoats embark.

Tramp tramp tramp came the soldiers, and soon they were marching past the Red Cock, where Harry and Martha had been joined on their bench by their friend Fred Lour. Harry remarked on how young the soldiers were; only boys, he said, coarse rough fellows, yes, but boys for all that, and Fred agreed, he said the sergeants filled them with ale in country inns and when they were drunk enlisted them for a shilling. On they came, four abreast, the sergeants shouting and cursing them for lazy useless dogs, and worse, and the officers on horseback, proud fellows in splendid coats and great coloured sashes across their breasts. On they came, rank after rank, company after company, hundreds of men and boys, then thousands; ten, fifteen, twenty minutes they marched past the Red Cock with no break in the ranks. Harry was made sad by the spectacle. They did not know where they were going, he said, nor why they were going there, but Martha felt no pity for those rough boys. Did not each one of them carry a musket? And would he not use it to kill a colonist? Harry supposed she was right. They watched as the first ranks of redcoats marched up the gangplank and disappeared below decks. A little later there was some disturbance in the crowd, they could hear men shouting for the American cause, scuffles broke out, and Harry, who feared riot above all things, rose to his feet and with Martha beside him, her arm in his, set off back to Smithfield, after saying good-day to Fred

Lour, who thought he might stay awhile and see what happened, make a little mayhem of his own, perhaps.

Such was the temper of their days, in the spring of 1774. But now something altered in Harry's behaviour, and my uncle was at a loss to explain it. Harry had grown 'despondent', he said. Despondent? Why would Harry grow despondent? What had changed? Had he, perhaps, dreamed of Grace Foy, after Lord Drogo's question that recent night? No answer was forthcoming, and I suspected my uncle was again withholding information from me.

But it seems that soon after Drogo's visit Harry began to leave the Angel at night, and did not return for hours. I could well believe that he wanted to escape the constriction of those shabby rooms, but Martha was filled with a profound apprehension at this development, for it had never been her father's habit to leave her alone and go out by night, and Harry, surely, was aware of this.

Where he went nobody knew. I imagine him striking out for the fields to the north of Smithfield, or perhaps crossing the river and making his way into the countryside beyond Southwark. But wherever he went, that big shambling figure must first have passed through gloomy courts, and winding alleys, ever darker and more scuttling, and heard soft siren voices from doorways, from windows, from cellars, calling to him to come in, come down, come drink –

But I imagine he ignored them, for it was not drink he craved, nor the company of women. No, I imagine he reached open fields, and at last filled his labouring lungs with air that was free of the filth of the town. Perhaps he found a great tree, an oak in the middle of a field of wheat that cast a pool of shade in the moonlight, and perhaps he sank down beneath it, and gazed at the night sky and dreamed of America –? But whatever it was he did in those lost hours, he returned to the Angel at first light, and found Martha sitting up waiting for him. With what tenderness did father and daughter then embrace!

It became a frequent occurrence, Harry's aimless nocturnal rambling, and I think he may have wandered some nights for miles along the river, and perhaps come upon the hay barges moored down by London Bridge, the boys sprawled sleeping on their harvest in the moonlight, with not a care beyond the getting of a fair price for their hay and drinking some London ale before returning into the countryside. What yearning we may glimpse in Harry's heart when he saw such a scene – could this be why he grew 'despondent'? He wished only to live as a free man upon the fruits of his labour, and grow old in the natural rhythms of the earth; instead of which he was cursed, so he felt, always to be an object of disgust, or horror, which is only disgust with a portion of fear superadded – always to be in the eyes of the world a monster. He sometimes talked to Martha of these things, by night, in his room, and in the candlelight his eyes shone with unshed tears, and she knew he ached and bled and raged in his heart not merely because he wished these things for himself, but because he wished them for her too.

One night he took a drink. I suppose the temptation, down on the docks, by the great ships with their masts rising slender in the moonlight, and the men and women loudly spilling out of the riverside taverns and cellars – in the end it was too much for him. He took a pot of ale. He intended that it be only the one. Oh, but there were men drinking there who had such stories to tell, and being men who had seen much of the world, and were not easily surprised, they accepted him and made no more than passing friendly inquiry as to his spine. That he had read so much, that he was an educated man, a poet, this mattered not at all, for Harry Peake was entirely without pride or presumption. No, what mattered was that they did not see him as a monster. They made no gesture of exclusion, and he was able to sit with them and smoke his pipe, and drink his ale, and listen with deep pleasure as tales were told of foreign shores, and the voyages undertaken to reach those shores, and the men who worked the ships that sailed there. Then came the songs, and the hornpipes, the jigs and the fiddles, and Harry Peake in silly beery disarray was soon cavorting like a boy among these sons of the sea.

And what a sorry sight, when at last he returned in the full glare of the morning! For with the coming of day the brief idyll that darkness and drink had permitted – it vanished; and home at last the poet must come, the heady fumes of the night no longer magic, now no more than an aching pain in an irritable brain, compounded by the guilt he felt at having succumbed to temptation; that guilt tempered in its turn by anger that he must always deny himself the pleasures enjoyed by other men; though sweetened withal, I believe, by the secret unspoken prospect of enjoying it all once more, when darkness fell.

Martha did not reproach him, but told him that she had not slept, such had been her anxiety for his safety; and detecting by the smell of him that he had drunk only ale, and been made soft and sleepy by it, asked him to think hard upon what he was doing, and what greater harm it might lead him into. This last annoyed Harry, who wanted only to sleep and be free of the pain in his head and the compound of unhappy feelings that had arisen in him; and he raised his voice in anger, glaring at her with grief and fury before stumbling to his bed and pulling closed his curtain. He lay there separate from her, moaning quietly and sweating out the fluids of the night in the full stifling heat of noon.

He awoke in a state of great sadness, having dreamed of the fire in which Grace Foy perished; and not, I believe, for the first time. For an hour Martha attempted to cheer him but to no avail. He was inconsolable. All lost, he cried, and the idea set off an association of thoughts that confirmed a deep-lying conviction in him of his own worthlessness. Martha suggested that they walk by the docks but Harry said no, and then declared he would never work in this damn sink again, never again would he show his back.

'Then what are we to do?' said Martha, but she received no answer, and she left him to himself.

She paced her room in a state of some agitation. Several hours passed. She could not go to him, for he had locked the door between their rooms. She shouted at him through the door, but still received no answer. This had never happened before, never had he locked her out – locked her *in*, rather, for the only door giving on to the passage and the stairs was in his room – and again she asked herself what was to become of them, if he would not work? For this, she knew, was no idle threat on Harry's part, Harry was not a man who made idle threats. Her mind at once raced to the worst of all possible outcomes. Were they to join the growing ranks of ragged castaways who begged and thieved in the streets of London, until gin, or hunger, or disease, or the gallows ended their misery for good?

8

In the days that followed Martha remained deeply alarmed by her father's mood. Never before had she seen him so cast down, and not merely cast down, something in him had died. She stood before him and gazed long and hard into his eyes as he sat, one evening, staring into the empty fireplace, and where once she had always found a spark of gentle recognition, even when he was deeply preoccupied – where once he would absently reach a hand toward her, and gather her into his arms, and seat her in his lap, without disturbing his meditation – now it seemed he did not see her at all. So extensive was the destruction wrought in that man's soul by the awakened memory of the loss he had suffered, and the grief and guilt attendant upon that loss, there was little capacity left to sustain the love of his daughter.

Martha demanded nothing of him. She understood that he must be allowed to ruminate to the full upon the tragedy, which for many years he had consigned to the cellars of his mind, whence the memory of it had now suddenly emerged; he must ruminate on it, she believed, before he could rise again with fresh resolve. Fred Lour appeared as usual, but Harry sent him away, insisting that he would never again submit himself to public display, and instructing him to cancel all performances. So Fred and Martha left Harry to grieve in peace, and went off about the town together.

Early one morning a few days later Martha entered her father's room and found him asleep, fully clothed, on the bed. On the floor beside the bed were half-a-dozen empty bottles. She sank on to a chair and covered her face with her hands. At last she looked up, and gazed at her father sprawled there, stinking of wine and snoring loudly. She was too young ever to remember seeing him in this condition, but she remembered well enough him speaking about the evil of drink, and about his own weakness.

Harry woke up some hours later, put his feet on the floor, but could get no further, and sat there groaning and clutching his head. Martha went to him with hot tea and murmured quietly to him as he sipped it, and he nodded, and after a time he turned to her with the tears streaming down his face and pulled her to his breast and held her there, moaning and rocking. Soon enough he had recovered sufficiently to make his way to his wash bowl and there, having stripped off his shirt, he doused his head in cold water and then lifted it with a shout, flung his head up so that the water showered off him, and the shout he shouted was: 'Never again!' – and shortly after: 'I am not beat yet!' – and more in this vein, and Martha looked on with a smile that was by no means free of anxiety. I think he was probably still drunk.

Ah, but there he stood bent over his bowl, and in the late afternoon sunlight the ridged hump of his back seemed almost translucent, so delicate a structure was it, like a fin, the skin so white, stretched taut upon its fragile outcrop of flaring bone. It was seldom that Harry took his shirt off in front of Martha, and she was fascinated by his spine. Watching him, loving the sheer strength and bigness of him, she did not see it as abnormal, and could, rather, believe she inhabited a world in which all men had ridged spines, and her father's the most handsome of them all. It was so unfair; and him so handsome, as he stood bowed over his bowl and sponged from his body the sweat and filth of the night.

For some days, said my uncle, resuming his narrative, Harry was as good as his word. He seemed to be shifting his gaze from the terrible wound which had opened in his heart, and was expressing tentative sentiments of hope. He even began to write a little, although he remained adamant in his refusal to perform in the taproom below. But what mattered now, as Martha told him, was that he bear up under his misfortune, and begin to make some plan for the future, and not drink.

A return, then, to the routine of their old life, Harry smoking his pipe and reading newspapers in the coffee shops, often lifting his head and drifting into distant contemplative reverie; and Martha going about her tasks, her washing and darning, her sweeping and cleaning, husbanding the small reserve of money they possessed. In the evening Harry would tell her what he had read that day, and through directed argument, with patience and humour, instructed his daughter in the practice of thinking so that, as he said, she might learn to distinguish Reason from that which merely masqueraded as Reason; and of the latter, he said, the world was full. Only by Reason – Reason tempered with natural benevolence – could any person, he said, man or woman, hope to live peaceably with others; and without the constraints, he might well have added, of governments, or churches, or kings.

He told her about the argument between the colonists and the crown, saying darkly that war would surely come soon; and hearing this I asked my uncle what Harry thought about the coming war, this man who hated violence? My uncle sniffed. It displeased him, he said, to have to tell me this, but Harry sided with the rebels. He had been an early advocate of American independence from the Empire, and he understood that blood must be shed for that independence to be won. And rightly so, I thought, though I did not say this to my clucking frowning uncle.

Lord Drogo came once to visit Harry during this period. As before, he came with William in the small black carriage with the coat-of-arms in flaking gold leaf on the door; as before, Clyte was their driver; and as before, they arrived at the Angel at twilight. Finding that there was no performance, his lordship sent my uncle upstairs to request an audience; which Harry granted.

The distinguished visitors spent almost an hour with Harry in his room. Lord Drogo wished to examine his spine, and did so. I asked my uncle what it looked like; and it has always seemed to me to be distinctly sinister that William Tree, although a surgeon, was in agreement with Martha in the strange idea that *Harry's spine was beautiful.*

Beautiful –?

But why, he cried, should it not be? Was it not constituted of flesh and bone, such as all our bodies are made of? This question he put to me in a tone of spry challenge, but I would not argue with him. And was this spine, he said, so strange, after all? Those struts and ribs of bone, were they not forms found in all of Nature, and indeed in the human form, although disposed elsewhere and otherwise? Why by this mere accident of organization must we think him ugly, or grotesque, or monstrous? Were he a landscape we would not be slow to pronounce him sublime!

He peered at me with rare earnest sincerity, but I had no answer for him. Harry was no landscape, he was a man. Why then must his life be twisted so far from what others had, on account of his back?

Martha saw the visitors as they were leaving, having stationed herself outside her father's door so as to hear what she could of what went on inside. Drogo nodded at her with cold disdain and went on down the staircase. My uncle William paused, however, and asked her how she did, and Martha was unable to hold her feelings in check, but told him all their recent misfortune.

My uncle said that on glimpsing the depth of her distress he resolved there and then that he would be a friend to this unhappy girl. He took her chin in his hand, he said, and looked into her eyes, and told her with great seriousness that if ever she were in need, she must come to him, and he would help her. Oh, I can see the old man now, as he dwelled upon this offer of help he made, still quite as intoxicated with his own gallantry as he was fifty years before! There he sat, dwarfed in his great armchair, sitting up with no small effort to be sure I understood what he had done, and in his excitement spilling his wine.

'I liked the girl, you see,' he cried, fixing me with a watery eye, and lifting a trembling hand, 'she had spirit!'

He talked on through the night. Again I sat in rapt attention, attempting to make sense of his digressions and asides, and to allow for what I was now beginning to recognize as a subtle attempt to

67

misrepresent the truth of the thing and make me believe that Lord Drogo was interested solely in the welfare of Harry Peake. About this last I was starting to harbour serious doubts, which were not allayed by the description he gave me of the visit Harry made to Drogo Hall later that summer. For my uncle would have me believe that Harry was welcomed, that he was treated with respect. My own construction was somewhat different, and I will tell you why.

I had begun to ponder Harry's decision not to show himself in the taproom of the Angel. This of course was why he was impelled to cross the Lambeth Marsh to Drogo Hall, Joseph Goat having not been slow to remind him that a man in search of pleasure by night will avoid a house where none is to be had; making it clear that Harry's refusal to work was damaging the interest of the house, which was Joseph Goat's interest. Harry must work, or he must pay for his board and lodging in full; and if he did neither, he would soon find himself unwelcome at the Angel.

But this was on the material level only. What intrigued me about the poet was his soul. And it is my conclusion that Harry Peake, in the wake of Lord Drogo's first visit, and the recurrence of his dreams of the Port Jethro fire, had changed, and the man who before had willingly painted his face, and indulged the coarse curiosity of the public, so as to make restitution for the death of his wife – that man now shuddered with revulsion at the very thought of such self-exposure. In short, his penance was over.

His penance was over. He had atoned for his sin. The man he had been was no more, this is my conclusion; a new man had begun to come into being, that man intent now upon turning his mind to higher matters of the spirit, and thus, in a sense, a weaker man than his predecessor. Harry was attempting to forge a new relation to his twisted spine. He was coming to understand that his body was but an accidental membrane sheathing a soul that in all its proportions and lineaments was not disfigured. His brief period of confusion and despair had opened his eyes, and he could not go back to what he was. I can find no other reason for this most independent of men to walk out to Drogo Hall and ask for money.

Now it seems Lord Drogo was that day entertaining a group of medical men, and that on being informed by my uncle William that Harry Peake had come to the house seeking an interview with him, he left his guests and came to the poet where he waited in the hall, having at once guessed the reason for his presence there. He quickly confirmed that, yes, Harry came as a supplicant, and made clear that he would be willing to help him, and generously at that; but that he asked one favour in return.

What was Harry to say? The long walk across the Lambeth Marsh, and the approach to the great house, were enough to rock the resolution of the stoutest heart, and put a man in a subordinate position before he had even encountered the master. When his lordship agreed to answer the request put to him, and then asked but one favour, the petitioner would of course accede at once. And what was that favour? Merely, said Lord Drogo, that he might show Harry's back to a group of medical men; purely, of course, that the advancement of learning may go forward, that the good doctors may be fully apprised of Nature's variety in the matter of twisted spines. Harry Peake's misgivings were overwhelmed by the sense of indebtedness that he felt toward Lord Drogo; and so he agreed.

Oh, the presumption, the arrogance of inherited privilege! I can only imagine the humiliation Harry suffered. But that it was extreme, given the fragile state of his soul at that time, is amply indicated by his subsequent behaviour. My uncle described how he was stripped of his shirt and brought into the Theatre of Anatomy, where a group of perhaps fifteen doctors had assembled. And I imagine that Lord Drogo, who had been friendly enough to Harry when talking to him in the great hall outside the theatre, became at once brisk and cold, he became the man of science attending to what was nothing more than a specimen. Harry's history, as he had given it to Lord Drogo, was recounted in stark, abbreviated form; his story of how he had been born deformed was mentioned, and much laughter was heard in the amphitheatre at the very idea of great shadows being responsible for anything but great nonsense.

But I wonder, now – was it such nonsense? Must we all now defer to the upstart Reason, and bend the knee before His Precocious Majesty? – and ignore the promptings of an ancient Knowledge which has guided mankind since the dawn of time? – why should not a great shadow, glimpsed in terror by a pregnant woman, deform the foetus in her womb? Does it not make eminent sense? To me, yes, it does – but enough. Harry Peake, hearing himself mocked in front of men of vastly more formal education than himself, and feeling himself more monstrous, as Lord Drogo turned him this way and that before the company, pointing out this or that feature of his spine, than he ever did when showing himself in the taproom of an inn – Harry suffered more in that hour, I believe, than he had suffered in the previous ten years. He became no more than a bent back. Man he was not. Of humanity he had none. He was cattle, worse than cattle, for his value lay only in that which was abnormal.

When Lord Drogo had finished, the doctors came forward to examine for themselves the anatomical curiosity. They fingered his spine, they measured it, they probed and kneaded and squeezed it. They asked him questions, but not as if he were a man, as if he were the mere porter or guardian of his own deformity! They talked among themselves of what they saw and what they thought of him as though he were not present. And when they had satisfied their curiosity, Lord Drogo dismissed Harry with a wave of his hand, and my uncle William took him to the kitchen and there gave him money, and a plate of food, and a glass of wine.

A glass of wine. Harry left Drogo Hall with money in his pocket and rage in his heart. He had his money, but he had sold his soul for it, so he felt, he had allowed himself to be handled as an animal, and all that distinguishes the animal from the man is the soul, no? He had for that interminable hour in the Theatre of Anatomy been a creature devoid of a soul. They had purchased his soul, and he had agreed to the terms of the contract. He was dirtied by the transaction, brought low by it; he felt himself a nothing, as he walked away from Drogo Hall that day, and set his steps across the

Lambeth Marsh toward the distant spires of the town; and with the taste of wine on his lips, and money in his pocket, he was soon established in a tavern, and by nightfall he had moved on to gin.

The rest may be predicted.

9

Is it premature to voice my suspicions as to what Lord Drogo truly wanted from Harry Peake? It was not a simple matter of examining his spine, nor of displaying it to his medical friends. No, Drogo had a far more – imperial – project in view. I believe he wanted to *own* Harry's spine. He wanted him for his Museum of Anatomy, he wanted him among his exhibits. Not so unusual a thing in those days, when any anatomist of distinction prided himself on his collection of anatomical curiosities, and vied with his peers in the range and oddity of the specimens he could display. Lord Drogo was no better than the rest, and I believe it had occurred to him when first he heard Clyte read the handbill discovered in the pocket of Mary Magdalen Smith, that here might be his *pièce de résistance* – the skeleton of the Cripplegate Monster.

Was he disappointed in Harry's backbone? Was it not as floridly bent as he had hoped? This was not a question I could ask my uncle William. But whatever the expectation, nobody could deny that here was a man with a most peculiar spinal formation; and Drogo wanted it. What then of my uncle William? Was he innocent of all this? I do not think he could have been. I think he was as complicit in Drogo's designs as Clyte was. He knew what was happening, he knew that Harry was the object of Lord Drogo's ambition. What none of them could have predicted of course was that Harry should then have come out to Drogo Hall to ask for money. But see how Drogo capitalized on his good fortune! See how he humiliated the poet, when he was at his most vulnerable! And see how my uncle William, having given poor Harry the money he asked for, sent him on his way *with a glass of wine*. You may imagine the scepticism with which I attended my uncle's narration after I had reached these conclusions.

That glass of wine led him by nightfall to move on to gin, and Harry Peake was no match for a bottle of gin. A bottle of hock, a

72

pot of ale, of these he had shown himself the equal, when he drank for an hour or two and then came home. But the gin, no, with the gin it was different, and it was bad gin they drank in those days, distilled fast, a crude and impure liquor. It masked his soul, or killed it, rather, for the period of the intoxication; and it had the effect then of urging him to renew the intoxication before it had worn off properly, before the fumes had cleared, so it was that much harder for him, when he did become sober, to recover his own self, and resume life in the person he had been.

But he did not become sober for a number of days, nor did he return to the Angel during that time. When he did come back, he was in a most pitiable condition indeed. All the money he had had from Lord Drogo was spent, and so was he. His humanity was burned up inside him, he was nothing but ashes and heat, smouldering with bitterness, now and then flaring without warning, then just as suddenly subsiding into a state of muttering introspection. Explosive energies seethed and roiled within his torched frame, within the ruin he had made of himself in his few days down by the docks.

Martha had heard her father talk often, in his sober years, about what drink did to him. He said there was a demon at work in him when he drank, he said he could see it, a ghastly black creature that sat on top of him, that hunkered slavering on his spine, urging him to fresh excess, and him a hollow thing in which the demon words reverberated and turned to din without meaning, and nothing left inside him with which to oppose its malign influence. That help must come from Martha. She must never, he said, allow him to drink. It was a responsibility that should never have been placed upon the shoulders of one so young. They were broad shoulders, Martha's, and she bravely attempted to do what he asked. But in the end the demon was too strong for her.

Each night of his absence she went into the town to look for him. It was nasty perilous work. A man on gin tends to drift eastward, and the further east a man goes, the lower he sinks. She searched the pot-houses and night-cellars around the docks, to which she guessed he would gravitate, given his old deep attraction to the river. She had only to open the door of those places and glimpse what lay within – the thick smoke, the lifted faces, the haunted eyes – for the insults, the compliments, the invitations, the curses to be flung at her like so many darts dipped in filth. In she went however, fixed in her resolve, she moved through the gloom until she was sure he was not there, and then on to the next one.

At last she found him. Emerging at dawn on to a deserted dock, by way of a covered alley with an arched opening, she saw a disused wharf stretching into the river on ancient mossy spiles. A light mist lay on the river, the few ships at anchor were spectral and un-moving in the stream. At the end of the wharf sat a humped figure singing a broken ballad. There was a bottle beside him on the planks.

She approached with some diffidence. Halfway out along the wharf, the damp rotten planks sagging and splintering beneath her feet, he heard her. Wheeling his head about with painful slowness he watched his daughter approach. His eyes were red smears in shadowy caverns, and a hopeless, amiable grin pulled apart his jaw and lent him the appearance of a donkey. He lifted a hand and shouted what might have been: 'Hail the dawn!'

Martha could not know his temper. She picked her way along the wharf until she was close to him.

'Father,' she said.

Nothing.

'Father, you must come home now.'

A streaming confusion of words from Harry now, an incompre-hensible stew in which could be detected scraps of poetry and fragments of thought, but all mixed in with nonsense like chunks of beef in a puddle of vomitus. The tone, however – the tone remained friendly.

'I've come to take you home, father.'

A last few sputtering ribbons of indigestible verbiage. Then silence. He spoke not to her but direct to the river, which was calm and oily where the mist in patches opened upon its surface. The great head sank forward now, and the hands were limply folded in the lap. A bell clanged mournfully from a ship in the stream, its masts and cross-trees visible above the mist. A breeze came up, and the vessels rocked gently at their moorings. The head sank forward, and the great back lifted. He had no coat, his shirt was torn open at the throat and somewhere he had lost a shoe. Then with a shake of the shaggy head he sat up straight and stretched his arms high above his head, and opened his jaws to yawn, and take in a few large gulps of the morning. He turned then toward Martha.

'Home, is it?' he said, absently scratching his chin.

'Home, father.'

There came now something in Latin, and then, with no small effort, and a good deal of pain, he managed to winch himself on to a knee, and from there, after a heaving pause of several seconds, to his feet. He swayed a moment, like a tree when the saw has come clean through, but the trunk retains a precarious balance on its stump; then flung out an arm, and held on to Martha's shoulder; and thus crutched by his daughter he began the slow grim lurch through the morning to Cripplegate.

For some days he barely stirred from his room. He was not drinking hard now. He had gin by him, but he took it sparingly; sufficient to maintain the smouldering husks of a morbid vitality. He paced the floor. He read, and at times scribbled furiously at his table, though he destroyed much of what he wrote, setting it afire in the grate. Martha watched him with wary eyes, ever-vigilant, awaiting an explosion she feared could come at any time from this stooped glowering figure with the dead red eyes. She was living with a wild creature of unpredictable temper; when would it show its claws, its fangs, in anger?

Martha watched her father in his decline with a grief and at times a rage that remained, however, impotent, for he refused to tolerate for a moment any attempt she made to interfere with his drinking. Ah, she watched the man; she should have watched the bottle. Had she properly understood the pattern of his drinking she would have anticipated the crisis. For there came a quickening, as he tired of whatever control was employed in maintaining the brooding semi-intoxication of the last several days. Now came a day – it was a Sunday – when she heard, in the early evening, just as twilight descended, and the murmur from the taproom below grew loud, and the first songs were sung to the first scrapings of the fiddle – a sudden shout from his room.

She looked up from her stitching. Muffled curses through the door now; he was in pain. This she had been dreading, that while he was in this gin-sodden condition he should suffer an attack of those torments of the spine which at intervals felled him and left him in a state of wrecked exhaustion. With gin in him, what then would happen when the pain came? Would it drive him into a frenzy, into mania proper; and what was he capable of then?

She put aside her work and crossed the room to her father's door, and without knocking she went in. There had indeed been a sudden increase in his drinking, and it had been accompanied, so it appeared, by a furious bout of writing. Sheets of paper were scattered all over the table, every sheet covered with his distinctive flowing hand, and not a few stained with spilt gin. There were papers on the floor, and no attempt had been made to gather or collate them, as though the act of writing was what mattered here rather than the verse generated, if verse it was; as though he were attempting to expel the demon through the medium of ink, and the more furiously he wrote the more gin he must drink to sustain the flow.

But he had been brought to an abrupt stop. He stood swaying over the table, staring at his thumb, from which blood was gouting on to his papers, staring at it with his lips pulled back from his teeth and his eyes wide with horror. He was obstructed even in his attempt to empty his poor teeming brain of its frenzy! Quills he had worn down and thrown aside were scattered on the floor, along with the shavings from repeated sharpenings of their nibs; and now in his sharpening he had sliced open his thumb. Blood spouting everywhere, on to his shirt, on to the table, and on to the sheets of writing, where it mingled with the fresh ink, creating blots and rivers of red and black.

Martha ran to him with a cry of alarm, pushed him back down in his chair, seized tight his thumb and held it aloft. Harry sat there dumbly, staring at his table, as Martha bandaged the wound with a handkerchief. He seemed then to awaken to his surroundings: the papers, the blood, the quills, the bottles, the ink.

'Am I mad?' he murmured, frowning, lifting a sheet of his own writing and trying to read it. He shook his head as though unable to comprehend what the words meant. He looked at Martha. 'Am I mad? What is the matter with me?'

My poor Martha, the tears were flowing unchecked now, at this first sign in so many days of his reason returning.

'No, father, no,' she cried, 'not mad, no; drunk is all, only drunk.'

'Only drunk,' he said, absently lifting his hand once more as Martha directed him to. 'For how long?' he said.

'Some days.'

'Oh God.'

At this point he laid his face on the table, among his sodden verses, and wrapped his fingers together on top of his skull; and Martha stroked her father's head as he sobbed into the table.

'Is it the ballad?' she whispered; and at the sound of her voice a wonderful event occurred. Her father's head came up off the table and he stared at her and for the first time in what seemed an eternity – *saw* her. He saw her.

'Martha,' he said, and lifted his bandaged hand to his tear-stained face, so that all his mouth and jaw were covered by his fingers, but his eyes gazed at her direct. And gone, gone, the deadness! It was him.

'Martha,' he said again, and pushing back his chair, opened his arms to her. She clambered into his lap and threw her arms around his neck and clung to him.

'Is it over?' she whispered.

Her father's face was buried in her shoulder, her head was pressed against his great head, held tight by his fingers. He murmured into her shoulder and her face filled with hope at the thought that it was over, and he was his own self again.

He was very tired. Martha led him into her own room and had him take his shirt off, and washed him as he sat nodding and dozing in the chair, and every moment he threatened to fall asleep and topple on to the floor. She put him into her own bed and then set about making order of the chaos he had created. She stood his jugs and bottles in ranks by the door, and organized the papers strewn about the room. Harry had made no attempt to number his pages or otherwise indicate their sequence, nor was that flowing hand legible as it once had been. Under the influence of gin, letters, whole words, strings of words even, had bled into each other so there was no telling where the one ended and the next began, this difficulty exacerbated by the smudging of ash from his pipe, the holes burned by falling embers, and elsewhere blots and runnings where gin or blood or tears had mingled with the ink. She would make out perhaps three or four words, a phrase, a sentence, then lose its meaning because she was unable to understand what it led to and where it had come from. It was a wild incoherent screed, and after some minutes of inspection, in which she tried to elicit some meaning from the soiled pages, it occurred to her that perhaps they had no meaning at all, beyond the flickering transient impulses of a mind unmoored and exiled from reason and mastered, rather, by the demon resident in a bottle of gin.

So she gathered them up, and flung sawdust on those still damp, and made a pile of them, and left them in the middle of his table with the ink bottle on top as a paperweight, and beside it the jar containing his uncut quills; then went into the other room. She dragged the chair to the bedside and sat there listening to the snores of an exhausted man surrendering at last to sleep.

It may be true that what a king is in the moral universe, a monster is in the physical, and that Harry Peake, in gin, behaved with all the violent intemperance of a tyrant. This is how my uncle would have it, and perhaps he attempted to impose this view on Martha too. Later, after she reached America, I believe she came to understand why her father acted as he did, and understanding, forgave him. But at the time, in London, in the late summer of 1774, she could not simply wait for the day when Harry, drunk, did serious damage to himself or to her.

For it was not over, Martha soon realized this; she had tried to convince herself that this was but some transient condition, some temporary disturbance of the soul which her father would shake off as a dog shakes off water; or which would simply pass over like a patch of bad weather. But no. She saw that it would never be over; she would have been unable to say why she knew this, but she had seen a man begin to try and change his nature, to forget who he was and what he had been, and move toward some new state or stage of being. He had glimpsed it; he had touched the lodestar of his own soul, and knew its heft and value; and he had thought that he could change his destiny and make himself anew.

He could not. For he remained trapped within the grotesque body. The world still knew him for a monster. However fresh the springs of the spirit within him, this could not be overcome, for this, his body, in the eyes of the world *was* his nature; and glimpsing this, in his bitterness, and spite, he had jettisoned his humanity and *embraced the monster*. Martha understood this as a child understands such things: darkly, in the obscure regions of the mind, those places from which occasionally truth will rise without preamble or argument. But that truth did not ravage her as perhaps it might have done, and for one simple reason: her father loved her. She cared for nothing else, and this I believe to be the very engine of her fate, that in all the tumult of her childhood he had been home and harbour, the source of love. She had seen it when he looked at her and the deadness was gone; and this, to her, poor child, was all that mattered.

The last sobering lasted no longer than the one before, and by then it had become clear to Martha that her father was sinking fast. My uncle said he did not wish to weary me with Harry's later outrages, suffice that despite all his good intentions in the wake of the last bout, he had resumed drinking. He brooded in his room for hours at a time, he paced the floor like a creature in a cage. Martha listened through the door as he moaned to himself in the night. Sometimes he thumped the wall so hard with his fist that the plaster was dislodged on her side, and clouds of powder drifted about in the moonlight. She had been growing more and more apprehensive, she had even tried to tell him that he had been seduced by a phantom, and was not the world full of that which merely masqueraded as Reason? Was there better magic in the bottle than in the embrace of a loving daughter? All this she said to him, but he paid no attention, instead he left her, and went clattering off down the stairs, for in truth he was now at war with love, only darkness answered to his temper now.

Martha sat in his room, waiting for him to return, and for the first time she quarrelled with herself, she told herself it was her fault he went off drinking, why could she not stop him? This brought her to tears, but in a moment her grief turned to passionate indignation and she reminded herself how hard she had thought about what she should do, and with nobody to advise her she could only do what her common sense told her was right, and how unjust, how bitter, to think that this was *her* fault –!

And now, said my uncle William – it was three in the morning, I remember hearing the old clock chime the hours in the hallway below – now comes one of the blackest episodes in the whole unhappy tale. Martha was awoken late that night by the sound of muffled grunting, and the creak and scream of woodwork in motion, the sound of a ship under sail, so it seemed, or some other great timbered machine. She sat up in her bed, straining to hear, and all at once the creaking stopped. She heard a voice, her father's, raised in anger, and then came another voice, a woman's voice, and in that voice she heard terror.

Martha ran to the door between the two rooms and pressed her ear to it. She heard her father shouting incoherently; then silence; then all at once a bottle shattering against a wall. She flung open the door. The room was dark, only one candle was burning. Her father sat naked on the side of his bed, bent forward and breathing hard, his back like a huge pale hood thrown up behind him, rising and falling as his lungs laboured, and his great horse-penis hanging black in the shadows between his legs. As Martha stared in astonishment from the doorway his head lifted and he glared at her from eyes that were blazing with drink and rage, and there was something else there too, that same deadness she had seen in him before, that black opacity in which she could find no reflection of herself, no answering flicker of feeling, as though he were a stranger, or worse, a creature not fully human, one possessed by brute animal instinct and with no higher faculty capable of employing reason or sympathy to temper its impulse.

That impulse had but a moment before been one of violence. Now Martha glimpsed a movement, and all at once she saw standing in the corner of the dark room the shadowy figure of a woman, clutching a chair as though to defend herself from attack – and it was Sal Goat, beefy Sal! She was panting hard. The candle flame caught a dull glint from the tin in her mouth. Martha felt her skin go cold; never had her father brought a woman back to their lodgings before. But her next impulse was for Sal's safety.

'Get out, Sal!' she whispered; then more loudly, 'Go!'

Sal Goat coolly hitched her skirt up with one hand and with her eyes never leaving Harry she moved to the door into the passage. At the door she flung a curse at him and was gone.

Martha at once went to her father, who sat staring fixed at the wall where the wine still streamed down the plaster. His jaw was working, bone grinding on bone, as though he searched for words, as though the animal nature dimly groped for what was yet human within its clouded brain. There he sat, breathing heavy, his hands clamped to his bare knees and his feet planted wide apart on the floorboards such that he seemed a piece of snorting statuary, a braced and strutted thing that burned within, and could be set in violent motion again, given due cause.

All at once he became aware of Martha in her nightshirt. His laboured breathing was the only sound in that room that reeked of wine and violence, in which the very air seemed throbbing and alive and in tumult still with his rage. Martha's weary temper frayed at last, she felt she could stand no more, and it was with an anger that had been fermenting in her for weeks that she began to berate him for the bottle smashed against the wall –

Harry's head snapped up. His eyes now burned as with the very fires of Hell – windows of Hell, his eyes were now, at the sound of Martha's voice. Oh, and what happened next would never be forgotten, I believe, by either one of them. He rose from the bed with a grunt and in one swooping step had seized up his daughter and held her before him, Martha clamped now and struggling in her father's huge hands, shouting into her father's face, that face twisted with fury, fumes of bad gin surging from between his bitter lips, the horse-penis up stiff now, hard as a rock and all athrob, great thick thing it was pushing at her thighs. All at once with a deliberate grunt he slammed her against the wall, with such force that the air was dashed from the girl's body.

The bruises on her upper arms, the distinct and separate marks of her father's fingers, would take many days to fade. She was screaming now, as Harry brought his face in close to hers, the burning eyes, the grinding teeth, the rage, the gin – and the next thing was Sal Goat running at him with a broomstick, screaming at him to let Martha go – she thought he would bite the girl's head off, bite her head off and throw her out of the window! For there was passion enough in him that the deed would be done in the impulse of an instant and then forever regretted.

Sal Goat flailed at Harry as if she were beating a carpet, and he took a step backwards, stumbling over the chair she had flung down earlier. He released Martha, who scrambled away, Sal seizing her by the wrist and dragging her into the other room, glancing as she did so at Harry, where he sat now on the floor with his head in his hands, oblivious to their withdrawal. A moment later, with Martha sobbing loudly on the bed, Sal pushed a chair up against the door. It could not have stopped him had he chosen to come through, but some gesture of defence seemed necessary.

They did nothing that night. They did not try to reach the passage, for they feared rousing him to fresh violence. They lay in bed watching the door. After a while they heard him moving around, and Sal grew alarmed.

'He will sleep it off,' whispered Martha, as the two girls clung together beneath the bedclothes, 'then he will be himself again.'

They held each other close, and at last they fell asleep.

No further movement was heard that night. When Martha awoke it was broad daylight, and she was alone. She saw that the chair Sal had pushed against the door was no longer there. A little later Sal appeared.

'He has gone out,' she said. 'He has swept away the broken glass. He has put the room to rights.'

Some comfort this, not much.

He returned in the late afternoon, she heard him come in. The door between their rooms was not locked. It swung open. He stood in the doorway, huge and crumpled and broken. He tried to talk but he could not. Martha gazed at him with steady eyes.

'What do you want?' she said.

His voice was barely more than a whisper. 'I want to be forgiven.'

He sank to his knees in the doorway, not without pain, and opened his arms. He stank of drink and tobacco and worse.

'Martha,' he whispered, 'I am sorry.'

Martha was silent.

'Forgive me.'

Silence.

Harry's face was a damp mess, running with tears, and with the dilute grime he had attracted to himself in the hours of his dissipation. Martha stood by the window. He gave out a sort of choked sob and, with one hand on the door frame for support, rose unsteadily to his feet. Martha shrank back. Harry gazed at her with a face of such piteous misery that her heart was ripped wide open by it; but she did not move. He turned then and withdrew into his own room, and the door closed softly behind him. A little later he thumped the wall hard; then he clattered off down the staircase, and she knew that when he returned he would not be sober.

And so ended the second night of my uncle's storytelling. He would have continued, I know; fuelled by whatever drug it was that sustained the vital flame in him, he would have talked till dawn about his demented poet and the poet's handsome daughter, but I could not have listened. I was exhausted. Unlike him, I had risen at an early hour of the morning and now I could barely keep my eyes open. Pleading fatigue, I asked if we might go on tomorrow.

The old man took this to be a lamentable lack of stamina on my part. He was wearing, that night, a maroon velvet smoking jacket beneath his dressing gown, and maroon velvet slippers; and on his head a curious sort of skullcap with a silk tassel hanging down over his ear. This skullcap he now removed, and briskly rubbing his liver-spotted skull and its few wisps of hair, he said he supposed he could amuse himself until his own bedtime; and bade me goodnight.

Bad dreams again that night; and again I awoke shivering early in the morning, and at once leaped out of bed and threw on my clothes, those that I had not been sleeping in. Standing at the window, and rubbing my hands for warmth, I saw that the day was clear and cold, with only a few clouds off to the west, and I decided that I would take my horse out for a gallop across the marsh, so as to clear my mind of all the grim events I had been told of in the night. The house was as empty as it had been the day before. I made my way downstairs and out through the kitchen to the stables at the back without encountering a living soul, and saddled up without assistance. At that time I owned a brown cob, a good strong animal with a sweet disposition, and when I led her out of the stable and into the yard I knew she was as ready for a gallop as I was.

We trotted out through the village to the London road, where we turned to the south, and with just a touch she was off like the wind. Oh, it was a fine smoky morning, and it was more than fine to be galloping through that empty landscape, getting clear away from Drogo Hall and my ancient dusty uncle! The road was dry and we came along at a fine clip through stubble fields, in the distance ahead low hills crowned with leafless trees. After a few miles we turned off the main road and cantered along to a village where I was sure I would find a good breakfast.

And so I did; and a good fire, in front of which I warmed my bottom, then flung myself into a chair and stretched my legs before settling to a plate of steamed kidneys, Colchester oysters, bread and butter, and strong tea. Then I turned my chair to the fire once more, and pondered Harry Peake awhile, and turned over in my mind the suspicion I was harbouring as to Lord Drogo's designs upon the man, his desire to have his backbone for *display*; and all at once it occurred to me that behind one of those locked doors I had encountered in Drogo Hall, or at the bottom of a sealed staircase, Drogo's Museum of Anatomy *must still exist*. It must still exist, I realized, sitting bolt upright as the idea took hold, maintained by my uncle, and containing such horrors that I could barely imagine, but including the skeletal remains of Harry Peake. If I were to inherit Drogo Hall – and to this possibility my uncle had made only one oblique reference thus far – what lay in store for me, when I opened that room to the light of day? What monstrous things awaited me in the bowels of the house?

With these unsettling thoughts somewhat damping the good spirits engendered in me by the fresh air and the exertions of the morning, I left the inn to find that the day had grown overcast; and even as I trotted away I felt the first spots of rain. Uncertain whether we were in for a brief shower or a sustained downpour, I did not at once turn back to Drogo Hall, but continued to make for the high ground to the south.

An hour later I was standing with my horse beneath the flimsy cover of a few bare trees as the heavens opened on all sides and the rain came down in a torrent. In the distance I could see the rooftops of London, where the storm raged with still more fury. From out of the bellies of lowering black thunderclouds – those same clouds I had seen off to the west, and thought so harmless – came jagged flashes of lightning, followed a second later by the rumble of thunder. I was soon soaked through; and as there seemed little point in simply standing there beneath a leafless tree, I remounted and set off back to Drogo Hall.

The road was a quagmire now, and our progress was a good deal slower than it had been earlier. A sorry sight we made, I am sure, horse and rider both with heads bowed, chilled and dripping as we picked our way across the Lambeth Marsh in the rain, which by this point had settled to a steady downpour, and made the world obscure. When at last we reached Drogo Hall I was somewhat comforted to be met at the front steps by Percy with an umbrella, and a boy from the village, and while I was brought into the house with much clucking and sympathy, my poor wet cob was led off round the back to the stables.

But this was not a house in which a man was easily made warm and dry, after such a soaking as I had suffered; and although I was sat down by a fire with my feet in a tub of hot water, and given a steaming cup of tea laced with lemon and rum, I was soon sneezing and shivering and feeling distinctly feverish; and by the time my uncle had appeared, and assumed an attitude of brisk solicitude, I knew that I would be packed off to bed, and even that damp contraption seemed welcoming now. The fire was lit, a tray was prepared, and I settled among my dank bedclothes with my uncle perched on the chair by the bed.

He seemed cheered that I was giving him a bit of doctoring to do. He chattered away as I lay there barely able to comprehend him, but when I understood that he had resumed his narrative, as though we were as usual in his study below, I made an effort to grasp what he was saying. He was talking about Martha's flight from her father, and her eventual appearance here in Drogo Hall; and fevered though I was, I reacted to this development with a cry of alarm, and attempted to rise up out of my bed, as though by some effort of my own I could warn her of the danger! I wanted to tell her that Drogo meant her no good, he only craved her father's bones, his house was a trap from which she would never escape!

Some kind of delirium, I suppose; my uncle abruptly broke off, and a few minutes later Percy appeared with a small glass of some ill-smelling fluid which I was persuaded to drink; and within moments I was deeply asleep.

That night while her father was out Martha slipped away from the Angel. Through the hours of darkness she walked the streets. She heard the bell of an unknown church chiming the hours, was it St Giles? – and the incessant barking of a distant dog; and as she walked she reviewed in her mind's eye the chain of events since first she had come to Cripplegate Street with her father, examining each for some hint it might contain as to how she should go forward. She remembered my uncle William, and that man's face was all at once before her eyes, the face of a gentle man, a kind man – had he not looked upon her with favour, called her a fine girl, taken pains on both occasions to engage her in talk – and had he not told her that should she ever need his help she must come to him?

My uncle preened, I remember, as he told me this, for of course it reflected well upon him, at least it did in his view of the matter. But I no longer altogether trusted his memory, nor indeed his motives; though whether he was deliberately deceiving me, or unwittingly deceiving himself, this I had yet to establish, and weakened as I was with fever, and unable to leave my bed, there was little I could do now but listen in passive resignation as he went forward with the story.

II

In the early hours of the morning Martha set out for the Lambeth Marsh. She knew only that Drogo Hall lay somewhere in that vicinity. All she owned, all her books and clothes, were packed in her battered cabin trunk and left behind in the Angel. As to her state of mind, she should, I suppose, have been sunk in truly dismal spirits but somehow, perhaps it was the crisp damp tang of the mist in the early morning, somehow I cannot help feeling there was a spark or two of confidence in her as she set her steps to the west. She crossed the river over the new bridge at Westminster and was soon through the village on the Surrey bank, and on to the marsh itself.

The Lambeth Marsh in those days was in some part grazing land for sheep and cattle, but in the main was made up of bogs and fens and stands of reeds and bullrush; and though deadly treacherous to the traveller should she stray from the road at night, or fall foul of a highwayman, it was safely crossed in the daylight hours. In her greatcoat, then, and a cocked hat she had had from Fred so as to lend herself, in her vulnerable state, something of the masculine, Martha gazed out over an empty flat expanse of open marshy land, with here and there in the distance a cottage, a barn, a stand of trees to break the line of the horizon. She saw sheep, she saw wading birds, cranes and herons, others she could not identify. The road across the marsh was made of raised earth covered with gravel and buttressed at the sides with logs.

It was colder out there on the unprotected marsh than it had been in the town, and pulling her coat about her she set off due south. The sky was hazy and the mist clung to the marsh like a soft white sheet that drifted and thickened in places, such that the scene was leached of all clarity and definition and rendered oddly dreamlike in its indistinctness; earth and water, air and sky all come together in a diffuse milky immateriality. No bird cried out in that blank expanse, no sound was heard at all. Into the marsh Martha advanced, the buoyancy she had felt earlier now subdued by the whiteness and silence of this strange world. An hour later she reached the top of a shallow rise and in the distance, to the east, and sheltered by a low wooded hill, she made out a group of buildings clustered about a large white house. This was Drogo Hall.

Another hour and she could see it more clearly. Drogo Hall was an imposing building in those days, and small wonder it had intimidated her father. It was a large square house of white stone with a pillared portico, the whole a thing of elegant classical proportions in that style we would now call Early Georgian. It seemed to gaze out arrogantly, imperturbably over the marsh, like a monarch, perfect in the authority of its formal design, a piece of flawless reasoning in stone, although as yet unfinished, and hedged about with the builder's scaffolding. It did not stand alone, nor did the buildings around it conform to the austerities of its own cold logic. It was flanked by a Norman church with a spiky steeple, behind which lay a walled graveyard in whose high grass were crowded families of ancient tilting stones. There were cottages – outbuildings – a forge – an inn – a village, in short, huddled about the skirts of the great house, and out front a small lake in which Lord Drogo kept various species of foreign fish. And all these older buildings, some of which actually abutted and were a part of the fabric of Drogo Hall itself, the original hall, that is, were built in a manner suggestive not of the Age of Reason but of an earlier age, a Dark Age, rather – I speak of crockets and gargoyles, wavering roof lines and shaggy brickwork, turrets, and a tower, and Martha surely asked herself, was this queer hybrid house a sanctuary? Would she find shelter here from the storm of her father's madness?

Coming through the village she was regarded with frank suspicion; Lord Drogo's tenants recognized her for what she was, a supplicant, and as such seeking to appropriate a share in that patrician bounty they considered their own. She came round the lake, and shunning the front of the house with its sweeping staircase, its colonnades and high windows, made her way round the side of the building, where a man in a leather apron stopped her beneath an archway giving on to a cloistered alley that opened into a large courtyard with outbuildings on three sides. Martha told the man that she had come to see Dr William Tree, and he told her to come no further, he would inquire within. Martha asked him, did he not wish to know who she was?

'Who are you then?' he said.

'I am Martha Peake,' she said, and lifted her chin, for she was almost in tears, being close, at last, as she thought, to safety. 'Please tell him that I must speak to him at once.'

Martha waited beneath the arch for an hour, and it began to rain; she was glad to be off the marsh, where she would have been quickly soaked. She saw much activity both in and around the house, several men emerging from the top of a flight of stone steps from the cellars, carrying buckets; and a little later a wagon loaded with crates rumbled past her down the alley and into the courtyard, where those same men, having disposed of their buckets somewhere at the back of the house, then unloaded the crates in the rain and manhandled them into the house.

Several gentlemen on horseback arrived, clattering through the archway, past Martha and down the echoing alley before dismounting in the courtyard. Then some minutes later she saw a familiar figure standing at the top of the cellar steps in his shirt-sleeves, wiping his hands on his apron and gazing at her; and she at once ran to him, her greatcoat flapping behind her, and flung herself upon him.

My uncle William remembered the meeting well, or as well as he remembered anything. Martha had plainly been making a great effort of self-control for some time, he said, and she was now overwhelmed with relief to find a friend, as she thought. To see Martha overwhelmed, said my uncle dryly, was to see an instance of the tumultuary blood in full flow. She was some inches taller than him, and when she threw her arms around him it took some time for him to detach her from his person.

'Martha Peake,' he said at last, and here his recall was rich with detail. 'Now can I guess what brings you to Drogo Hall? I confess

I am not surprised to see you. Will you come in? Have you walked out from the town all this way? You must be famished. Let us see what we can find in the kitchen.'

And with that, he said, he had her follow him through a scullery and along a flagged passage, and so into a vast kitchen where half-a-dozen women were at work. He told me it was obvious that this plucky child (he always called her a child) was deeply frightened, and needed first to be brought among the women of the household, to be warmed and fed.

In a great hearth on the far side of the room a fire burned, various pots simmered on the hob, and a large dog lay sleeping on the stones before it; and hanging from racks and pulleys above, various creatures for those pots, rabbits and chickens, pheasants and fish.

'Patience Cogswell, what have you there for a hungry traveller?' said William, and a stout woman came forward sucking her teeth and straightening her cap; her hands were white with flour.

Ten minutes later Martha was seated at the end of a long table of scrubbed oak with benches down each side. She had before her a bowl of hot tripe soup, a plate of cold beef, a jug of milk. She made a hearty dinner of it while in low tones telling my uncle about her father's collapse. William had produced a white clay pipe and sucked at it now in a contemplative manner, nodding and frowning. Martha told him more than once she wanted him to understand the danger her father was in, for William remembered at one point taking the pipe from between his lips and saying gravely: 'And not only him, Martha, yourself too' – and her saying: 'Yes, without me, what then would become of him?'

My uncle William told me he set his elbows on the table, placed his chin in his hands, put his pipe between his teeth, and pondered the matter. He took out his pipe and rubbed the back of his neck. 'Martha,' he said at last, 'what am I to do with you?'

'It doesn't matter about me,' she said, 'I do not believe he will hurt me again. But he will hurt himself.'

'So I understand.'

'It is the drink. He cannot help it.'

'Then what will happen to him?'

Long pause here. 'I think,' she said, 'in a few days I will go back to him, and talk to him.'

'You are a brave girl, Martha Peake,' William said, 'and you are clever, and you have spirit – by God you have spirit, I have seen it.' He pressed his lips tight together in what, in my uncle, passed for a smile, and briefly patted her hand.

'I will help you, it is in my power to do so and I want to do so. But you will have to do what I say. This house may be out of the town, but much of the town comes to it. I will hide you here and you will stay out of sight. And then we will think what to do.'

Even after she reached America, and safety, Martha, I believe, still dreamed of Drogo Hall, and of its tenants, and of what occurred there; and in her dreams there was chaos and darkness and only fractured impressions, each one associated with strong feeling, dread, or terror, just as she experienced it as a bewildered girl of fifteen. They were days of great uncertainty, great fear. At first she feared what lay outside Drogo Hall, the things that howled on the Lambeth Marsh by night, and only later did she come to fear what lay *within* – what stood waiting in the dark places of that house, the endless echoing passages, the empty landings, the obscure staircases and sudden unexpected chambers she encountered when she was bold enough by daylight to make tentative exploration of this new world of hers.

Now, though, as she sat in that warm kitchen, having her hand stroked by my uncle William, and being told what a bold, clever, spirited girl she was, the relief was writ large and clear upon her face, and she felt a warm joy to be under William's protection, and under the roof of Drogo Hall.

12

I had been in bed for several days but I was at last beginning to feel stronger; and I asked my uncle if I could see the room where Martha Peake stayed during her time at Drogo Hall. Of course, he murmured, waving a regal hand, Percy will show you tomorrow. And so the next day Percy, in his dusty coat and breeches, led me out of the kitchen by way of a pantry which gave on to a narrow passage with a flagged stone floor, and so to another passage, and then up a twisting flight of stairs, and more gloomy passages and narrow stairs, until at last we fetched up in a tower, in an obscure west wing of the house neglected and untenanted for years; ever since, I imagined, Martha had been here, although I was not able to have Percy confirm this. Everywhere broken windows, great droopy swags of cobweb, thick thick dust, the droppings of bats, and mice, and other creatures that had made their home in this dilapidated region of the house. Gamely but grimly we plodded down those passages, and up those narrow twisting stone staircases, Percy and I, until at last he flung open a door and ushered me into what had once briefly been Martha's home.

It was a circular room, a tower room, long neglected, but with the vigorous application of a broom, and water and scrubbing brushes, I suppose it could have been made comfortable. What at once caught my attention was the window seat, set in an alcove three feet deep with a prospect clear across the marsh to the spires and towers of London, where in the dusk a few lights were already winking. I imagined my uncle leaving Martha here and returning with candles, soap, bed linen, firewood and other necessities. As for the bed, it was no servant's bed, it was vast, the dark wood of its heavy frame carved into a menagerie of creatures leaping and climbing among exotic vines that twisted up the posts and ran the length of the upper frame before descending to the headboard and there rioting in glorious grotesque profusion; and in my mind's eye

I saw Martha fling herself on to the mattress, to be at once lost in the dust that rose up from it in a cloud. Oh, it was only a tower room in a forgotten wing of an old, old house, but the thought that Martha Peake had lived here before she left for America, this was strangely exciting to me. Treading the same boards she had trod, I was able to inhabit her experience all the more intimately.

So this was the room my uncle moved her into. I imagined Martha, later that night, sitting alone by the fire and reviewing the day's events. Her relief was great; and as she sat there in the candlelight, darning her stockings perhaps, the needle catching the flame and throwing off sparks of light into the gloom, she thought: this is how it used to be, for us, of an evening. But how much has changed! Am I not harrowed by the loss of my father? Where is he, out there somewhere in the London night, at the mercy of some diabolical power that has choked his will, that squats upon his very soul – how can I darn stockings, all tranquil in the candlelight? But what choice do I have?

I understand now that Harry, by shifting as he had beyond the reach of reason – by embracing the monster – had, in a certain way, for Martha, died. But she persisted in thinking of him as he was before he turned against her, and even now her thoughts were only for his welfare; and with herself beyond his clutches he was, she believed, safe; and so, for a time, she was at peace. She slept soundly and awoke early and at once went to the window, where she clambered into the alcove on her knees and peered out at the first light as it came spreading across the marsh.

Martha set to work that first morning to make her quarters clean and comfortable. My uncle visited her at noon, she heard his footsteps ascending the narrow wooden staircase for some minutes before he reached her room. She ran down the passage to greet him, and this, he told me, gave him inordinate pleasure, to be treated by Martha as an uncle, almost as a father. He had a particular fondness for her, and she knew this, I suspect, and made sure, whenever he was present, to be at her most spirited.

He brought her further supplies of household necessities, and food from the kitchen; also some books, which she had asked for; and then she questioned him intently as to her security in the house, and he gave her reassurance, nodding his head as she poured forth her worries, and rubbing his neck, and then telling her what she needed to hear. She was much cheered by William's visit, and the time fled quickly by, and before she knew it she was lighting candles and dusk was creeping over the marsh. That night she saw Clyte below her window.

Clyte – that whispering principle of negation – that *resurrection man* – oh, he has long haunted me, he haunts me still! Thin as a rake, long of jaw and hollow of cheek, dressed in rusty black and no wig on his cropped blue skull, Clyte was the sort who moved always to the shadows, who sought the darkest part of any place he found himself in. He was a creature who *slunk*, who *stole away* before his person had properly been registered, who was known, in fact, more for his absence than his presence. This had much to do with the line of work he pursued – if work it can be called – but also with the very kidney of the man, for by nature he was more shadow than substance, an instrument of darkness who served a master in constant need of precisely the services Clyte alone could provide. I speak of course of Lord Drogo.

There she was, squeezed into her alcove in the window, her back pressed against one wall and the soles of her feet against the other, knees bent and arms wrapped about them, gazing across the marsh toward the town, when she caught from the corner of her eye some small movement in the shadows of the courtyard below. Glancing down, she saw him leaning against the wall with his legs crossed and his hands in his pockets – and staring straight up at the window! Martha had not a furtive bone in her body. Deception and subterfuge were alike alien to her. She did not pull back at once, like some guilty thing surprised, although perhaps she should have done.

No, she held his gaze – gaze, I call it, when what she saw, I imagine, what she locked eyes with, was, rather, a pair of slits which even in the gloom, even at that distance, were tiny glittering pinpricks of malevolence and lust – but after a second she pulled back, a fierce prickle of dread and alarm coursing the length of her spine, and a strong flush rising as the blood came up in her cheeks. She sat panting in the window alcove while these extraordinary physical reactions to the man subsided; and then, climbing down, she sat close to the fire. Clyte knew why she had fled her father, and that her father was ignorant of her whereabouts; and I strongly suspect that every instinct in Martha told her that this dark little creature meant her no good.

She did not sleep. Later that night, her imagination still excited by the appearance of Clyte, she tried to tell herself that she must put her trust in my uncle William, who would not allow her to be harmed by anybody, as she thought – not Clyte, not Drogo, not her father. This helped her. She had no great confidence that putting her trust in God would avail her much – if God was looking out for her, then why was she in this predicament at all? – but William Tree, he was another matter. William did not move in mysterious ways. William had offered her his protection. He had taken her under his wing. She had nothing to fear with William on her side.

Not so. Even my uncle admitted as much. He was a busy man, he said, and his duties in Lord Drogo's dissecting rooms were many and varied, with the result that, after settling Martha in the west wing, and issuing stern warnings, he vanished into the bowels of the house, by which I mean the cellars, sculleries and outhouses set aside for his lordship's anatomical work, and Martha lost sight of him. Knowing only when she was allowed to appear in the kitchen, and when she could put out her night-soil, and collect her water and firewood – and instructed never to show herself out-of-doors during daylight hours, nor in any other part of the house than those passages and staircases connecting the tower to the kitchen, and under no circumstances to attempt to make contact with Lord Drogo – who had not yet been apprised, William told her, of her presence under his roof, as William was waiting, so he said, for a 'felicitous opportunity' – she was left to herself.

Meanwhile Harry was scouring London for her. Her flight had convinced him beyond all reason of the truth of his suspicions, that is, that his daughter, with the help of Fred Lour, who had also disappeared, had robbed and deceived him. Other things, wild things, he also believed. He believed there must be still other men involved. Harry's picture of the world and how it worked was by this time as bent out of alignment as his spine. Since Martha had fled him there was no one to buttress him against the self-loathing and despair that now preyed upon him without cease. For as my uncle correctly said, if the world calls a man a monster, and there is nobody to contradict it, then that man, in his own eyes, becomes a monster; and who could love a monster? Surely any man, any normal man, of normal scale, and structure, and symmetry and proportion is preferable to a monster – hence Harry's conviction that Martha had fled with the help of other men; and hence, to compound the madness, jealousy of the most destructive kind, mindless and primitive, was now aroused in his tortured heart. Salt in the wound, worse than salt, a fresh wound, rather, a hundred times more excruciating than mere abandonment. Oh, Harry Peake's hell had yet to display the full measure of its torments.

But as he floundered in his sea of gin, as he clung like a castaway to this single splintered plank of an idea, someone came to him and hinted to him of Martha's whereabouts. Who could have done that? Only Clyte.

He crossed the marsh on foot. Martha was the first to see him, as he came forward alone against that flat, featureless waste. She was in her window, with a book, when she happened to glance up, and there he was, a mile away, just beginning to come up over the rise; and as soon as she saw those shoulders she knew it was him. Only her father had shoulders thrown so emphatically athwart as those were; only her father – and now the figure was over the rise and visible in all its lurching glory – had a spine which flared like a hood and *wrenched* those shoulders apart! He moved her to tears, that shuffling fellow out there on the marsh, that dear benighted man; and she was close to surrendering all caution, she wanted to run down the road and feel him sweep her up in his arms – but she pushed down the impulse, she pushed it down, though it cost her all she had, and with her face pressed to the window she silently wept, because she could see him coming and was unable to go to him lest he harm her.

But what was he doing now? He had reached a solitary stand of elms on the bank of a narrow ditch and settled himself at the foot of a tree. And what was he doing now? He was having a drink. He had taken from his pocket a bottle and he was having a drink. Then he put the bottle away, but he did not move. He was watching the house. He was sitting under a tree and staring at Drogo Hall, waiting for – what? For Martha to appear, so that he could rush down on her and tear her to pieces? Oh no. Not that.

Still the tears streamed down Martha's face. After a while she saw him get to his feet and resume his erratic progress. Was she the only one to see him? How could a big humped figure like that go unnoticed in a landscape devoid of any feature but a few trees? Surely the whole house must know he was coming?

'Oh God,' she whispered, 'what am I to do?'

But a moment later my uncle entered the room; and seeing Martha at the window, turning, now, startled, toward him, he said: 'So you know.'

'What am I to do, William?' she cried.

'Nothing, my dear, nothing at all. I came to tell you that. Do nothing. Lord Drogo will receive him. Your presence will not be revealed.'

'Is this sure, William?'

'On my honour.'

'Thank you, William. Thank you, thank you!'

He bowed, and left her.

What Martha should of course have remembered, but did not, were her own sentiments when, like her father, she had come on foot across the marsh, drawing ever closer to Drogo Hall, and quite uncertain as to the reception she could expect. To come as a petitioner to a great house is not for the faint of heart. The nearer the visitor approaches, the more imposing the building appears; the more imposing the building, the more intimidating the prospect;

so that by the time she actually reaches the house, her feelings of doubt and trepidation have become magnified, and whatever courage and purpose she may have started out with, by then it has long since dissipated. This is why lords and kings build great houses, so as to terrify their visitors.

And so it was for Harry Peake. Martha watched him from the window, careful that she herself could not be seen; and the closer he got, the slower and more haltingly uncertain his step, such that she was convinced he would at any moment turn back.

But then Lord Drogo came out to meet him.

Hearing this, I began to pay close attention not only to my uncle's words, but to the tone in which they were spoken. I suspected strongly that hidden meanings were secreted in this history of his, relative to Lord Drogo's ambitions; I listened to hear them betrayed. Drogo, he said, in his urgent fluting whisper, emerged from the front door and came briskly down the steps in shirtsleeves and breeches and advanced with a hand outstretched to where Martha's poor bewildered father stood waiting, somewhat unsteady, deeply uncertain, suspicious, hopeful, and, yes, proud – she saw it, she saw his jaw lift, felt the flare in the man as some heat arose from deep inside him, some idea of the soul that translated into a conviction, despite his exposed condition before this great house, of his essential manhood. Martha saw it; Francis Drogo saw it also. He understood what had brought him here and what it had cost him. He shook him warmly by the hand and, still gripping his hand, pointed toward the house, offered hospitality, made him welcome; and the two men went in.

Martha was in some distress now. She imagined she would be summoned to appear below, where his lordship, in a magnanimous gesture of misplaced condescension, would reunite the father with his daughter. Martha remembered what William had said, he had sworn on his honour that her presence would not be revealed. This calmed her down. This brought her round.

She made herself comfortable in her window once more. Twilight was stealing over the marsh, and with it a low mist, a clinging, seeping mist, and soon, she knew, the howling would begin; and she thought, surely Lord Drogo will not send my father home in the dark? She tried to imagine what was happening down in the hall, or the kitchen, or wherever it was that Lord Drogo saw fit to entertain a man like Harry Peake. Were they again speaking of his pain? No, more likely Harry was telling his story, telling his lordship of his ill fortune in raising a treacherous child who stole his money and ran off with another man, leaving him destitute. Was she here, he might ask, and Lord Drogo, she imagined – she hoped! – would respond with bluff surprise and amusement: 'Here, sir? Whatever makes you think she is here, sir?'

What would her father say to that? 'You showed us kindness, my lord, when we were last together. I suspect my daughter may presume on that kindness by coming to you now.'

'I wish she had, sir. Nothing would give me greater pleasure than to effect a meeting between you and your daughter, to some happy end. I remember the girl well. Spirited creature.'

What could her father do – argue with him, contradict him? His position would be delicate now. Swimming in gin as he was, could he muster the wit to keep his mouth shut and avoid giving offence? Not altogether; not as she heard it told later by William. Harry had apparently come straight to the point.

'Is she here, my lord?' he said.

Lord Drogo, had he chosen to, could have regarded this as a gross affront. He chose not to. William said that Lord Drogo had at once understood the extent of Harry's moral decline and knew him not to be responsible for all that he said. He was curious, in fact, as to how far gone in drink Harry was; Harry's state of health had become a matter of some importance to him, and yes indeed, I thought, so it should be. He glanced at William.

'We have not seen her, sir,' he said. 'She did not come to me.'

Now the poet's head, his rheumy bloodhound eyes, swung round to William.

'Not to you, my lord,' said Harry. 'To him.'

Drogo did not blink.

'We cannot help you, sir, neither myself nor William. She is not here. If you doubt my word, however' – and here he permitted a pause, so as to invite Harry to wave aside at once any suggestion that his lordship's word might be doubted – 'I offer you the freedom of my house.'

The invitation was made in tones which indicated that to accept would be an impertinence; and Harry, now, hesitated to antagonize Lord Drogo, from whom he had already had assistance and could hope to have more. He turned from William to his lordship, anger, confusion, desperation all working across his harrowed features.

'Forget her,' said Lord Drogo.

'She has stolen my money, my lord.'

'I shall give you money. Forget her.'

Imagine Martha's reaction when William told her all this! Harry was silent now. Had he the will for it, he could have searched the house from cellar to attic. Drogo's authority alone prevented him. He turned again to William, and again subjected him to a scrutiny which troubled him sorely, for my uncle disliked deception – so he claimed, ha! – particularly with a man in as pitiful a state as her father was; for he felt, so he said, a genuine sympathy for the man.

Darkness fell on Drogo Hall. Lights were lit, and in the kitchen there was much heat and noise and toil, as there was every night when Patience Cogswell prepared to feed the many and various individuals lodging in and around the great house. Martha waited in a state of no little apprehension.

Downstairs, Harry was explosive, said William. Every impulse, every intuition of that intelligent but befuddled man told him his daughter was here. But every impulse of caution and self-preservation told him to acquiesce in the lie he was being told. Fearless when sober, drunk he was reckless, and he might have pressed the point. But he did not.

Then Lord Drogo all at once clapped his hands and gave out a brisk bark of laughter. 'Enough, Harry Peake,' he cried, 'do not take on so, sir! Are you the first man who had his daughter run away from him? Many would think it a blessing. Come and eat, and we will talk more. Come!'

Lord Drogo was a charming man, when he chose to be so; he now affected the genial good heart of the rustic squire taking his guest to table, and he would brook no argument. Harry reluctantly relinquished his cause, albeit temporarily, and allowed himself to be led off to the dining room.

He slept in the house that night. Martha knew this because she was watching for him, and he did not appear. And as the hours passed, it became clear that he would not appear, not that night. The howling started up out on the marsh, and Martha stirred with unease. Around ten the wind freshened and soon was blowing hard, and it muffled the howling but aroused instead a symphony of strange noises there in the high regions of the tower in the west wing. Amid the creakings and thumpings and rattlings, the bangings and gustings and crashings, would she hear the approaching foot-steps – the laboured breathing outside the door –?

This is what she feared, poor Martha, who had learned at her father's knee to fear nothing. Now she would sit up and keep watch, so with book and candle she made herself comfortable in her window alcove as the wind came up ever stronger and howled among the turrets and chimneys of the old hall.

The hours passed and her eyelids grew heavy; she could concen-trate no longer on her book. As she sat there in the window she imagined herself the only soul in the house still alert. No longer infected with despair, and strangely soothed by the howling wind, and pleased to think that everyone in the house was asleep but her – she began to wish that her father would come. How she wanted to see him –! She still believed that she could drive out the madness that was in him. She would do it by the power of her love. He was not a free man. He did the will of another. From that other she would liberate him, she would restore him to himself, to the man he had been, the father she had known, the wise, gentle, melancholy poet in the warmth of whose love she had grown and flourished –

She fell asleep in the window and dreamed wildly; and waking at dawn, shivering with the cold, and stiff in every joint, she stumbled into bed fully clothed. When next she awoke it was broad daylight. She opened her eyes and sat up in the bed; then leaped out and dashed to the window, and peered out over the marsh. Some mist still, but clarity enough to see there was no one on the road.

A voice spoke from the open doorway.

'He left at dawn,' said my uncle William.

'At dawn –?' She turned toward him.

'You are safe now.'

Martha said nothing more. He had left at dawn – but she had awoken at dawn! She might have seen him, and if she had, she would, she knew, have gone out and run after him. And then what? Would she indeed have liberated him from his demon? In the cold morning light she still believed she could.

It was from my uncle William that she learned of her father having dined with Lord Drogo that night; how the great man had had William on one side of him, and Harry Peake on the other, at the head of the table in the grand dining room where in recent days I myself had more than once supped. There was nobody else present, and Harry had been treated, as an honoured guest, with every courtesy. They had drunk claret with the roast beef, and mead with the pheasant, and Riesling with the fish, and cider with the apple pie, and port with the nuts and cheese; and Harry, given the chance of conversation with a man of learning, seized upon it, and rose to the occasion, although fresh draughts of wine did nothing to improve his nerves. Every so often, said my uncle, there would be a sudden *bang!*, and plates and glasses rattled, as one or other of Harry's knees swung suddenly violently sideways into a leg of the table, an effect of old gin still sluicing about his body; or his fist would suddenly clench tight, quite involuntarily, or some odd spasm would seize upon his upper body and for a moment he was rocked back and forth with the force of it.

Lord Drogo observed all this, said William, with that intense curiosity he brought to bear on all pathological phenomena, and questioned Harry closely about the state of his health, in particular the effects of sustained gin drinking on the intellectual and poetic functions; after which they returned to matters of literature and history, and Harry Peake's powerful mind had little trouble overcoming the influence of the wine he had drunk; and then the two men parted for the night, Lord Drogo excusing himself on the pretext that he had further work to do, but inviting Harry to make free with his library, and to sleep in the house.

William accompanied his master down to the cellars, lighting their way with a branch of candles. Lord Drogo, despite his affability at table, then displayed considerable irritation toward my uncle.

'You are fortunate,' he said in tones of ice as they descended into the cellars, 'that our friend believed you.'

Lord Drogo of course referred to William's denial of Martha's presence in the house.

'Why should he not, my lord?'

'Do not play me for a fool, sir!' cried Drogo in a surge of sudden rage. Then, calmer: 'Do not play me for a fool. There is nothing in this house escapes me, do you not understand that? Keep her out of sight!' – and with that he stripped off his coat, and strapped on his apron, and went at his work with his usual ferocity.

So Lord Drogo knew about her after all. He knew about her, and tolerated her under his roof. Because at heart he was a good man who recognized that he had an obligation toward her? Or because it was in his interest that Harry Peake not revenge himself upon his daughter for some imaginary wrong she had done him? For if that were to happen, others would lay claim to Harry Peake and he would be lost to Lord Drogo for ever. Thus did I construe the meaning of his lordship's actions that night. He was prepared to protect Martha, this was clear enough, but not for her own sake, for her father's. Or rather, for his own.

My uncle went to the west wing early the next morning and told Martha all that had happened. She at once recognized that the risk to herself was if anything greater than it had been before.

'You have no relation, I suppose, who could shelter you? Somewhere your father could not find you?' said William, after he and Martha had worried at this question for several minutes.

Martha thought then of her brothers and sisters, and of the rest of her family in Cornwall. At times she remembered them as though she had parted from them but the day before, and was filled with a painful longing to see them again. But then she would not think of them for months at a time. She would not go to them now. Her father would soon find her if she did.

'My mother had an older sister,' she said doubtfully, 'Maddy Foy –'

'And where, pray,' said my uncle, 'does that good woman reside?'

13

Hard upon the big winds the night of Harry Peake's visit to Drogo Hall, said my uncle – the hour was late, still we talked on, each in our own way intent upon the outcome of the thing – came the first bad weather of the autumn. The sky was filled with large dark clouds that hung low overhead and roiled and galloped about in the wind before unleashing their waters in furious gusting storms that hammered the house without mercy, exposed as it was out there on the marsh. But though the house was exposed, said my uncle, isolated it was not, oh no; and despite the fact that the road across the marsh was reduced to a quagmire, and whole tracts of the Lambeth Marsh were under water, and the roofs of the old parts of Drogo Hall admitted the rain in a hundred places, still an unending stream of visitors made their way out there, seemingly drawn by one thing alone, and that was the genius of Francis Drogo.

They came from all over the country, and beyond. Martha often heard, as she crept about the house, for she had soon grown impatient, said my uncle, of her confinement, the broad incomprehensible gutturals of Scotsmen, and the lilt and trill of the Dublin men, all of whom, and many more besides, came to learn from his lordship. Then there was Cyrus Hamble, the American, a man remarkable for the plainness of his dress and, as Martha heard from her friends in the kitchen, his refusal to take strong drink. But for the most part the visitors were English doctors: dressed in sombre, heavy clothes, bewigged (though not elegantly so), equipped with silver-topped canes and narrow watchful eyes, and for the most part sober, they greeted one another in the entrance hall with sly formality, and observed with a scrupulous punctilio those delicate calibrations of rank and status so vital to the Englishman's sense of propriety. They then filed into the Theatre of Anatomy and listened with close attention as the great man of medicine cut up another poor devil who but an hour or two previous had worn King George's rope before being brought away by Clyte.

Drogo Hall was a house often permeated by strange smells. Later, in America, when the whiff of an unfamiliar nostrum or an exotic specific reached her nose, Martha was affected with all the strangeness and unhappiness of those dark days after she lost her father. But in Drogo Hall her inclination on detecting some rank incomprehensible odour as she crept along an unfamiliar corridor, was to follow it to its source; which was not easy, rank incomprehensible odours being as a rule closely attended at source by adults.

On one occasion she penetrated from the old west wing into the main body of the house, where her nostrils were all at once assailed with a most peculiar smell, one that she associated with overripe fruit; and tracking it with no little curiosity, she suddenly found herself at the head of the main staircase, a sweeping thing of grey stone which descended to the entrance hall with its vast fireplace, its hanging arms and armour, its flagged floor on which the heels of a man's boots could ring with a satisfying solidity. She crouched behind the balustrade, from which concealed position she peered down into the hall and identified the source of the horrid smell.

At the back of the hall a pair of tall doors stood slightly ajar beneath a shallow stone arch, and from beyond came a single voice, oddly amplified, and she knew the voice to be Lord Drogo's. Down the sweep of stone stairs she came. This was perilous now, for she had no place to hide herself should anyone appear. From the bottom of the stairs she must cross the hall to reach the tall doors out of which emanated both Lord Drogo's voice and the smell.

Without a second's hesitation Martha ran across the flagged stone floor and slid between the doors, so that she was neither in the hall nor in the room beyond, but in the shadow, rather, of the doors that stood ajar.

Ah, Drogo! In my mind's eye I can see him now, as Martha saw him that day so long ago – not as he was at the end, no, but as he was *then*, when he was in full possession of all his diabolical powers!

Physically he was unremarkable: not a tall man, but built firm and compact, with small hands, a large domed skull, and hair cropped to a grey-flecked stubble. A nose hooked and arched in the Imperial Roman manner, a prominent chin, an air of distinct forbidding authority even when, as now, he is without a wig or finery of any kind, and wearing a black leather apron, smeared and stained with the proud excrementa of a thousand operations, strapped on over a white shirt open at the throat with the sleeves rolled up above the elbows. There he stands in the well of a crowded semicircular room of steeply tiered seats with a gallery above, preparing to lecture to the eminent men of medicine of his day.

This is Lord Drogo's Theatre of Anatomy. As he stands there he does not meet the forty pair of eyes gazing down upon him with no little anticipation. This is a man acknowledged as one of the great surgeon-anatomists then at work in London, a man at ease in the company of Cheselden, Smellie, Pott, the Hunters – the giants. And his reputation he holds so dear that his every public appearance is a drama in which he must play his role to the hilt, and that role is – the great man of medicine!

Never married, and with no taint of scandal attaching, he possessed a capacity for hard work that was said to be extraordinary. And his curiosity toward all forms of life was legendary: he could be found at his table at four o'clock every morning, they said, already hard at it dissecting, for instance, a beetle, for no other reason than to acquire knowledge of the creature's anatomy. The fire in his eyes, his restless hands, his quick temper, the quickness of all his movements – he was in such haste – he had such *greed* – to know all that could be known, ignorance was to him anathema and he must overcome it through relentless application of reason to observed fact, and he disdained all that smacked of metaphysics.

Though he did not leave a book. He left a museum, but not a book. He collected abnormalities. He claimed that such phenomena, by displaying wrong action in a part, could illustrate normal function. Hence his interest in Harry Peake. Interest, I say – he pursued that man, dogged him to his death, ay, to his death, and beyond – !

So this is the man who stands now behind the table in the well of his crowded Theatre of Anatomy, and gazes down at a corpse fresh from Tyburn Field, courtesy, of course, of Clyte. He taps his knuckles on the table and the room falls silent. Without a word to his audience he touches the dead man's belly. He then brings his face down close to the body. He sniffs the length of it, small precise twitches of that hawk's beak of a nose. He then lays his ear upon the chest. He listens. As he listens he places a fingertip on the head of the penis. He remains in this curious position for several moments.

At last the great man of medicine lifts his head, and as he rakes the amphitheatre with a fierce stare that has several doctors shifting uneasily and turning their faces aside – Francis Drogo has friends here but he also has enemies, he knows who they are and they know he knows – he touches his fingertip to his lips, and registers the taste with a comical pucker.

'Gentlemen,' he says.

A pause. Utter silence. The voice is cultivated. Men strain to hear him.

'Let us cut this poor fellow open. Let us' – he pauses, he eyes the assembled doctors – 'see what he is made of.'

With that he stretches a hand, palm open, toward my uncle William – who has been standing to one side all the while – and William gives him the knife. God help him if it is not sharp as Old Scratch himself!

It seemed he would make the first cut now. But he paused, even as the tip of the knife sat snug in the notch in the dead man's sternum. Again he looked up at his audience.

'Gentlemen,' he said. 'I beg your leave. You came to see a man cut open, and cut open he shall be, and his every organ inspected as to its size, shape, situation and structure. Then we shall have the facts. But perhaps we are already in possession of facts relating to this man, and it is those facts we first should examine.'

There was some murmuring among the medical men. What new tack was this? These perorations of Lord Drogo were warmly anticipated by those who loved him. Others suffered silent resentment. Drogo put down his knife and examined the cadaver.

'We have lividity and swelling of the face. The eyelids are swollen and blue. The eyes themselves, gentlemen, are remarkable. They are red, and they protrude from their cavities. There is a bloody froth at the lips. The fists are clenched. There has been expulsion of faeces and urine. And one thing we would be foolish to overlook. There is a deep wound to the neck extending from below the left ear and under the chin. So deep is this wound that the vertebrae are exposed.'

Lord Drogo delicately peeled back the torn flesh and probed the wound with his fingers. Again there was some sniffing.

'Is it not a fact that a month ago this man rode a horse? I am aware that the horse was not his own, but we are not here to dissect his morals. That is the prerogative of a power superior even to that of Surgeons' Hall.'

Uneasy laughter here; Drogo was indulging his famously sardonic sense of humour. Why did he not cut? He had set down the knife and was leaning on the table on his palms and gazing frankly at his audience.

'A month ago he rode a horse. A week ago he entertained a certain lady in Newgate Gaol.'

All eyes shifted to the cadaver's genitalia.

'Was the lady sound?' said Drogo, laying a hand upon the private parts, not so private now. 'We shall see. But the point is, gentlemen, that he showed no sign of any sickness to suggest that within the week he would be – as we see him now.'

He lifted his hand and there was a brief murmur as every doctor in the Theatre of Anatomy contemplated the malodorous body on the table, whose pallor had assumed a distinct tinge of green.

'I employ a sensitive instrument, gentlemen.' He held up his hand, palm outwards. He laid it on the dead man's forehead. He said: 'Cold.'

He stood nodding at his audience, who now shuffled with some discomfort, suspecting themselves mocked.

'Cold. Gentlemen, this man has lost his vital heat. The loss of vital heat can have only one consequence.'

More nodding, more shuffling. Then a cane was tapped smartly on the floor and a voice from high in the amphitheatre, up in the gallery, an amused voice, a voice quite as cultivated as Drogo's, said: 'Come, my lord, do not tease us. Tell us what you mean to say.'

'Ah. Mr Eliot. You would have my meaning, would you? Well, I tell you, sir: the man is dead.'

Laughter here.

'The fact is self-evident, my lord.'

'And the cause of death? That too?'

'He's had his neck broke at Tyburn Tree.'

'But he has lost his vital heat. Now blood, surely, is responsible for the body's natural heat. Deprive a body of circulation and the external parts become cold. Ergo, the man is dead. What tree, sir?'

'You jest too subtle for me, my lord.'

'I only say, that to speak of a principle of vitality is a nonsense, when a fact is before us. He is cold. His neck is torn. So it is safe to infer that he has been hanged, and being hanged, asphyxiated. I reason it thus, from the use of these instruments' – he touched his eyes – 'these' – he lifted his hands – 'I have employed this' – his nose – 'these' – his ears – 'I have even used this' – he stuck out his tongue. 'Gentlemen, there are no vital principles here. The evidence of our senses, this is enough. The body is cold. It is dead. There is a severe wound to the neck. Modest things, gentlemen. Make no assumption. Question all theory. Above all, be sceptical.'

The expression on the faces of a number of men present suggested that this last advice had been heeded already.

'I am told that this man was sprightly over his last few days of life, but given to periods of anxious introspection. I am told he was prone to outbursts of sudden anger. No doubt a superfluity of the cold wet humour. Too much black bile discharging from the spleen. Best stick a clyster up his arsehole.'

This last was said with such ponderous gravity that the entire room roared, even those from whose lips the same words might have slipped easily but the day before. Many now warmed to Lord Drogo's theme, for it was at last becoming clear where he steered them.

'I should have liked to see his urine.'

The laughter is uneasy this time. These doctors take their urine seriously.

'Nonsense! The man was to be hanged and he knew it. This much we know. This is his *history*. This we remember, but nothing more, as we enter the chambers and alcoves' – here growing ironical once more – 'of the human mansion. So let us examine the organs within. Let us know their design, and infer their function. For if they exist in Nature, they must have both design' – and here he picked up the knife once more – 'and function.'

And thus the meagre philosophy of the great anatomist. No vital heat indeed! What then of passion? What of the flaming heart, *le coeur flamboyant*?

Martha stood in the shadow of the doorway of the Theatre of Anatomy, watching Lord Drogo as he set the knife in the notch at the base of the dead man's chest. She saw the blade sink into the flesh. She saw the blood well up and spill sluggish across the pallid skin. And then, behind her, she heard a noise. She turned. Squatting by the front door like a grotesquely embellished umbrella stand, and watching her with what she at once recognized as a kind of gloating contempt – it was, of course, Clyte. He lifted his hands from his knees and opened them wide, as though to say: What now?

Then he grinned at her, and she knew, too, what that grin expressed: lechery. Clyte was a lecher and Martha was the object of his lechery. Without taking her eyes off him for a second she boldly crossed the hall to the staircase, and still with her eyes fixed on the foul creature, who squatted there still, and still displayed his ghastly yellowing incisors at her, like the rabid runt of a sick vixen's litter – she darted up the stairs, not pausing until she reached the gallery at the top. There she turned again, and he was gone.

Her composure deserted her. She ran back to the west wing in a panic, pausing only when she reached her door, and there brought herself under control.

She sat that night in the window, watching the marsh in the

moonlight, alert to movement in the yard below; but there was none. She was confused and frightened by what she had seen that day, and she had no one to whom she could confide her feelings. Would God protect her? Doubtful. Could my uncle William? Doubtful also, if the suspicion was aroused in her, as it had certainly been aroused in me, that her father was bound for the dissecting table in Lord Drogo's Theatre of Anatomy, and that her own presence in Drogo Hall would be instrumental in bringing about that abomination.

14

I had grown stronger under the care of my uncle, but he advised me to stay in bed a few days longer; these marsh fevers, he said, had a way of turning putrid unless a proper term of convalescence was observed. So I lay abed, and despite some aching in my joints, and a persistent headache, and the occasional bout of delirium, enjoyed a welcome respite from my duties in town. I perused volumes of history and literature from the library downstairs, and undertook some light correspondence. And late every afternoon, as the light thickened over the marsh outside my window, there came a knock on the door, and then in came the mothlike Percy, wheeling a clanking contraption of metal and wood which contained various bottles and glasses, pipes and jars, that were adequate to my needs and, more important, those of my uncle, during the hours of narrative that were to follow. Candles were lit, fresh coal was laid on the fire, and when all was in readiness – my uncle's chair must be positioned just so, lest he strain his eyes with an excess of gloom, or take a chill from being placed at too great a distance from the fire – Percy rang a small silver bell and, a few minutes later, in shuffled the old man in his tasselled skullcap and velvet slippers, and I would lay back into my pillows as his story once more rolled over my sceptic ear.

I now knew that plans had been laid for Martha's departure. One night William spoke to her about what was to happen.

'You cannot stay here,' he said. 'He is sure to find you. Lord Drogo encourages him to visit again.'

Martha was silent. She could not but feel that events had slipped beyond her control, and her desperation, I believe, was fuelled by wild thoughts that came to her as she sat watching the marsh by night, and filled her with forebodings about the man who sheltered her.

'He knows you are here,' whispered my uncle. 'You must get far, far away from here, somewhere he will never follow you.'

Martha said nothing.

'You are not safe here,' he hissed, insistent, 'he has said he will murder you, you have heard it yourself. He came here to find you, and but for me he would have done.'

Still she said nothing. She would not look at him. But at last, unable any longer to hold her tongue, and my uncle still insisting that she agree with him, she told him she did not believe that her father intended to murder anybody. Nor did she intend to let anyone murder him! – though whether she said this I do not know.

Oh, but then William let her have it! He reminded her of what the gin did to him, what it turned him into, what he had done under its influence, his inability to control himself in spite of all good intentions, and more in this vein, such that Martha was overwhelmed by the very flood of it, and no longer knew what she thought or believed or wanted; although she was aware, even as reason told her that what he said was true, she was aware, said William, for he knew her well by this time, so he claimed, of a small hard nut in her heart that would not be dislodged, and that nut was her love of her father, and her belief in his goodness; and she also believed that he would never hurt her again. But it was no argument, and she did not say it.

'Where am I to go then?' she said.

'America.'

Martha lifted her head. America! At the sound of the word a flood of incoherent ideas, and half-glimpsed images, and strange alien passions swept rapidly over the girl, strong, wild feelings she could not identify, nor even say whether they were pleasurable or not. The sound of the word, and the seriousness, the awe with which my uncle William spoke it – America. America. She murmured it under his breath. There was power, there was magic in it, the word *America*. Ah, but there was terror in it also!

'He could not follow you there. He need never know where you had gone,' said William.

All at once Martha laid her head on the table and hammered on the wood with her fists.

'But you would be *safe*!' cried William.

He sat down beside her and stroked the back of her head. Martha would not lift her face. He kept talking to her, he kept stroking her head, and after a little while she sat up and said with some petulance: 'How should I go to America? I have not enough money.'

'We will help you.'

She rubbed her eyes. America. Despite her reluctance she wanted to go to America, the very prospect of it thrilled her beyond words. But to go for this reason, for this reason alone, to escape her father – it was too cruel.

'When?' she said.

'Soon.'

She pondered this.

'A new life,' said William.

But this was killing her! How could she tell my uncle that although such words thrilled her to the very quick of her being, she could not freely embrace them, for there was a voice in her that added to each of them the words *without him*. A new life *without him*. The New World *without him*. America – *without him*. It was too much for her, and she turned to William with arms outstretched, he took her to his breast, his old eyes shining at the memory of it, as a small pellucid droplet of liquid phlegm hung trembling from the tip of his thin red nose. So they comforted one another, and after a while they were quiet, and able to think over these dramatic developments with some composure.

Harry had often talked to Martha about the colonies, indeed they had friends in Smithfield who spoke of little else. America was for these men and women a country in which English liberties, long neglected at home, and fallen into decay, stood every good chance of flourishing. If the Americans should rise against the king – and in truth, it was muttered, such words being treasonous, what need had they of a king, that prospering people? – Harry and Martha would not be alone in supporting them. Had not Edmund Burke spoken for them all, when he rose in the House of Commons to defend the industry and ingenuity of the people of New England, and deplored King George's attempts to constrain that people's trade, and then their freedoms?

Now Martha was to go and live among them; but without her father, who had taught her to admire them, and who was, it was said, a sort of American himself, and was even called *Harry America* by some, having created in his ballad of Joseph Tresilian the very type of the defiant patriot. It was too bitter to be thought of – she would go to America without her father, because her father in his madness believed her to be his enemy! So yes, Martha was divided – torn, rather – by my uncle's proposal, but she decided, wisely, to say nothing yet of her reluctance and her doubts.

The American plan was a well-kept secret in Drogo Hall. Letters were dispatched to the colonies, where Martha's aunt, Maddy Foy, lived in New Morrock, a small fishing port some way north of Boston. She must sail soon, while the weather still permitted, and William took it upon himself to arrange her passage; and so, while these preparations went forward, poor Martha swung violently between a wild anticipation of her imminent journey to the New World, and the grim knowledge that somewhere out there her father, who now had the ear of Lord Drogo, and had been told he could come to the house whenever he chose – and who believed, moreover, that his daughter was under this very roof – wandered the Lambeth Marsh.

Poor confused child! I saw it all, I knew what Drogo wanted, he wanted Harry Peake to return to Drogo Hall, and Martha was the lure. If it meant that he must give her shelter, then he would do so, it was nothing to him, she was but poultry exposed that the fox may be taken. But to prevent Harry carrying her off – which Drogo most emphatically did not wish to happen – then she must be removed elsewhere; which was why my uncle was packing her off to the colonies.

15

Ah, but Harry Peake was not to be had so easily – he was no nobleman's dupe! He came out on to the marsh but he did not visit the house again, for all he wanted was to see his Martha. In his desperate loneliness and misery I believe he forgot for a time his wild conviction of her treachery; but not knowing how to reach her, he wandered the marsh by night, he came around the house, never showing himself, staying clear of the dogs, and of Clyte, who was always active in the hours of darkness. No, he did not want to storm the citadel and carry her off, but he did want her to know he was out there, that he was out there waiting for her.

How could Martha have known this? I have no idea, and neither did my uncle. But she knew it, because one night she stayed awake, waiting until the house was asleep, and then she slipped out of bed, and throwing on her greatcoat over her nightshirt – the coat she had had from her father, and which, though it stank of tobacco still, and the sleeves were so long she had to fold the cuffs back several times to get her fingers out, was yet a good warm coat for a chill September night – and with her boots and stockings on, and a shawl over her head, and her hair all brushed out and spilling down her back – she was tolerably warm for the vigil that lay ahead.

She rubbed her hands before the fire, which was dying, then clambered into her window alcove and there arranged herself as comfortably as she could. It was a clear night, and there was a moon, and she knew, somehow, that this night she would discover for certain if he was out there or not.

Moonlight seemed to bleach the marsh, to render it palely gleaming, this tract of waterland that stretched for miles in all directions, its ghostly haunted vastness broken only by the occasional stark outline of a leafless elm, and now and then the flicker and flare of the will-o'-the-wisp. This night it was silent. Nothing was moving. Only the mist, delicate as gossamer, stuff of dreams, coiled and drifted in the low-lying bogs where standing water gave back the moon's reflection in strips and bars of tainted radiance. In the distance the town was no more than a dark massy presence with tiny scattered spots of light; and nothing in any other direction. Martha sat in her high window with her arms wrapped round her knees and watched over it all. She had a candle with her in the window: she was a beacon, shining in the night; if he was out there, he would see her.

Oh, but she found it hard, after an hour or two, to stay awake. Her head would start to slide off her knees and she would wake with a start, not knowing how long she had been asleep, a minute or an hour, until she saw how the candle burned; and then once more she looked out over the marsh, so still in the clear cold moonlight.

But soon she was fast asleep, curled up in her big bed with the birds and the lizards scuttling about in the foliage on the headboard.

Three nights later she saw him. There was heavy cloud that night, and some fog, for they had had rain that evening, and a wind, too, and the marsh was very different from what it had been a few nights earlier, altogether darker and wilder, alive with movement, though there was no saying what that movement was, wind on water, shifting fog, animals, spirits, or man. He was among the elm trees. Martha's candle was burning, her beacon was lit. He did not move, merely stood there among the trees gazing straight up at the house.

She was ready. She was wearing her greatcoat. With her boots clutched in one hand, the candlestick in the other, she stepped silently to the door and, turning the key, for now she locked herself in at night, she slipped out into the corridor, where she set down the candle and pulled her boots on. Then away she went down the staircase and through the dark passages of the west wing, then down to a door that opened into the courtyard below her window, where she put out the candle and hid it behind a barrel. Clyte was now the problem, him and the dogs; but as she crept along the wall she heard nothing but the soughing of the wind out on the marsh.

She pressed her back against the bricks for a few minutes, then darted across the yard to a gate that opened into a walled garden behind the stables where she knew she should be safe. Again she paused; again she heard nothing to alarm her. Then she was running, clinging to the deeper shadows by the wall, until she reached the far end, where a sturdy trellis fastened to the brickwork gave her an easy climb up over the wall, and a simple drop to the ground on the far side.

Only a fence or two now separated her from the marsh itself, and the stand of elms where she had earlier seen a tall bent figure among the trees. Then she was running, or squelching rather, across a cow pasture, mud splashing her nightshirt, the greatcoat streaming out behind her. She was slipping and sliding but determined to reach the fence on the far side without once stopping.

She reached it. She hung there, panting. She glanced over her shoulder: nothing pursued her. She glanced about her: nothing moved. In the darkness – heavy clouds had rolled across the moon – the stand of elms was a dense black mass half-a-mile away. She could see no figure there now. The ground between was boggy and uneven, a dangerous place to cross on a dark night after rain. What was that to Martha Peake? She would pick her way with care. Off she went with beating heart, slow and cautious, feeling her way among tufted clumps of earth with dark mucky pools between, and she had to step from one to the next but not before testing with her boot that it was firm enough to take her weight. Perilous work; and more than once she slipped and felt her leg sink in up to the knee, and she hauled it clear but not without difficulty, for the ooze clung and sucked at her, eager to take her down.

Now there was some noise on the marsh, her own: her cries of surprise and frustration, her grunts of exertion, the ghastly sucking sounds of her leg being hauled up out of the bog. She couldn't help it. She didn't care. She was determined to reach the stand of elms where the ground was higher and she had seen, so she thought, her father waiting for her.

The grassy hillocks grew fewer and farther apart and she was scrambling now from one to the next, clawing in the darkness with her hands to secure if not firm footing, at least a grip on something solid. She was wet to her groin. Her greatcoat now dragged about her like a damp sack, a burden she would happily have abandoned but for the wind, which was beginning to spit cold rain in her face. The half-mile from the fence to the trees now seemed a very Atlantic in its vastness. She may have wept but she did not stop. She could not stop. She had no confidence in her ability to turn herself around and find the way back. She had at least the trees in front of her now, she could see where she was going. But she could not see her father.

It grew worse. She was wading through bog now, but slowly, painfully slowly, it was all she could do to keep moving, to get a boot up and out of the bog and take another step. She was wet and cold and miserable. Her strength was flagging. A wave of despair swept over her –

Then she saw him! She saw him. He was tramping toward her through the muck as though it were no more than a puddle. It splattered about him as he came shouldering through. A moment later he had her round the waist and was lifting her clear of the mud, and turning and ploughing back the way he had come, and a little later still they heaved up on to firmer ground and he set her down among the elms. She sat there panting. He squatted at the foot of a tree. He looked old and thin and ill. He had lost several teeth. His cheeks were sunken, his long black hair was matted with dirt and straw, his clothes were in rags. His eyes shone with a peculiar brightness: gin, she thought. His hands trembled. He looked wild. He looked mad. Her father. But the monster was not in him, no, it was his own soul she glimpsed burning dimly within.

'I knew you were out here,' she said. She was filled with a quiet happiness. 'I knew you were watching the house.'

For a long time he said nothing. Then, at last: 'Are you reading your books?' His voice was changed; cracked and husky now, but still it sounded like old leather.

She did not find the question odd. 'I read his books,' she said. 'He has a library.'

'I know it.'

'Aren't you cold?'

'No.'

'I am.'

He had fewer clothes on than she had, but he pulled the cold damp girl to him and wrapped his arms around her. He was very smelly. She wanted to tell him about America but she could not.

'Do you mean to murder me?' she whispered, clutching his collar.

This provoked a hoarse hack of laughter. He shook his head.

'I have gone mad, Martha. At times I cannot account for what I do. But I have no wish to kill you.'

'What will you do?'

No answer to this.

'Are you still living at the Angel?'

'No.'

'Will you visit Lord Drogo again?'

'Drogo!'

His grip on her tightened. He struggled with his anger, she felt it rising in him. She was shivering now, her teeth were chattering.

'I will take you back,' he said, growing suddenly quiet again. 'When I am not mad I think of you.'

'I think of you too.'

'Better forget me.'

'No!'

She shifted herself about in his arms until she could look him in the face, and as she did so the clouds fled from the moon and she saw him for a few seconds with some clarity. The face she saw before her in the moonlight was more scored and hatched with pain than ever, and about the eyes there was a sort of hollowing, a deepening of the sockets and a strange clearness of the brow that somehow unmistakably spelled lunacy. Even Martha, child though she was, could read that; oh, and a hundred other signs of a weakening fibre, the twitching, the muttering that went on constantly under his breath; the hand that trembled in the darkness above her head, and then returned, like a bird disturbed from the nest, to encircle her waist and hold her close. Tears shone damply in his eyes.

'Does your back still hurt?' she said.

'I have no more care of pain.'

She rubbed her cheek against his face. There was a thick beard on him and it scratched her. She pulled back sharply with a cry.

A little later he led her back to the house, bringing her round the boggy part, firm ground all the way. They held hands, and a strange sight they would surely have made, had there been any eye to see them, the big shuffling humpback in rags, and his daughter, in greatcoat and boots, and with mud to her waist, out beneath an angry sky, at the dead of night, walking hand in hand in a marsh. Close to the house he left her, and she stood by the wall watching him as he lumbered toward the London road. She found her way back to her room without mishap, where she cleaned herself as best she could before climbing into bed. It seemed all a dream, and perhaps it would have been, but for the mud she had brought back with her and the burn on her cheek where she had rubbed against his beard.

In the morning the bed was filthy and my uncle was in a state of no little irritation when he discovered that she had gone out on the marsh in the night. She did not tell him about meeting her father. She told him she liked to go out at night, and this made him angry. There were dogs, he said, wild dogs, did she not hear them howling? Martha reassured him, although it irked her sorely that he should attempt to lord it over her like this. But she avoided promising to stay inside the house at night.

And this is how it started, the strange late phase in Martha's relationship with her father. It was unfortunate that her expedition out of doors should have been discovered so quickly, for at one blow she had lost her guardian's trust. William knew well enough that she was a wilful, headstrong girl, but he had presumed she understood the precariousness of her situation in Drogo Hall, and that she would not jeopardize her tenuous security by rash acts.

Now, he said, he was not so sure. That night, when she was settled in her room, he locked the door himself, and pocketed the key. In the days that followed he continued this practice, and by these means gave her little chance to get out of the house and look for Harry in the marsh. She could only keep a vigil in her window alcove, watch for him and pray he would be patient, that he would wait for her. She did not expect this surveillance of William's to be sustained for many days, and sure enough, once he began bringing her books about America from Lord Drogo's library, he became himself so engrossed in them, sitting with her of an evening, that he soon forgot to lock her in and she was gradually able to return to her old independent ways.

Still, it was daunting to go out on to the marsh at night, although it was not difficult during the day to slip across the courtyard and into the walled garden, which was almost always deserted at this time of the year, with little growing there but witch-hazel and catkin; and from there she would make exploratory sweeps of the surrounding country. In this way she first came upon the graveyard.

16

It was another of those dismal and overcast afternoons of which they had so many that autumn; and having used the trellis at the far end of the walled garden to get out into the fields, she skirted round the back of Drogo Hall, using what cover she found out there. She had no idea what the other wing looked like, beyond her memory of the church with the thin steeple standing off to the right as you approached the house on the London road, and which connected it in both body and spirit to the village clustered about its walls.

So she made a wide arc out behind the house, where the land was elevated and dry, and scattered with stones and boulders, and covered in short coarse grass on which Lord Drogo's sheep grazed, their droppings heaped in piles like the cannonballs of some lilliputian artillery. Cold winds came sweeping over those pastures and cut her to the bone, and there was little more than a crumbling stone wall to break their force. Martha kept low behind the wall until she was well off to the far side where the land began to climb, gently at first and then more steeply, the slope heavily wooded with fir and ash. Once in the shelter of the trees she could move more quickly, and soon she had climbed far enough up the hill that she could pause and survey the world spread below her.

She had a clear view of the house, the village, and the marsh; London was but a faint grey smoky mass in the distance. She saw the roofs of Drogo Hall, the shallow slope of roof of the new house with its white balustrade, and around it the steep-pitched gables of the older adjoining structures, moss between the slates, chimneys rising in clusters, fine octagonal stacks with lancet openings, all patterned, moulded, gargoyled even, and in strange contrast to the austere lines of the new white building rising among them. The church, too, from this fresh point of vantage, was a thing of simple, soaring grace, and older, in turn, than the house it served. And there behind it, tucked away, hidden between the church itself and the hillside on which Martha now sat, was the graveyard.

The grass was high between the cracked and fallen stones, and the wall surrounding it was six feet high and overhung on the church side by the boughs of great trees. There was a gate in the wall, and Martha at once realized that here was a place close to Drogo Hall which nobody visited, the high grass was ample indication of that. It was protected by a wall and accessible through a gate on the wooded side. She made her way back down the slope to the gate, which she was able to push open easily, and then for an hour she wandered among the tombstones and read their inscriptions, most of which however had faded with time, now nothing more than faint smudged marks on old pocked stone. Although there was one structure which rose from the high grass at the far end of the graveyard, and seemed to dominate among these ancient tombs, and that, of course, was the Vault of the Drogoes.

Martha left the graveyard as dusk was coming on, and in the thickening light she returned the way she had come, through the trees and then across the pasture at the back of the house. Approaching the walled garden she heard a brief sharp whistle from over by the elms where she had met Harry that first night. It was him; he was there; and she ran to him and flung her arms about him where he stood beneath a tree, just as she had first seen him from her window. He was not sober. He was fuddled, and gentle, and did little but cradle his bottle and grin at her. Breathlessly she told him of her discovery of the graveyard, and he nodded happily, and said he knew the place, and she told him she would be there tomorrow in the afternoon. More happy nodding, another hug, another endearment, and she had to leave him there, and make her way, with many a backward glance, across the field to the walled garden; and when, some minutes later, she reached her room, she climbed at once into the window alcove and peered out.

Did she see him? In the late twilight she could not be sure. Where did he go? Where did he sleep? How did he eat? What did he do for money for gin? That poor, shambling, benighted fellow, she was wracked with anguish at the thought of him shuffling about the streets of London with nobody to protect or succour him. And in her anguish there was guilt. Despite everything, she knew she should help him, but she did not know how.

The next day the weather was unchanged, and having done her chores she left William poring over the diaries of a gentleman-planter from Virginia, and his account of that colony's pestilential swamps, and retraced her steps of yesterday afternoon. Oh, and he was there, he was there, sitting with his back against a gravestone and smoking a white clay pipe with a broken stem. She sat down beside him and they talked, and as they talked they ate, for she had smuggled from the kitchen some cold beef and pickles. He told her something of his life since last they had been together in the Angel. With sadness he described how he had reacted to her flight from the Angel, and his eyes were pools of misery as he stared at the grass growing over the stones.

Martha asked him if he had really said he would kill her. He lifted his eyebrows a little and gave a small shake of the head. He did not know. He supposed it likely. He certainly remembered having the conviction that she had taken his money. She asked him if he still believed that; and now the great head came round and he peered at her closely. He asked her if she *had* taken it, and she told him that of course she had not taken his money, did he really think she would do such a thing? This she asked him with some heat. She was no thief! She would not think of stealing from him!

She said all this – and then she saw it; she saw it rise all at once in his eyes, and for a moment or two he seemed to shake off the blanket of fuddlement he had assumed as a sort of protective garment, so it seemed, and his whole being burned with a mad black flame. He had told her he was mad, that at times he could not account for his actions. Now she saw the madness. Now she saw the monster. Now she believed him. She had forgotten it, she had forgotten that it had frightened her so much that she was flying to America to escape it. Oh, it frightened her now, and she scrambled away from him, but more than that it mystified her.

Where did it come from? How did he sustain it, this mad hatred? – and this was the thought she came away with, after their first meeting in the graveyard.

All this I heard as I lay in bed and struggled against the depredations of the marsh fever I had contracted in the rain the day I rode out from Drogo Hall. I should say, rather, in the interest of that candour I have tried to bring to this history, that all this I *believe* I heard while lying abed; for at times my mind wandered in delirium, and waking, sweating, from the brief fitful dozes which followed upon such episodes, I could not be sure that what I remembered had actually been told me by my uncle, or was, rather, mere tissue I had manufactured to flesh the bare bones of his own spare narrative.

It matters little; for I had by this time plumbed the depths to which Martha and Harry had been sunk in their misfortune, and when my uncle was not with me I began to scribble the outlines of the thing into a small notebook I carried always upon my person. That notebook provided a valuable aid to me in the subsequent composition of this history. A few fevered jottings, clawed from the chaos that illness wreaks in the mind, and from which a full rich body of memory springs forth, at leisure, and in retrospect, I have subjected to the rigours both of reason and of the sympathetic passions, and thus rendered coherent.

A few days later William told Martha that he had secured her passage aboard an American vessel called the *Plimoth* which sailed for Boston in ten days' time; and that letters had already been dispatched to New Morrock informing her relations of it. William had assiduously laboured to encourage in Martha an enthusiasm for the American plan. Often in the late afternoon they sat at the table with their heads together over a book or a print or a map, and at night he regaled her, unwisely in my opinion, with startling anecdotes about white women seized by savages, and extraordinary feats of survival in the Wilderness; though he spoke also of the paradise of clean water and clean air and good cheap arable land that awaited the intrepid settler on the frontier, a theme familiar to her from her father's dream of America, and his poetry.

But Martha was too preoccupied, too full of conflicting feelings properly to give herself over to these ideas. Of course she wished to be stirred by stories of the New World, but at the same time she could not forget her father's welfare, about which William made little further mention.

I believe she came to despise my uncle for this. I believe she thought him heartless and cold. She grew to think that he felt nothing for the sufferings of the poor old wreckage she spent her afternoons with in the graveyard. And with this thought, I believe, so did the first impulse of rebellion arise in her heart.

But then came a most sinister development. Coming away from the graveyard late one afternoon, she discovered Clyte leaning against the wall by the gate and smoking a short black pipe.

'What do you want?' she cried, shocked to come upon him like that, and recoiling as though she had almost trod on a snake. He did not answer, all he gave her was a display of those dog's teeth of his, yellow and pointed and out of all proportion to the weaselly thin face with its stubbled skull and eyes like slits of oil. She asked him again, and again he shook his head, and she went back to the house in a state of great unease. Clyte was not spying on her, she realized, he was spying on her father, and what he learned he passed on to Lord Drogo.

Why did this disturb her? Because she suspected that Lord Drogo meant her father no good, and that Clyte was his agent in whatever scheme was being hatched in the cellars of Drogo Hall? Harry had not dined with his lordship apart from that one night, so if he could not be lured in by a warm fire and good talk, as apparently he could not, then he must be tracked by Clyte, this was Martha's surmise. When next she saw her father she warned him to beware of Clyte but he seemed unconcerned, he grinned the toothless donkey grin and she could not guess what was in his mind.

Martha grew quiet as the moment of departure drew near. I believe my uncle knew she was seeing her father, for Clyte would surely have told him, but he did not know of her dilemma, nor did he hear the pitiful sounds of that lost girl weeping into her pillow each night. All those years of happiness and calm, all swept away in the space of a few weeks, it was little wonder her heart had at first frozen over with the shock of it. And little wonder that when the ice began to crack she would be overcome with grief.

Ah, but out of that grief emerged a decision: I will not go. This is my conviction. I will not go. William knew nothing of it, when I suggested it, but why would he? She would have hidden it from him, of course she would.

And so the last days passed. William spoke to her of the rigours of an Atlantic crossing so late in the season, and much else besides, and Martha listened, though her mind and heart were now decided against an American future. She remained committed, rather, to the skeletal figure haunting the marsh, whom she continued to meet in the graveyard. The day of departure from Drogo Hall was now imminent, and Martha was determined to see her father the night she was to leave the house, and tell him of the plan she had made. She could not leave him. She felt she did little enough for that poor man, and if that little were taken away, then what would be left? He would surely die. He never told her about his life in the town, nor did he answer her questions as to how he fed himself, and where he slept, and by what means he had money, but it was not hard to guess these things. Did Clyte know? He probably did. He too haunted the marsh, watching, always watching, and Martha had no doubt that he followed her father back to whatever sordid night-cellar he spent the night in, after drinking his fill of bad gin.

But these last days he had not been drinking, and was instead sunk in a weary, watchful state of melancholy, almost as though he knew she was about to leave him. And it was that night, the last time she saw him, that a catastrophe befell her whose repercussions she would feel for the rest of her short life.

It happened in the graveyard. The night was windy, and the moon was obscured by clouds. Martha had slipped out of Drogo Hall unobserved, and tramped up the hill, and found him slumped against his customary headstone and stinking foully of gin. She had never seen him so bad. He lay there staring into the high branches of the graveyard elms as they whipped and thrashed about in the wind. The jug was corked and lay beside him in the grass. He raised himself as she approached, lifted an arm and called to her to lie beside him.

She had so much to tell him! She had made her decision, she could not leave him, she would stay, she would help him, they would be together as they had been before. But oh, she was shocked at his appearance. At their last meeting he had been sober for three days, and she had glimpsed the faint outline of the real man within, and upon that glimpse she had begun to build – again! – a small tentative structure of hope. That hope was now dashed. The strength he had acquired in his brief period of sobriety had been put to service in the work of drinking, and with the drinking had come, once more, the turning to the darkness, the embrace of the monster, the disdain of love in the face of a world that would not love him but denied his humanity, rather, and pushed him out.

Martha settled herself in the grass beside him with some apprehension, wrapping her arms round her knees as he rambled at the sky. She made no attempt to understand his dark chaotic chains of thought, all commingled with a scrap of Milton, a snatch of his own verse, fragments of memory rising like tiny silvered fish then sinking for ever to the depths below. He began upon the fire, and oh, there was for him no forgetting the fire, the fire he had caused in his drunkenness that took Grace Foy's life and ruined his own. Despite his incoherence, the slur and garble of his muttering, he did not fail to arouse in Martha, when she remembered the death of her mother, feelings of the most profound grief, and soon he had her weeping, and he, sentimental creature that he was, and all the more so when in drink, he wept with her, tears of gin, and they were soon clutching each other in their unhappiness as Martha stroked his face, and kissed him over and over, and attempted through her own tears to find some words of comfort for him.

That was when he turned. The animal passion flared up like a bed of coals deep in the furnace of his being, and he was so far beyond the reach of reason – so defiantly had he turned his face from the light – that he did not know her as his daughter and his friend, she was nothing but a creature weaker than himself on whom the aroused passion intended now to spend its force. He did not know who she was, he did not hear her screams, he did not heed the fingernails she buried in his face, this sudden conflagration deep in his animal body burned so fierce there was nothing in him now but a storm of lust that must *out* – and Martha was its object. He overwhelmed her without difficulty, he pinned her down, and her struggles were to no avail as he hoisted her skirt then freed from his ragged breeches that great horse-penis of his, now thick as a fisted arm –

She did not know what happened to him when he was done with her. She ran away from him through the graveyard, through the shrieking wind and the flailing trees, beneath the moonless sky, sick and bleeding and desperate only to reach the sanctuary of her room. She burst in through the door and flung herself on the bed. When she had recovered a little she washed herself in the shadowy recess of the room, and found on her body and her garments eloquent marks of what she had been made to endure; and by then her plan to slip away from Drogo Hall that very night, and join her father, lay in ruins.

Nor was this the worst of it. For in her shame, in her pollution, she fastened on that which was to her even more terrible than the rape itself, and that was the deep sure knowledge that when her father spent himself inside her she had conceived his child.

CAPE MORROCK

A thin joist of a spine never yet upheld a full and noble soul.

HERMAN MELVILLE

17

My uncle's story had been growing darker and more terrible with every fresh burden he loaded upon the young shoulders of Martha Peake, but this was too much.

'What? Conceived his child?' I cried, rearing up from the bed and thoroughly startling the old man. 'And she *knew*?'

Seemingly she did. Women often do, or so William would have me believe. There is, he said, a sort of *leaping* sensation in the womb, which is felt as the leaping of life. And everything that followed, everything that Martha suffered in America, was the direct consequence of it – of, that is, her father's act of brutal ravage in a dark graveyard not a stone's throw from the very room in which I now lay in weakened and feverish condition as my uncle fluttered in wild-eyed excitement at the horror of what he was telling me.

Go on, go on, I cried!

Ah, but Martha could not think of staying now, I reflected, as he talked on, Harry had made a mockery of her hopes, revealed them for the empty fantasies they were, shown himself a brute, worse than a brute, even brutes – did not Tom Paine say it himself? – even brutes do not devour their young.

I saw her kneeling in a patch of moonlight by the window of her tower room in the west wing of Drogo Hall. No tears flood down her face, as she packs her few possessions into the small trunk that followed her from the Angel, she is, rather, dry-eyed, stony-faced, no apparent anger, only a furious concentration on what she is doing. She descends the staircase canted backwards, clutching the leather straps of her trunk, not an easy thing, for it is dark, the stairs are narrow and uneven, the old stone treacherously smooth in places. Draped in her dragging greatcoat, step by clumsy step she struggles down to the bottom.

She reaches the courtyard. The storm has blown itself out, and the moon is intermittently visible through the ragged clouds that drift across a night sky which seems rinsed, now, and exhausted. In the shadows of the courtyard with his back to her stands a slight figure in a bulky riding coat, his hat pulled low over his face, attending to a pair of horses harnessed to the black carriage. It rocks on its springs as the horses shift and stamp, but there is almost no sound, for the wheels are bound in rags, as are the horses' hooves; an old smuggler's trick. The figure turns, and it is of course my uncle William.

Martha pulls open the door of the carriage and pushes the trunk in, then climbs in after. William gets up on to the cab and the carriage shudders into motion. As they roll out of the courtyard Martha sits forward to pull the window blind aside an inch or two and look out across the marsh, fearing any sign of discovery which might impede her flight. For a moment the moonlight falls full upon her upturned face, and it is not hard to imagine the stark stony sorrow there; then she sinks back into the gloom of the carriage's interior.

These are the minutes of greatest danger, and they pass with unspeakable slowness. If Harry is still conscious, if he has not passed out against a headstone in the graveyard, he might well be watching the house, alert for this very occurrence, an attempt by his daughter once more to escape him. And if he does see the black carriage moving out of the shadows of the house, will he not come down to the road and attempt to stop it? Seize the bridle, throw William aside, haul open the door, reach in for her –?

The carriage rumbles around the side of the house, the horses splashing through the puddles, then out past the lake. The hooves and wheels though muffled seem thunderous to Martha, but no shout comes, no sound of pursuit, no sign at all that her departure is detected. Perhaps Harry does indeed see them, perhaps he stands among the trees on the hillside, a shadow among shadows, and watches them go, and does nothing – but then, does she not have Clyte to fear as well; will the little gargoyle, knowing his master's scheme, allow Martha simply to slip away from Drogo Hall – or does he no longer need her, and the bound wheels and hooves are all a masquerade for Martha's benefit, to arouse in her a false perception of her own desperate predicament? – oh, the plotting was devious, devious, wheels within wheels –

At last they reach the road at the far end of the village, and there, in the darkness beneath the trees, William solemnly climbs down and removes the rags from hoof and wheel. The last of the clouds drifts into the east and now beneath a full moon and a clear sky they move off across the marsh at a good brisk trot. Soon the horses are going at the gallop, and the black carriage sways and lurches as they toss their manes and lift their jaws to the moon, and their flashing hooves splatter through the puddles, throwing up showers of mud and water. Martha, flung this way and that in the rocking carriage, turns her head, and through a small oval opening in the canvas behind her she sees the rearing form of Drogo Hall etched sharp and black against the sky, but receding from her, growing smaller with every moment. She has no reason to think she will ever see the accursed place again.

The carriage raced across the Lambeth Marsh, and after some time Martha heard a tolling bell. Her head lifted, and a faint light of hope sprang up in her face. By God she had pluck! Only hours before, the one man she had ever loved had subjected her to the most vile and violent attack, and her poor heart must have been in an utter chaos of shock and revulsion – and she was in bodily pain, yes, she had been assaulted with great force – her world was upended, and here she was, about to leave England for a country of which she knew little beyond that her own countrymen were preparing to make war upon it! Yet she showed nothing of this to my uncle. He discovered only much later what Harry did to her in the graveyard.

They crossed the river at Westminster and were soon clattering along cobblestoned streets. She heard men shouting, bodies buffeted against the carriage, and at each blow Martha's own body stiffened, as though she had taken the impact directly, as though even the slightest shock had the power to awaken the recent outrage she had suffered, and undo the numbness that was already stealing over her soul. When the carriage at last came to a halt it was light outside, and she emerged blinking on to the London docks. Then, with the trunk carried between them, and many an anxious glance cast this way and that, they hurried across the crowded quay and into a narrow alley and so to a public house, where shortly afterwards my uncle left her. Martha spent the rest of the day in a small room at the top of the house, waiting for him to return.

What she endured over the next hours it is hard to imagine; but because her mind could not at once contemplate the shock of what she had just suffered, I believe she maintained a sort of eerie stillness, for a while; but then, becoming suddenly fearful, she paced and fretted, she talked to herself, she wept, she hammered the table with her fist; at last making herself calm again, and sitting silently at the window watching the ships, her heart and mind a blank; until the panic came again. But she did not leave the room.

At last William returned, and they left the house together. Hurrying across the quay, with their coats wrapped about them, and their heads covered against spying eyes, they reached a flight of old stone steps which descended the seawall to the river, where a boat was tied up to a ring in the stone. To the west the sky was a glowing mass of piled grey clouds, lit from within by the sinking sun, and rising against it the masts of the massed merchant shipping. William helped Martha down the steps and at the bottom, in a damp gusty wind, with the choppy grey waters lapping at their feet, they embraced. It began to rain.

Out on the river small vessels slid under the bows of large, and the darkening sky was netted with ropes and rigging. Flags and ensigns stirred at the mastheads. Martha was suddenly overcome; for a second the crust round her heart broke open, and she made a strange, strangled cry. She seized William round the neck and pulled him to her. She hugged him fiercely. When they broke apart the tears were coursing down my uncle's cheeks as well.

'God speed you, Martha Peake,' he whispered.

Martha clambered into the boat, where a waterman with a red kerchief tied about his skull sat waiting to take up the oars. Huddled now in the depths of her greatcoat, only a strand or two of hair escaping from under her old cocked hat, she settled herself in the boat as William stowed the trunk behind her in the stern. The lanthorn was lit, the waterman pushed off, and then she was out in the river, ships towering like buildings on all sides of her and casting great shadows in the dusk.

The waterman pulled with easy strokes, murmuring a song to himself, as the oars cleft the dark unquiet water. The further out he rowed the fresher the wind grew, and soon it was gusting strongly, spitting rain in their faces. Martha's hair was flying out from under her hat and plastering itself all over her face. She closed her eyes and lifted her head and in her mind she told the wind it could do what it wanted, she didn't care any more, and if it wanted to blow her all the way to America then it could. After a while, and the sky now darker still, the boat drew close to a brig with two masts, a great looming thing, one of several such vessels rocking at anchor in the middle of the river, and she saw it was the *Plimoth*.

Then she twisted around and, peering back at the shore, tried to catch sight of William. Through the gloom, through the shifting chaos of rope and spar she found again the flight of steps she had put off from. On the quay braziers were burning now, lamps glowed dull yellow in the windows of warehouses, all light was splintered in the dank wet dusk. At the top of the steps she believed she could make out the motionless figure of William Tree, his arm lifted above his head in a sort of salute. She lifted her hand and answered his salute, then turned back and cried out to the waterman to pull harder – harder, for the love of God!

The waterman pulled, the wind blew stronger, night came on. Where was Harry? Was he even then lurching down to the river, shouting for a boat, rearing from the prow like an agent of Nemesis sent to obstruct his daughter's escape to America and vent again his awful passion upon her –

But he did not come. He was out there somewhere, perhaps he was on the docks, perhaps he even saw her; but he did not show himself. And Martha, having clambered up a rope ladder to the deck of the *Plimoth*, and been hauled aboard by an American sailor, stood at the rail while her trunk came up after her, and contemplated the last of London. She began to tremble. She was seized with a great convulsion of the heart, she gasped with pain as though she had been kicked, such was the force of it, and a hand went at once to her belly, while with the other hand she held herself upright against the rail. It was nothing, she told herself, as she was taken below to join her fellow passengers in steerage, but it was not nothing, it was a sudden gust of heat in the icy numbness settling upon her spirit, the first grim augury of the misery and guilt that would come to haunt her for her desertion of her father.

18

Upon Martha's plight I would have much time to ponder in the days to come. I left her safe aboard the *Plimoth* as the waterman, having delivered his passenger, pulled away through the darkness, long oars sweeping and dipping, for the lights of the shore. Now it was to her father that my thoughts fled; and I could not but wonder, when Harry next opened his eyes – when next he sobered, and remembered what he had done – what wild interior landscape of hellish guilt was then revealed to him? Even a man of unbent strength and fortitude would stumble and fall, so what was I to think of Harry's prospect, enfeebled in the moral part as he was by gin and isolation? Then all at once I saw his prospect, and again I rose up from my bed, seized by a premonition, as with terrible clarity I glimpsed him in my mind's eye far out on the Lambeth Marsh, far in the distance on some desolate tract where only wild dogs and crows lived, where the cold winds cut across the empty land and flapped his rags about him – strung up on a dead tree and turning slowly on the end of a rope!

My uncle peered at me with keen bright eyes. He told me to rest. Rest? I had no need of rest! Did Harry hang himself from a tree? The old man denied it, but his assurances did little to settle the storm aroused in me and later, after Percy had come to me with a sleeping draught, I dreamed wildly of Harry's death out on the Lambeth Marsh.

But on awakening I thought: there was – there must have been – some small flickering ember of self-love that smouldered still in his charred soul, by which dim glow he found a reason not to hang himself. Did he first sink into darkness and intoxication in some night-cellar, not returning to the surface world for some days? Did he attempt to extinguish the voice of his conscience, and pursue the oblivion which drink holds out to those who lack the will to destroy themselves at a single stroke? I do not know; I think it likely.

*

I can only imagine, never having crossed the Atlantic myself, what Martha endured for the next weeks, down in the hold where poor emigrant families were crowded together and only rarely allowed to come up into the fresh air. It was late in the season and the weather was bad. There was disease rampant on the lower decks, and the air was foul with the stink of rotting hemp and damp timbers; there was the awfulness of the night-soil buckets, and the seasickness, and the ceaseless wailing misery of the children. The crack of flapping sails, the massive screaming beams, heavy seas dashed with immense force against the pitching hull – all of it reduced Martha at times, I believe, to a state of such distress that she slept fitfully at best, and waking in the darkness, on her narrow bunk, mere inches from the planking of the bunk above, and no glimmer of light in that fetid space to tell her she was not entombed, she was terrified; and in her terror she wrapped her arms about her knees and huddled there shivering. Hers was a spoiled body, in her own eyes, and she wanted to be held.

At other times, when the captain allowed the passengers up on deck, I see her standing by the rail in the late afternoon, wrapped in her greatcoat, numb within and gazing out to sea. She was disturbed by the sea, by its restless violence and careless power, and the American sailors, I believe, were amused by her, and asked her did she pine for a sweetheart left behind in England? She roused herself sufficiently to tell them there was nothing in England for which she pined, the very opposite, she said, her thoughts were all with what lay ahead, with America.

But it was not true. She did not think about America, for all through the voyage her womb remained dry; and so she became certain she had indeed conceived. She lay on her back on the hard bunk and spread her hands across her belly. She lacked any ability to awaken feeling in herself for this new life nested inside her, as she herself lay nested in the darkness in the belly of the ship, which heaved and yawed through the North Atlantic swells, vessel within vessel within vessel.

*

Seven weeks the voyage took. Martha spoke little, and held aloof from her companions in the hold, poor English families themselves uncertain and subdued; her eyes were turned inward, she was occupied with her own unhappy thoughts and feelings to the exclusion of all else. This blankness and passivity, this apparent unfeelingness in the face of catastrophe, all this was merely a mask she wore, I believe, while she adapted herself to her new condition. I believe she was consumed, at times, by the most passionate hatred of her father; but I believe she also came to understand, at some profound level of her being – in her soul, I mean – why he had committed the outrage against her, and understanding, determined that her love for him would not be extinguished. This was no act of the will, it was barely even conscious; it was, rather, the accommodation of her spirit to the compulsion to love him. She had no choice but to love him, nor had she ever questioned that compulsion; and so in her mind a new picture of her father began to form, a picture she would protect from the memory of his crime just as his child would be cherished and protected while it grew in her womb.

I said this to my uncle. He was having none of it, he snorted and told me he knew little of what Martha Peake suffered in America; and, he might have added, for it was there in his tone, cared less. And I reflected, not for the first time, on the diminishing interest, the indifference, even, in the old man's account of Martha, this in strong contrast to the copious attention he paid her father. And although I had yet to uncover the mystery he seemed so avid to preserve, I was aware of a swelling irritation, even as I lay abed recuperating from the marsh fever, at his crude attempt to manipulate my credulity. For I was by now convinced that my own understanding of the events he sketched was closer by far to the true heart of the matter than his own inadequate interpretation.

So I pressed the point, I asked him again, did he not think that Martha wanted to forget what her father had done to her? He sighed. He shrugged. He admitted he thought it possible. He knew little of what Martha suffered in America, he said, and it was so long ago, and her letters had not given any sort of a clear picture of her life there –

But where *are* these letters, I cried!

Some flapping of his hand here, and pursing of the lips, and gazing at the ceiling; but for once I was not to be deterred, and with some vehemence, sitting bolt upright in my bed, I requested, nay, I *demanded* that he show them to me! At last he met my eye, and with a sigh he shook his little bell.

Percy duly appeared.

'Bring the letters,' murmured William.

Percy cocked his head, lifted an eyebrow. Things unspoken passed between them.

'Bring them.'

Percy bowed and left us. We waited in silence, William sniffing and sighing, and busying himself with a large handkerchief, my own thoughts growing impatient now at the prospect of at last glimpsing something more intimately connected with Martha Peake than the phantasms of my uncle's ailing memory. Reading what she herself had written, this would illuminate my understanding, as a stormswept night is illuminated by lightning – I would *know* her, I felt, I would know her for who she truly was, and I would learn, too, of those events in America of which my uncle, naturally, had no direct knowledge. And how much more capable was I, I thought, to grasp the import of what she had written, than he with his failing powers of mind –!

Oh, but I was sorely disappointed. Sorely disappointed. When Percy returned, and placed a small tin box in my uncle's hands, I saw at once that it could not contain much of a correspondence. Nor did it, when at last he unlocked the box, and took from it a small packet of letters; which had been so corrupted by time, and damp, and neglect that I knew I would be fortunate to discover much that was legible within. He handed me the letters, and with trembling fingers I untied the ribbon which bound them; and even as I did so they began to fall apart.

Fragments. As I picked with growing desperation through those crumbling scraps all I had was fragments. But oh, so tantalizing! –

and I turned to my uncle, even as I groped about in the blankets to gather them up, and begged him to help me make a whole of what now was little more than a heap of stained, brittle scraps of paper the colour of damp tobacco, and with only the faintest signs of Martha's hand upon them, those signs mere shadows – ghosts! – of the mind, the heart, the *presence* of that once ardent spirit!

'Ah no, Ambrose,' he murmured. 'No, I cannot do more.'

I began to protest; a hand was lifted, and this time I fell silent.

'I am an old man, Ambrose. Spare me this labour. You have what you wanted.'

And with that I had to be satisfied. He left me soon after, and I lay abed in some dejection, frustrated in my enterprise and unable to understand why so little care had been taken of Martha's letters. But as the hours passed, and the fire burned low in the hearth, and the wind rose in the trees outside the window, I began to feel – and it is often thus with me that the night will bring a fresh clarity to what, by day, has been obscure – I began to feel that all was not lost; that with the aid of these crumbling scraps, and the exercise of my own sympathetic passions, there might yet be a way of coming at the knowledge of what Martha Peake did in America, and what was done to her; and I came at last to the decision that, like Martha, I would go on alone. I would write her story myself. Armed with these fragments I would trust to my own intuitive grasp of the drift and meaning of her experiences in America, and give them life with my pen.

What choice had I? If Martha Peake's story were to be told – and I had heard enough by now to know that it must be told, and her place in American history fixed for all time – then only I could tell it. I rang for Percy and had him replenish my inkpot, and my medicines, and struggling to my table, with a blanket round my shoulders, I went to work with fresh resolve.

With the sea spray frozen in the rigging – I wrote – and icicles hanging in clusters from the shrouds, one clear cold late October morning the *Plimoth* at last came into Massachusetts Bay. When land was sighted the steerage hatches were opened, and the passengers came shuffling up on deck, those who had survived the voyage; and chilled to the bone though they were, great was their excitement, and they cheered loud and long. Greater still was their relief that they would soon be done with wormy bread and bad beef, and would sleep no more on hard dank bunks. Already the air smelled different, it smelled of soil, of trees, of smoke, and for all Martha's despondency there arose in her a surge, if not of joy, of faint dull hope at the thought of stepping on to dry land. Gulls swooped about the ship, and in the distance Boston was no more than a smoky blur, but as the *Plimoth* stood in toward the harbour the features of the town became ever more distinct, its hills and houses, its wharves and steeples, all hedged round by the masts of ships.

The day was clear, the wind gusting offshore, and the smell of woodsmoke grew stronger. As they passed among the islands seals barked at them from the rocks and slid in groups into the icy waters; and there was Castle William, its battery studded with cannon, and a company of redcoats passing through the gates. Over the fort the Union Jack flapped and cracked in the wind.

Martha stood at the rail among the other ragged exiles. Boston was like no town she had ever seen, its neat wooden houses and forest of steeples all trimly contained among hills and water – so unlike London, which sprawls in every direction like a great squat toad! Smoke rose from a thousand chimneys into the cold air, and now she could see the big British ships of the line anchored across the mouth of the inner harbour, and skimming and wheeling among them a host of smaller vessels, coasting craft and the like. One of those vessels, a single-masted cutter with white sails billowing fore and aft, was now seen to be clearing the harbour mouth.

Now, it is my belief that aboard this vessel was an officer of the British army then billeted in Boston, a man called Giles Hawkins. It is a name I discovered in several of Martha's letters, or in the remains of them, rather, and it took no great skill on my part to recognize its importance to her; for that name, each time it appeared, was printed in capital letters. It is because this man played so large a part in Martha's life in North America that I introduce him here. For it was aboard the *Plimoth*, I believe, that Martha first encountered him.

As I see him, Giles Hawkins had something of the fighting cock about him, he was small, portly and pugnacious, and his duty, this day, was to inform the master of the *Plimoth*, an ill-tempered Nantucket mariner called Daniel Bowditch, that he, Bowditch, could not bring his vessel into Boston Harbour. Having come alongside the *Plimoth*, and climbed aboard, Captain Hawkins discharged this duty in a loud, ringing voice such that he was heard by everyone on deck. Up on the bridge Daniel Bowditch turned red.

'And why not?' cried the apoplectic Nantucketer.

'Because the port of Boston is closed.'

'By whose order?'

'By the King's order, sir!'

He had flashing blue eyes, this stocky Englishman, and he stood there in the wind, staring up at the enraged Yankee sea captain, with his chin jutting out like a bulldog's, as Daniel Bowditch expressed sentiments that would have got him hanged in England. Captain Hawkins heard him out.

'Duly noted,' he then said, and turned to the listening passengers. He announced that before allowing them ashore he would inter view each of them below. He then ordered the ship to be searched, and the company of redcoats he had brought aboard with him moved forward and opened the hatches, and clattered down to the lower decks.

I need not describe the profound unease all this aroused among the wretched families clustered there on deck, men and women who had spent all they had to get themselves and their children to the New World; and imagine Martha's feelings! Having crossed the North Atlantic, was she now to be sent back to England on the whim of this one man? Little wonder she printed his name in block capitals!

The mood aboard the *Plimoth* grew uglier by the minute as each family in turn went below to the captain's cabin in the poop, which the Englishman had commandeered for his purpose, and showed their papers.

Martha Peake was left to last. Exhausted though she was by the voyage, dirty and stinking after the grim weeks confined below, she made some order of her hair, she squared her shoulders, and down the staircase she went and stepped into the captain's quarters in a temper apparently robust and unafraid.

Captain Giles Hawkins sat in the corner of the room in deep shadow. He was less terrifying at close quarters than he had been on deck, for here he had no need to strut and shout, but with some civility, rather, he told Martha to shut the door and then asked her name. His voice was at once familiar to her, it was like an English hedge, clipped and cultivated, such as she had often heard in the mouths of bucks and rakes who frequented the low London taverns for the dubious pleasure of swimming in alien currents. But this was no fop; Captain Hawkins possessed the peculiar easy charm that Martha would later come to understand as the mannered affability of the English gentleman harnessed to the seasoned army officer's habit of command, and the two not in conflict. Not such a rare type, but new to Martha, and although he showed her kindness she did not, at first, trust him.

With the door closed, and her eyes adjusting to the gloom, she could see him better; and he could see her. He sat back in the captain's chair, the ferocity of his features softened somewhat, his plump booted legs crossed as he mended his windblown wig with a small tortoiseshell comb. When Martha said her name he leaned forward and scribbled it on the list before him, then tossed the quill into the inkpot. For a moment or two he sat frowning at it, as though he knew the name but was unable to place it. He looked up, gazed at her, and then asked her: 'Why are you here, Martha Peake?'

Martha could not stand upright in the little cabin, she was too tall for it. The mariner's lamp swung to and fro from the beam close to her head as the *Plimoth* rode gently on her anchor cables. She noticed Captain Bowditch's charts rolled up and pushed into pigeonholes along the wall. The shriek of the gulls came faintly through the closed porthole.

'I have come to live with my mother's sister and her family.'

'Have you no family in England?'

'No.'

'Your mother and father?'

'They are dead.'

'I am sorry for you. Sit down, Martha.'

This she had not expected, nor that he should then give her a small glass of the captain's rum. He told her his name was Giles Hawkins, and that he was a Somerset man, and Martha said she knew the county, she had passed through it as a child on her way to London.

'As a child?' he then said. 'And are you not a child now, Martha Peake?'

No, she was not.

They talked then of Cornwall, and somehow, she did not know how it happened, she found herself telling him the story of her mother's death. Ah, but it must be remembered that after the weeks at sea – and given her late ordeal in England – Martha responded with strong feeling to a warm smile and a kindly voice, she could not help herself. She had the strength of character to stand alone, but she was not accustomed to it, and Giles Hawkins saw this at once. I believe she aroused a real sympathy in him, and that he questioned her closely about her family in America so as to assure himself that she would be cared for when she went ashore. But he was, at the same time, part of an occupying force in a rebellious colony, and he knew Martha's uncle for an influential merchant, and a patriot; and his display of fatherly concern masked, I believe, a shrewd probing of the girl. Martha had nothing of value to tell him, of course, nonetheless it was a complicated transaction, which culminated in Martha shedding tears, and Captain Hawkins comforting her as he would one of his own daughters.

Later I told my uncle that this I imagined to be what passed between Giles Hawkins and Martha Peake at their first meeting. The old man may have wished to be spared the labour of thinking about Martha any more, but he was not slow to criticize my own account of her experience. At once, and with some heat, he contradicted me. Could I not imagine an Englishman offering simple kindness to a young creature in distress, as Martha was? Did I think he was *bound* to attempt to take advantage of her?

Frankly, I said, yes, I did.

He frowned at me then looked away. He rubbed his thumb against his fingers in his agitation, and made small inarticulate noises as he licked his lips with little rapid flickers of his dry old tongue. And did I think Martha so foolish that she would not see this? Did I not remember the glorious destiny which she was even then approaching? Why, this was the girl who would save the Revolution – was she not made of sterner stuff than a mere –

Child?

You said it, I did not! Is this your heroine? Is this your proud rebel?

I shrugged. It was not the character of Martha Peake he defended, but that of the English officer. I did not trouble to point this out to him.

The Boston waterfront was as crowded with people as the harbour was with shipping. Martha was brought in with the last passengers, sitting on her trunk in the stern of the boat. She heard men shouting from ship to shore and shore to ship as the gulls flapped and screamed overhead. All was movement and noise, and then they were gliding in, and a rope was flung up on to the wharf. She waited her turn to climb up the short wooden ladder and set foot on the New World. Her trunk came up after her, and there at last she stood, gazing about her with some astonishment as her fellow exiles clambered up on to the wharf beside her, some to be met by tearful relatives, others, like herself, stranded there, bewildered. She could hear drumming not far off, over the hubbub of dockside commerce, and a whistling fife, and she knew it for the fife and drum of the redcoats. The Americans paid her no notice at all, but thronged about, doing their business, merchants and clerks, porters and carters, such as might be seen any day on the London docks, although these men were larger, leaner, louder, their voices strange to her ear and their clothing coarse and homespun. There were some wigs to be seen, but many preferred to grow their hair long and tie it at the back with a scrap of ribbon. Martha seized up her trunk by the straps, and weak though she was after her time at sea, off she plodded down Long Wharf to the crowded street that fronted the harbour.

And did Giles Hawkins lean on the taff-rail of his cutter, and watch her as she disappeared into the crowd? Oh, I believe he did. I believe he did.

But such figures she glimpsed then, in her first minutes in Boston –! She had read about the savages of North America, she had seen illustrations of them; but to meet them at once in the flesh, this was something else, and she slowed and set down her trunk and gawped at a group of Iroquois braves who stood silently staring out across the harbour to the open sea. Dressed from head to toe in the skins of animals, with long-barrelled muskets at their sides, knives and hatchets in their belts, their garments beaded and feathered, and with wild shaggy manes of black hair sprouting from the crowns of their shaved skulls, they seemed to Martha not so much savages, in their dignity, and stature, and straightness, as princes. She was later told that these men were employed by the British as scouts and trackers in the forests to the north.

There were still more people milling about on the dock than on the wharf, and they were an agitated crowd, for moving through them in a small tight squad were a dozen redcoats, an officer on horseback riding alongside them. At the head of this tight little column stepped the drummer she had heard, a boy ten years old beating out a brisk tattoo; and as the redcoats passed by they were closely watched by various clusters of men on the dock who seemed to have no business to do, but were waiting, so it appeared, for something to happen.

Martha was familiar with this, men standing in doorways, on street corners, waiting and watching, though for what they might be waiting and watching here in Boston she had no idea. Young men for the most part, they stood about in small groups outside shops and taverns, and their mood was easy to read, they were mocking, and their mockery was directed at the redcoats. They muttered together and shouted to one another, they laughed loudly, they moved about from group to group, all the while watched carefully by the officer on horseback as he rode by. Even the busy merchants paused, and regarded him and his soldiers with undisguised contempt.

All this I gleaned from the fragments of what I took to be Martha's first letters from America; for nowhere could I find a date, nor any other indication of the sequence in which the letters had arrived at Drogo Hall. But it was, I felt, enough, and I was confident that what I imagined was indeed what Martha observed that blustery day in the autumn of 1774; and observing it, remembered what she had heard of Massachusetts, of how the province had renounced allegiance to the crown some weeks before and been placed under martial law. And as her curiosity came sparking faintly to life she sensed a rising emotion in her heart, she did not know what it was, exactly, but it responded to what she was seeing and hearing all about her on the Boston dock that day. But she had no chance to think more about it, for all at once she heard her name called.

19

After her weeks at sea Martha was not an impressive spectacle. She was bedraggled and exhausted. She was pale from lack of sunlight and fresh food, her hair was matted, her clothes filthy and stinking. She had lost a tooth and she itched all over with ship-lice.

'Martha Peake!'

There it came again, through all the noise of the port, and as she peered about her she saw a broad-shouldered youth as tall as her father detach himself from a group of men standing around a capstan and come loping toward her down the dock. Martha stood by her trunk clutching her hat to her head for the breeze off the harbour was brisk. The big lad advancing on her was dressed in a sturdy brown coat which flapped about him over a high-buttoned waistcoat; black breeches; black stockings; solid muddy leather shoes without buckles, and a cocked hat pushed to the back of his head so the peak pointed at the sky. His long hair was pulled back from high in the middle of his forehead and tied in a ponytail with a blue ribbon. She watched him come, she saw how he jigged through the crowd, a grin on his face, this strong loose-limbed fellow just a year or two older than herself. He fetched up in front of her, panting slightly, set his hands on his hips, and looked her up and down with some amusement.

'Cousin,' he said.

He then swept his hat off his head and made a grovelling mockery of an Englishman's formal bow. There was life and spirit in his shining eyes, those eyes set deep in a wide, ruddy, big-chinned face, and Martha stared at him with mild astonishment, thinking, is this an American? But he did not displease her; until, that is, he seemed to catch a whiff of her, and all at once slapped a hand, not clean, to his face, and peered at her as though uncertain he had the right girl here.

'I believe you to be Martha Peake,' he said.

'Who are you?' she said.

'I am Adam Rind, eldest son of Silas Rind, Esquire, of New Morrock, in the Massachusetts Bay Colony, to which King Charles granted the charter in the Year of Our Lord sixteen hundred and twenty-nine.'

He could talk, then.

'Are you to carry my trunk?'

To this imperious question he responded with a large grin, a large display of large discoloured teeth that aroused at last a small smile in Martha's stern countenance.

'She favours me,' he said, and took her hand gravely. He made a small sober bow. 'There is my father, sitting up in that fine wagon with his servant. He trembles at your coming.'

He pointed at a high sturdy wagon drawn up outside a chandler's shop, a team of four horses harnessed to it. People were passing along the dock between them, and she could not clearly see the figure to whom her cousin pointed, for he was leaning down from the buckboard in close conversation with some men in the street. Up on the wagon beside him sat a Negro in a blue coat whom Adam identified as his father's servant Caesar, and his own good friend. He then hoisted Martha's trunk on to his shoulder and offered her his arm, but she would not take it. They set off across the busy street, she with her shabby English greatcoat flapping about her.

'How do you like Boston?' he cried, and then, in a tone of mock cultivation: 'A damn fine town but for all the bloody English in it' – and still pushing briskly on, he turned to her and again gave her the horsey grin. Martha wondered whether he ate oats and had to be rubbed down at the end of the day.

Now Silas Rind was a good deal more formidable than his husky son. Let me attempt to classify the parts of that complicated man, as I have come to understand him. I know something of the Puritan temperament, I believe, and I suspect that Silas Rind had a distinct tendency toward the introspection of that sect, being a man who restlessly scoured and abluted the dark impulses of his masculine heart. But he was not narrow, no, he had a good mind, he was curious about all branches of learning, and he could converse with ease with the best-educated men in Boston, many of whom were his friends. Then, too, he had a vigorous instinct for commerce, and had grown rich from his various enterprises; and he was, in addition, a fierce patriot, long outraged at the despotism of a distant empire and a distant king. These aspects of his character were not at war with one another. Rather, his several commitments to virtue, to learning, to commerce, and to the political future of his country, these coexisted in complex balance one with the other, no part becoming dominant but some other part would moderate it. As for his person, he was a lean, dark, broody sort of a man of middling height and middling age, dressed in a plain brown coat and breeches. He wore no wig, his hair gathered at the back in a simple blue ribbon like his son's.

He climbed down off the wagon and they shook hands, he and Martha, and had a good long look at one another. His eyes at once told her that a temper was in him that she never wanted directed at her; though this thought was enough to arouse in Martha the distinct whisper of a desire to challenge him. He asked her about her voyage, all the while scanning the crowd on the dock, which allowed her the opportunity to inspect him more closely. It was as though the broad, raw-boned features of the son were here glimpsed in an original which bore marks of a natural nobility lost in transmission across the generation. He had a high forehead and temple, a hawklike nose, thin lips clamped tight, a firm jaw; and the handsome bones of this fine proud head admirably framed its manly features. It occurred to Martha that if he ever became her enemy he would surely destroy her, but there was withal a sort of confidence to him that she liked, even a wintry warmth. She told him that the *Plimoth* had not been allowed to unload its cargo. She suspected that this would anger him, and it did. He lifted his eyes and gazed into the sky as though an explanation of this folly was written in the clouds. He frowned at her, and she knew he was contemplating her Englishness, asking himself how deep it went. Ah well, Martha Peake, he said, a new home, eh? A new home in New England.

Then she was taken to Foley's Tavern, a dark wooden house near the docks, where they were to spend the night before setting off for New Morrock early the next morning.

It is fruitless to speculate as to what Silas Rind expected to meet on Long Wharf that day in the person of Martha Peake. In the autumn of 1774 the English were roundly despised in Boston, or rather their king was, him and the soldiers he had sent to occupy the town. My uncle was vague as to what he had written to Silas Rind, beyond that Martha was in the most grave peril and had to flee England. But it occurs to me now that even before her arrival her plight had earned her the sympathy of her American relatives, who were themselves in a sense in a similar predicament. So whether or not they were sensible of the particulars of her situation, they knew at least that she was in bad trouble through no fault of her own; and I can imagine Silas telling his friends that this English girl was no less the victim of cruelty and misfortune than they were themselves.

Several of those friends arrived at Foley's as the New Morrock party was finishing an early supper. In they came, four or five men who were, to Martha's eye, like Silas himself, serious, sober, unsmiling men. They sat down and subjected the weary Martha to a close scrutiny as she cleared the plates from the table. When she returned from the kitchen they were in close conversation over a bottle of rum, and spoke too low for her to make much sense of what they said. She settled herself by the window and watched the street, yawning, eager for her bed but as yet uncertain where she was to sleep. Adam cast a number of glances in his cousin's direction, but he did not leave the table, intent as he was on what the men were saying.

Then she saw Silas Rind lean over to his son and whisper something in his ear; and Adam nodded, and pushed his chair back, and came and sat down next to her at the window. He was serious now, his mood in accord with that of the men at the table. He laid a hand on hers and told her he understood how strange it must be for her, thus to arrive in a country she did not know, which was even then approaching a great crisis, perhaps its greatest ever.

'Will there be war, then?' she asked him, withdrawing her hand.

He said there would be, that they had gone too far to turn back now. Even as he said it, his manly gravity began to crumble and the raw excitement of the youth shone through.

'But have you an army?'

'We will have an army. Would that we had a navy too.'

'And are all the colonies united now?'

'You understand our situation, Martha Peake. No, we are not united, which is why we go slow.'

He stretched his long legs, crossed them at the ankle and regarded her with some interest from those lively eyes of his. He tore a splinter from the table and began to pick his teeth with it.

'My father,' he said, 'is not aware that you are familiar with the difficulties we face.'

'We have not spoken properly to one another.'

'So are you a friend of ours?'

'I am no friend of England, sir!'

'Then you are with us.'

Grinning now he offered her his hand, and she took it. He rose to his feet and stood nodding at her. He then returned to the men at the table. Martha frowned. Had she just joined a rebellion against the king? She supposed she had. Was she now a traitor to her country? She rather thought she was. She liked the idea, yes, it gave her an odd feeling of comfort, to think she was a rebel and a traitor and an enemy of the crown. Perhaps, she thought, this was the one place in the world where a girl might yet meet with kindness and understanding; a girl, that is, in the kind of trouble she was in.

The journey to New Morrock took the best part of five days, and what Martha remembered of it – what I was able, that is, to make of her account of it, from those first letters of hers, or rather, from what my uncle remembered of them before they fell to pieces –

beyond a constant jolting over rough roads, and the steaming horses, and the cold weather, and the thunderstorms – was the endless depths of forest they passed through as they made their way north. Though these they did not properly penetrate until the second or third day. The first day, after leaving Boston at dawn, they passed through towns that rang with the sound of hammers and saws. New houses and barns and churches were going up on every side. She saw fields recently harvested, their furrows straight and their fences in good repair, and men, women and children hard at work in those fields. The Americans she encountered were hardy, industrious folk, raw-boned and sinewy, dressed in plain garments and somewhat taciturn in manner, so there was always, somehow, to Martha's taste, the distinct tang of *vinegar* about them. But she saw none of that idleness and debauchery that so disfigures the English countryside, and reflects so ill upon our national character, and I remember mentioning this to my uncle when first we spoke of America.

He was a cynical fellow, my uncle William, and at times he affected a weariness of the world and a most bleak view of the human nature; and how he acquired this character I do not know but I suspect that a lifetime spent among cadavers had something to do with it. He sniffed at my enthusiasm and observed tartly that the American, by nature, in his experience, was no better than the Englishman, and that he himself would rather die in Surrey than the Kaaterskill Mountains; so I did not press the point. But on reflection I see that this difference of opinion marked the beginning of our long disagreement on the subject of America, and of the meaning of the Revolution in particular.

Martha was thrown together with Adam Rind for a good deal of the journey. Silas and Caesar always had men to see in the towns and villages through which they passed, and preferred to sit up front when they travelled. At such times she talked to her cousin about the colonists' argument with the king, and he told her with a rising passion of the various outrages the British had committed to his certain knowledge; many of which involved the impounding of an American vessel, and the impressment into the navy of men who had defied the naval blockade – had not a number of his friends in New Morrock – had not he himself? – narrowly escaped just such a fate? In the course of these conversations Martha discovered that despite his clowning temper her cousin had an ardent enthusiasm for the fighting they all seemed certain was soon to come; nor did it occur to him, after their talk in Foley's that night, that she might feel different.

For this she was grateful. She did not properly understand what was happening here. She knew only that she would soon face her own great crisis, when it became apparent that she was with child, but without husband.

'Cousin Martha,' said Adam one morning, as they bumped along an old ox track, with fields on either side and mountains in the distance, the two of them stretched out upon sacks of grain in the back of the open wagon, gazing up at the clouds with their hands behind their heads.

'Cousin Adam.'

'Cousin Martha, are you not happy to have left England behind you?'

'I am not happy to have left those I loved.'

'Ah, so you loved.'

Martha had grown fond of this odd cousin of hers, and already thought of him as a kind of brother. She groaned at this weak sally, and did not answer him. He tried again.

'But is not England rotten with luxury and vice?'

'There are good people in England,' she said, purely for the sake of being contrary, 'as there are everywhere.'

'Why then do they abuse us so? We only want what is ours by natural right.'

Martha lifted herself on to an elbow and peered at him. She had heard this phrase before, her father had used it.

'What is a natural right?' she said.

'Why, what is ours because we are men.'

'I am not a man.' She paused. 'Nor are you.'

Now he too rose on an elbow. His anger was not a man's anger but a boy's. He spluttered. He began to tell her what he could do with an axe, with a gun, with a horse –

'But are you a man, for all that?'

'What is a man, then, tell me that, Martha Peake?'

Martha thought of her father. He was a man. Could she tell her cousin about him? Oh, but she wanted to, how she wanted to tell him about Harry, and how he was brought low, and what he had suffered – and then all at once the confusion, and anguish, and rage were rising in her, almost overwhelming her – and as she pushed these feelings away, pushed them down, she glimpsed something of what had mystified her.

'Is it a man's natural right to be judged not for his body but his character?'

'Of course!'

'Then I believe in natural rights.'

'And so do I!'

His own anger departed as quickly as it had come, and gave way once more to lazy amusement. But still he sat up on his elbow gazing at her, a spark in his eye.

'So we are in agreement,' he said.

'We are,' said Martha; and with that he flung himself back on the sacks and lay there grinning at the sky.

By the afternoon of the third day they had left the rolling farmland and neat white villages far behind them, and had entered a wild region of hills and forest that stretched as far as the eye could see, and off to the west a range of mountains rising like a spinal column from the great broad back of the land. How civilized the English countryside has become, I reflected, in comparison to the giant landscape I aroused in my imagination, those magnificent tracts of wilderness Martha passed through, for in England the woodlands have largely disappeared, and what remains of the countryside is enclosed by fences and hedgerows; and what is worse, we are afflicted by a plague of mills and collieries, with high brick chimneys that belch out clouds of black smoke and sulphur.

But America, now this was stuff for the soul, this truly was God's country, and soon they had plunged into a dense forest whose dying autumnal foliage was as fiercely aflame with colour as any painter could desire. Did Martha glory in the majesty of it all, the great trees crowding in upon the shoulders of their narrow road, that now dropped into steep dank ravines with gurgling brooks rushing over rocks and rotting tree trunks, and now climbed on to broad plateaux from which the surrounding country offered itself to the eye for miles around, vast sweeping vistas of gold and scarlet, and no sign anywhere of the hand of man, save, perhaps, for a scrap of white, far below, the jibsail of a gundalo on some distant river, or a rough log cabin in a valley by a stream, with a thin plume of woodsmoke rising from its chimney? I do not know; she had much besides the landscape to occupy her thoughts. But when she forgot her troubles I imagine her heart did lift, that she did gaze with wonder and awe at this natural grandeur, and remembered, perhaps, her father's descriptions of it in his ballad of the tyrant Sea.

On the afternoon of the fifth day, after a spell of fine weather, the clouds moved in and the heavens opened; and so torrentially did the rain come down that not even the forest canopy could save them from a drenching. It cleared after an hour and they were able to continue on their way; Martha, soaked and wretched, and by this time deeply unhappy with her lot, and Adam, dripping and grinning, saying to her that it was surely a fine thing for an English girl like herself to be caught in a real American rainstorm. The road was slick and muddy now, and the going was slow indeed. The afternoon was well advanced, and the light was starting to fade, and still Martha had seen no sign that they were close to any human settlement. But she would not display weakness by asking questions of the men.

Dusk was coming on and bats swooped and flitted through the gloom before them. Every minute the woods seemed to crowd in closer upon them. The desolate howling of the wolves in the forest did little for the temper of the horses, nor for Martha's either. A half-hour later it was dark, and Martha was convinced they were lost in the depths of a wild and chartless forest, where they would perish and be eaten by wild animals. But even as she thought this thought she became aware of a dull roar, distant but sustained, and she strained to identify it. Then she had it, it was the ocean, they were close to the ocean, and in a sudden access of joy she shouted to Adam that this road would surely bring them out on the coast –!

But the road continued to deteriorate, and was soon little better than a cart track, mired in mud and puddles and treacherous with roots, stumps, and ruts. The moon rose into the evening sky, and after the grim damp obscurity of the last miles they now had at least a pale lunar glow sifting through the boughs high above their heads. It was close to midnight when at last they emerged from the forest on to a ledge of rock overlooking the ocean.

Martha gazed down in wonder and relief. The coastline was a wide jagged arc from north to south, with at either end a headland rearing like a sentinel. Tatters of black cloud flew across the sky and concealed the moon, but then all at once the clouds parted, and the moonlight shone full upon a small fishing port huddled in the most sheltered cove along this wild coast. There must have been a hundred houses down there, with narrow twisting alleys between, narrow wharves stretching out to the deep water, fishing boats tied up at the wharves and scattered about the harbour. There were buildings on stilts around the dock, and a thin white spike of a steeple rising from the church. The bay beyond was dotted with islands, and beyond the bay the moonlight spilled out across the vastness of the heaving black Atlantic.

But as Martha looked down on those slumbering houses, I now wonder, did she know a tremor of unease? Did she perhaps remember Cornwall? Was there a sense of foreboding, even, a feeling that this was a town without welcome or warmth, jealous of what little it had clawed from the cold black sea that gives life, and just as surely takes it back – was she gripped by the conviction that she had stumbled upon a place of the dead? I do not know; it is possible, given all that followed.

The wagon lurched to a halt, there on the headland, and

Martha with a shiver flung off these sombre thoughts and climbed down. Adam stood beside her and the pair of them gazed at the dark place below. She told him something of her unease, for after five days together she had fallen into the habit of sharing her thoughts with him, those that did not touch upon her father, or her child.

'But the forest,' he said, 'is darker by far than whatever may await you below.'

She told him she did not fear the forest.

'Nor anything it contains?'

'No, nor that.'

He laughed then, turning away, but glancing back at her every few moments such that she began to feel her temper rising and knew she should soon shout at him. But she told herself that her cousin was a foolish boy who always spoke in jest.

Slowly they descended the hill, and came into New Morrock over the old flint road across the mudflats. Then there was a bewildering crowd of strangers – her aunt Maddy, the children, various others – who brought Martha into their home and made her welcome.

Her sleep was only once disturbed, that first night in New Morrock. She was awoken by a sound from outside the house. She sat up in bed and had no idea where she was; then, remembering, and hearing the murmur of men's voices, she padded across to the window, between the beds of her sleeping cousins. The window looked out over a barn. There was a moon that night, and by its light she saw Silas Rind directly beneath her with a man in a greatcoat to his ankles, his collar up by his ears, and a cocked hat pulled so low she could see nothing of his face. In his hand he gripped a riding whip, which he slapped softly against his leg as he spoke, while Silas frowned and nodded.

Then the barn door opened and Caesar emerged leading a horse saddled and bridled for the road. The stranger shook the hands of both Silas and Caesar then swung himself into the saddle and touched the whip to the horse's flank. He cantered gently out of the yard. Silas turned back to the house, and Caesar returned to the barn. It all reminded Martha of her childhood, she remembered her father, in Port Jethro, and visitors who similarly came in the night and left before dawn. She got back into bed and was at once asleep.

20

All this I discussed with my uncle, and he supposed, he said, that this was how it might have happened, there was little here he could take exception to. It was *plausible*, he allowed, his tone suggesting that plausibility was but a poor cousin to *truth*. But truth being a prize beyond our grasp – as I then said to him – then plausibility, surely, was as good as we could hope for?

To this question came no reply but rather a series of pinchings and pursings about the mouth and nostrils expressive of resignation and fatigue. Hardly encouraging, but I pressed on; and what I pressed on with was Silas Rind and his family. Born with nothing, I began, Silas had made a fortune in the cod fishery, then built a large house some way above the harbour on a lot of several acres backing on to the forest, where his family was spared the stench that rose from the waterfront when the tide was low and the mudflats were exposed to the wind off the harbour. It was a solid foursquare wooden house sheathed in grey shingles and streaked with salt from the many storms it had endured. It had a gambrel roof and a small tower where Silas could gaze out to sea with his spyglass and look for his returning vessels. The inside of the house was organized round a great stone chimney with fireplaces in several rooms, the main one in the kitchen. Maddy Rind had pots perpetually boiling on the kitchen fire, and that large room, the heart of the house, saw endless cleaning and washing, chopping and skinning, all the multitude of tasks the household required; with which she had the help of her daughters and her neighbours, who this day were avid with curiosity to see the English arrival.

Maddy Rind made no complaint about being forever occupied with the running of a large house, and the care of young children, and the demands of an autocrat husband – Silas, that is – to whom she had come from Cornwall as an indentured servant, and later married when his first wife died. But despite her air of constant harried distraction, Maddy Rind reminded Martha strongly of her mother; and she felt an immediate loving affection for this tall thin restless aunt of hers, and lost no time in expressing it, in both looks and words. Maddy in turn welcomed her niece with great warmth, and was eager to know all that had happened to her, having heard only vague scraps of rumour over the years. And so, that first morning in New Morrock, they sat together at the kitchen table with Maddy's eldest daughter Sara, and Martha told them about her childhood in Port Jethro, and the death of her mother.

Maddy Rind remembered her sister Grace as though they had parted but a week before; and as Martha talked of the fire, Maddy grew distraught, and covered her face with her hands. Sara Rind, however, who was a few months younger than Martha, sat dry-eyed as she listened, and when Martha described how her father had been injured trying to save Grace from the flames, Sara interrupted her.

'But it was he who started the fire.'

'He did not mean to.'

'But had he not been drunk it would never have happened.'

'I am not defending him, I am telling you what he suffered!'

'And did Grace Foy not suffer more?'

The two girls had risen to their feet. Sara was as tall as Martha, but where Martha was fleshy and ample, Sara was lean and slender and bony. She had long, pale features, and dark shining eyes, and a head of raven hair; a striking creature, with an intensity of manner only rarely glimpsed in her bluff brother; and she saw no reason now to mask her thoughts from this new English cousin of hers, to whom she had already formed a strong dislike. But Maddy at once seized her daughter's hand and clasped it to Martha's, and though Sara tried to pull away, her mother held her fast. Maddy gazed from one to the other with astonishment.

'Is this how you mean to treat one another?' she cried. 'Have we not enough enemies that we must make more, and under our own roof?'

'I do not see that I must feel pity –'

'Enough, Sara!'

Maddy turned sharply toward her daughter but Sara did not flinch.

'You will say no more!'

'I will speak my mind!'

And with that she tore her hand from her mother's grip and ran from the room.

The first service Maddy Rind performed for Martha was to transform her from what she had been to something more like her own daughters. Martha had come off the *Plimoth* with her clothes in dire disrepair, held together by her own stitching, done in bad light below decks with a blunt sailcloth needle and coarse black thread begged from a sailor. Her body was covered with sores and bruises, and after the journey from Boston she was filthier even than she had been when she disembarked. Her teeth hurt and her hair was falling out in places. At least she was healthy, or rather, despite all she had been through, she was not afflicted by any flux or fever.

Maddy Rind and her younger daughters, both of whom were as dark and slender as Sara, were warmly dismayed at the condition of their English cousin, and later that first morning Martha was taken out and had her rags stripped off her, even her linen, such as it was. There she stood, shivering in the wind behind the house, plump, ruddy, and buxom in her nakedness, and she took no small pleasure in being thoroughly scrubbed with hot soapy water in the big iron washtub in the yard. She was then hurried back into the kitchen, wrapped in a towel, and in front of the fire Maddy rubbed various ointments and salves into her skin, while the girls brushed out her long red hair, which was clean now, and picked free of lice.

She was given a cotton shift and a dress of thick dark wool, high at the neck and tight to the waist, which fitted her well, and an apron, and a cap, and new boots and grey worsted stockings that came up her thighs. Also a shawl; and Maddy Rind then demanded her old clothes so that she could burn them. Martha happily surrendered all but her cocked hat and her muddy greatcoat, which still smelled of tobacco and London rain, and was now permeated with the odours of the *Plimoth* as well. She could not give that up, it was connected to her father, and however violently she may have swung between hatred and longing for Harry she clung to his greatcoat with a blind wilful dogged unflinching insistence.

Her younger cousins clustered about her and it was agreed by all that now she looked just like one of them. And so she did, she was a Cape Morrock woman with cap and apron and bell-like skirt from waist to floor. She was given a comb and a small mirror, and her own candlestick, and other small items for her toilet. Maddy said that Martha Peake had to be set up as a young lady of the town, for to this rank she was surely accustomed, and they all howled with laughter at the idea of anything of the world of fashion counting for much in New Morrock. But she now had a wardrobe and a clean bed and much else to be thankful for besides, and when all was complete she sat by the fire and laughed with the sheer joy of feeling once more like a human being rather than a wild creature in flight; and she forgot for a time her growing worry about the child in her womb. Maddy and her daughters were moved by her emotion and they too laughed. Then they hugged one another and tearfully told Martha she was welcome, and a part of their family now. Sara Rind took no part in any of this.

At supper all the Rinds came together at the long table in the kitchen with Silas at the head. What a collection was there, and Martha was somewhat shy, particularly as so many of them were so very curious about her. Maddy had put her beside Sara, but Sara continued cold and aloof. Sara's two younger sisters, and her two brothers besides Adam, all sat at the table; also present was Caesar, and a man who worked for Silas called Grizzel Apthorp. Then there was Silas's brother, Joshua Rind, the doctor.

He was much respected in the town, this Joshua, as Martha would discover. A small spry fellow with long silver hair swept back off a shining dome of forehead, he resembled his brother but seemed made on a smaller scale, was quicker with his tongue, and had not Silas's magisterial gravity. The doctor had arrived at the house before supper, limping on account of his gouty foot, so that he could look Martha over with what he called a medical eye. In the course of his examination he gave her a few pats and squeezes before declaring her a fine healthy strapping girl who needed only a little feeding up. Martha was less than happy to have Joshua Rind's fingers wandering over her person, for her body had secrets it must conceal, and she believed he wanted to get under her clothes with those fingers of his. They were a doctor's fingers, but they were also a man's fingers, and for men's fingers she had an abhorrence now.

Joshua Rind wore thin, wire-framed spectacles on the end of his beaky nose, and he had once, during the war with the French, lanced a boil on the neck of George Washington; and he would, if Martha liked, show her the instrument with which he had performed the operation. The Virginian had a strong-smelling discharge in the boil, said the doctor, a putrid symptom he had since learned to associate with the qualities of moral fortitude and incorruptibility.

Silas Rind at his own table surprised Martha by becoming almost voluble, and indulging a dry, salty humour. He first muttered a brief grace then welcomed Martha and introduced her to all his children, whom she had of course already met by this time; and in the course of these introductions he indulged his humour at their expense. He then spoke about the unfortunate state of affairs existing between Martha's country and his own, talking of 'her' government and 'her' king, and shy though she was to be among so many strangers, after a little of this she grew irritated and told her uncle pretty sharply that they were nothing to do with her, it was not 'her' government, she hated them as passionately as he did.

Silas was amused by this retort, for I do not believe his own children were much in the habit of contradicting him, with perhaps the exception of Sara. After that, each time he repeated the slur he would add – 'though Martha Peake disclaims all responsibility for the wretches' – to general amusement. I believe he was simply trying to draw out, at that first meal, what opinions if any Martha held about the colonies, and their argument with the king. Was she sympathetic to their cause, he wanted to know, or must he convert her to it?

Oh, but Martha had no thought of causes – she was hungry! She had for weeks had little but oatmeal and bad beef, and now there was roast venison and cod pie and boiled vegetables and milk, and there was more than enough of everything. She ate and refilled her plate, and but for the one outburst spoke not a word unless spoken to, but gazed around her with frank curiosity and listened closely to all that was said. But not until some time later did she have the answer to the question that most intrigued her: who was the man who came in the night to confer with Silas behind the house, and then rode away? Where had he come from, and what was his business? His business, she would learn, was treason; and Silas Rind, merchant, was complicit in that treason.

For several days Martha was excused all household tasks and given leave to wander at will. She was most aware, those first days, of the presence of the sea. The recent weeks aboard ship had been uncomfortable, to say the least of it, but now the sea no longer held her to its will, it no longer flung her about or made her ill as it had during the voyage. Now it was spread out beneath her, and she was on dry land high above it, so that however it raged, with whatever force it flung its great waves against the rocks, and smashed at the walls of black cliff rising sheer from coves and seashore along the coast, it could not harm her. Instead it provided an unending spectacle of power and grandeur, and she was exhilarated by the surge and flow of those waters; the immoderate enthusiasm she felt for the turmoil of this wild stretch of the North Atlantic arising, I believe, from her own condition.

This then is how I see her, her first days in America, usually up on the great cliff, Black Brock, large high white clouds pushing across the sky and the gulls wheeling around a solitary boat returning from a late-season run in defiance of the blockade. There she stands, wrapped in her greatcoat, her cocked hat pulled low on her forehead against the wind, staring out to the horizon and thinking of her father, thinking of Harry, mad and wild, wandering the wilderness around Drogo Hall. She cannot prevent the revulsion and horror rising in her as she remembers what he did to her, nor her anger – nor, at times, the burning irrepressible desire to *kill him*! – but at the same time he is her father, her *father*, and she holds grimly to this, and tells herself she must forge a fresh link with him, this link an act of the mind and the will, so as to keep him alive, to prevent him drifting off and disappearing into the Lambeth Marsh and ceasing to be real to her any more. She tells herself she must not forget him, and she furiously nods her head – though how could she forget him, with his child in her womb? – as the wind plucks at her hair and brings the tears streaming from her eyes with the salt it flings in her face. She looks out over a dark and turbulent sea, and closer in, the harbour, then the town, close-packed wooden houses in which dwell a community of strangers – of Americans! – who do not know her, nor she them.

When it grows so cold she can stand it no longer, and the light is thickening in the mountains, and thunderheads begin to gather among the peaks, she makes her way back down the side of the cliff to the house, where the day's work is ending and the family is gathering in the great kitchen. There is a loose, rough harmony in the Rind household, each one taking responsibility for a task necessary for the common good, and her aunt Maddy overseeing it all; and her uncle, preoccupied as he always is with his business and his politics, the two now grown inseparable, staring off into the distance as he stands with an elbow on the mantel, smoking his pipe and clutching a glass of Tobago rum, unconscious of his surroundings until some loud noise from a petulant child has him frowning and barking irritably for a little order, *if you please* –

One night Silas talked to the table at large of their duty to Martha. She was a part of the family now, he told them, and Martha had the impression, as the Rind children gazed silently at their father, that he had spoken to them already on this subject. And it was then that he turned to Martha and asked her to tell them what had happened to her during her last weeks in England.

For this she was not prepared. She could say nothing. Her uncle said he meant the period after she left Cripplegate Street, and he coaxed her gently to speak. So she talked about her father and how he had become mad and tried to do her harm, and how she had had to flee to Drogo Hall; she said nothing of the rape. Ah, but it took little, now, to make Martha weep when she thought of those days, and soon Maddy Rind and her daughters were weeping with her, as was Sara, who until that moment had shown Martha only coldness. But when she glimpsed the horrors her cousin had endured, she could sustain her enmity no longer; and as Martha glanced about the table she saw in the candlelight that the tears shone also in Silas's eyes. She could not help herself, she rose from her chair and ran to her uncle and flung her arms about his neck and sobbed her thanks into his shoulder. He patted her, he murmured words of comfort, then he stood her up before him and gazed into her streaming face.

'You are among friends now, Martha Peake,' he said. 'You have come to us at a critical time, and there is darkness ahead for all of us before we can live as we wish to in America. But if you are with us, we will never abandon you.'

Then with all the family – not least the stricken Sara – gazing intently at her, she found herself assuring Silas with no little passion that yes, she was with them, she did not ever want to be abandoned again, for this, now, was her family, this was her country, she would never leave!

Martha never forgot the events of that evening. Had she any last lingering sentiment of affection for England it was dissipated that night. If there was a place where welcome was made to a lost creature in flight – and welcome so generous, so honest as this – then that place must surely be called home. She turned it over in her mind in the following days, and convinced herself she had found her home, that America was her home. And then she told herself: and it will be complete when my father has recaptured his reason and we are together once more.

That was her dearest wish. Despite all that had happened she wanted to see him again. She looked for the ship that would bring him to her. On Black Brock she looked for it, and at other times she stood at the end of the wharf and waited for it to appear in the bay. When the weather was foul she climbed into the tower at the top of the house and kept her vigil there. Many ships she observed out to sea, in those first days, and all of them English ships, but never his. She did not despair. She held his arrival in some future in her mind, a future of which she never doubted, nor was she impatient of its coming. She believed he knew that she was waiting for him, and she believed he would come when he was his own self once more, and no longer dangerous to her.

21

I had spent five days in my uncle's house. I was now, with the aid of his medicines, almost recovered from the fever I had contracted out on the Lambeth Marsh, and had fallen into the habit of writing through the night, after we separated in the small hours, and sleeping most of the day – I had, in short, adopted his own nocturnal rhythm, the quicker to arrive at the end of the thing and ride away from Drogo Hall, leave the accursed place behind me for ever.

No, I would never return, this decision had been maturing over the days I had spent there, and the expectation I had once entertained of inheriting it, this I had abandoned. I wanted nothing more to do with that unhappy pile, once the story was over. And why? I am not a suggestible man, and my imagination, while strong, is disciplined; I would have you bear that in mind when I tell you: some creature walked in Drogo Hall by night; though whether living or dead I could not know.

I do not say this lightly. I have examined the facts, I have turned the thing over in my mind, I have heeded the empirical methods of Drogo himself, his exhortation to scepticism, his reliance on the senses alone, stripped of all obfuscating theoretical impedimenta – and still the answer is the same. And my evidence? It was the sounds, to begin with, the tramping footsteps distinctly audible in distant corridors. Oh, I remember all too clearly when it started, I believe it was the second night I spent under my uncle's roof, and he was describing to me the poet's early days in London, when he and Martha were living in simple, sober contentment at the top of the Angel in Cripplegate Street, and she was maturing into her young womanhood. Even as the old man rambled on, his narrative stream broken only by a frequent recourse to the decanter, and the occasional ministrations of his man Percy, who like an old dame fussed about his master, adjusting the blanket on his knees and stoking up the fire, in terror that the doctor might take a chill – so yes, there was old William Tree, one claw quivering in the firelight – when all at once he stopped dead, his white-wisped head twitching as his eyes darted from side to side – and I heard it too, the clump of boots sounding faintly down far-off halls and staircases of the house – sounding down the very years, as it seemed! – and himself plainly in a state of acute alarm.

'What is that?' I said, rising to my feet. 'Have you a visitor? An intruder, perhaps?' – and I thought at once of the pistol I had brought with me across the marsh, which at that moment lay wrapped in a dark blue velvet cloth, in a walnut box, in the drawer of the table at the side of my bed.

'Sit down!' hissed the old man with some heat, and in a tone I had not imagined him capable of, so brisk and peremptory was it – that I at once obeyed, and sank back into my chair, by now as alarmed as he was. When I attempted a question he silenced me in a manner no less forceful, and I was thus constrained to sit, like him, and listen, as the ghostly clumping footsteps tramped their dusty corridor and at last faded away in a charged and trembling silence. With some courage I spoke once more.

'Who was it?' I whispered; for I knew the slinking Percy to be incapable of such a footfall; and at that very moment a coal fell in the fire – a heap of sparks leaped up – and the clock in the hallway struck three.

'It was nobody,' said my uncle, when the chimes died away, still sitting up rigid, his large batlike ears perceptibly straining to catch every last crumb of sound to be had in this mausoleum of a house.

'Nobody?' said I.

He turned to me then.

'Nobody!' he cried hoarsely. 'There is nobody here, do you understand me, Ambrose?'

'Then what –'

But I was not allowed to finish the question. He silenced me with a ferocious glare, a lifting of the head and a great flashing of the eye, there in the gloom, with but a coal fire and a few candles burning. Later, in my room, I asked myself what this could mean, and his 'nobody' rang still in my head with all the fierce conviction he had invested in the word; and I asked myself, did he mean it? Could that footfall have been caused by 'nobody'? Who then was this 'nobody' who tramped the corridors of Drogo Hall at the dead of night, for tramp he did – *I heard him with my own ears.*

Thus did it begin. There was, however, so much else to occupy my mind in the hours and days that followed – I mean of course the story of Martha Peake – that I gave little further thought to the *nobody* who had so disturbed my uncle. Until, that is, the next time I heard him.

I was lying abed, sweating freely, convulsed with fever and barely able to lift a hand to my wine glass. Again it was very late at night, and my uncle had left me only a short time before. I could not sleep, for the medicines he prescribed me, which I drank without inquiring as to what they were, had the unfortunate effect of stimulating my mind, even as they brought on the sweating that he assured me was essential to rid my body of the toxins with which I had been infected on the marsh. So there I lay, turning my head from side to side as the perspiration streamed from my pores and soaked through the bedsheets and into the blankets. My mind wandered freely, throwing up vivid pictures of Martha in flight from her mad father – Martha taking ship for America – Martha's first glimpse of New Morrock, from the top of the cliff they called Black Brock – when all at once my reverie was broken by that same tramping footfall I had heard two nights before.

I ceased my restless turning in the bed. Martha Peake vanished from my mind. My senses were at once concentrated on the sound, for this time it issued not from some distant corridor, no, it was far closer than that, by God it was very close indeed, there was somebody outside my door! I lay there in a terror, the sweat now coming off me in sheets, and I doubted I had the strength to rise from my bed, and cross the room – pistol in hand! – to discover once and for all who it was that moved about the house by night, who this *nobody* was who had plainly alarmed my uncle as much as he now did me! I flung a hand out and groped for the drawer in the bedside table, but succeeded only in knocking over my wine glass – it shattered on the floorboards – then all was silent once more.

What did this mean? Had he fled, whoever, or whatever, he was? Or did he even now lurk outside my door, the shattering glass having alerted him to my presence here within? I was seized with desperation, and with desperation came strength, strength I did not know I possessed. I struggled out of my soaking bed, I opened the drawer – a single candle had been left burning, and a few dim embers still glowed in the fireplace – and with trembling fingers I unlocked the walnut box and took from it my pistol. With no small difficulty I then primed and loaded the weapon – cocked it – and thus armed, in my nightshirt, fevered, trembling and terrified, I advanced to the door of my bedroom – paused a second, listening – heard nothing – flung open the door, and stepped into the passage, ready to fire!

Nobody was there. A window some way down the passage admitted a shaft of moonlight, and I was able to confirm that in the grey gloom no lurking figure waited to fall on me and do me harm. I advanced a few steps along the passage to be certain; it was deserted –

And then – a noise – a door creaked slowly open at the far end of the passage! My heart was pealing like a dozen church bells. I lifted the pistol, my finger trembling on the trigger – the pistol shook wildly as I raised it as high as my shoulder – I gripped my wrist in a vain attempt to still the tremor –

Then coming through the door, a candlestick held aloft, and followed a moment later by Percy – it was my uncle. With some relief I lowered the pistol.

'Dear boy,' he cried, 'whatever are you doing? Back to bed at once!'

'He was here!' I cried. 'He was outside my door!'

With Percy close behind him my uncle came shuffling along the passage. He wore a dressing gown that seemed to have been cut from an old carpet, or a set of curtains, on his feet his Turkish slippers, and the red nightcap askew on his skull. I cried out wildly once more that I had heard a man outside my door, but no, no, there is nobody here but us; and without further ado he shepherded me back to bed, having taken my pistol from me and replaced it in the drawer by my bed. He laid a hand on my febrile brow, while Percy mixed a sleeping draught. I was not disturbed again.

The next morning I was much recovered, the events of the night having seemingly provoked the fever to its crisis. I was permitted to get up for a few hours in the late afternoon, and as soon as I was left alone in my room I looked to see if my pistol had been confiscated. It had not.

I joined my uncle in his study that evening. He was vague, he seemed distracted, and I assumed he was troubled, as I was, at these recent occurrences in the night. Nonetheless I began at once to question him about Martha, and I remember his truculent insistence that he was too tired for this American adventure, as he called it. So I desisted, somewhat offended by the brusqueness of his manner toward me.

After several minutes of uneasy silence, himself making curious sucking noises with his mouth, while I glared frowning at the fire, he at last looked up and resumed talking as though no interruption had occurred. But he did not talk about Martha, his mind was busy, rather, with the fate of her father; for while he had had no involvement in Martha's life after arranging her passage to America, he had played a large part in Harry's last days, instrumental as he was in the furthering of Lord Drogo's black scheme; and uneasy slept the conscience of that close and secretive man, so uneasy, in fact, that he was *haunted* by what he had done –! And here it came to me with a clap of thunder, and a dazzling jag of light – *this* was the source and origin of the mysterious footfall in the night: deep in the ancient gloom of Drogo Hall a restless spirit, with work unfinished, was stirring to life! But if so – what sort of spirit – and *what sort of work*?

This came as no small shock, I must tell you. What to do now? I sat forward in my chair as my mind raced forward, a flurry of ideas, questions, possibilities tumbling into the light, but nothing certain, I must know more, I must wait and be sure. I decided to let my uncle go forward with Harry's story before I challenged him. I decided to show him nothing of what I now knew, or suspected I knew. And so we went forward; that is, he rambled, often erratically, over the matter at hand, with many a digression and, as always, a frequent application to the Hollands and water, while I, later, in my room, gave literary flesh to what I had heard, bringing to bear upon his few sticks of ill-remembered fact the full powers of imagination – intuition – sympathy – and art – that as a sometime poet I possessed in no small measure. Thus did his sticks come to life; thus did they flower.

22

So what of Harry, what of that poor lost fellow? This I have thought about a good deal, what happened to Harry Peake after Martha left Drogo Hall, and I have not been helped by my uncle, who I fear did not steer me straight in this. I suspect that when Martha fled Drogo Hall, Harry did indeed watch the black carriage cross the marsh in the moonlight, but made no attempt to intercept it. I believe he remained in the graveyard all that night, and I cannot imagine what he suffered. He did not commit suicide, William has assured me of this and I am inclined, at least on this point, to take him at his word. If he did not commit suicide then he must have gone on, but newly burdened, with a fresh load of guilt to carry on his bent spine, and it is a measure of the man's spirit that he *could* go on, that life, for all the bitter fruit he had tasted, seemed still the better thing – because of Martha? Because while she lived, he would love her, he must love her? Perhaps he would never see her again, but what he desired no longer mattered. It was for him only to love her, and whether or not that act of love, sustained as long as he drew breath, did any *good* – this he could not know. This he must take on trust. What choice had he? His love might be of some use to her, wherever she was, and he had not the right to deny her it, he had lost the right – and it must have cost him dear, to recognize this – to turn his face to the darkness.

Thus I imagine the wordless currents of the spirit of the ragged madman slumped among the gravestones on the hill above Drogo Hall. Come the dawn, and the last of the gin dissipated, he knows she has gone. It is time for him to leave this place, there is nothing more for him here. I see him then, as the first light steals over the marsh, a faint figure moving through the mist, limping off toward the town, whose distant domes and steeples can be picked out now against the grey sky.

Ah, but he is not alone, there is movement in the trees above the road, and as he tramps back to London a dark figure shadows him. It is, of course, Clyte. The little gargoyle has not been distracted by Martha's flight, for it is not Martha he is after. The wind comes up and there is a touch of ice in it this morning, and Harry Peake clutches his thin coat about him. He is sober now, and he feels the cold. Winter is coming on.

Winter was coming on in Cape Morrock too, and Martha would have felt it, as she adapted herself to her new life among the Americans, she would have felt the ice in the wind, and seen a growing fury in the restless sea. That coast had given many of its men to the sea, and in the long hours of darkness, when the winter storms battered the cape, the firesides and taverns of the town were alive with stories of those who had perished and those who had been driven mad by the sea, of whom there were more than a few in the history of New Morrock. Martha listened, and remembered how her father used to talk to her about Cornwall, the men he had known there, their own stories.

I remember my uncle puffing away at his pipe one night in Drogo Hall, his eyes dim and faraway, and I knew he was reliving old arguments, he was back in the 1770s, for he had been talking about the Americans and, to my astonishment, with some sympathy. I remember how he shook his head, more with sadness, I believe, than anger, when I asked him if the king had been wrong in his actions toward the colonies; and I then remarked that Martha surely shared his opinion.

At the mention of her name the old man winced, he distinctly winced; and I thought, what raw thing have I fingered here?

Oh, she was for the American cause, he said, after a moment or two, cross now, sour again; was she not her father's daughter?

But it was not only Harry who spoke to her of these matters, I said. There was her uncle, and others, too –?

Here he gazed at me through narrowed eyes. He knew what I was after. He nodded once or twice. Adam Rind, he murmured, oh yes. Of all the proud rebels in Massachusetts, he was the one who fanned the flames of rebellion in the heart of Martha Peake.

This was what I had suspected.

One morning that fall, carrying buckets of steaming hot water from the kitchen to the washtubs outside, where her aunt Maddy was scrubbing sheets and linen, Martha paused and straightened her back, pressing her hands in just above her buttocks, and pushing out her belly, feeling for the secret creature in her womb; and as she stood thus, gazing out over the sea, Adam came up beside her and told her he was going down to the dock and did she want to come with him?

Yes, she did, she did indeed, so she asked her aunt and was told she could; and Sara would come too, for the two girls had made their peace now and were fast becoming the best of friends. She pulled on her boots and flung on her greatcoat and cocked hat and off they went, arm in arm, herself in the middle and a cousin on either side.

What a dirty town it was! As they came down the hill they stepped over fish heads and rotting vegetables in which pigs and dogs rooted freely. It was a clear cold day with a strong salty breeze off the harbour, and when they reached the bottom of the hill they were among the fishermen's houses, ramshackle structures with woodsmoke drifting from their crooked chimneys and bleached bones nailed to their doors, whales' jaws and the like. Crab pots were piled up against the walls, also gaffs and harpoons, whose function Adam began to explain to her, till she told him sharply she came from Cornwall, she knew what a gaff was for; and indeed, all she saw that day reminded her of Port Jethro, and in her nostrils the strong rank fishy smell from the flukes where the cod were dried on the rocks nearby.

They met people shuffling off to the dock, or leaning in the doorways of their workshops, big men with long hair and thick beards, and Adam introduced Martha to various of them, Dan Pierce and his brother Nat, who had the tavern; John van Horn, captain of Silas's trading vessel, the *Lady Ann*; Ben Clapsaddle, Henry Coffin, Mr Crow, the minister. All were friendly, in their gruff way, except the minister, who regarded her, unsmiling, from ice-blue eyes as though he were drawing back the curtains of her soul so as to take a look inside.

Then they were on Front Street, and there was the harbour. Between the wharves were crowded a great number of fishing boats, sloops for the most part, stubby-masted vessels with two jibs flying from the bowsprit. They saw men talking in small groups on the dock, and women with pipes in their mouths stitching nets; but no boats were going out. Adam spoke with fierce indignation, his arm sweeping across the scene, saying, here are men who should be out fishing, here are seaworthy fishing boats, and here – with a large flourish at the Atlantic – fish! A multitude of fish! It is because of the British that we are idle when we should be catching fish! But Sara and Martha were in no mood for Adam's fervour, and told him to mind his manners, they did not wish to be *harangued*.

They stopped at the forge. The smithy was hard at work, his fire going strong and sparks flying everywhere as he hammered like a very Vulcan. He had straightened out a twisted gun barrel for Adam, who now stood admiring the man's handiwork, lifting the musket to his shoulder and sighting down the length of it, muttering about damned redcoats.

Beside the forge a narrow alley snaked off between small wooden houses built close together, and the three made their way up the hill, Adam with his gun on his shoulder. Sara left them halfway up, having errands of her own to run; and Adam returned – he could not help it! – to the topic which had so inflamed him on the dock, that his friends and neighbours were prevented from going to sea and doing the work that men of Cape Morrock had done for the last hundred years!

What is it you catch? Martha asked him.

Cod! he cried. It was cod they caught, which they salted down in barrels and sold in the sugar islands. They came away with sugar and molasses, he said, and made rum from it – here waving a hand at a large building in the town, which Martha would later learn was his father's distillery. And what did they do with the rum? They sold the rum in Africa, said Adam, and came away with, oh – he was vague – various goods – and here my uncle William wheezed with malice – slavers, were they, he cried, these Sons of Liberty? – I ignored this troublesome interruption – which they then sold to those same plantations where they bartered their salt cod. And in this way, said Adam, men grow rich. But now your king threatens our prosperity by levying taxes which obstruct our trade and turn us into smugglers. Small wonder we talk of taking up arms to assert our natural rights!

Martha frowned as she listened to this. She had realized the first time she saw it that the cape was well-suited to the requirements of the smuggler, pocked and fissured as it was with natural harbours; so she said this to Adam now, asking him did they not know how to evade the navy, as Cornishmen knew how to evade the Excise?

Oh, and Adam's pride was stung by this, and soon he was telling her how John van Horn, and Grizzel Apthorp, and Brockden Coffin, and Dan Pierce and others like them – had he himself not crewed aboard the *Lady Ann* many a time? – how Cape Morrock men had run the blockade, how they had come through under cover of darkness, or fog, or storm, and slipped into concealed bays and coves where their cargo was swiftly unloaded, crates and barrels transferred into wagons which then, by night, were hauled to magazines and depots throughout the colony; and it was not sugar and molasses they brought in now, he told her, oh no, it was powder, and cannon, and muskets, and ball! And who do you think, he said, is the man who organizes the landing of all such contraband on the cape?

Who?

Silas Rind.

This must surely have astonished Martha, to discover that her uncle pursued her father's old occupation. She told Adam this, and the cousins then spent a happy afternoon talking about the ways of smugglers. Adam later mentioned this to his father; and such was Silas's respect for Martha Peake, he allowed Adam to invite her to a landing planned for some nights hence so she could tell him later what she thought –

Tell him what she thought? *Tell him what she thought?*

This, of course, was my uncle again; I was giving him my account of Martha's quickening friendship with Adam Rind, and knowing only that she had indeed attended a landing with him, I had surmised that Silas must have wished to know her –

The old man was robust in his rejection of this conjecture. Why on earth, he said, would Silas do such a thing? Is not *secrecy* the first rule of the smuggler? Why reveal his secrets to this girl – a new-comer, and English withal?

Because he trusted her –

Trusted her my fat bladder! Trusted her? He trusted no one! Ambrose, use your brains! If you have any left. No, Silas Rind was up to something. That, or Adam brought her along without consulting him.

But as to what Silas might have been 'up to', on this my uncle would not be drawn, and merely muttered at me to go on, get on with it, if I must.

The upshot was, I said, somewhat shaken, the upshot was, that late one afternoon that autumn Martha rode up the coast with Adam, perched behind him on his black mare, her arms wrapped around his waist, to Scup Head, a high rocky headland behind which was concealed a deep narrow channel that a half-mile inland opened into a pool fed by waterfalls and enclosed by steep cliffs, and on the far side a gently shelving beach of black sand. The forest grew thickly to the edge of this narrow beach, and a track ran back into the forest, which some miles further on quietly merged with the Boston road.

Adam and Martha paused on the cliff above the hidden cove in the last light of an autumn day, and there beneath them, lying at anchor, was the *Lady Ann*. All sail had been furled, and the mainmast rose like a crucifix needle from the schooner's trim hull, throwing long reflections across the still dark waters. A fire of driftwood blazed on the beach and two men stood in a rowing boat tied up to the vessel, Caesar and another man, and with lifted arms silently received the powder kegs handed down to them by the crew. They loaded the boat to the gunwales, then Caesar sat to the oars and rowed to shore, where four men waited on the beach.

In they waded up to their knees and lifted the kegs from the boat. They carried them up the beach to a farm wagon hitched to a team of oxen. And all in utter silence, only the soft plash of oar in the black water, and the splashing of the men in the surf; and Martha, on the cliff above, dared not speak, dared not disturb the stillness of the place, nor the solemn activity going on below.

They rode round the headland then picked their way down a path through the woods to the beach. They went ahead of the wagon as it lurched up the track into the forest. It was dank and chill among the ancient trees, and they soon dismounted, the better to warn the others of the ruts and stumps ahead. Slowly through the deepening gloom the wagon bumped along the track. Night fell and they moved through darkness, no moonlight to help them, and several times the men had to put their shoulders to the wagon, when the oxen foundered or a wheel snagged, and Adam and Martha threw their weight behind the wheel with the others.

At last they glimpsed lights through the trees. For several minutes Martha had been aware of a dull muted roar from off in the woods up ahead, a sound that had insinuated itself so subtly into her mind she did not know when it had started. Then there were shouts, and men with torches coming down the track to meet them, and as they drew closer a long low shed came into view. This was Silas's sawmill, and the dull roar was the rushing of the cataract that drove the mill's great wheel.

As Silas's men unloaded the wagon and carried the kegs into the sawmill they threw long strange shadows in the torchlight. Adam stood by the wide doors of the mill and counted the kegs and crates as they were carried in. The great wheel, shadowy within its scaffolding of logs and planking, was unmoving, and as the moon rose over the trees Martha stood by the creek and saw in the river far below the long flat boats that once had carried her uncle's milled lumber downstream to the sea. She imagined those craft with powder kegs and crates of arms lashed to them, and with that thought the prospect of the fire and destruction to come was all at once brought home to her.

Later, when Silas questioned her as to what she had seen that night – my uncle snorted at this, but allowed me to continue – she told him that in Cornwall the free-trader worked solely for profit, whereas Silas's men worked for a cause, and worked all the better for that reason. Silas appeared satisfied with this. My uncle William merely lifted an eyebrow. I could tell he still thought that sly old Silas was 'up to' something, and that I was a damn fool not to see it.

The weather grew colder and the sky was often heavy with rolling banks of low grey cloud, and the sea turned an angry dark green, black at times, and so turbulent that the fishing boats, those few that would risk the blockade, rarely went out any more. The people of Cape Morrock made their preparations for the rigours of the season to come. They set about securing their houses and barns against winter storms. Boats were dragged to the stony beach hard by the harbour wall, then hauled above the winter tideline and tied up to iron rings in the wall. Maddy Rind inspected her larder and her pantry, counting the crocks of pickled fish and jars of fruit she had laid up over the summer, and everywhere fires were lit in smokehouses, and the last of the season's fish and meat was cured. When the wind was right the air was filled with smells that set Martha thinking with some passion of her dinner, for she was hungry all the time now.

They burned prodigious quantities of firewood in the kitchen, and the several woodsheds on the property had to be filled before the snow came and drifted deep on the forest floor. Glimpsing these facts of Martha's new life, I could not but reflect on how close to the elements these people lived – closer certainly than I did in Drogo Hall, where I sat by night writing this account of Martha's American life in a very storm of creative energy, my back to a blazing fire and a bottle of claret to hand!

But no, clinging to a cliffside with their faces to the sea, and the forest and the mountains at their backs, they had created plenty from this wilderness, and from their surplus had established a thriving commerce. Seeing this through the eyes of Martha Peake, it is easy to imagine how a flame kindled to life within her, a rebel flame, a patriot flame; ah, but tempered, always tempered, by the uneasy thought of the child growing in her womb –

Then one day she awoke to the sound of chopping from the back of the house. Going at once to the window, she saw Adam in the yard below, in boots and breeches only, hard at work splitting logs beside the barn. After each blow of the axe he bent down and tossed the chunks of cleft wood into a basket, and she smiled to see his long hair flopping about, and the muscles of his broad white back as they lumped and gleamed in the wintry sunlight. His breath was like smoke in the cold morning air and the sweat came steaming off him in waves. After some minutes he felt her eyes upon him, for he suddenly turned and saw her there in her nightshirt, with her hair tumbling loose about her shoulders. She at once flung wide the window and shouted some nonsense at him, and he laughed right back then leaned on his axe gazing up at her, panting, and pushing damp strands of hair off his face.

Later she went with him to the barn, and there, in the crisp chill of a November dusk, in the smoky gloom, with the smell of horses thick in their nostrils, and the stamping and snuffling and whinnying all around, she gave him to understand by the general arrangement of her person that she was to be kissed.

He hesitated for only a second or two. Then he seized her in his arms – and she took some seizing, did Martha, she was a big girl – but Adam was bigger – and knocking the wind out of her, he crushed her to his strong young chest! She lifted her laughing face to his, and with some urgency, and no little intensity, he pressed his lips to hers; and when after some moments she began to fight for breath, he released her with a cry of alarm, fearing he had hurt her. She assured him he had not, but that he must allow her to breathe occasionally. He kissed her again, and this time was more tender. Martha's heart was beating fast, her blood was in turmoil. She pulled away from him, she leaned her back against a beam, and with her eyes afire, and smiling broadly, she set her legs apart, she lifted her arms, and linked her fingers behind her head. She had been kissed before, and she had been handled before, but never in quite the way she was now, never with such passionate uncertainty.

After some minutes more of this she put her palms on Adam's chest and pushed him back. She did not meet his ardent gaze, but toyed instead with the buttons of his shirt.

'Forgive me,' he said, 'I was overcome.'

'I will not,' she said.

Then he kissed her again. His hand was on her hip, on her buttocks, on her thighs – she thought she would melt, she thought she would fall down! – but neither of these things happened. There was another kiss, and another – would there be no end to this kissing? Her breathing was shallow, her heart beating faster than ever, she was flushed scarlet and glad to be in the shadows where he could not see it. There was a great warmth inside her, and a great rank dampness between them –

'We must stop,' he whispered, and she was on the point of asking him why, indeed the word had risen to her lips, and would have flown out, but some impulse of – what? – prudence, calculation – certainly not virtue! – whatever it was, she paid heed to it and said, breathlessly, 'Indeed, sir, we must, and I must be at home' – and with that she ran off, leaving him to pace the barn with his breeches bulging and the buttons of his shirt undone all down his chest.

She slept but little that night! She ran upstairs without a candle, her skirt lifted and her hair streaming out behind her. She lay awake with the curtains open and stared at the clouds moving across the moon, and rehearsed in her mind all the details of her evening since she had gone out to the barn. His face before her, his hands on her body, his arms crushing her to him, bending her spine as if she were a sapling! Then her own arms flung about his neck, and her face lifted to his, opening to his, and then the great liquid warmth rising from her womb and filling her whole body, so she had to cleave to him if she were not to fall down in a swoon! Oh, she could not be doing with any of that, she would not be overcome –! What would have happened had she allowed the kissing to continue, this she could not imagine, or rather she could imagine, all too well, which is why she slept so little that turbulent night.

*

Ah, they were young, their animal spirits were healthy, and often after that they met in the barn, high in the gloom beneath the great rafters, amid bound bales of straw where they could not be seen; and they found no good reason to be prudent, nor virtuous either. Afterwards they would fall back in the straw, laughing, and then they would talk. Martha told him stories about her father, stories of the old days before the gin and the madness.

'By God I hope he comes soon,' said Adam one night, as he rose from the bale on which they lay, a beam of moonlight by chance shafting through the rafters to cover him in a cold yellow glow. 'There are others like him all over the Europe,' he said, 'and when it is time they will join us in their thousands –'

Martha pushed him down on the straw. Much dishevelled beneath her open greatcoat, she straddled him with her legs and set her elbows either side of his neck, and gazed into his eyes from but an inch or two above him. The old familiar grin appeared, and the boyish belligerence faded. Adam's moods shifted and changed like wind on water, and could be read as clearly. He reached up and unpicked the loose knot of her hair, so it fell forward and spread across his face. Martha pushed it aside and set her chin on his chin, their lips an inch apart. Again the mood changed. There was silence now, their thoughts confused by the sudden warmth in their bodies as she spread her fingers across his cheeks and hungrily kissed him –

Thus do I imagine those young lovers, in the very dawn of the Revolution!

23

In the wake of my uncle's recent outburst when I had, it seems, been insufficiently cynical of Silas Rind's motives, I was less than expansive in the account I gave him of Martha's blooming romance. I suspected he would say: 'Romance? *Romance?*' – then mock me for a naif, and tell me that Martha's motives were no less self-interested than her uncle's; and having no desire to hear that brave girl's honour assailed I restricted my construction to the pages of my journal. There I allowed the thing to flower – though not, of course, without those obstacles that dog the course of all lovers, but give the thing such sweetness in the consummation.

Hungrily I sifted through the crumbling American letters, seeking some stray word or phrase that might throw light upon the matter; though with little success. But as I sifted, peering by candlelight at Martha's faded handwriting, something rather strange, and wonderful, occurred. For I began to notice, here and there, in the margins of the letters, a drawing she had made, and then repeated, over and over, as though attempting to perfect it. It was a simple thing, a rounded form, anatomical, I supposed, a bended knee, or a breast, perhaps – or a belly. And all at once I saw it – a swelling, spherical belly – a pregnant belly – she was drawing her own belly! Again and again she had sketched that which she must conceal, and so revealed her secret, perhaps not even aware that she did so. I do not believe my uncle ever noticed these little simple drawings Martha made of her belly, but I did; and they endeared her to me all the more.

They slipped away from the house whenever they could; not together, of course, for they had to be careful. And if Caesar was busy in the barn then they walked up into the woods, or climbed Black Brock and stamped about on top of the cliff, shouting at the

British warships on the horizon. One afternoon he took her to the Old Burying Ground, a large sloping field on the north side of the road down to the harbour. There on a stony windswept hillside the grass clung close to the slope and the grave markers were of wood, the whole exposed and barren place girdled by a wandering picket fence. Victims of war were laid to rest there, victims of disease and, most numerously, of the sea, and it became a favourite pastime for Adam and Martha to drift about among the graves reading aloud the stories of disaster. A great storm ten years previously had claimed the lives of seventeen men from four boats. A storm of a different kind carried off every member of a family who farmed a valley in the back country, when the father went mad and murdered them one by one with an axe. He walked into the woods and was never seen again. There were victims of the smallpox, the yellow fever, the scarlet fever and the windy fever, and one old woman called Jephtha Stocking who died of boils. Adam and Martha sat by her grave and gazed out to sea, conjuring visions of death by boils. Martha at this period, that is, the late autumn of 1774, was as happy I believe as she had been since leaving England. Were her wounds healing? They were, and Adam did not disturb that slow work going forward in her soul, as she buried the memory of the Harry who had raped her, and raised instead a suffering Harry, a blighted and persecuted Harry, Harry the victim of cruelty and intolerance in that hated place of despots, that *England* –! And then the thought of his unborn child would cast her down into fear and uncertainty once more.

Ah, but they did not go unobserved. In this small world eyes were always watching, tongues whispering, small minds busy with scandal and malice. Martha's friendship with Adam Rind had aroused strong resentment in certain of the townspeople, and she was made aware of it the day she celebrated her first Thanksgiving in America.

The morning dawned damp and cloudy, a strong breeze off the sea that spat rain against the windows and promised worse by nightfall. Adam had brought in turkeys from the forest, which were plucked and cleaned by the women, and now as they roasted in the fire they filled the house with smells which Martha had never smelled before. By noon the house was crowded, the men gathered in Silas's parlour drinking Tobago rum and smoking Virginia tobacco as they talked about one thing only, that being the present public emergency. Martha made it her task to replenish the men's glasses as they talked, and in this way she overheard much of what they were saying. She heard Nat Pierce loud with indignation that when twenty thousand patriots marched on Boston, Samuel Adams turned them back. Silas was in regular correspondence with Mr Adams, and supported him now, saying that the moment to strike had not yet arrived. He argued that there were many in the colonies who had not come as far along the road to arms as had the people of Massachusetts. He feared they would fight on the side of the British. He feared a civil war, which the patriots would surely lose.

Joshua Rind was present. As his brother talked of those men in other colonies who would remain loyal to the crown, he interrupted, saying: 'Civil war? I think not, Silas. I think a revolutionary war.'

'Will we have a revolution then, Joshua?'

'God help us, I believe we will,' said the doctor, 'and if we lose it we shall all be off to London to wear the king's rope.'

He gingerly fingered his throat.

Also present was the minister, the small, thin, excitable John Crow, who worked alongside the other men six days of the week, and drilled with the militia up on Colchester Fields. This Thanksgiving Day he had preached a blistering sermon, taking as his text the first verse of Lamentations, and voicing the memorable sentiment that Resistance to Tyranny was Obedience to God. Now he spoke with no less ardour about the stupidity of the British government.

'Free trade is all we ever asked!' he cried in tones he usually employed to depict the rigours of Hell. 'They grew rich, they would have grown richer, selling their goods in America, but no, they must tax us, and they will lose the profits of trade, and they will not get their taxes either. Why are they blind?'

'The king is mad,' said Nat Pierce, and spat a gob into the fire, where it hissed like a snake.

'They have deformed the constitution,' said Joshua Rind. 'Theirs is an old rotten state, and our own health demands we separate ourselves from them before we become sick with their distemper.'

Still fingering his throat he frowned most darkly.

'And they think us raw, cowardly men!' he then cried. 'They think we will easily be beat in the field!'

'But that is all to the good,' murmured Silas, pushing himself off the mantel and pacing the floor, the other men all watching him now as Martha filled their glasses from her jug.

'We shudder at the prospect of blood, and rightly so. But we are in a state of nature now, and we must take up arms against them. Not yet, however. We must await the moment. Then you will have your revolution, Joshua.'

Martha had filled their glasses, her jug was empty, but still she dawdled by the door, unwilling to be out of the room if something truly dramatic was said. But she heard no more then, for Sara came looking for her, saying she was needed in the kitchen. Reluctantly Martha returned to the women, who were occupied with tasks that were at once of lesser and greater importance than those being discussed by the men; that is, they were making the dinner. The back door was propped wide open but even so the room was hot and steamy and full of the smells of roasting turkey, and her aunt Maddy was basting the birds as the other goodwives of New Morrock worked around her, and the children were put to work too, laying the table and pulling corks from bottles and the like.

Here the mood was different. As the women worked they talked, and they talked of their husbands and brothers and sons, and in their voices Martha heard the fears that none of the men dared speak aloud. They feared that a great army would come, an army of men deeper blooded in war and better armed than their own men, an army that had seen battle in much of the world and had always emerged victorious. They did not doubt their men's courage,

196

but they knew they were not soldiers, they were fishermen and farmers, rather, and although many of the older men had served in the war against the French they had been commanded by English officers. Now those same officers would be ranged against them. The women in Maddy Rind's kitchen did not deceive themselves. They saw no good reason to believe that the patriot cause would be victorious when the smoke cleared and the last of the bodies was hauled away in a cart.

Martha heard all this with growing agitation, for she believed the colonists must take up arms, no other course was open to them, this she had learned from her father; and if in some part of her mind a voice told her that it was not her place to speak her thoughts, she paid it no attention.

'But they will not be beat,' she burst out at last, 'why do you say such things?'

There was a sudden silence, a sudden stillness in that steamy kitchen.

'Martha,' said her aunt Maddy, in her kindly, worried way; but she was interrupted by a sour widow called Purity Clapsaddle.

'Martha Peake,' said Goodwife Clapsaddle in a sneering tone which dripped with spite and contempt. 'And what does our English cousin think she knows?'

Now Martha had never concerned herself much with what others thought of her, this too she had learned from her father. Small wonder then that she had taken little notice of the reaction to her arrival of those beyond the Rind family circle, in particular women like Purity Clapsaddle and her daughter Ann, a girl of Martha's age with a spirit as pinched and pickled in brine as her mother's, and who was also in Maddy Rind's kitchen that Thanksgiving Day.

'What do I know?' retorted Martha. 'I know that your men will risk their necks on an English gallows so you can live as free people here.'

The sentiment was not new. It was spoken a hundred times a day in the kitchens and taverns of New Morrock. But these women did not expect to be told such a thing, in such a way, by a newcomer, a stranger – an English stranger! Nor was this Martha's worst offence in their eyes. She and Adam had been seen up in the Old Burying Ground together, and it was much talked of that he had taken her with him to his father's sawmill the night the *Lady Ann* was landed under Scup Head. Adam Rind was the eldest son of the richest man in town. The question of whom he would marry had long engaged the busy tongues of the New Morrock goodwives. Among those thought to be a suitable match was Purity Clapsaddle's daughter Ann; and although Adam had shown little interest in Ann Clapsaddle, older wiser heads were quietly confident that good sense would prevail. Until, that is, this red-haired English hussy threw all their calculations into disarray.

'And you know better, do you?' said Purity Clapsaddle, moving toward Martha with flames of malice leaping from her eyes. 'You who have come here with the stink of London still upon you.'

'English whore,' said Ann Clapsaddle, as her mother stood bristling and jutting at Martha, who had straightened up from the fire and stood now with her chin up glaring at this little snake of a woman spitting poison at her. Her colour was up, and her face was as red as her hair. The other women stared at Martha with fierce stony eyes, all but Sara, who at once ran to her cousin's side, and Maddy, who was astonished at what was going on in her own kitchen.

'Ann, you be silent!' cried Maddy.

'She shall not be silent,' hissed Purity Clapsaddle, 'and neither shall I. You scarlet creature –'

What would have happened next, had not the men at that moment been heard shuffling out of Silas's parlour, their voices loud with joy at the smells coming from the kitchen, I do not know. But in an instant the women were back at their work and the men were rumbling in, rubbing their hands, none of them with any idea that but a moment before Martha had almost been set upon by their own wives and daughters.

In stamped the men, then, their spirits well-lifted with rum and the heady talk of revolt. Now they bantered with their womenfolk and were chided like children, and laughed it off, buoyed with the feeling that great doings were afoot. Martha's temper subsided, in her mind she consigned the Clapsaddle women to a place of darkness, and paid attention once more to the men. Later it occurred to her that if she could arouse such anger merely with her words, what would happen when her belly started to show?

The weeks went by, the weather grew colder, and it became ever more difficult for Martha to hide her condition. The day after Thanksgiving Sara had come to her and told her that she must never doubt the love and friendship that she, Sara, felt for her. Martha was much affected by this, as she had been by Sara's coming to her side during the argument in the kitchen. She saw something of her own spirit in this girl, something of the adamantine element, and by God she wanted a friend. The two embraced, they clung together, Sara was surprised by Martha's strength of feeling but she returned it, for she had recognized a quality in her cousin, she could not describe it precisely, a sort of wholeness, a directness, an unshakeable integrity of purpose; Sara had it too, I believe, but hers was an inner flame, whereas Martha's whole being was imbued with it, she gave it off to the world as the sun gives heat, and she could no more hide her nature than change it. Sara loved her for it, and she also feared for her. One day when the two were washing linen in the great tub behind the house, Martha suddenly felt weak and had to sit down. Sara wanted to fetch her uncle Joshua, but Martha could not allow her to. Sara began to insist, and Martha shyly told her she was with child.

Sara was at once full of curiosity, and asked if she might listen to the child's heartbeat. There was nothing to hear, cried Martha, laughing now, but her cousin would not be denied, and so they went into the barn and Martha pulled up her skirt, and Sara laid her head on her belly. After some moments, and with shining eyes, she told Martha she had heard her baby's heart beating. Martha said this was surely not possible, but Sara, laughing, insisted it was true, and as Martha pulled her skirt down, Sara stopped her hand and asked to hear it again. Martha allowed her, then pushed her off and sat up, and as Sara lay there dreamily gazing at her cousin she said her breasts were bigger than they had been when she arrived from England. Martha told her this was because of the child, and they hugged one another, laughing like a pair of happy lovers.

Some days later the two girls were wandering barefoot along the seashore at low tide on a cold and overcast day. They were carrying a basket between them into which they tossed anything they could find in the way of crabs and mussels. The sand was cold and gritty beneath their feet, and a breeze was coming off the sea in short damp chilly gusts. Martha must have told Sara something of her fear at the prospect of her belly betraying her, and Sara was silent for a while. Then she spoke.

'I know who the father is,' she said.

Martha stopped in her tracks.

'Who?' she whispered.

The girl smiled shyly at her.

'Who?' shouted Martha, and Sara shrank away from her.

'Sara, who?' said Martha, gently now.

'Adam,' said Sara. 'It is Adam. You must tell him, and he will marry you.' Poor dear Sara, it all seemed so simple to her.

Martha said nothing more, and hid her confusion by stooping to seize up from a rock pool a little scuttling crab, and dropped it in her basket with the rest.

Martha found that the swelling of her belly went unnoticed if she wore her clothes loose and tied her apron slack, and invented frequent reasons to haul on her boots and greatcoat and work in the yard. She spent many a frosty morning that winter out behind the house, up to her elbows in a basin of hot water and lye, her face flushed red with cold and steam, scrubbing sheets and shirts so as to escape the kitchen, and the goodwives of New Morrock, who went in and out of each other's houses with bewildering frequency, having some kind of sixth sense as to when extra pairs of hands were wanted.

But she was always in the house after dark, and several times during this period a man on horseback cantered into the yard, and Silas would go hurrying out to meet him. A minute or two later the rider came stamping into the kitchen, a heavy leather satchel on his shoulder, his face white with cold, frost in his beard, and rubbing his chilled hands over the fire as the women prepared hot food and drink for him. Having warmed himself at the fire, and created muddy puddles where the snow melted off his boots, he would be led off by Silas to his parlour, and there the two men would shut themselves in. When Martha carried in the tray the stranger would instantly cover up the papers spread on the table, and all talk ceased until she had left the room. In vain Martha pressed her ear against the door to discover what they talked about, for the doors in her uncle's house were built solid and no sound passed through them. But once, as she was closing the door behind her, she heard the stranger say to her uncle: 'That is your English girl then, Silas?'

She did not hear what Silas replied, for as she held the door open a crack he said loudly: 'Close the door, Martha' – and she had no choice but to obey.

With each fall of snow the road to Boston became more impassable. By the beginning of January 1775 they had seen the last of that winter's riders. The ocean was no more friendly than the forest, storms coming up quickly and lashing the cape with great fury before passing on out to sea, but a few intrepid vessels crept up and down the coast in the lulls between the storms, few of them British, for the enemy preferred to keep his shipping safe in Boston harbour now. Only through these brave sailors was Silas kept abreast of the proceedings of the committee in Boston. In this way he learned that the petition sent to the king, demanding the crown's recognition of the colonists' rights, had been ignored. It was one more insult. Silas was quietly elated.

'Now they understand,' he said. 'Now they know what sort of men we are dealing with.'

For he wished it to be brought home to men in the other colonies that the British had no interest in seeking a peaceful resolution but intended, rather, to *punish* them, for presuming to challenge their masters in London.

It was in this climate of at times unbearably tense anticipation that Martha Peake continued to guard her secret. She calculated that she would come to term in the late spring or early summer, by which time she hoped that the people around her would have events of greater importance to occupy them than her little bastard. But then the situation was dramatically changed, and not by any action of her own. Adam discovered that she was with child. Sara told him.

They had been in the woods together seeing to Adam's traps. He told his sister that when he had a son he would give him his own land to clear and build upon. He had turned eighteen just before the Thanksgiving holiday, and he passionately resented that he still lived under his father's roof. So Sara asked him if he had decided who he wanted to marry, and Adam said: 'Martha Peake, of course.'

Martha was upstairs changing sheets and airing the bedrooms when Sara came to her and reported this. She then admitted that she had told Adam that his cousin would soon have need of a husband, and on being pressed, had told him why.

Martha let out a cry and sank on to the bed. After a moment she asked her cousin what Adam had said to that.

Nothing. A great shout of joy was all.

'Joy?' said Martha.

Sara nodded, and Martha at once understood that Adam assumed the child to be his own. Had this possibility not occurred to her before? Indeed, had it not coloured her feelings for Adam from the start? My uncle William would have it so, but I believe not. For I do not think Martha capable of such base calculation in a matter of the heart.

'So he wants the child,' she said.

'Oh yes,' said Sara, beginning to see how badly she had blundered.

Martha gazed at her a moment then looked away. She would not let Sara see what she was thinking. She resumed her work, and cast her cousin only a sour glance as she went at another bolster, throwing wide the window and letting a blast of icy air into the room, and thumping the bolster hard on the sill.

'Go away,' said Martha. 'I have work to do.'

Sara ran from the room. As soon as the door closed behind her Martha pulled shut the window and sank on to the bed and began to think of what this meant to her; to her, yes, and to her unborn child. And for the first time, I believe, she thought of her child not as a sinful secret, nor as the manifestation of the evil done to her by her father, but as a living being, rather, who one day soon would require her protection in an uncertain and unfriendly world.

Adam Rind was by nature generous, and his generosity had a practical cast to it. As soon as the weather turned cold he had given Martha a fur hat that kept her head warm all that winter. Everyone wore fur in New Morrock but nobody had a hat as handsome as hers, for it came from a creature with a pelt of shining, flawless whiteness. When she put on her white fur hat, stitched by Adam's own hand, she felt like the Empress of all the Russias, so rich and thick and soft was that fur.

The next day was Sunday, and Martha went to church with the family and she wore her white fur hat. It was ill-suited to her greatcoat of course, which by this time had been patched and darned a hundred times, beaten with a broom like a mule, streaked with salt and faded grey like the shingles on Silas Rind's house; but clad thus in fur hat and greatcoat, and stout leather boots, and her plump white face framed by the wild wisps and hanks of hair that, do what she might with pins and combs, would never be contained, so eager were those rebel tresses to be free, as it seemed, in this place where the word *liberty* was never long absent from any pair of lips – thus attired, I say, she tramped down the hill with her cousins as the bell chimed in the steeple, and the gulls screamed about the harbour, and from out of the houses emerged the good people of the town to go to church and pray for the destruction of their enemies. The day was bright and cold, the sky a steady blue, the sea running fast in the harbour below, and the snow still thick on the ground where the feet of men and horses and oxen had not trampled it to slush and mud. Sara – who had since been forgiven for her indiscretion – walked by her side, her arm linked in her cousin's, this at Martha's request as she had no wish yet to talk to Adam.

Ah, the poor lad. It was hard not to feel for him, and I had a great sympathy for what Martha was putting him through. For a day now he had been desperate to secure a moment alone with her and she had not allowed it, keeping herself always out of his reach, even when in the same room as him. And how his eyes burned on her! His sisters were not slow to notice this, but even their delight at such evidence of romantic feeling could not embarrass him, so ardent was he with this news he had had from Sara. But Martha was not ready, she was far from ready, and she kept Sara by her every minute she could, it was the least the girl could do to protect her, having precipitated her into this dilemma at the outset. Sara was as distraught as Adam was! She hated to arouse Martha's displeasure!

But after the service Sara promptly disappeared; and Adam was quick to seize his opportunity. As Martha trudged through the slush in her fur hat she heard him come up behind her, and then he was at her side. He gripped her arm and they marched on up the hill together.

'But is it true,' he said, with a passionate urgency, 'what Sara told me?'

She turned to him. They were close to the house, and she had no doubt they were observed.

'I cannot talk to you in the public road like this,' she said. 'We will meet later and you will know everything.'

'But where?'

'I will tell you. Now I must go in.'

And with that she ran away from him, and the last glimpse she had of his face, as she went into the house, it was alive with longing and hope.

She had created for herself a brief interval in which to cast about for some solution but it was in vain, she could see no way out.

She would have to allow him to think the child was his, and she would have to marry him. That they should each lose their freedom for a lie –! But for him at least the sacrifice would not appear as such, but rather as the fulfilment of his heart's desire. Though did it truly not occur to him, I asked myself, that he might not be the father?

I thought not. Had he seen more of the world, had he spent any time in a city – had he grown up in London! – the thought would most certainly have occurred to him; but I believe he did not think the thought, for he was uncorrupted, he was clean; and it was cleanly that he declared his love. They met in the barn later that day. Martha, wrapped in horse blankets, sat shivering in the gloom as Adam paced the floor and made his declaration. Out it came in a great inchoate gush, how Sara had told him the news that had made him the happiest man alive, how he would build her a house when the war was over, and how they would live there in peace and grow rich and old surrounded by their children, and their grandchildren, and more yet in this vein; and when he had finished he stood waiting for her answer. She looked up and told him to sit beside her. She then sank into silence.

'Martha?' he said at last.

She turned away.

'Will you then?' he said.

With her eyes cast down on the floor of the barn, where a tiny puddle of water had frozen, and by some small miracle escaped the boots and hoofs that had trod the barn all day – she nodded her head.

He leaped to his feet and with a tiny splintering sound the ice was crushed into muddy splinters as he lifted her to her feet and enfolded her in his arms, and for a second she felt her own bones going the way of the frozen puddle. He whispered her name half-a-dozen times and then she pulled away, and gazing solemnly into the wild streaming happiness of the boy's face she asked him only that he say nothing for a few days, and he didn't care, he would have agreed to anything.

They stayed in the barn a little longer and then she told him how cold she was and he hurried her back across the yard with his coat around her shoulders and into the kitchen and the fire. Everyone looked up as they came in but nobody said a word, and when the younger girls could restrain themselves no longer, and began to whisper and snort, Silas silenced them with a short bark – 'Enough!'

24

And so another night in Drogo Hall came to an end. Again I had written through the hours of darkness and now, as I rose from my chair and stretched my stiff limbs, I saw the dawn was already picking at the old stiff curtains. I hauled them back and flung open the windows to admit the damp air of the early morning. My room looked out over the stableyard at the back of the house, out to the fields beyond, and the marsh, where a dank white mist hung low to the ground and obscured the distant prospect. I filled my lungs and leaned on my hands on the sill, and allowed my thoughts for some moments to linger on my uncle William, and his strange ideas about the Revolution, ideas which influenced his attitude to Martha Peake, and created distortions in his narrative that I have only with some difficulty been able to correct.

We had argued again, I am afraid. I believe he provoked me for the sheer sport of it, and I daresay I should have refused to be drawn, but he had a way of introducing into our conversations ideas that inflamed me, that set me raging before I realized what he was doing. Earlier in the night he had remarked that only Britain, alone among the nations of the world, had produced a constitution that guaranteed the individual's liberty against the power of the state.

I began at once to protest, but he asked me what other country had delivered both liberty and order to so many for so long?

Again I began to protest, again he cut me off, saying why did I support an attack on such a nation, merely because a particular set of ministers was corrupt and greedy? Did the Americans truly believe that with their few small communities strung along the Atlantic seaboard, each with its differing interests, they could create a system of government with none of these flaws?

I retorted that this vaunted British liberty of his was more fantasy than fact, and that the bulk of the British people still had no vote to cast in the election of its parliament.

So did I believe, he said, that America, in its system of government, would be *perfect*? Why should America be the exception to the rule of nations?

Because, I cried, it is her destiny!

At once my uncle fell silent, as did I. Where had this come from? It sounded like Adam Rind, or even Tom Paine. Did I believe it? I suppose I did, for I had said it loud enough. My uncle began to wheeze with happy scorn. Oh, her *destiny*, he said, his voice dripping with acid sarcasm. Destiny, is it now? Providence smiles upon the earnest smuggler, eh?

Earnest smuggler, I said, returning his sarcasm with equal acidity, was it an earnest smuggler who drove the redcoats back down the road from Concord that day? Was it an earnest smuggler who prevailed at Trenton, at Saratoga, at Yorktown? Who held together at Valley Forge over the course of a bitter cold hard winter when he had no boots, no rum, and no blanket? Who inspired the world with his defiance of the arbitrary power of an empire, who declared his independence at the risk of life and fortune, who forged a republic from a disparate group of colonies with little in common but a taste for liberty – indeed, I cried, who forged a republic which one day – one day! – will lead all the nations of the world as they clamour for those freedoms every American enjoys by natural right? If this, I cried, is America's inevitable necessity, her predetermined course, if this is her destiny – then, yes, I cried, it is!

My uncle was silent once more, his sly filmy eyes darting from my red impassioned features – I had risen to my feet in the course of this outburst, and stood now, breathing heavy, with my back to the fire – and then away. Your sentiment, he said at last, grows hotter, I see, as the history progresses.

And what man of feelings would not?

Man of feeling, yes, murmured the old man, as he picked up his little bell and shook it with some violence.

I flung myself into a chair and snorted loudly. Angrily, I examined my fingernails. Simpering Percy appeared, and was put to work with glass and decanter. I excused myself soon after, and as I closed the door I heard from within the room what could only have been the malicious tittering of those two old ruins. It cut me to the quick, thus to be abused behind my back; seething, I stormed off to my room, and there seized up my quill and composed myself for narrative.

Trapped, said my uncle William, when next we took up the story together, and I described how Adam proposed to Martha in the barn. Silas Rind saw it, said my uncle, he knew all was not as it should be.

Trapped? I said. Trapped? But how could Silas know? Had he glimpsed how Martha swelled beneath her apron? Was it written on her face? She was then in the first bloom of her young womanhood, I said, and her skin, I know, for you have wasted no opportunity of telling me, was envied by English girls, for by great good fortune she had escaped the pox – could he tell it from her *skin*?

Ah, said my uncle, with a weasel smile, she had a milky skin before she left England, yes, but that milky skin would now be *creamy* – did she not pore over it, each morning, with her little looking-glass propped on the windowsill, and a strong winter light reflecting off a fresh fall of snow in the night? Did she not examine her face for what it showed the world of this, this – a low cackle here – this wondrous little living being within? Was it not soft and white, her face, translucent almost, and plump with health; her throat delicately veined in blue; and her eyes possessed of a sleepy contentment that belied the anxiety she felt as she endlessly pondered her predicament, as you yourself have so often asserted? And her rebellious red hair, did it not gleam with a lustrous well-being, and all in all, he said – enjoying himself now – did she not give off the look of a well-fed creature in the very thick and marrow of fertility? Eh? No, she looked pregnant, Ambrose, pregnant, for the source of this plump creamy glow of hers was the *foetus in utero* all snug and complete and growing stronger every day. And if her uncle – said my uncle – did not see it for himself, his brother the doctor would not for a moment imagine Martha Peake to be anything other than what she was, a healthy pregnant girl.

He glared at me triumphant.

But they would assume, would they not, said I, that Martha's unborn child was Adam's?

Would they? Though she had conceived the child back in England? Had they not the arithmetic for it, these world-shaking smugglers of yours?

The next day Joshua Rind came to the house and settled himself beside the fire in the kitchen with a long white pipe and a tumbler of rum. Martha was at the table scouring pewter, keeping her head down and her eyes on her work. Joshua sighed as he eased his gouty foot on to a stool, and murmured to any who would listen that this was the hardest winter he had endured in his more than forty years, not because it was cold, and his horse made such heavy weather of it when he was called out to a remote farm, and the rivers were impossible to ford, and on and on in this vein – no, it was the hardest winter because they could do little but await the great event that would surely occur in the spring.

Martha looked up startled at these words, thinking only of a great event that would occur to *her* in the spring – and the doctor caught it, his little eyes sparked behind their spectacles, and Martha saw the trick, she saw how he spoke with a double meaning so as to arouse such a reaction in her. He had succeeded. He had stolen a glimpse into her soul. It reminded her of how his fingers had wandered over her body when first he had examined her.

He asked her then was she well?, did she require physic of him?, and when she told him no, she required nothing of him, he pulled on his pipe and nodded and said no more. They could hear muskets cracking in the woods behind the house, where the militia drilled, and Joshua remarked that Adam had become as good a shot as his father. As Martha bent low over her pewter she could feel the blood come rushing to her cheeks and knew her face was flushed as red as her rebel hair.

That night she was summoned to her uncle's sanctum. Here was a girl with good broad shoulders and a character as strong and stalwart as any American's, but what Silas Rind now said to her tested that character to the limit. He told her that Adam had come to him and declared that he loved her, that he wished to marry her, and that she was carrying his child. What did she have to say?

What indeed? Silas sat back in his great chair with his arms folded and contemplated Martha with a small wintry smile that was not without a particle or two of warmth. He asked her did she feel for Adam as he apparently felt for her? Martha had prepared herself for such a question, she had her answer ready. She did not love Adam Rind, not as he loved her, and for that reason alone she would never have married him. But circumstance constrained her now, and she had to think of her unborn child. He must have a father, and she a husband, if their way forward in the New World were not to be blighted from the outset. She had no choice in the matter. Lowering her eyes, and welcoming the rush of blood to her cheeks that came not, as Silas imagined, from modesty and shame, but rather from the effort of deception she was making, she said she did feel as Adam felt.

Silas sat nodding his head, watching her, permitting nothing more than that chill smile to touch his shadowed features. A few seconds passed, an interminable interval of silence it seemed to Martha; and then, as she had seen him do before at such moments, he roused himself suddenly with an exclamation.

'I am pleased,' he cried, sitting forward, setting his hands on his knees and thrusting his head at her in the candlelight, and she saw then that he was smiling broadly.

'If you love him, I welcome you into my family,' he said. 'And I will tell you something else, Martha Peake' – he spoke her full name with dry amusement, an indication that he was indeed pleased – 'I have been hoping for such a union since first you arrived in this country. You are a strong young woman and we will need you in the days to come. Give us sons, Martha Peake, we need sons.'

She could not look at him when he said this, and down went her head once more, up came the rebel blood.

'Forgive me,' he cried, seeing this, 'give us daughters then, if you prefer. So long as they are strong Americans, eh? Come, we will go to the kitchen. Adam is in an agony.'

Adam's joy knew no bounds, now that he was free to express it. And was it, Martha wondered, as she found herself being warmly embraced by the girls, was it really so little she had won here? She would be the wife of the son of the first man in town, and her child would have a security she had never known; no, nor her father either, who was born a bastard and made a monster. So she began to think she had done well after all. She sat in the firelight with happy Adam beside her, and her uncle standing over her, and everyone wreathed in smiles, and she thought – all will be well.

Only then did it occur to her to look for Joshua Rind; and there he was, outside the family circle, leaning against the wall in the shadows with his arms folded across his chest, watching her with an expression not of delight but of scorn.

Martha was now permitted a brief period of calm, and as though in harmony with her new mood the weather became unseasonably mild. The snow began to melt, and though the winds still blew wet and cold, and the sea lashed the coast with its accustomed ill-humour, and the fire was banked high in the hearth of an evening, something in the morning air, something in the light, suggested if not spring then at least the hint of a possibility of the beginning of the end of winter. And as the old season died, and Martha prepared for her wedding in the spring, she was at last liberated from the necessity of keeping her condition concealed. She showed off her belly to her aunt and her cousins, she allowed herself to be treated with special consideration, to be excused the heavy work, to be fed and rested as one who carried not only the future of the family but also – and this was a reflection of that strange, fraught season – the very future of the country, as though she carried *America herself* in her womb. But no, it was simply that the child of a patriot, himself the child of a patriot, in the last weeks of the peace had a near-sacred status among the people of the town; and Martha discovered she had become, if not popular, accepted, at least.

Though not by all. A number of women, Purity Clapsaddle and her daughter Ann being foremost among them, remained her adamant antagonists, hating her for her English trickery, as they saw it, in capturing the heart of Adam Rind. They concealed their hatred when they were in Maddy Rind's kitchen, but Martha was aware, when she was down at the port, of the hissing and muttering that followed her. She paid it no notice. She believed she had a far more dangerous enemy in New Morrock, and that was Joshua Rind.

One day, seeking solitude in which she might unburden herself with no hostile eye upon her, she climbed up on to Black Brock, where she had spent so much time in the fall. A stiff wind was blowing and the sky was grey, but strips and streaks of pale watery sunlight here and there broke through the clouds and for the first time in months it was possible to be outdoors without being chilled or soaked to the bone. Even the character of the Atlantic seemed changed, for a brisk sea was running, dark green with whitecaps, a sea that surely invited the intrepid privateer to make a dash down the coast in defiance of the blockade. But she saw no sail out there on the horizon, and so much watery waste was almost enough to lull her into believing all the world was as desolate and empty, as devoid of passion and conflict as the rolling waters and stately clouds of this North Atlantic seacoast.

Ah, but in the affairs of men a climax was approaching. Shots would soon be fired, blood spilt. That blustery afternoon when Martha gazed out to sea from the top of Black Brock was the last day of February 1775.

She would have no more such expeditions, for soon she found it difficult to make her way up and down the steep paths on to the flat places atop the cliffs and headlands. So she walked on the seashore, close to the chill salt Atlantic breakers as they came flooding and frothing across the black sand and the pebbles, to be then sucked back into the ocean's belly leaving flotsam and bladderwrack and great bulbed tendrils of seaweed beached and shining damply in their wake, the froth blinking on the sand until the next wave came hissing in. The sound of it too, and the wind catching at her skirt and her hair, and the gulls wheeling and screaming about her – somewhere deep in her body she heard a call which answered the sea, it came from the small sea she carried within her own body, in which was floated her own precious cargo, smuggled into America under the very eyes of the authorities! – such whims and follies would often slip into her mind and briefly distract her from the planning, the reasoning, the worrying and watching which were the occupations she was accustomed to practise, treading her parlous path among the colonists even as they prepared to rush blazing down the high road to liberty. That, or extinction.

Her breasts and belly astonished her daily now. Her child moved and kicked inside her, a sensation that filled her with a joy she could not compare to any experience she had known before. Maddy Rind and the other women looked after her with brisk skill, and whatever misgivings any of them had about her character, these were set aside as they looked to the business of ensuring the health of the little American in her womb. Martha was happy to submit to their ministrations and instructions. These women had seen many an infant safe into the world, and she knew they would do no less for hers.

Soon the road to Boston was open once more and men on horseback set out on the hundred-mile journey every day or so. The movement of shipping remained dangerous, and reports came in of vessels searched and impounded by British ships. More men were impressed into the British navy straight off American fishing boats, further outrages to add to the daily lengthening list.

Martha saw the first of many departures when a group of Cape Morrock men marched off from the dock one morning. In the fighting to come, which would often demand of the patriot army that they cross bodies of water under cover of darkness so as to avoid confrontation with the British, or engage the British while preserving the element of surprise, the seamanship of men from Cape Morrock and elsewhere on the Rum Coast would more than once be the saving of the Continental Army.

How it would begin, none of them could know. But that it would come soon, nobody was in any doubt at all. There was talk now that the militia would be called up soon and brought close to Boston so as to join there with a larger force; and a new idea began to dominate all talk in the Rind kitchen, that the British would attempt to destroy New England at the earliest opportunity, perhaps this very spring, for this was where the loudest of rebel voices were to be heard. Put down New England and the other colonies would soon come into line – this must be the British plan, and to do that, to cut New England off from the rest of the country, control of the Hudson River was vital. If the British held the Hudson the country would be cut into two parts, which they could then subdue one after the other at their leisure. They already controlled the Atlantic coast. They must not be allowed to control the Hudson also. If they did, the people of New England would be caught in a vice and surely crushed.

25

I was pacing about my uncle's room while Percy fussed with the old man's blanket, mulling the plight of the Americans – caught in a vice, and surely crushed! – when I found myself standing at the fireplace absently gazing at the painting of Harry Peake. It was not the first time I had stared up into those harrowed features, but now a question arose in my mind, and I did not understand why it had not occurred to me before. The man in the picture had a straight back. Behind me the usual clucking and muttering went on, and as I turned to ask the question my uncle gave out a high-pitched yelp of irritation as Percy tightened his cravat, and flapped at him like an angry goose. I turned back to the painting; and saw what I had overlooked before, that amid the leafy excesses of its gilt frame a tiny brass nameplate was screwed into the woodwork.

I peered at it. I had some difficulty reading it, for it had seen neither cloth nor polish for many years. But even as I deciphered the faded copperplate my uncle spoke the words I read there.

' "The American Within." '

The American within – Harry Peake with his back straight. I seized upon its meaning at once, of course, but who had commissioned the portrait – how had the artist known what Harry looked like – was it done after his death? I turned again and found my uncle gazing at me with glittering eyes.

'I wonder you did not see it before,' he said. 'I made a wager with Percy that you would not. He has more faith in your intelligence than I do.'

A dry wheeze here. I nodded wearily, I had grown used to these merry barbs of his.

'Lord Drogo commissioned the painting,' he said, 'and titled it himself. And he it was who gave the painter Harry's likeness.'

This statement raised more questions than it answered, but I set them aside for the time being.

'Did Harry believe,' I said, 'that there was an American inside him who looked like that?'

'Harry came to believe that his spirit was American, and that it was an accident of birth and circumstance that made him an Englishman. I Ie felt he was trapped in England as he was trapped in his body.'

'He knew by then where Martha had gone?'

'It was a comfort to him. At times he tormented himself that he was not with her in America, but no, it gave him comfort. Odd, eh, Ambrose?'

Comfort? I turned again to the painting. This was how Harry saw himself; or rather, how Lord Drogo saw him. But I knew better than to pursue the subject, for my uncle always became evasive and oblique when I tried to establish what happened to Harry after Martha left England. He had something to hide, and he made no attempt to pretend otherwise, which did not surprise me. Harry Peake's last days were miserable indeed, and my uncle bore a large responsibility for that misery; in his position I should have been oblique and evasive myself. Still, there was a certain poetic beauty in the depiction of that tragic figure in his self-made identity with the American people. So much of what they suffered, he suffered. So much of what they aspired to, he aspired to. And his broad back, with its ridge of peaks down the spine – was it not the very image, in miniature, of the land itself? Was he not himself a *living map* of America? Oh, he would have fought alongside them, he would have spoken out in their assemblies, he would have given his life, had they asked it of him. As it was, he had given his daughter. Was this the reason this most tortured of Englishmen was comforted to know that he had driven his daughter into the arms of the Americans, indeed into the very teeth of their revolution? I believe it was. I believe that in his last days he found comfort in the thought that whatever of him was in his daughter, it was now with the Americans.

Although I doubt he knew that what there was of him in his daughter was a foetus, and that this, his unborn child, was the real American within –!

Then came a most dramatic development.

26

Now here was an occasion when I might have expected my uncle's assistance, for the incident I must next recount involves no moot question of republican principle, being a matter of *espionage*, rather. But the old man was most reluctant to tell me what he knew, and became truculent when I pressed him; and for no good reason that I could see, beyond the usual sport he had in frustrating me. What I had learned from the letters was this: that late in the afternoon of an unsettled day in the March of 1775 a dank salt fog came down on the cape, and within an hour all that could be seen of New Morrock were a few yellowy patches where lamps in windows down by the port shone weakly into the gathering gloom.

The next morning the fog had lifted a little, but still it clung to the trees up behind the house, and hung like a curtain at the harbour wall a half-mile out from the dock. From the hill the town was visible through a thin scrim of mist. Figures could be glimpsed moving about on the dock, and among the boats pulled up on the shingle nearby. But there was a muffled aspect to the world, and in the Rind household they moved about quietly, and spoke little, all strangely affected by the weather, all but the younger children, who were eager to be out. It was an hour or so after they had risen, with the day's work well started, that Silas came in and told them that something peculiar was going on below, and Martha, lumbering at once to the window, saw that a crowd of people was forming down on Front Street, all of them staring out to sea, though nothing was visible beyond the harbour. The children were at once impatient to go down the hill, so Martha and Sara took them off.

Even before they reached the port they began to hear strange noises carrying across the water – a loud creaky rumbling that spoke of timber and rope, and could surely belong only to a vessel of some kind, and then a *grunting*, and a slow, muffled plashing, as of oars; and then what sounded like shouting, these various sounds all indistinct, all thick-blanketed in the wet fog so as to suggest a picture of men, timber, hemp, boat; but what men? What boat?

On the dock the people of New Morrock turned murmuring to one another, but none attempted to halloo the vessel, nor did anyone pull a boat down the shingle and row out across the harbour. No, they stood and watched, and Martha was soon aware that several members of the militia had come down to the dock with their muskets. And so in silence they waited for the creaking thing bearing down on them through the fog. Then it emerged, and they gazed at it in astonishment.

It was a large rowboat filled with men, crowded to the gunwales with men, men heaped on men, ragged, desperate men, straining at the oars, and moving forward with the incoming tide with huge effort. From the stern of this overloaded boat, which sat so low in the water that even in the calm of the harbour the sea slopped in over the sides – from the stern, where a single stout figure stood over the others, manning the tiller, a clutch of ropes were stretched taut, hauling some greater vessel through the fog behind them.

The men in the boat turned with shouts and cries, rising up and waving as they glimpsed the dock and the waiting townspeople, the oars flailing wildly now, several men tumbling into the sea and striking out for shore, others clinging to the sides of the boat and flinging their arms in the air. Some shouting came from the dock, when it was observed that among the men crowded into the boat were several who wore the familiar red coat of the king's army. Boys ran back into town to raise the alarm, but it was at once clear that if these redcoats wished to fight they chose an odd way of coming at their enemy.

Once more silence fell upon the watching Americans. Sara slipped her arm into Martha's and the cousins drew close together. Silas, mounted on horseback, clattered on to the dock now, followed by the remainder of the militia, Nat Pierce directing them into ranks.

Then all at once the prow of a ship broke through the fog. A cry from the people on the dock, who at once pressed forward on all sides, but were held back by the militia. The prow of a sloop – for sloop she was, and a sloop-of-war at that – towered over the crowded boat, and it was strange indeed to see the great height and bulk of the empty vessel dwarfing the boatload of men below, her figurehead the deep-breasted torso of a queen. On she came, this flightless bird of the sea, and it was at once clear to the watching crowd why she was towed: she had lost her mainmast. Though not her flag; the Union Jack hung limp and tattered from her bowsprit.

Silas sat deathly still upon his horse, and about his pressed lips flickered a suggestion of wry contempt. There was laughter now among the waiting crowd, for here came the hated English, the enemy, the oppressor, but unmanned, unmasted, and undone. Martha glanced about her and soon found Adam among the ranks of the militia, tall as any man there and his hair tumbling out from under his hat. The militia stood stolidly to attention on the dock, their muskets shouldered, but the mood of the people around them was charged with derisive antagonism at the sight of the broken ship and its labouring crew. Then all at once Martha fell silent, her eyes fixed on the bare-chested officer at the tiller of the rowboat. For she knew him, yes, she knew him – he was Captain Hawkins.

Captain Hawkins. Oh, she remembered that combative little man, she remembered how he had strode about the bridge of an American ship and given orders to the master of that ship; and she remembered his utter assurance, his confidence in the authority of his uniform, and his own proud self, and it aroused in her a mixture of warm emotions, for she also remembered his kindness to her in the captain's cabin, more than kindness, a genuine paternal sympathy. Now he had his own spy-glass to his eye, as he stood at the tiller and coolly surveyed the dock, the town beyond, the hill, the cliff, and the forest above, where the fog still hung heavy in the trees.

At last the spy-glass came to rest, and it was evident upon what it rested: the single mounted figure on the dock; and Silas in turn gazed at the gazing officer.

The children grew quiet and stood close to their parents as they stared out across the harbour at the overcrowded boat and the looming vessel it dragged through the misty water in its wake.

*

It was another hour before the boat approached Rind's Wharf, where men now stood ready to take the ropes flung from her bow and haul her in. English sailors and English soldiers, soaked and chilled after their long night at sea, scrambled wearily on to the planks, and a moment later their officer joined them. He stepped out of the boat unafraid, seemingly unwearied by his ordeal, and gazed keenly about him at the silent Americans.

The militia stood in ranks at Silas's back, still with arms shouldered. Giles Hawkins strode down the wharf to the laughter of the watching Americans, his chest bare and his breeches soaked, but his head high and his gaze firm. He spoke a few words to Silas and lifted his hand. No one on the dock could hear what he said, and for a long moment they waited for Silas's response. If there were some present who wished to see Silas spurn the Englishman's hand, if there were even a few present who would have the militia march these wretched men off to some quiet cove and stand them up before a firing squad – none spoke, for Silas had already made it known how he wished them to conduct themselves. They waited in silence, and there was barely a murmur when Silas leaned forward in the saddle and gave the Englishman his hand.

The family were all in the kitchen when Silas came home late in the afternoon. He wore an expression Martha had come to know well, the angry, set, sober face he seemed always to bring back from Pierce's. He came in through the scullery and his eye sought first not his wife but Martha, and the look he gave her alarmed her, for she found it difficult to read, there was in it something quizzical – sceptical – irritable also – but approving withal, or at least suggesting a sort of dark amusement. He did not trouble to make clear what he meant by it, for he sat down without a word, and only when he had eaten did he tell them what they might expect in the days to come.

The *Queen Charlotte* – for this was the name of the sloop, and a hated name too, Charlotte being the king's wife – had been on patrol up the coast. The ship's master, an Englishman unfamiliar with these waters, had been surprised by a storm out to sea: waves thirty foot high and a gale that came up without warning and tore through his canvas before he could get any men aloft, all this in the middle of the night and no moon to help them see what they were doing. Four men coming up out of the hatchway before the mast were lost at once, swept overboard by a sudden great wave; and it must be said there was no heart in Maddy Rind's kitchen so hard set against England that it did not feel pity for those poor sailors.

It took the wind a very few minutes to bring down the mainmast, which lay across the deck with its rigging all tangled and the loose shrouds flapping wildly like some great white gliding creature brought up from the deep. Still the wild nor'easter clawed and howled about the vessel, and it was then that Giles Hawkins had struggled up on deck with an axe, and amid the shrieking fury of the storm he hacked the mainmast free of its splintered base and cut loose the rigging. Liberated of her burden the ship found some measure of stability, and somehow they survived the night; and the following morning were driven toward the coast before the wind died away and they found themselves adrift in the fog.

Captain Hawkins, said Silas, was then faced with a hard necessity: he must strip the *Queen Charlotte* of her cannon and dump them overboard, and put his men in the boat, which by chance had not been swept away in the night. Then they would haul her to some natural harbour.

'And,' said Silas, one eyebrow lifted, and with a curl to his lip, 'by great good fortune they found shelter with us.'

'What now?' said Adam.

'What now indeed,' said Silas; and told him that the *Queen Charlotte* must be refitted in New Morrock before she could return to Boston.

'Refitted here,' said Caesar.

Silas nodded, his chin on his hands.

'A new mast,' said Adam. 'Sailcloth and rigging.'

Silas nodded. Martha glanced from father to son, but could not read what else passed between them.

'And the redcoats?'

'I have put them in the George.'

This was an old dilapidated wooden structure on stilts, down the far end of Front Street. It had prospered in the days before Nat Pierce opened his establishment. Only a very few of the old fishermen continued to drink in the George, the reason for its unpopularity being its name. Now it was to be used as a billet for the soldiers. A greater irritant to the inflamed passions of this patriot town would be hard to imagine, and Adam said so.

'Those passions,' said Silas, 'must be contained.'

There were only the two voices now, Silas's and Adam's, and the others in the kitchen stayed quiet and still, all but Sara, who moved around lighting the lamps. Silas did not have to tell his son that if the militia attacked the redcoats it would set the colony ablaze. A massacre on that scale could not be concealed.

Adam pondered, then said: 'What does the Englishman say?'

'He is with me,' said Silas. 'There must be no trouble. You must all help me.'

He looked round the table, looked closely in the lamplight into the faces of his worried family. His gaze came to rest on Martha. 'Much depends on it. Perhaps everything.'

Late that night Martha lay awake and stared at the ceiling, where a stray shaft of moonlight had picked out a long pale rectangular patch on the plaster. Her hands were under her nightshirt, on her belly. Silas's words turned in her mind. Much depends on it. Perhaps everything. What was everything, America? Was America everything? To her it had become so. America was the world into which her child would be born. But as she thought of Giles Hawkins she felt a profound unease, for she had not admitted to Silas that she knew the man.

The next morning New Morrock awoke to the knowledge that it now sheltered a detachment of redcoats and a crew of English seamen in the port. The redcoats were billeted in the George and the seamen were aboard the *Queen Charlotte*, and Martha was not alone that morning in running at once to the window and looking down to the harbour, and the hulk tied up off the end of Rind's Wharf. The weather, instead of throwing up tempests and hurricanes to match the passions that simmered in every heart that day, instead unfolded the first of a string of still, cold, cloudless days in which the world in its physical vestments shone forth with a terrible clarity, the most vivid element of that shining world being the faded red coats of the English soldiers as they emerged from their billet on Front Street. That, and the *Queen Charlotte*, visible to every household in the town, so that not for a second could they forget this monstrous broken alien vessel riding at anchor in their harbour.

When Martha went downstairs Silas had already gone out. She spoke briefly to Adam before he too left the house. Dear good Adam, he stole what moments he could with his love before kissing her at the back door then hurrying off down the hill to Pierce's. There he was publicly delegated by his father to lead a squad of redcoats into the woods to select a good straight pine for a main-mast; and it surprised nobody that he set off to the south, away from Scup Head, away from his father's sawmill, with Caesar at his side and the soldiers in rank behind them.

Now Martha began to glimpse the delicacy of the predicament into which Silas Rind was plunged by the arrival of the *Queen Charlotte*. She spoke to Sara, and came to understand the necessity Silas faced of making an ally of the Englishman, almost indeed a friend. The *Lady Ann* was moored behind Scup Head, just a few miles away, and not far off the sawmill was packed to the roof beams with materials of war. Silas wanted no suspicions aroused. He did not want those redcoats out searching the countryside. He wanted them away from New Morrock as quick as possible, and as they could not leave until their ship was refitted, he had sent them off into the woods for a mast, and given Captain Hawkins his word there would be no ambush.

27

There was no ambush, and late in the afternoon came the news that a tree had been felled and trimmed; they would go back the next day with horses and chains to drag it out. The family was sitting down to dinner when Adam and Caesar returned to the house, and Silas told them they had done well. They then fell to their food and Silas said nothing more.

Not until the meal was over and the table was being cleared did he make his announcement. To general astonishment he told them that Captain Hawkins would be coming to the house that night, and would they all please show a civil face to the man. This he said in that dry, grim way of his that was not without humour, but it was that desiccated humour which Martha now recognized as a Massachusetts variation on a certain laconic English wit. Silas Rind was a man of some severity, even in his levity.

Her heart sank. She had no desire to confront the man again; he was a British officer, and any connection with him must compromise her. She had a wild hope that she might be able to avoid him when he came, but that hope was soon dashed, for Silas was looking at her as he had the day before, and she could have no doubt that some scheme was afoot that concerned her. She was not surprised then, when the meal ended, that Silas asked her if she would come to his room. Without waiting for an answer he rose to his feet and left the kitchen and Martha, also rising, and casting a look at her aunt, so as to excuse herself, followed him out with lowered eyes and the sensation of moving through quicksand.

He was in his parlour, in his great chair, and she stood before him with all the humility of the family dependant in the presence of the master. It was a room in which she had rarely felt at ease, particularly at night, when the dark leatherbound tomes crowding the bookcases, and the black panelling on the walls, and the glass cases and stoppered jars that gleamed on the high shelves, all exhaled the heady forbidding fumes of male knowledge, male mysteries, male power. And there in his great chair, that great carved throne of his authority, with his stout-shod feet planted firmly on his own firm floor, and his big strong hands with the black hairs fleeced across their backs laid flat on the arms of the chair, and his face all crags and clefts in the shadows – oh, Martha Peake was a girl of strong heart, but Silas Rind, when he waxed severe, he put the fear of God in her.

But she showed nothing of this, she stood before him in a guise of meekness and willed the child in her belly to be still. What he had to say to her was simple but it confused her all the same. He wished her to be present when Captain Hawkins came. She asked him why. He said that she had known more Englishmen than he had, and that she could judge the captain's intentions. I want, he said, another pair of eyes.

Silas, I believe, did not deceive with skill on this occasion. He said these words with a certain shrugging vagueness, as though they occurred to him in the moment of speaking. Martha sensed at once that he had another purpose, which he wished to hide from her. She began to say she knew nothing of army officers, but he lifted a hand and she fell silent. They heard a footfall on the path outside the house, and Silas went to the window.

'He is here,' he said. 'Sit in that chair, Martha. Say nothing unless I address you. Listen close, and afterwards you will tell me what you think of him.'

'Yes sir,' said Martha, and retired to the back of the room where he directed her.

The captain was brought into the parlour and on being introduced to Martha betrayed only the slightest hesitation of recognition; and said nothing. It seems he grasped at once the delicacy of her position, an English girl alone among the colonists. He wore a powder-blue coat streaked with salt and less than splendid. His bulldog features were grave, composed, watchful.

'Captain Hawkins,' said Silas, 'this is Martha Peake, my niece. She is lately come from England, and advises me in matters that concern your country. I value her judgement. You will not mind if she is present at our conversation.'

Martha saw that Captain Hawkins found it as implausible as she did that Silas Rind should seek the advice of a girl, but he showed nothing of it. He bent over her hand, as she rose from her chair, and as his head came up she saw his eyebrows lift, and his eyes gleamed in the candle flame as he caught the creamy flawless radiance of her skin; and there was, too, I believe, in his eyes, a whisper of friendship, a warm memory of the hour they had spent together aboard the *Plimoth*.

'Mistress Peake, honoured,' he murmured, and there it was, the peculiar rich cadence of his accent.

'Captain Hawkins,' said she, keeping her eyes down, for she wanted no traffic of looks and lashes here in her uncle's sanctum.

The two men then threw back some rum – she should have liked to drink some rum herself, but was not offered it – and Silas led the captain to the far end of the room where Martha could not hear what they said. She had the opportunity then to examine Giles Hawkins at her leisure; and there was, she saw it now, as he patronized Silas, and played the English gentleman, an arrogant streak in him, a pridefulness that set him apart from those he considered his social inferiors; her uncle, it was clear, being one such. You must play him, she thought, like a big fat trout, glimpsing the vanity that lay behind his pride.

But was this not what her uncle was doing, even as Martha thought the thought? He knew it before she did – that there was one thing only the captain did not see clearly, and that was himself! So she watched Silas impersonate the rustic colonial, she watched him flatter the captain, but with such subtlety that nobody who did not know Silas Rind for the man he was would see it. Silas Rind did not grin at Englishmen! He did not scratch his head, nor slap another man on the shoulder, and he certainly never showed the effects of a glass or two of rum; but now he was doing all these things, and the Englishman watched him with an amused condescension that confirmed him in his assumption of his own superiority.

Then Silas was calling Martha over, telling her to go to the kitchen and fill the jug, and as she took it from him he grasped her by the cheek and turned her toward the captain, saying something about the flowers of England, and she guessed at once that he wanted her to show his guest how she bridled at being thus handled, but was forced to endure it – and the anger blazed up in the Englishman's eye, but he, like her, could not show it under Silas's own roof – and in that moment a new sympathy was born in him, as he saw Martha Peake as a maiden trapped in the house of a monster, the maiden an English maiden, and the monster – American.

She knew it for the bold tactic it was. Silas wanted the Englishman not to know his strength. He must think Silas a boor and a fool, and he must sail away from New Morrock believing the colonists a set of coarse buffoons incapable of fighting a war. Thus did Martha reason it as she left the room with the empty jug and filled it from the keg in the kitchen.

They were again deep in talk when she returned, and from what she could hear she understood Silas to be warning the captain that the men in the town were hard to control, and the less the British soldiers showed themselves the less the risk of confrontation, which neither of them wanted. The captain was nodding his head as his eye strayed from Silas to Martha, and she knew the bait was taken, the hook was in.

Thus far Martha had played her uncle's game. Now, as she poured each man another tot, she asked herself: and what is my game here? What am I to have from all this? And then she thought: it is not what I want that matters any more, but what my child wants – what can I do here in his best interest?

Later that night, in bed, her hands on her belly to keep him warm, she reflected that her child's presence within her had again changed the direction of her thoughts, indeed their very nature.

But before she got to bed she had still to navigate the treacherous waters below. Captain Hawkins and her uncle completed their business and the Englishman left soon after, though not before once more taking Martha's hand to his lips, and again his eyes spoke with some eloquence as his head came up. Nor was Silas blind to this. He saw him out. When he returned he sank into his chair and his head fell back and for a few seconds he closed his eyes. He sighed. Then he sat up.

'Ah, Martha,' he said. 'Martha Peake. If you knew what all this costs me.' He gazed at her a moment, his fingers drumming on the arms of the chair. 'Perhaps you do,' he said. 'But I am pleased with you. Now tell me, what did you make of that fine fat enemy of ours?'

Martha had had but a few minutes to prepare herself for this question. But she knew it was the interest of her unborn child she served now. I am weak, she told herself, I must survive if I am to protect him, and so I must ally myself with the strong party. She had decided in those few minutes to ally herself with Silas. So once more, deeper now, ever deeper, did she come over to the American side. For it had occurred to her that she might have gone with Giles Hawkins, had she so chosen.

She picked her words with some care. 'His pride makes him blind,' she said. 'He is not a match for you, sir.'

There was a silence. Had she said too much? Had she flattered when she should have been silent? But no; all was well. There came a brief loud shout of laughter and Silas leaped up and crossed the room with outstretched hands.

'You have it all!' he cried, pulling her to her feet. 'You understand me, Martha Peake! Of all the children in this house, you alone understand me.'

For a few seconds he held her hands and with narrow bright eyes and a small tight smile, his head pushed forward and his whole body tense and trembling with the impulse of his soul, which was toward Martha, he gazed into her eyes. She held his gaze and kept it from the secret thoughts within.

'Good!' he cried, dropping her hands. 'Good. Now we will talk. Sit. Listen.'

The next morning Martha was the first in the kitchen after her aunt. She tended the fire, which was allowed to burn low through the night, and got the water started in the big kettle. She had not slept well. The conversation with her uncle after the captain's departure had left her worried and confused, uncertain how she was to manoeuvre among the men and still protect herself and her child. When she had gone to the kitchen to fill the jug, she had found Adam and Caesar seated at the table. She had hurried across the room to the rum keg and Adam had risen to his feet, his face alive with questions, eager to know what was going forward, but she could only say that they wanted more rum.

'But what are they saying?' he cried.

The two men gazed at her in silent expectation. Under the scrutiny of their eyes she was clumsy with the spigot, and as she wiped up the spilled rum she said she did not know what was being said for they spoke too quietly. Later she slipped upstairs to bed without encountering Adam, and fortunately her cousins were all fast asleep.

But there was no avoiding him for long. He waylaid her later in the morning, behind the house, as he was about to go off into the woods, and he would not listen when she told him that she must get back to her work in the kitchen. He was hurt not to have been asked to attend the meeting of his father and Captain Hawkins, and the fact of Martha's presence there, and her long private conversation with Silas after the Englishman had left, all this was a further insult. He wanted to know what had transpired, and Martha saw nothing for it but to tell him the truth.

'Your father has bound me to say nothing,' she said. 'I have given him my promise.'

'And have you not given me your promise too?' cried Adam. Oh, she had never seen him so distraught! That his father should bind his Martha with promises of silence −! She had not properly known men's jealousy before, beyond the unnatural rage she had observed in her father during his madness. Adam did not understand why she was not plain and open with him, and she hated having to be politic with him, she felt a powerful reluctance, a repugnance, even, to deceive him. So she seized his hands and said with some passion: 'Yes, I have given you my promise too. And if you would have me honour that promise, you must see that only with your father's permission can I break my promise to him. Ask it him! If he will release me, I will tell you everything.'

She knew as she said it that Silas Rind would never release her from her promise. Caesar stood waiting with the horses, and Adam left her, a little relieved, at least, by this evidence of the desperation she so plainly felt.

28

I paced my room and pondered these developments. My uncle, as I say, would tell me nothing of these events, and grew caustic with me at the mere mention of them. Nor would he acknowledge the extent of Martha's difficulties. The night after the Englishman's visit to the Rind house, Martha, on Silas's instructions, went down the hill to visit an old widow woman who lived near the George, taking her four jars of her aunt's pickles and a jug of her uncle's rum. It was a windy night, the moon not yet risen, and the sea rattled on the shingle and crashed against the harbour wall. She was making her way home up a narrow twisting street behind the tavern when she heard someone softly calling her name. She turned to discover Giles Hawkins standing in a doorway in the shadows.

This she had dreaded. She tried to hurry on, but he called her again and asked her if her uncle was well. She said he was. He then said that as the night was dark, might he escort her to her house?

They made their way up through the town. The captain told her he was concerned for her welfare, he wanted to know how she fared among the colonials, he asked her did they mistreat her because she was English. 'An unhappy story,' he said, 'to lose both your parents, and live among strangers so far from home.' He made no mention of her pregnant belly.

'Not unhappy at all,' she said. 'It pleased me to leave England. I am an American now.'

'An American, are you?'

She noticed as they came up the empty street, the little fishermen's houses pressed close together on either side, and a narrow strip of cloudy night sky overhead, that he glanced constantly about him, into alleys and doorways, and up at windows and roofs, as though he anticipated being at any moment ambushed.

'Have no fear,' said Martha, 'you are safe with me.'

This made him laugh quietly.

'Indebted to you, madam,' he said. 'Let me offer in return to serve you as a soldier and a gentleman.'

'An English gentleman,' she said. 'But it is from English gentlemen that I shall soon require protection.'

'Let us hope,' he murmured, 'that it will not come to that.'

'You can hope,' said Martha.

They were up among the big houses by this time, where the merchants and sea captains lived, and as the moon rose over the forest, and spread a pale light on the world, they stopped and turned to look down on the harbour and the sea beyond. They were beneath an ancient oak tree, and cloaked in the gloom of its great bare boughs. The captain turned to her.

'You say this is your home now.'

'It is.'

'It need not be.'

'Where else would I go?'

'I could carry you back to Boston with me. I could find you a place with an English family there.'

'As a servant?'

'At first, yes.'

What did he mean? Was she to be a servant? Or was she, rather, to be his whore? We may imagine how Martha Peake would respond to such an invitation, if indeed it was an invitation; but once again she was politic. She did not lose her temper. She was civil.

'It is not possible, sir. I am to be married here.'

'Ah. That is too bad.'

'It is not too bad for me.'

Silas and Adam were still up when she returned to the house, the pair of them in lamplight occupied with the cleaning of a musket, which had been dismantled and its parts spread across an oilskin on the table. As she hurried through the kitchen Adam watched her with hungry eyes, and Silas flung a quick dark glance in her direction.

The next day she tried to go about her duties in the normal way.

She took the children down to the dock but did not push to the front of the crowd, as she had the day before, to watch the men at work on the *Queen Charlotte*'s mainmast. No, this time she hung back and instead watched the captain as he moved about on the wharf. Had he meant what she imagined he meant, the night before? She was less sure in the cold light of day. She gazed at him now, strong brisk capable man he was, his voice ringing out clear and clipped as he strode about in his white breeches, issuing orders to his men. And he saw her, of course he did, and his eyes suggested nothing that would dishonour her, he seemed again the honest fatherly man she had met aboard the *Plimoth*.

She found more errands to perform after dark, again on Silas's instructions. The old widow woman, Hezebiah Scunthorpe, whose husband had been carried off by the windy fever earlier in the winter, was again the object of her charity. And again Giles Hawkins intercepted her as she made her way home. She did not betray the suspicion he had aroused in her the previous night, instead she played the innocent, and steered the conversation toward topics military and political. She told him what Silas wanted him to hear – that is, that no war preparations were afoot on the cape – and asked him the question Silas wanted answered, in her own way, of course, so as to conceal her true purpose, that question concerning the destination of the British fleet, when it left Boston; but the captain revealed little, he smiled indulgently, rather, for he saw her game at once.

He then startled her, he startled her greatly, by asking if her father was called Harry. Taken by surprise she at once said yes. What did he know of Harry Peake?

'We are talking of the humpbacked Cornishman who fell in with the Earl of Drogo?' he then said, and she said, yes, yes – 'for the love of God, sir, tell me what you know!'

Oh, but to hear him talked of by another person, to hear news of him –!

'Little enough.'

They were sitting in an empty stable in back of the saltworks, for the night was wet. Martha in her excitement had seized the captain's sleeve, her face was close to his, her eyes implored him!

'Tell me!'

'And what,' says he, in kindly tones – in *silken* tones – 'will you tell me in return?'

29

The captain had indeed heard something of Harry Peake, ah but it lacked any of the detail Martha craved and it smacked, rather, of the gossip of the clubs, an anecdote to amuse the dandies, or prompt Horace Walpole to a bon mot for the pleasure of one of his old women. It was correct in its broad essential, but it missed the pathos, the tragedy even of the conclusions I myself had reached. After Martha left Drogo Hall Harry sank fast, I believe, which is not surprising, given how little he had to cleave to, those final days. Martha had been his last hope, the one true prop or strut to which he might have clung in his extremity, and she had fled him. This then was what he had come to, he had driven away all who had once been his friends, nor had he any clear prospect of regaining his footing and rising from the depths. He wandered the streets of London, his only buttress against encroaching darkness his own frail will.

But even after he had taken to the streets I saw him returning time and again to the Lambeth Marsh, to search for Martha in the boggy fields around Drogo Hall; and failing to find her, was unable, in his grief, to believe that she had left him, unable even to contemplate the idea. I saw him sitting all night in the graveyard behind the church, rocking back and forth, keening with misery for his lost child, and when I thought of Harry keening I heard the wolves in the forest behind Black Brock. Easy enough then to imagine this broken man being approached by Clyte – Clyte! – and lured into the house, perhaps with false promises of Martha's presence within. Lord Drogo would then have sat with him, talked to him quietly, soothed his spirit – and made him an offer.

Yes, made him an offer; and although Harry Peake had lost the right to turn his face to the darkness, turn it he did, for he had not the moral wherewithal to refuse Drogo's offer. This was what Giles Hawkins was about to tell Martha, and the prospect horrified him,

I believe, when he saw what he had aroused in her by talking of her father. He hesitated, he searched for some way out, but she demanded that he speak plainly.

'But my dear,' he said, 'did no word reach you of this? All London knows it.'

'But knows *what*?' she cried, for he had spoken only in the broad generality. 'For the love of God tell me what you know!'

'Very well,' he said. 'They call him Harry America –'

'I know it!' she cried. 'Go on!'

'They say Harry America sold his bones to Lord Drogo for the price of a bottle of gin.'

That was all he had heard. It was all Martha needed to know. At once she saw it, she saw what I had seen all along, why Lord Drogo had first come to the Angel, why he had shown such interest in her father, why he had acquiesced in Martha being sheltered in Drogo Hall. There was no impulse of benevolence there, Francis Drogo had known what he wanted the moment he first clapped eyes on Harry Peake. He wanted his bones. He wanted his skeleton so that he could mount it as an anatomical curiosity and install it in his museum. He had used Martha to lure her father to Drogo Hall and, knowing how rapidly he was sinking, had waited until he was within his grasp.

Then he had made his offer.

Oh, and Martha well knew poor Harry was in no state to refuse! After she had fled from him nothing remained but gin. Gin cost money, and Drogo was offering him money, money enough to drown in gin. And for what? For that which he would have no further need of when he was dead, I mean his bones. Harry did not decide the issue, for he had dissipated his freedom, and now obeyed the dictates of necessity. Who was master, him or Nature? Nature. Not hard to imagine what happened next. A contract was produced, and I saw my uncle William being present for this part of it, summoned by Clyte as Harry and Lord Drogo sat at wine in the great dining room, the aristocrat doctor and the broken poet who could still however muster wit enough to converse with an educated man.

In came William, less than sanguine, perhaps, about the bargain being struck by his Mephisophelean master, or perhaps not, perhaps he had connived at it from the start; and he carefully laid the contract and quills on the table, the sealing wax, Drogo's stamp. With little more than a glance at the document Harry put his name to it. How much time did Drogo imagine Harry had left? Whatever the estimate, it must now be amended by the sea of gin that would be purchased and consumed by a man with money in his pocket. What did he get, twenty guineas, fifty? Drogo would have good cause to be generous. The more Harry drank, the quicker death would come, the sooner Drogo could extract from his sodden flesh the strange misshapen bones within.

Drogo was generous, Harry signed away his bones, they sealed the arrangement with a bottle. Did Harry stumble out on to the Lambeth Marsh that same night, the coin clinking in his pocket, to seek out the nearest gin shop? I fear so. Martha, an ocean away, just recently arrived in America, was ignorant of all this of course, and a flame of hope still burned in her, I believe, a scene perhaps occurring to her imagination in which William secretly went after Harry, told him what had become of his daughter, urged him to eschew the gin shop and instead take ship for America – was such a thing possible? Would William have dared his master's wrath in such a manner? Would his tenderness for Martha prompt him to this humane act? And if it did, would Harry hear him out, and follow his bidding, and somehow find the means to cross the Atlantic and come to her? All of this she had imagined, stamping about Black Brock those first weeks; and then she would ask herself – was he *at that very moment* somewhere in America and making his way through the wilderness to find her? Oh, she had to believe it, all was otherwise dust and horror –

But that wild hope was now dashed. He had sold his bones for a bottle of gin.

There was worse to come however. Giles Hawkins told her this only after she had given him what he wanted, that is, all she had learned the day she rode with Adam to Scup Head, intelligence regarding powder, muskets, cannon, men. Desperate for news of her father, poor Martha could no longer play the politic game, and spilled it all out in a rush. So her bad news cost her dear. She stayed with the captain not a moment longer, and with his words still ringing in her ears she made her way home in a state of great distress. She composed herself before she went into her uncle's house and made some order of her clothing and her hair. She came into the kitchen and was met by Silas. His face was dark and unreadable. He asked her to come to his room.

And thus did I construe the sad business, sitting till dawn in my room in Drogo Hall, scribbling furiously, in a very frenzy of historical reconstruction, and all the while growing deeper outraged at the treachery of the old man who fluted and whistled away downstairs, and concealed the true facts of the matter from me, indeed would have me believe that he and Drogo meant only to do well by Harry Peake! On I scribbled, till the dawn was breaking, and the story every hour opened fresh depths of depravity and betrayal to my horrified eye. I was not sure how I would greet my uncle, when next we spoke. I decided that I would say nothing of the conclusions I had arrived at, but allow him instead to exhaust this tissue of lies – his account of Harry's life, I mean – then tear it down for the false thing it was.

30

April 1775, and it was in the midst of uncertainty and rumour and fear that Martha Peake was married to Adam Rind. The town had been talking about it for weeks, I believe because they wanted to forget, however briefly, the imminent horrors that consumed all their thoughts but could never be spoken of lest they sow seeds of despair in each other's hearts. This they had learned from Mr Crow, he had been preaching the lesson from his pulpit every Sunday. Now he was preaching at Martha's wedding, telling his congregation what this wedding meant, it meant new life – and who could doubt it, I imagined the women whispering to one another, as they nodded at Martha's belly – and new life, said Mr Crow, is as a bulwark against the storm of death we know to be approaching.

An audible groan rose from the pews at this, but he silenced it with a lifted hand and told them, in hushed tones, that it was for the sake of this life that they must pass through the coming storm.

'And when the storm is over,' he said, his voice rising, 'and its black and bloody clouds no longer fill the sky, and a faint watery sun is glimpsed at last' – then, his voice dropping – 'it is upon the heads of the young that its first light will fall.'

A silence here, and Martha heard in his words: they are fighting for my child, and for his sake they forgive me everything, my Englishness, my difference, my manifest carnality. She would wear no red badge of shame as had the women of Cape Morrock disgraced by their bellies a hundred years before, no, something older than religion and deeper than shame was aroused here. She had become a kind of emblem, at least to some. But it was scant comfort, and she would dearly have loved to share with Sara the information she had had from Captain Hawkins, that stark and ghastly rumour; but she dared tell no one what had passed between him and herself. Oh, my poor dear Martha, she must have seen it all, the hideous drama on the Lambeth Marsh, long since concluded, perhaps, she could not know. The news brought by Captain Hawkins was old news, and by the time she heard it the thing may well have been decided, and her father dead, as the captain assumed him to be. For what was to prevent Clyte dispatching him some dark night on the marsh? Who would miss him, who would go searching for his hacked corpse in the cellars of Drogo Hall? He was at their mercy.

These were the nightmare visions that haunted Martha, I believe, even as she knew a sort of quiet glory as Adam Rind's betrothed, and the expectant mother of Silas Rind's first grandchild. Nothing of her torment was apparent, however, in the flushed young woman who stood before the minister that day. The words were spoken, the ring was given, and Martha Peake stepped away from the altar a married woman.

Bride and groom made their way down the aisle, and from the steeple came a sudden pealing of the church bells, and the people of New Morrock emerged from the church to crowd about them, handsome couple they were, Adam so clear and happy, eager unclouded American youth with his blooming swollen bride beside him – what a fine young man he was becoming! He was tall, and straight as a sapling, with a good long leg and a strong back, and as I thought of him – I was downstairs with my uncle, who at that moment was removing the stopper from the decanter and pouring himself a large one – it was hard not to recall the words of Henry Adams. I gazed at the ceiling.

'"Stripped for the hardest work",' I murmured, '"every muscle firm and elastic, every ounce of brain ready for use, and not a trace of superfluous flesh on his nervous and supple body, the American stood in the world a new order of man."'

Muffled snort from my uncle, but yes, that was Adam Rind. He wore a black coat cut from a bolt of Manchester velvet he had come upon in his father's warehouse, and begged a piece of; breeches to match, fine black cotton stockings, and his hair tied back with a blue velvet ribbon. With this handsome American husband on her arm, and an American baby in her womb – as they all thought – Martha, that day, and despite her private sorrows, believed that in the eyes of her neighbours she had ceased to be English, that she had finally, properly, irrevocably come over to the American side. Who could doubt that at last she was one of them? Ah, there were some, there were still some who hated her.

But today was her day, as she emerged into chill sunlight and a cold wind, under a sky in which rainclouds were massing in force over the mountains to the west. The militia was there, ready to march for one of its own; there was young Thomas Coffin with the drum slung over his shoulder, rattling off a brisk martial rhythm as two Irish lads from up the Morrock River piped away on their fifes, and with the appearance of the bride and groom they marched off down the hill, muskets shouldered and backs straight, Silas on horseback at their head, and the congregation following after, clutching at hat and skirt as the wind came gusting off the harbour, sweeping the thick slimy briny kelpy stench of the mudflats up the hill in waves. Together they all struggled down the hill to Pierce's Tavern.

When Martha awoke the next morning, in a bed not her own, she had beside her the unconscious body of Adam Rind. For a second she was filled with alarm, until she remembered that he was now her husband. He had had more wine than he was accustomed to, and he had got drunk. She had watched him carefully, and taken little herself; having seen the effects of drink on her father she was suddenly afraid that she would glimpse the same demon showing its foul face here too – and hideous was the thought that it moved among a people who wanted only to be free of the taint of Europe's corruption!

Then she remembered how Adam had become merely raucous, in a soldierly way, and soon after grew sleepy, and soon after that laid his head on his arms and snored peacefully as the older men talked on and laughed at him quietly, and the women murmured to Martha that she need expect little from her husband this night, and in their smiles lay the thought unspoken, that there had been nights when he was not unmanned by drink, did she not have the belly to prove it? But it was not with malice that they smiled and whispered and kissed her, and she discovered at last that she was no different, no worse than they were. Not one of them had gone a virgin to the altar, and not a few were pregnant, though not until this night, her wedding night, was she admitted into this deeper truth of life in New Morrock. And again she felt it, that she had come over to these people and was one of them. And forgetting her grief for an hour or two, she allowed herself a tentative confidence that all at last would be well.

That all would be well? She lay beside her snoring husband in the early morning and wondered at her foolishness. All would be well? The world was about to go up in flames! The roads were open, men were marching, men were massing, muskets and cannon and powder were stored and waiting in a thousand barns and sawmills and distilleries; they sat on a powder keg that required but a spark and the end of the world would be upon them! All was well? But in a way it was. She could do nothing more for her father, it was over, she had learned his fate from Captain Hawkins, and Captain Hawkins, thankfully – for she did not care to dwell upon what she had revealed to him, and had not yet admitted to herself the gravity of those disclosures – Captain Hawkins had sailed away. All she could do now was go forward with the Americans, and assure the survival of her child. She was not alone any more.

31

The spark came, the powder keg exploded, and the end of the world was upon them; the end of the old world, that is. Sitting by the fire with my uncle, snug and warm, *foeti in utero* in Drogo Hall, with a storm howling about the chimneys of the old pile and the great event long since decided – a redemption from tyranny won – and the promise of America no longer a dream, merely – it took a strong imagination to see how it must have been for them, back in the April of 1775, when news first reached them of the slaughter at Lexington Green.

I grew passionate, I admit it, as I recalled the events of that day, or the account of them, rather, that as a child I had had from my mother, for I was not alive when the Revolution began. My uncle William was, of course. He was here in Drogo Hall, where the last act in the tragedy of Harry Peake was still playing out; and as I have more than once suggested, he did not share my own view of the patriots' struggle, he saw the whole affair as a family squabble which had been allowed to get out of hand.

Were we not all Anglo-Saxons, this was his line; why take up arms? Reasonable Englishmen do not resort to *revolution*! They do not go to war with their own countrymen, people of their own *blood*! Even savages do not make war upon their *families*! In his view it was a feckless band of Boston hotheads who had turned a simple civil dispute about smuggling into a war of independence. They should have been hanged at the outset, Adams and the rest, and that would have been an end to it. The colonies would still be ours. Asked to sum up in one word his opinion of the greatest event in history since the birth of Christ, that word was: unnecessary.

I never gave up trying to make him see the light. I hoped to rouse him with the picture I had in my mind's eye of the Lexington militia, sturdy farmers gathering on the green in the hours before the dawn, having been woken by pealing church bells and the news that a thousand redcoats were marching north to seize the gunpowder they believed to be cached in Concord. Oh, and they had waited in the darkness, men not unlike the men of Cape Morrock, until at last they heard what they had been dreading to hear, the faint trill of the fife, the distant beating of the drums, the grim and awful tramping of a thousand marching men!

An event long expected will often surprise the mind with the force of the shock of its eventual occurrence. So it was with the outbreak of war. They knew it was coming, they had been preparing for it for months, but the day a rider brought the news from Lexington, and as it rapidly spread through New Morrock and into the surrounding country, a great change came over the people. I believe what they felt in the first days was simple terror; Martha did, I am sure, I see her hands flying to her face, and then to her womb – her heart gave a kind of kick the blood drained from her face. Had she had *hope*? Had *hope* lain coiled in her heart in the darkness where she could not see it? Hope that the parliament in London would draw back from making war on its colonies, that the king, the father, would not shed his children's blood? Martha Peake, had she properly examined her unspoken assumption, that no father will attack his child, would have seen at once, from her own experience, that it was not so. But her poor father was mad, made mad by drink, and before that by deformity and misfortune, and his violence she understood, and understanding, forgave. But this, this was against Nature, this was a deliberate war of parent against child, the very deliberation of it was what frightened her. I said this to my uncle and he sniffed with scorn.

But did they not expect it, he said? Had not Lord North two months earlier moved a bill through the parliament declaring the province of Massachusetts to be in a state of rebellion?

Yes, I said, with some bitterness, and had not the king signed it at St James's Palace in a mood of celebration, his royal pleasure spiked with contempt of the colonists?

But those who are in a state of rebellion will rebel, said my uncle, and when they do so they must expect to be fired on by soldiers.

I frowned darkly. I shook my head.

Over the days that followed the rest of the story came in bit by bit, to be slowly assembled into a whole as they mulled and argued over it in the kitchens and taverns of Cape Morrock. They could not get enough of the redcoats' inglorious retreat from Concord, and the valour of the men and women who fought them every inch of the way, throwing up ambush after ambush as the British column limped back along the twisting narrow road to Boston – they were not so fearsome when the battle went against them! And if they had not been rescued, reinforced, that is, by a full brigade, with cannon, that came out of Boston to help them, they would have been destroyed.

News of these events was soon arousing patriots not only in New England but in all the colonies, and the courage of the people of Massachusetts gave heart to all who feared that their liberties were at mortal risk from the military occupation of their country.

Men in their hundreds were making for Boston now, where on the high ground around the town fortifications were going up and an army was coming into being, despite the fact that it had no uniforms, no cannon, and no leader. The British were under siege, and with no provisions arriving by road they had to live on salt cod. This gave them pleasure in New Morrock, where they knew all about the joys of salt cod. And when news of the British defeat reached London, friends of the American cause rejoiced at it, but the king proclaimed a British victory. This caused still greater amusement, this fresh display of royal folly.

And what of Martha? I am, and I say this without apology, although I can quite well imagine my uncle's toothless cynic's grin, I am a man of strong romantic sensibility, and I find it all too easy to be swept along on the torrent of fervour with which the Americans set about their revolution. It would be simple then to forget, that in the stuff and matter of the lives of the individuals caught up in the swift dangerous currents of this history, all was not quite so straightforward as it appears through the gauzy veil of hindsight.

And how true this is of Martha. When I think of her position on the eve of Lexington Green, before that first shot was fired, and the world was changed for ever – I glimpse a young woman at last stitched into the fabric of family and community and never again, so it would seem, to play the fugitive, the stranger, the sinner. And being one of them now, as she thought, she did what she could for the Revolution, which was not as much as she would have liked to do, for she was huge and ungainly, and easily tired, so vigorous were the demands of her unborn child.

For she saw that the women must rise to the occasion now. The men would go to war, some had gone already, but the life of the town must not suffer by their absence. And so for the women these were days of endless toil, not only at those activities which sustained their families in time of peace, no, they must also be taught to defend themselves. They were to be taught how to use firearms. Martha insisted on taking part in these drills, despite being so far gone in her pregnancy, determined as she was to learn how to fire a musket properly.

Then with the news from Lexington and Concord her feelings were at once swinging wildly about like a boat unmoored in the wind, her heart the tiller! For an hour she was calm, resolute, secure in the belief that the justice of the cause would secure an American victory. An hour later she was terrified, she saw only death and fire and smoke, and out of that smoke came first the faint tramp of marching feet – then a faintly beating drum, a single distant fife – then through the swirling mists the first glimpse of soldiers in faded red coats with muskets on their shoulders, and on the face of every man of them a brutish grin of hatred and lust such as she had seen on the face of Clyte, most hideous Englishman of them all! A thousand Clytes advancing on the women of New Morrock, coming down out of the woods in smoke and mist as the women ran out of their houses and lifted their flintlocks, but oh, to little avail against King George's soldiers, who overran the globe like wild dogs!

Then she would remember that the redcoats were far from indestructible, had they not fallen in their hundreds on the road back to Boston, did they not bleed and die like Americans, when a hail of musket fire ploughed their flesh? Our men are a match for them, she thought, they did well at Concord and will do better in the months to come, as they grow more artful in the ways of war. And having driven out the enemy they will return to their homes, and we will live in peace and plenty in our own free and independent land. And you, she thought, talking to her unborn child, as had become her habit, you will inherit all this, you will be the first citizen of the New World. At such times he gave her strength, and she told herself, it is for you, for you, for you – and pushed away the knowledge that the cause was already betrayed.

Events began to move now at a quickening tempo. News came that Captain Benedict Arnold of New Haven proposed to take a party of men to the lakes above the headwaters of the Hudson, and seize the cannon from the British garrison at Fort Ticonderoga. The call went out for volunteers, and among the men from New Morrock who came forward was Adam Rind.

Martha felt a great ghastly lurch in her belly when he told her this, and a rising in her throat, and the blood came rushing into her face, the strength of this reaction surprising even herself: and her own uneasy conscience played no small part in her distress, for she felt, somehow, in some powerful, wordless way, that her treachery would recoil upon her husband. Poor Adam, he was unable to meet her eye, and she was so shocked she could barely speak! Not for long. She argued with him, she wept tears of rage, she shouted at him, and at last his head lifted and with blazing eyes he told her the war would be lost before it was properly begun, for the want of a few cannon.

'A few cannon?' she cried. 'You think it a matter only of a few cannon? Have you not thought what a cannon can do to a man? Or a musket discharged into a man's face? Or a bayonet stuck in his guts?' Such injuries she had never considered until this moment, but hearing the boy talk so foolishly her imagination took fire and she quickly terrified the pair of them.

But he had already spoken of his plan to Silas, and he could not withdraw now. So Martha went to her uncle to ask him to forbid

Adam to go. Ah, such misdirected feeling, in one who always saw things true – thus did the knowledge of her treachery distort the motions of her heart. Silas heard her out, his eyes hooded, his chin resting on his fingertips, there in his great chair in the flickering masculine gloom of his sanctum. He heard her out and then allowed a silence, before saying at last: 'I believe him to be stronger than you think.'

'He is not strong!' she cried. 'He is a boy!'

'Is he not your husband?'

'He is my husband but he is not yet a man!'

Silas began quietly to laugh at this, which made her angrier still, and for some moments she could not speak. She rose from her chair and paced back and forth waddled, rather – scarlet with frustration.

'Perhaps you cannot see how he has changed.'

'How has he changed?' She sat down heavily. She was no longer capable of storming about a room. 'He is still a boy, and you are sending him to do a man's work and risk his life.'

'How does a boy become a man?'

'He grows to it, like a tree.'

'We have not time to grow our men like trees.'

'So you send him to his death.'

'We have all chosen to risk our lives. You have so chosen, Martha. You could have gone with the English officer. You chose to stay.'

Did nothing escape this man? Did he see into all the workings of her heart? No, not all its workings, he surely did not see her violation of the trust he had reposed in her.

'He is a boy!' she wailed.

'He must be allowed his choice. He has made it.'

She was sobbing now. Oh, she hated to give any man the satisfaction of seeing her weep, but since her child had begun to grow inside her she could not control her feelings as she once had. Silas had her come to him and took her on his lap, where she wept silently into his shoulder. As he stroked her hair he told her she had nothing to fear, this expedition would meet little resistance from the British, for they were not expecting a move of such boldness from the American side.

'They think us fools,' he murmured. 'You know that, Martha, you helped me give the Englishman that lie. They do not know we are coming. There are only a few men at the fort, and we shall take them by surprise. Adam will come to no harm.'

By this point she was more liquid than solid, and she could not think, she could not argue, her will was turned to porridge. Sniffling wetly she mumbled, 'No?'

'No.'

'And you will go too,' she wailed, 'and what will I do then?'

He pushed her gently from his shoulder so as to gaze into her splotched wet red mess of a face and asked her: 'Do you not think first of your husband?'

Mess though she was, she saw the danger here.

'Yes, yes,' she cried, 'but he is young!'

'And I will perish because I am not?'

Nothing for it but to wail and bury her head once more in his shoulder, crying, 'I don't know, I don't know!'

'Martha,' he said, 'this is not you. Where is my brave daughter, who understands me better than all the rest? Where is the girl who fled a madman and came to this country alone? You crave safety for those you love, but that is because you are with child. It is your nature now not to fight but to protect. This will pass. After your child is born you will remember that we must face dangers greater than anything Adam is about to meet.'

She had no argument left in her. She had done what she could. Oh, but to think of Adam off in the mountains of New York –!

'Martha Peake,' murmured Silas, and laid a hand on her great belly. Then he laughed shortly and his eyebrows lifted. 'Martha Peake? You are Martha Rind now. You are my daughter.'

She said nothing to this. She did not like it at all. She climbed down clumsily from Silas's lap. She had resolved that whatever the world called her she would not abandon her father's name. She would add her husband's name to her own but she would not displace her father, and she intended to inform Adam and Silas of this when she was stronger. Martha Rind Peake, this is how she would be known.

Early one wet and dismal morning Adam joined a group of militiamen marching to Boston. From there he would travel on to join Captain Arnold's expedition to Fort Ticonderoga. They were cheered on their way, and then the women of the Rind family turned to one another with pale grave faces. Martha was strong now, she did not weep. Few men were left in New Morrock, and of those few the able-bodied would be gone within days. Then it would be only the women to hold the town until the men returned. None of them was afraid that day. I believe women are never afraid when they know what must be done. Martha was not afraid. Adam was gone, poor brave boy, and Silas would be gone in a day or two, but Martha remained calm. She had stilled the voice of anxiety within her, and once more convinced herself that all would be well.

The last of the militia left two days later, Silas with them on his horse, his cloak billowing about him, and on his proud head a large black tricorn hat with silver edging and a blue cockade. Once again the women gathered outside Pierce's Tavern. A clear brisk day, and it was strange, the women were saying, and not for the first time, to be by the harbour on such a day in April and not see the boats going out. Many a goodwife cast her eyes seaward then turned away, shaking her head; all life was in disorder. The men formed up, Silas strode about giving instructions, inspecting this and that, until all was ready.

Then he came over to his womenfolk where they stood in a group on the dock with their shawls clutched about them in the wind. There were wordless embraces, kisses and tears, and Martha he left almost to the last.

'Martha Peake,' he said, and took her hands and gazed into her face as he had so often done before, as the wind picked at her hair and set it fluttering about her face, to which the blood now rushed from the fullness of her heart, and the emotions warring within it! She gazed back at him, holding his fingers tight and wanting only to fling her arms around his neck and tell him to be careful! But his gravity prevented her. He told her he wanted a strong and healthy grandchild, would she see to it? She would. He wanted his household to keep faith with the cause no matter what happened, would she see to it? She would. He wanted them all waiting when he came home from the war, would she see to that too? Oh she would, she would –! Then he swung himself on to his horse and cast a glance out to sea. Removing his hat, he murmured a brief prayer.

Then after saying a last tender farewell to his wife he turned his horse and cried to his men to go forward. Off they marched, off up the hill, and the women wandered after. The drum was beating a lively tattoo, the fife trilled a lilting light air, and there was laughter now amid the tears as the small boys ran alongside their fathers and brothers and uncles, and among the women a brief hope arose as they glimpsed in the step of the men and heard in the fife and drum a spirit that would surely carry them through the darkness to come. Martha knew now she could keep the promises Silas had asked her to, and that he would come home to a fine grandson and a family intact, a household united and sustained in his absence by hope and resolve. Caesar took up the rear of the column, and the last Martha saw of them was that man's broad back as the road turned off through the woods up the hill and the whistling fife grew fainter and fainter and then was heard no more.

32

For Martha and the other women the waiting began. With all the men gone off to Boston – save Joshua Rind, whose gouty foot made him unfit for service – there were no riders from Mr Adams, as there used to be; they could not spare riders just to keep the women informed, and so the women lived in ignorance of what was happening on the hills above Boston. They could only speculate, and try to convince themselves that the British would sue for peace, having seen the resistance at Concord, and being trapped in Boston under the American guns, what few there were.

So there they sat by the fire of an evening, busy with their needles in the candlelight, murmuring to one another about the men of the household and the men of the town, finding good reasons why each would be sure to acquit himself well in this business. Often the doctor sat with them, so there was at least one less empty seat at the table, and silently smoked his long white pipe; and the candle flame caught the women's flashing needles and threw out little sharp splinters of light as they stitched and stitched and with their hearts and their words made their men safe, one by one; and then they went back to the beginning and made them safe all over again.

The nights were more difficult, and Martha soon moved back in with her cousins rather than be alone in the bed she had shared with her husband. Still the night brought its terrors. The girls fell asleep quickly, leaving her to gaze from her pillow at the sky, to watch the moon racing among the clouds, and think of what would befall them all but particularly poor Adam, who was least able of any of them, so she thought, to survive the dangers he would face.

Would some good man look out for him, take him under his wing, this stripling boy? He gave her much worry, she felt he should never have been allowed to go, she daily grew less able to hold out hope for his return; and the thought that she might never see him again, this filled her with the utmost wretchedness and despair. His welfare was hers to vouchsafe, and she had lost him, she had allowed him to slip off into the Revolution, to be swept away into the howling wilderness of the Upper Hudson Valley and the lakes beyond – oh, he would perish, she was sure of it, and she would carry the shame of it to her grave. To think of him tramping through the wilderness for days and days and at the end being part of an assault on a fortress garrisoned by redcoats –! He would not survive it, he would perish if not from a musket ball then from weakness or sickness or a hundred other perils of the north woods. He would be scalped!

She would have made herself busy, the better to keep from brooding on these things; though such brooding was, in truth, but an expression of that anxiety which had gnawed at her heart since her last encounter with Giles Hawkins. Ah, but her condition prevented her doing little more now than sitting by the fire with her needle, and Joshua Rind was quick to notice her low spirits. She admitted they came of concern for her husband, and the doctor reassured her, telling her that Adam was stronger than she gave him credit for.

Could she believe this? She tried to, but whenever she saw him in her mind's eye he was the soft, tender, curious boy to whom she had taught the lessons of love high among the hay bales in the barn behind the house; or up in the woods, in a bed of leaves, himself filled with delight at discovering pleasure he had never dreamed of, living in his father's stern house, with the long shadow of his Puritan ancestors cast always across his soul. Was she wrong to believe that she knew him better and saw him more clearly than this gouty doctor? The boy who had clung weeping to her in a transport of ecstasy when first she had brought him to the height and climax of passion? Was she wrong to think that this tender youth would surely perish in the woods?

Nobody will ever take you from me, this was the promise she had made to her unborn child. But somebody would take him from her, and soon, too, for she had almost come to term. She had been visited several times by Hester Winthrop the midwife, who seemingly had delivered every infant in New Morrock for the past forty years. She had strange ways, old Hester, but the women of the town attested to her great art at pulling them out whole and screaming, and few were lost, they said, mother or child, with Mistress Winthrop attending. She was a vast ancient crone with a black mole the size of a penny on her upper lip from which sprouted a cluster of black hairs, and what few teeth remained in that collapsing jaw were yellow with decay. She carried about her compendious person numerous malodorous herbs and plants which she gathered in the forest, and she would produce from deep within her many layers of shawl and skirt a few stems or leaves of some green or brown or black thing and make a tea of it, which must be drunk no matter how foul the taste and stink of it. She had probed and poked Martha with her bent old fingers, the soil of her garden caked thick beneath the nails, and pronounced her strong and the boy within – she was at once certain of his sex, you see – as 'curious big'. Mistress Winthrop eyed her with some interest, from under her shaggy brows, and Martha did not know what she meant by 'curious big'.

She thought no more of it; she was eager now to be done with this pregnancy of hers, she wanted to move again, do her work, get outside, climb the hill – be mistress of her own body, which more and more felt like a ponderous great ship heaving into harbour, holds bursting with cargo and her planking beginning to split. Darling boy, she thought, I am weary of carrying you, I want you out in the world where I can hold you in my arms and gaze into your eyes and find your father there.

The day grew near and now she could only sprawl in her uncle's great chair, which had been carried into the kitchen, no other chair being big enough for the galleon Martha Peake had become. She lay there panting and flushed as the child stirred and kicked inside her, as eager, I believe, to be out, as Martha was to have him out. She drank what she could of Hester Winthrop's tea and poured away the rest. Her cousins were far more excited than she was. She had not the strength for excitement, she had ceased to be herself, she had become a simple docile creature capable of nothing but the rudimentary functions of a cow. She was a cow, in her own eyes, she was a beached whale – you have done to me, she murmured to her belly, what no man ever has, you have made me soft and slow and dull and stupid. Her emotions began to grow vague, and in those last days of her pregnancy she could barely arouse anxiety for Adam at all, or for her father, or for the American army gathered on the hills round Boston. She ate and slept and little else.

She awoke on the first day of May, to heavy rain and thunder, and sensed at once that he was ready; yes, and she sensed too that it would be a slow and stately progress, his entry into the world, and she did not hurry to send word to Mistress Winthrop, but waited until noon, sure that they would be many hours about the business. She was in her uncle's great chair when her water broke, buckets of it, and her aunt Maddy became at once brisk with authority and dispatched her daughters on various errands, Sara to get the great kettle boiling on the fire, Ann for clean sheets and towels, Hester to summon the goodwives who would assist Mistress Winthrop in her work. She did not trouble to send word to Joshua Rind, this was woman's work, but none of them doubted that the doctor would make an appearance regardless. As for Martha, she was ordered to bed, with warming pans, and told not to move, and the bedroom became for the next hours a busy place indeed, the very eye of a storm of womanly activity that matched the lashing rain and thunder and the gusts of a freshening gale, and Martha was happy for all the attention, not because she felt she needed it – it is surely not so very hard to push a baby out of your belly, she thought – but because it marked her child's birth for the profoundly solemn occasion it was.

And so she allowed herself to lie languid on a great heap of pillows, feeling in her warm clean nightshirt like a queen of sorts and reflecting on what sweet pleasure it was to have others waiting on her, alert to every whim and desire that she may chance to entertain. Maddy Rind saw this and remarked that she had better not get used to it, it was her child they attended, all she must do is stay alive, as he would shortly want her milk, and after the buckets of water that had flowed in the great chair he was sure to be a big one.

Soon enough he announced his intention of dominating this drama as muscular events beyond Martha's control dispelled her pleasant languor and had her heaving and sweating and crying out with pain. Mistress Winthrop now held the floor but did little as yet, taking Martha's hands tightly in her own and murmuring words she could not understand, she was so intent on trying to obey the manifest demands of her own body. Mistress Winthrop continued to murmur to her, and all Martha knew from her murmuring, for she was working hard, harder than she remembered working in all her life, was that all was well, all was going forward as it should.

She was pushing now, and the pushing seemed never to end, and strong as she was she had to stop every minute to catch her breath. Her aunt Maddy hovered over her and wiped the sweat off her face, which she was later told had turned a shade of red so deep it had never before been seen on human skin. Scarlet, then, wet with sweat and God knows what other nameless fluids that had seeped or flooded from her, surrounded by watchful murmuring women as the wind hammered at the windows and the house creaked like a ship, and aware now and then of Hester Winthrop's fingers down beneath the tented sheets, she tried to push a great thing out of what she knew to be an impossibly narrow opening, and it was like forcing a pig through a fence, the pain of it warning her that the fence must splinter for the pig to get through; and she was so sore and tender down there that the thought of her body being torn open filled her with terror, soon forgotten in the sheer bloody labour of sustaining the rhythm of her heaving muscles, which continued to perform the task given them by nature with scant regard for her pain. She was soon desperate for it to be over, and when next she paused and had her face wiped she weakly asked how much longer and heard a cackle from the midwife and a muttered response that gave her no great reassurance, something about a pumpkin.

It got worse. There was some screaming, she barely heard it herself, and in a small calm place in her mind she wondered who was screaming, and why they were screaming, and why nobody gave them comfort, but it was her, it was her, she was no longer a rational conscious being but a woman utterly under the tyranny of her own body. And so it went on, seemingly for ever – and then it changed! It changed. There was an intense sudden pain as though a hot poker had been thrust against her sex, there was a hideous sensation of *ripping* – and after that a sort of relief, for the first time a lessening in the intolerable pressure within her, but she could not rest, she could not pause, even, the contractions were coming closer and closer now, and when she cried out to the midwife the old woman did not cackle but said they were on the last mile, for his head had appeared, and a big one it was too.

His head! In the waves of relief all commingled with pain that came with the appearance of his head she seemed to recover her ability to think thoughts and feel feelings other than mere effort and torment, for the very idea of his head filled her with wild joy, his head, his body, his heart, his mind, his soul, so ran her thoughts – it was then that the promise of this child with which she had lived so long gave way to an idea a thousand times more powerful, which was his real and actual *presence*, her child, her son, and it was with *him* that she worked now to finish the business, she was now a *mother* helping her child in his first enterprise, and she spoke to him, whether in her mind or out loud, whether with clarity or in gasps and cries she did not know, but from then on they worked together, Martha Peake and her little Harry, and she whispered, Harry, Harry, come now, Harry, be strong, Harry, this time, Harry –

By now the storm had passed, the rain fell steady on the roof and all the world was wet. It was growing dark outside. Lamps were lit and one of the women said quietly that the doctor waited below, should he be wanted. Mistress Winthrop only snorted and asked for wine, and still working, peered down at Martha and asked her how she did. Martha, panting, told her she did well and the midwife said she was a strong girl and they should soon be done. The rest was completed an hour later, by which time Martha was exhausted, and her brief ecstasy of communion with her son had passed, as again the sheer labour of the thing obliterated the possibility of all other sensation. She heard him screaming! She heard his first tiny screams, and she struggled up from the pillow with what little strength remained to her to get a glimpse of him. There was silence in the room now, for Martha's baby had soon stopped screaming and instead spluttered and sneezed, his eyes tight shut like a little monkey and his tiny fists clenched. The women stood gazing at him and said nothing.

Darkness had fallen, the wind had dropped, and in the wavering candle flame Martha saw that all was not as it should be, that Hester Winthrop was frowning and clucking as she turned the infant about in her old clawed hands and the blood and the slime and some curious white stuff dripped off his slathered little body, and the cord from his belly yet hung between them. Martha propped herself up on her elbows, and as she gazed, exhausted, at her child, she saw with a flare of strange joy that he was indeed a little Harry, he had his father's spine.

DROGO HALL

Of its own beauty is the mind diseased,
And fevers into false creation.

BYRON

33

Francis Drogo had been dead for many years, this my uncle had told me, and I had no reason to doubt him. Yet one had the sense (and Drogo Hall is not the only house, in my experience, to have nourished the spirit of a late dominant master) – one had the sense that the house was not yet empty of him, or that he was not yet ready to quit it, for his presence still hung heavy about the place; and William and Percy being mere feeders upon the sepulchral animation of the house, there was little vitality beyond my own to help dispel these ghostly intimations of a former time. The footfall I had heard outside my room in the night: I had turned the thing over in my mind, I had examined it from every possible point of vantage, and no other explanation was satisfactory.

Once already I had left my room in the early morning, during that period of exalted creation, as I now think of it, when Martha gave birth, and with my pistol in my pocket I had come downstairs into the entrance hall and spent some time in Drogo's Theatre of Anatomy, where the bodies of Mary Magdalen Smith and countless others had come under the master's knife, and the steep-tiered benches rising in a semi-circle almost to the ceiling were filled with doctors all of whom had long since passed away. I found it thick with dust and festooned with cobwebs, the early sunshine that drifted through the bespattered skylight providing but meagre illumination for any operation that might now be attempted on the dissecting table below, where the blood of Drogo's cadavers had stained the woodwork black in patches. There was much scuttling behind the wainscots and panelling, and the tiny bones of a small bird that had somehow found its way into the room, and then been unable to get out again, lay scattered among a few feathers in the dust and droppings on the floor.

The door creaked loudly when first I entered, and the boards groaned as I descended into the well of the room. The air was stale and stank of mildew, and it was not hard to imagine those eminent men of medical science coming to this grim place to hear his lordship lecture, and see him cut. A recessed door, leading, I believe, to the cellars, was locked, and having no idea where its key was kept I determined to find another way to get down there. And why? For this reason. I had come to the conviction that there remained one service I could still perform for Harry Peake. For yes, in the last hours my mind had ranged widely across the matter of this history, and I had arrived at an understanding of the final weeks of that poor man's life.

Clyte, I feel sure, was always present, Clyte would never have let Harry out of his sight, after the contract was signed, but tracked him across the marsh and through the town, lurking in the shadows in the night cellars where Harry spent Drogo's coin, watching over him when he sank into stupor, and later following him back out on to the Lambeth Marsh; Harry having forgotten, if he had ever truly known it, that his daughter had fled from Drogo Hall for ever. And with every day that passed, so did the weather worsen. The rain that fell on the marsh was cold and hard, and not even the bullish strength that had sustained him this long, not even his giant constitution could withstand the cruel autumn rainstorms, nor the scything winds; and he weakened. But knowing what I did of the man, I could not believe that even in a weakened state he would willingly give himself to the darkness at the end. No, I believe there arose in him a last magnificent impulse of defiance, a rising of the spirit, and with it a turning away from the diabolical bargain he had made with Drogo, and with that, perhaps – and here I truly speculate, for I myself have not the Christian faith, I worship in a very different church – with that recognition of the frailty of his own will – a turning toward God? Toward a merciful saviour? Not as uncommon as you might imagine, in men who find themselves as utterly alone as Harry was, as they draw near to death.

And if he did indeed turn, did a prospect open in his benighted mind, indeed more than a prospect, a vision – a vision of the Last Day, the dead everywhere rising from their graves, to stand before the Lord and be judged? I think it not impossible. Harry Peake, having failed to achieve the spiritual renewal he once thought could be his; having failed to overcome the mortal antagonist, his own body; and having with that failure sunk to the depths of Nature, become a prisoner of Nature – Harry Peake, I believe, glimpsed at the last the possibility of redemption. He glimpsed a way to stand before the Almighty and seek election to Paradise. And I believe that he then went to Drogo, and pleaded with him to be released from his contract – and Drogo said no. Drogo denied him. Drogo had paid for those bones, and he would have them.

What then – a rage, a great wild storm of destruction that had Drogo and William retreating up the staircase, and Clyte cowering in some high place, atop a lofty wardrobe, like a distressed bat, while Harry laid about him in a fury? I think not. I think when Harry saw the chance of redemption he became quiet, he sobered, he wished to keep the idea before him with some clarity. So no, no great act of destruction, instead he crossed the hall and walked out of the front door and down the steps and on to the marsh; and Clyte, from a distance, with caution and cunning, was, as ever, his shadow. And when Harry's time came, when alone, in some cold damp garret room, he turned his face to the wall – Clyte was below, waiting for him in the small black carriage.

So Harry went to his death without even the comfort of believing that he would rise again on the Last Day, to stand whole and shining before the God of Love. But I would defy my uncle, yes, and Clyte, and Drogo most of all, I would give Harry that comfort, I would take his scavenged bones and secure a Christian burial for them, and where? – in the old graveyard by the church.

Ah, but first I had to find them. That morning while the house slept I had done little more than explore those rooms and corridors that were not locked against me. Everywhere I came upon the remnants of Drogo's fine furnishings, phantom glimpses of what the house had been in its days of glory. Neglect and damp were responsible for the damage, for not only did the house stand chill and unheated winter after rainy winter, with the exception of the few rooms my uncle used, but the roofs leaked in various places and no effort had been made to repair them. This accounted for the smell of mildew and the presence of lichen and moss clinging to the floorboards and creeping up the walls. Many of the old Turkey carpets had been ruined, and as for the great paintings, the old masters and such, smoked by time and clustering thickly in baroque gilded frames on Drogo's walls and staircases – on close inspection, with the aid of a good wax candle, I found them to be covered with a soft furry coat of black lichen which seemed to feed upon the oil in the paintwork.

Nor had Drogo's collection of statuary escaped the parasites. Fine sculptures of classical figures standing in handsome long rows along the corridors of the public rooms downstairs were discoloured and patchy, colonized like so much else of the house by the creeping lichens that needed only a good damp climate, a cool temperature, and gloom, to flourish and proliferate; and it occurred to me, when first I became aware of the extent of the damage done here by damp, that this house would be hard to burn down. All that was flammable – furniture, carpets, bedclothes, the many thousands of Drogo's books, including the old ones shelved behind glass – the very stuff and fabric of the house – it would be impossible to set fire to it, and whatever end fate had chosen for Drogo Hall, a charred ruin it would never be.

Thus my thoughts in the long reaches of the night, thoughts that I could not of course share with my uncle William, for he had been complicit in all this – had he not produced the inkpot and quill when the contract was signed? Was he not desperate to see Harry as the crowning achievement of the Museum of Anatomy? Did he not eagerly feed his master's appetite for strange bones? So when next I saw him – I still had not located the museum – when next we met, as we did each day at four, in his study, to continue with this edifice of history we were constructing, which encompassed now the first phase of the struggle of the American people to free themselves from precisely the sort of imperial bondage that Drogo practised on Harry Peake – when next we met I was more than ever guarded, circumspect, alert to every devious shift and feint in what the old man said, always correcting against the bias, against the *skew*, groping through the boggy twilight of obfuscation for the truths that gleamed like pearls within!

34

Martha Peake sat up in her bloody bed with her arms stretched out to her newborn son and the tears streaming down her cheeks as her heart overflowed with waves of love of a power and purity she had never known before. They wanted to take him and swaddle him before she could have him but she cried out fiercely, her fatigue and pain forgotten, and the women at last shifted their astonished eyes from her child to herself and hearing her claiming him, looked at one another, and even Maddy Rind for once did not know what to do.

But Hester Winthrop did. She came to the bed with the infant in her arms and tenderly gave him to Martha. She received him with wondering gratitude and sank back on her pillows with her little Harry on her breast and her fingers on his tiny spine. What a mess he was! She took an edge of the sheet and wiped his head clean – his skull was covered in a fine soft down of the palest red imaginable – and then she wiped his back, and how could she think of that delicate flare of tiny bone as a flaw, the thought did not occur to her, he was beautiful, he was a kind of miracle, inexplicable, a mystery, she would not have believed anything so perfect could be created in this world had he not been lying in her arms, alive. Asleep! He had fallen asleep! He made her laugh, little man exhausted by his labours when it was she who had done all the work!

He slept. She stroked the great soft dome of his skull, she stroked his little curved twig of a backbone, she wept and laughed and clucked and murmured and when at last she looked up, the women stood in a clutch in the candlelight gazing at her, all but Mistress Winthrop, who was busy with her herb bag.

'He is called Harry,' she whispered, for she did not want to wake him. None of the women uttered a word.

'What's the matter?' she whispered. Still nothing. She grew alarmed.

'What's wrong?' she said. 'Is he not well?'

'He is well,' said Mistress Winthrop, not looking up.

'Then what is it?'

Maddy Rind spoke at last. 'It is this, Martha, we are surprised, we did not expect –'

'What?' She truly did not understand.

'His back,' she said, and fell silent, gazing at Martha now with damp eyes that seemed imploring or compassionate, she could not tell which.

'He has my father's back,' she said.

'But what a sad thing,' said Maddy Rind, sitting by the bed, laying a hand on Martha's cheek, gazing at her with eyes like pools, she was that close to tears.

'I am not sad,' said Martha.

'But think of Adam.'

Adam? What had he to do with this? She was perplexed, but it was a mere breath of a breeze on the deep strong warm wordless flow of love that rose inside her. This talk of Adam was unimportant, she had her son in her arms! She turned away from her aunt and gazed once more at the little miraculous being asleep on her breast. She smelled his skin and felt his tiny shallow gulps of breath. Was that all? If he was strong and well as Mistress Winthrop said, what else mattered? Maddy Rind glanced at the other women and they turned away and one after another silently left the room.

Maddy then stood gazing uncertainly down at Martha, and Martha was filled with love for her too. She took her aunt's hand and brought it to her lips. She thanked her. She glowed, she was radiant, she was all love. Maddy smiled down at her niece but her forehead was a knot of worried questions. Martha tried to reassure her, she laid her aunt's hand gently on her baby's skull and covered it with her own.

'Adam will be happy,' she said.

'I hope so, Martha,' said Maddy. She sat down again and still stroking his head, stared hard at the sleeping infant.

'I hope so,' she said again, and still Martha heard those worried questions in her voice.

*

A little later Martha's cousins were allowed to come and see her infant son. They did not stand back as the women had, they were curious, they were filled with wonder, they were adoring. They looked at Martha with new eyes, they had not dreamed their loud cousin from England could create a little being with eyes and hands who spluttered and clenched his tiny fingers, who had hair as soft as spun silk and skin as clear as light. Very gently they traced the curve of the little hump on his back, and were astonished at how soft the little bones were. They declared him perfect and Martha lay there bathing in their pleasure and allowed Sara to hold him in her arms, and oh, she was so careful, there was no need to warn her what a precious cargo she held. She gazed down at his face with great seriousness.

'Little man,' she whispered.

None of the women had asked to hold him, but the Rind girls were eager to, and as one by one they lifted him into their arms Martha wondered why the women had behaved so strangely. Did they think the child bewitched? Did they think the hand of Satan was in the making of his backbone? She had heard similar nonsense in her few months in New Morrock, for the beliefs of a century past lived on in certain minds which had had no benefit of education – did they think she had lain with the devil? It suddenly made her want to shout with laughter, that an idea so ridiculous could still be taken seriously when a new age of reason was teaching men that old beliefs, like old systems of government, must be swept away – and for a minute or two a passion stirred in her, a spark or two drifted up from the slumbering embers – until she remembered again the infant in her arms; and when this blindly groping little creature sought her breast and began to suckle, she lay back and thought of nothing, and all ideas of Progress and Reason slipped away like so many pieces of flotsam drifting on the tide.

Three days she remained in bed and she would not let Harry out of her sight despite all attempts on the part of her aunt to take him away from her. Joshua Rind came up to tell her what was customary in the first days after birth, but she told him she did not give a fig for custom, she only cared for her son, and that she intended to look after him herself. The doctor examined Harry's spine, he peered at it through his spectacles, he frowned at it and tentatively touched it with a finger, then threw a glance at Martha that at once convinced her that he too thought she had had congress with the devil. When she said this he became embarrassed and said no no no, but in such a way that she suspected he had entertained the idea, or one similar to it. He pronounced no judgement on her Harry and went away still frowning, after patting her hand and absently congratulating her on bringing a healthy American boy into the world.

'He will be named for his father, then?' he said, pausing at the door. Martha lifted her head from the pillow. He would be named for his father, of course he would, he had been already; but the doctor meant Adam.

'He will be named for my father,' she said, and the doctor nodded and left the room.

He was not impressed with this nephew of his, the backbone troubled him it was plain to see, but Martha knew that in time he and the rest of them would come to see her son as she did, and then it would not matter what shape his back was. She did not say this yet, she knew the reputation young mothers had for creating grand illusions about unremarkable infants, but her Harry was different. This was no foolish illusion. There was greatness in him even then, and she did not need to explain this to others, it would become clear to them all in time.

Three days she lay abed; and then she could lay there no longer, even though she was still stitched up with catgut where Harry had torn her, the stitching done swiftly and neatly by her aunt Maddy, and the wound not yet fully healed. She was sore, but she could move about, and what pleasure it was to have her body as it used to be, no longer vast and bovine. Harry was an easy child to care for, he never cried, he slept sound, and if his hunger for her milk left her red and tender she did not care, it was for him and he was welcome to it all. He quickly lost the blindly wrinkled appearance of the first hours and became instead a placid handsome baby with a huge wispy red skull and tiny perfect limbs. She had always to lay him on his belly when he slept, for fear he would crush his spine.

But what a beautiful spine it was! The morning after the night he was born Martha made an extraordinary discovery about her baby's spine.

She had slept deep and long after her labours. In a clean nightshirt, and between clean sheets, her body bathed and stitched and her sore parts smeared with ointments, she had sunk into the most blessed oblivion she had ever known. Harry had slept beside her in a crib on rockers which in its time had served all the Rind children. She awoke to a day of wind and blue sky, the storm having passed out to sea leaving the air and the land cleansed and fresh.

For a second on awakening she did not know what had happened to her and why she hurt; then she sat up and leaned over to the crib, which she had pulled close to the bed before falling asleep, and found her son lying on his belly and stirring into wakefulness, his face all squeezed tight, his little hands groping about him. And then he yawned, he yawned hugely, she was delighted by this great yawn and clapped her hands to her face lest she shout out with joy and frighten him! He yawned, and then he opened his eyes.

Martha heaved herself gingerly out from under the sheets and sitting on the edge of the bed, lifted him out of his crib. He made not a sound. He gazed at her with an expression of profound contentment in which she thought she glimpsed a hint of a spark of interest in the large female beaming at him with eyes filled with tears. They were alone together for the first time. Feeling the warmth of his mother's body he closed his eyes and lay against her breast, and did this with such utter *trust* that she was unable now to hold back the tears and they rolled down her face even as she smiled and murmured and stroked his soft head. She could hear her cousins in the yard below, she could see the sky, big white clouds kicking along before the wind, she knew days like this and loved the salty freshness they brought; so she stood up, painfully, and carried him to the window. It was the first day of his life!

She showed him the world. That is, she showed him as much of the world as could be seen from the back of Silas Rind's house, that much world comprising a yard, a well, a barn, a broad field that Silas and Caesar had cleared with their own hands, a wall they had built with stones dug up from the earth in that field, three grazing horses, a wagon, several outhouses and woodsheds, an old boat up on blocks, a vegetable garden with a high fence to keep out the deer, and beyond that the forest, where the first foliage created a distant canvas of shimmering greenness, and the high boughs tossed in the wind. Beyond the forest lay the mountains, still with snow on their peaks, huge indomitable mountains, and beyond them more mountains, and beyond them still more, and great river valleys between filled with good rich pasture and game, on and on into the west, all of it America, and Martha said this to her son.

'America,' she whispered, as Harry blinked at the world. 'Springtime,' she whispered. 'And there,' she whispered, 'friends.'

The three girls had seen them at the window, they had been watching for them, and now they stood waving and calling out, 'Good morning, Harry!' But it was too much for him, America and springtime and friends, all on his first morning, and his face puckered like a prune, he let out a wail, so Martha went back to bed and produced from inside her nightshirt a large breast. Harry laid to with a will.

It was not until later, when he was fed, and had slept again, that she made her discovery. She was again standing with him at the window, and his nightshirt had slipped off his shoulders so he was bare from the waist up. As she held him against the glass the light of the day streamed in and she saw that so delicate was the little structure of flared bone lifting from his spine, so fragile and porous the membrane of skin stretched over it, that it let through the light, it was translucent, it seemed almost to glow, to shine, it seemed ethereal, a thing without substance or mass, for within she could distinguish each of the tiny white bones of its construction. Later, as he grew, his skin lost its translucency and she never saw those tiny bones again. But that day she saw her child's spine through a film of skin as fine as the finest muslin, and she knew at once that this was no stigma, nor a piece of mere clumsiness in the work of careless Nature, no, it was given him to mark him out from other men, and she would teach him to carry it with pride.

35

So the first days passed. Little Harry groped and blinked and fed and slept and rarely showed any sign of discontent, and life went on in a town without men, the women providing what they had been told the Revolution required of them – that is, that they be the alert second line but also the peaceful embodiment of continuity. Though Martha was at this time so deeply occupied with her infant and his welfare that her stronger passions were entirely diverted from the cause.

Silas, it seemed, was well, camped with his men on a hill above Charlestown, but of Adam nothing was known, the expedition to Ticonderoga having sent back no messengers to report its progress. Maddy Rind worried about her son coming home to find his child a humpback, but Martha knew Adam's nature, he was a good boy and would share her delight in the child, believing himself the father.

Then one day it occurred to Martha that it was not Adam's reaction to the infant that worried her aunt, *but Maddy's own*. She saw how Maddy never picked him up, how she watched him with troubled eyes, and how, when Martha tried to make her see him as she did, her aunt turned away and went off about her tasks. All at once she suspected that Maddy had been listening to the old women, and had decided that this little monster of Martha's could not have come from the seed of a Rind.

This was a bad shock. This frightened her. She knew how the ignorant reacted to those who differed from them in some marked way, how they subdued the disorder they felt by invoking the figure of the monster, had she not seen what they did to her father? Now they would do it to her son. But the thought of it only stiffened her resolve. For there was a bedrock of dogged resistance in Martha Peake that would see her fight to the last breath for that which she loved; and she would die for her son, of this she was certain. She did not care about herself, let them revile her as much as they wanted, just so long as Harry could find shelter in her shadow.

In time the little rocking crib came down to the kitchen, and there Harry spent his days as the women went about their work around him. Martha was pleased to have the company of her cousins, for they did not share their mother's aversion to her child. They continued to declare him perfect, and lifted him from his crib with such tenderness it filled her with deep joy to see it. The older women watched with sidelong glances, or from lowered eyes, and she did not try to guess what new strange notions they had invented to explain to each other why his spine was deformed. It was not easy to live beneath a constant cloud of suspicion but she was equal to it, and believed it would change as soon as the men came back.

Whenever they were alone together Martha whispered her fears to Harry, and her hopes too. She took him with her when she first left the house and walked down to the dock with Sara, to learn what news there was from Boston. And she was aware at once that the changed attitude toward her in Maddy Rind's kitchen was shared by other women in the town, who sat working on the boats in the sunshine, but turned away when Martha and Sara approached, and watched them as they passed, then whispered to one another behind their hands, spitting into the harbour and touching the various talismans they secreted in the depths of their scaly clothing.

Martha had seen how the Americans celebrated the birth of a child, the impression they gave that each new American strengthened their claims and prospects on this continent; as though they knew they were engaged in a great act of creation, and that with every new child they acquired another pair of hands to assist in the task. Another American mind, another American heart, another American back; but it seemed they wanted nothing to do with her Harry's back. So she displayed him to the world all the more proudly, hurt and angered by their cruelty but determined not to show it.

She stood with her baby at the end of Rind's Wharf, arm in arm with Sara, and gazed out to sea. No doubt the women believed she was thinking warmly of England, but no, she was damning them all to hell, and she told Sara she did not care what they thought of her, she had faced hardships a hundred times worse than the malign idiocy of old women who had never read a book. But she regretted most bitterly that the fierce joy she had in her son was soured by the hostility of these certain elements of the town. She stared out to sea with her child in her arms and prayed for the men to come back. Everything would change when the men came back.

The Congress met in Philadelphia in May. They had much to discuss. John Adams faced men from other colonies who believed there was still some point in trying to negotiate with the king. How Martha snorted when she heard this! The English would not let them go without a fight, she felt she knew them well enough by now. The idea of liberty may have arisen in England, but there it had withered on the branch because the English continued to bow the head and kiss the boot of men whose power and wealth came from the accident of birth, no more than that. As if a man's value, his virtue, his character could be inherited from his father and not *earned*! Whereas here in the New World it did not matter who your father was; and just as well, thought Martha, when she reflected on her own child's paternity.

Meanwhile the patriot army sat by its campfires on the hills above Boston and waited. In New Morrock the women talked of politics and food supplies and had to be content with what few scraps of either came their way. With many of the boats still out of the water, and the men who sailed them far away, the cod that fed the town and created its wealth remained at liberty in the sea. Sara, with mischievous intent to annoy her mother, declared at supper one night, as they made another frugal meal of corn and potatoes, that cod had rights too.

'We are surely no better than the tyrant on the throne of England if we use them solely for our own needs and pleasure,' she said. 'Perhaps,' she said, 'after the war, the cod will be allowed to create a republic in the sea.'

Martha thought this very amusing, but her aunt sniffed, while Joshua Rind peered at Sara over his little spectacles and asked her, was she serious? When she told him that indeed she was, he said he would attempt to make peace with his conscience and remain a republican among men but a tyrant in the matter of fish. Hester Rind then declared that she would eat no more potatoes, for did not potatoes have rights too? This presented a problem, said Sara, for if people starved to preserve the liberty of potatoes, then the republic of potatoes would be lost, for there would be nobody to plant them and dig them.

Joshua Rind then remarked that the king undoubtedly regarded his colonial subjects as potatoes and justified abusing their rights for the same reason. They decided that alas, potatoes must be deprived of their liberty if the race of potatoes was to survive. They were all tyrants, said Sara, all of them having devoured their potatoes, then added that only Harry was innocent, for he took nourishment from his mother's breast and this did not affect her liberty at all.

At the mention of Harry's innocence Martha caught a sharp glance from her aunt Maddy; such talk did not go on when Silas was present! Rising to clear the table she suggested to the doctor that he stop talking rubbish about potatoes and tell them what he had heard of the doings of the Congress.

There was news, said Joshua, important news, and they were all at once impatient to know what it was. Joshua Rind, gouty rooster among the hens, enjoyed moments of power like this, and he took his time charging up that dreadful stinky white pipe of his with the tiny quantity of tobacco he allowed himself in these days of general shortage. Having lit it with a taper, and inhaled the only decent mouthful he was likely to get from it, he looked round the table and at last told them that Mr Adams – not Silas's Mr Adams, the other one, John Adams – in his wisdom John Adams had put forward for General of the Continental Army not his old friend Mr Hancock, but George Washington of Virginia.

Martha gave a shout of joy that startled them all. Sara asked her why she was happy and she told her. George Washington was a most passionate friend of liberty, she said. He was a tall well-made man, she said, with broad shoulders, and he rode a horse well. Joshua Rind said dryly he knew many tall men who rode a horse well. But Martha had long held a picture in her mind of George Washington, and had come to believe he was a man like her father. Not bent and anguished, no, but with her father's spirit, whole and straight, the new man rising – the American within.

I sat at my table that night with pen poised and dripping and thought of the portrait of Harry Peake hanging in my uncle's study. I am my mother's son and I too have an American within, but oh, he is trapped, as Harry's American was trapped; and like Harry's American he can only be conjured to life in art, which of course is no life at all!

36

The next they heard – the next *I* heard, the following day, my uncle, to my astonishment, having decided to take up the reins of the story once more, and carry it through to the end, so he said, claiming it had all 'come back' to him – the next they heard, he said, George Washington had arrived at Dorchester Heights and taken command of the Continental Army, while down below – in the besieged town of Boston, he meant – the British were suffering terrible hardship. The flux raged, order was breaking down, floggings and executions every day, houses torn down for firewood, horses butchered for food, and still the troopships promised for the army's evacuation failed to appear. The only Americans left in Boston, he said, were loyalists and traitors and a few rebel spies.

And in New Morrock?

Ah, New Morrock. Some shaking of the head here. Some drumming of the fingers. Flux there too, he said, Joshua Rind went from house to house but there was little he could do. Nothing to eat! A few scraps of salt pork, a few early vegetables, what fish they could catch in the harbour. And that, said my uncle, here assuming the gravest of tones, and looking me straight in the eye, was how things stood when two British sloops appeared out to sea early one morning in June.

Now this really was the most extraordinary thing. Not the British sloops – their arrival might have been anticipated – no, I mean my uncle William involving himself once more in what he had always dismissed as 'the American adventure'. I was at a loss to explain it. And he did not speak in a scornful manner, nor was there any of the hesitation you might expect in a man whose memory was stirring to life after a long period of slumbering inactivity. He spoke, rather, in a way I had not heard him speak before: slowly, clearly, and with great seriousness, such that I set down my glass and sat forward, listening close, all my faculties concentrated upon what he said.

The townspeople, he began, became aware at first light of the presence of the enemy vessels, when the church bell started ringing before its time and woke them from sleep. They had long been prepared for this. Martha had heard the men talking about the chances of the *Lady Ann* or another vessel being intercepted and searched on her way in; or, in some moment of indiscretion, a Cape Morrock man being overheard by some loyalist spy; and they had argued over what tactics the militia should employ, if a British ship did come.

But they had no militia now. The militia was a part of the Continental Army a hundred miles away. Nor had they much in the way of weapons, nor any clear idea what they could do to oppose a British landing party other than blaze away at them from their houses. In the Rind household there were two muskets, two pistols and an old blunderbuss, all primed and loaded and standing against the wall by the window at the front of the house, and if the soldiers came the women intended to fire on them, as they had been taught to. There was haste and some panic in the town as the church bell rang, and the two ships, out close to the horizon, were now seen to be making for the coast under full sail. By good fortune a few men who had come up from Boston were still in the town, and a meeting was called in the church.

Joshua Rind sent a boy up to the house to tell them to come at once, so Martha bundled Harry in her shawl, and she and Sara hurried out with the rest. Five minutes later they were standing at the back of the church among the other women and children. Dan Pierce, brother of Nat, attempted to keep order, but it was not a tranquil meeting. The first excitement had subsided somewhat, but the church was alive with anger and fear. Some were angry that Silas Rind had left none of his militiamen behind, although this line of argument was quickly abandoned, planning rather then recrimination being required now. Some said they should simply surrender, so that they might save their homes and live to fight another day, but this idea did not catch the spirit of the women, who discovered once they had come together that they were in no mood to concede a thing to the British, let alone meekly surrender. The mood softened somewhat when Joshua suggested they evacuate the town, simply collect what they could carry in the way of food and bedding and go south on foot. This plan was more attractive but it raised a serious question, and the women rose one after another to speak to it: what would happen to the very young, the aged, and the sick?

Martha, said my uncle, his voice heavy with feeling now, and his old eyes shining in the firelight, listened to all this with growing horror. She could no longer pretend to herself that her conversation with Giles Hawkins had been inconsequential. There was little doubt in her mind now as to what those ships had come for. She stood there with Harry in her arms, apparently listening intently to all that was said, but in fact hearing not a word, aware instead only of the storm of feeling within her. Oh, a great, great sorrow – she did not want this place smashed up by the British, she did not want these people turned out of their houses and forced to suffer God knows what ravages at the hands of men whose brutality was familiar to them all – they were women and children, with a mere handful of old muskets between them, what could they do against a company of redcoats? And this, said my uncle, was the question to which the town meeting was attempting to find an answer – when all at once the door of the church was hauled open, and a boy ran in, clutching a spy-glass and shouting something about the ships!

Here the old man paused for some moments, breathing fast.

Confusion now, he whispered, when he had composed himself once more, as all debate ceased and the women cried at the boy to tell what he knew, but the poor lad was soon bewildered, no sooner starting to answer a question than another was flung at him, and after a minute or two he simply stood there in the aisle with his mouth hanging open. Then Dan Pierce called him up to the front and at once there was silence. The boy walked between the silent pews and when he reached the front of the church he was sat down in a chair and Dan Pierce spoke to him quietly, then listened to the boy's whispered reply.

Dan Pierce straightened up, frowning, and turned to face the people. He was a big raw-boned fisherman with a face so burnt by the sun and blasted by the wind it resembled old boot leather. He gazed at them for a second and the silence grew profound.

'This boy,' he said, 'has seen the names of the British ships.'

They waited.

'One is called the *Bristol*.'

The name meant nothing.

'The other is the *Queen Charlotte*.'

Uproar at this – the *Charlotte*! Oh, now Martha's heart sank utterly, and she felt the colour rise in her cheeks. All the women were talking at once, and it seemed they were reaching the same conclusion. They were turning to where Martha stood at the back of the church, they were pointing at her, their faces were distorted by hatred and rage, on their lips was one name only – and that was hers!

37

Martha Peake shrank against the back wall of the church clutching her infant to her breast; and it was at this dramatic juncture in the history, with herself seemingly undone at last, that my uncle, gasping for breath, lifted a trembling finger, and pleading fatigue – declared it was enough, and shook his little bell!

A small cry escaped my lips, as I lurched forward in my chair, twitching, in a very *fervour* of desperation to know what happened next – barely had he resumed the narrative, and already he was tiring! I begged him not to leave me like this, but he sighed, and shook his head, and I knew there was no point in harassing him once he had begun to fade. I paced the floor as he sat waiting for Percy to come and take him off to bed. I myself was not in the least tired, having ingested a liberal dose of the medicines I took nightly now so as to avoid a recurrence of the marsh fever.

My mind worked quickly. I watched as old bent Percy came shuffling in, mumbling to himself, clutching a lamp, a sparse white stubble on his cheekbones and a line of spittle down his chin. William was ready for him. They had a sort of ritual, a sort of mating dance in which my uncle would seize Percy's arms and then, rocking himself backwards and forwards, build sufficient momentum to launch himself out of his chair, to be held and steadied by Percy, the pair having first reeled back together before finding their balance and at the last standing panting face to face in the weak glow of the fire. Then they hobbled off out the door, William gripping Percy's arm and Percy holding up the lamp before them. Muttering and wheezing they shuffled away down the darkened corridor in a small flickering nimbus of gloomy lamplight.

I watched them go, then closed the door and strode about the room, a glass in my hand, pausing to stir up the fire, replace my uncle's rug on his chair, and gaze a moment or two at the portrait of Harry Peake, who had gazed down at me these last nights with what I now understood to be *supplication*. Yes, I had at last fathomed the mystery of the great knotted brow, of the deep dark eyes, the grim set jaw. It is, perhaps, the most dangerous of illusions, to imagine that one can ever know another human being, particularly a dead one; but at that moment I felt I knew Harry Peake.

The moon had set when I left the house, the sky was that eerie starless blue of the hour before the dawn, the air was chill and the ground damp. Faint coils and tendrils of an early mist drifted over the gravel and weeds, and off among the trees a bird cried out, there was a scuffling in the branches, then silence. Drogo Hall loomed over me vast and dark. Keeping to the shadows by the wall I made my way with some stealth to the courtyard at the back of the building, sure that I would find there a set of steps down to the cellars where the bodies were prepared. Had not Martha Peake entered the house by way of those steps, when first she fled her father and came to Drogo Hall?

They were there; but disused these twenty years, and overgrown with grass and moss and weeds, and treacherous with slime underfoot. I descended with great trepidation, feeling my way, my hands on the bricks, the soles of my boots tentative on the slippery stones. I reached the bottom and the darkness was total, and in my nostrils a rank stench of putrefaction, as though dead things had been left there to soften to carrion to be eaten. I pushed at the door; it did not budge. I pushed again; it was shut tight and unyielding. I pushed for the third time, harder now, and it scraped an inch inward, the bottom of the door rotted away in places with damp, and grating horribly on the uneven stone floor. Then I put my shoulder to it, and a moment later had it wide enough that I could squeeze sideways into the pitch blackness within.

Heart thumping now, blood racing in my veins, I stood inside the cellar to which I had been unable to gain access from above. The air was stale, dead, foetid. From my pocket I took a stub of candle and a flint, and in a moment I had a small flame in the darkness, though at first it gave me no sense of what kind of place I had entered. Why am I here, what do I hope to find in these foul-smelling cellars – is his museum, in truth, here below? These were questions I had already pondered, and having searched Drogo Hall without success, both the house itself and the older buildings which clung to its walls, I had suddenly seized upon this dawning insight, that once Drogo possessed the bones of Harry Peake he would wish to display them only to a trusted few, fearing to make public the fact that the great haunted poet, as familiar a London figure in his decline as in his better days, had fallen into his lordship's clutches and been boiled down for a skeleton.

I moved forward slowly over old damp flagstones, my stubby candle held before me, and giving me only walls of brick and stone. A vast deep brooding silence suffused this desolate subterranean place, but like all vast deep brooding silences after some minutes it betrayed to the ear a host of small sounds which together consti-tuted that silence, and as I edged uncertainly forward I now became aware of a symphony of tiny furtive scrapings, distant creaks and timbered wheezings, vague throbs which vanished when I brought my senses to bear upon them and which might well have issued from within my own bodily edifice. What large old house is not an asylum for myriad species of bird, mammal and insect life: the delicate twilight pipistrelles in the attic, the sparrows and martins, the rats, mice, moths, beetles, weevils, lice, mites, fleas, earwigs and spiders – oh, many many spiders – not to say, in this wet place, toads, natterjack toads, all these the house supported as well as its two old men and a number of elderly feral cats dedicated to gluttony and sloth rather than any useful predatory work. Given this organic fibre in the very walls and beams, floors and chimneys, attics and drains of Drogo Hall, then any silence one heard at dead of night was in reality alive with discreet activity, and my ear soon became attuned to it. That noisy silence was then shattered by a huge muffled distant *thump*.

I froze. I was aware of a sort of tremor briefly running through the building around me, transmitted beam by beam and stone by stone in an instant and then gone, followed by a silence that was for some seconds absolute – before the scratchings and scamperings, the borings and chewings and throbbings resumed. Rigid, petrified,

I watched my candle flame tremble in the cold air and then burn steady again. The sound was not repeated. I dared not move. Surely a great beam had fallen? Some vast solid piece of timbered furniture come down upon a planked floor in a remote chamber? A block of stone toppled from the battlements, to plunge to a courtyard below?

I began to move forward once more, a sick sensation of fluids in disorder churning within me, my hand unsteady and my hair prickling upon my scalp, as I summoned every last part of courage my heart would furnish me for this suddenly parlous undertaking.

I need not weary you with the horrors of my exploration that night, my slow advance through the chill malodorous passages that riddled the vaults and cellars of Drogo Hall, suffice that when I came upon the door I knew, despite the profound obscurity that pressed upon me from all sides, despite the panic that rose constantly from within my own mind, suppressed only by the most vigorous exercise of the will – despite all this I knew at once, when I encountered it in a small vaulted chamber, flanked by iron sconces set into the wall, studded and sturdy within its recessed arch – that through this door lay the dark heart of this malignant dying house where Drogo's treasure was laid up, the heaped booty of a lifetime of plundering in the name of science – ha!

I paused, panting, before the door; I set my candle to the sconces, and was rewarded with a crackle of tarry flame, a plummet of black smoke, and a flaring illumination which, dim though it was, was brighter by far than what I had had from my stub of candle. I sat a moment on a bench of cold stone, bent forward with my hands on my knees and my head turned toward the door. I knew what I would find within; or rather, I dreaded to have confirmed that which I anticipated finding within, for over the days and nights I had been in Drogo Hall I had spent many hours resurrecting the past, making a sense and order of it, enough time, certainly, to glimpse the inevitable end to which this history had been drawing ever closer.

Harry Peake had been the victim of Drogo and Clyte. He had died with a bottle of gin in his hand; or perhaps they could not wait for the gin to do its work, poison being too slow for them, and had lured him into the big house instead, and some howling midnight Clyte did the deed himself; I do not know. But in my mind's eye I could see what he had become, I saw his bones all brown and yellowy from the rapid boiling away of the flesh, and constructed anew, an articulated skeleton with screws and wires in his joints to hold him all together. I saw him in a glass cabinet in the central gallery of Lord Drogo's Museum of Anatomy, displayed in such a manner that every visitor could examine at his leisure the structural peculiarities of the spine. There he would be, old Harry, with an iron rod to keep him upright and a hundred tiny screws drilled into his bony matter that he might stand in death as he never stood in life –

I had opened the door without much difficulty, and pushed it back across the flagstones sufficient that the flaring light from the smoking sconces cast a dim glow into the museum beyond; and I had gone in, at last, I thought, to confront the skeletal remains of Harry Peake. I wandered down a gallery lined the length of both vaulted walls with ancient glass-fronted cabinets, thick now with dust and cobwebs and fingery incursions of that familiar black lichen which, being wiped or scraped away with my sleeve, revealed the rotting trophies of Drogo's organic researches, his restless probing into the very structure of those creatures he had slaughtered and dissected and labelled and organized and displayed; all now turning to slime.

Yes, slime. For when first I had pushed open the museum door I had been met with a soft *whoosh!*, like a gasp, the last breath of spirit escaping its long confinement in this deathly cell, leaving behind only dank emptiness. And with that final exhalation those specimens began the last rapid movement of their decay, spoiling even as I peered at them with my candle to the glass, structure collapsing and tissue turning viscous until nothing remained but the husks and ichors of a hundred plundered organs. Oh, there were bony specimens too, the skeletal claw of a grizzly bear, the skull of a hydrocephalic cretin, the amputated shinbone of a syphilitic Negro. But no high cabinet stood in place of honour with

Harry's bones within, no giant humpback skeleton reared like a lord over the lower specimens. No, I was deceived, he was elsewhere, I had penetrated Drogo's house – Drogo's *soul!* – to its depths, so I thought; but I had not gone deep enough.

He was not there. He was not there. I had failed to see the thing whole, I had missed a fragment, I had erred in my estimate of Harry's courage, perhaps, or of Drogo's cunning. The bones were elsewhere.

And so I shuffled out of the Museum of Anatomy, and pulled the door behind me, so all could rest in peace within. It creaked and screamed on its ancient hinges as it scraped across the flagstones, it resisted my force, and I paused, the better to seize hold of the iron ring. And then, in the silence, with a last flare in the shivering gloom, one wall sconce in the ante-chamber gave out with a sputtering sigh – and then, a second later, the other – and in the sudden darkness, *a hand fell on my shoulder.*

38

Martha shrank against the wall of the church clutching Harry to her breast. She was aware of Sara close beside her, reaching an arm round her shoulders, as hissing and whispering rose all about them, women emerging from pews and pushing toward them. Some small object was flung at her, a pebble, I believe; it struck her temple, and that stung her to life. She stepped forward, shaking off Sara's arm, cheeks blazing and eyes on fire, and shouted at them did they think this was *her* doing? Oh, and a chorus of insults, a chorus of *yes* to this and she shouted her denial with all the force in her body. Little Harry was wide awake now and screaming, and she hitched him higher in her arms so they could scream at them together. The women screamed back, their insults were hideous, unspeakable, *English whore* was the least of it, but she understood they would not touch her with an infant in her arms.

A few seconds later she was not so sure, as she felt fingers clutching at her shawl. Harry was wrapped in that shawl! She tore it free and turned in fury on a small vicious woman she had often seen on the dock but had never spoken to in her life. She felt someone pull at her hair, and whirled around, in a fury now, convinced that they would seize her child from her and tear them both to pieces, even as Sara flailed wildly at her attackers. It astonished Martha that so many were ready to presume her guilt on the strength of nothing more than the name of a ship! The whispers about Harry's back, was it this that inspired such hatred among the women that they would at once see her as a woman who not only had lain with Satan but was a *traitor*? She did not know what it was she shouted at them but it did not drive them off, they only shouted and hissed and spat at her the more, clawed at her clothes, her hair, taunted her, crowding in upon her, and again she shrank back against the wall, tightening her grip on her child –

Suddenly there came a roar from the front of the church, a roar so loud that they all turned, and saw Joshua Rind standing there hammering his stick on the floor and shouting for order. The doctor had authority here. He shouted at them to sit down and to Martha's astonishment they were cowed, they obeyed. She had never seen Joshua so angry! She had no idea he had it in him! She had forgotten he was a Rind, but now she saw what she had glimpsed in Silas, the dangerous quality she had been apprehensive of provoking in that complicated man. Now his brother the doctor by the sheer force of his character had silenced a churchful of angry women.

'That girl is not our enemy,' he shouted, 'our enemy is at hand!'

'She brought them here!'

'She is their spy!'

'She is their whore!'

The clamour rose to a shriek but once again the doctor silenced the women, and at last they turned their minds to the ships bearing down on their harbour, and but for a few looks of loathing cast her way, Martha was for the moment forgotten. Once he had their attention Joshua set about briskly reviewing their situation. Knowing the British army at first hand, he said, for he had fought in the last war, and knowing their current bitter hatred of the patriots and their cause, he believed they must expect harsh treatment.

'They will burn our houses,' he cried, 'and they will carry us off in their ships to Boston. Those who are able must get away from the town with all haste. Those who cannot go will gather here, in the church, where I will stay with you. I will plead for you here, in this church. No British officer will permit his men to harm those too weak or sick to leave.'

He could say no more; a great hubbub erupted, with some crying out in support of this plan, and others just as passionately opposed. Martha was badly shaken by her ordeal and felt a strong impulse to flee the church, but she did not, she stayed, thinking that to flee was to admit her guilt. She *was* guilty, but none of these women knew it, her conversation with Giles Hawkins in the saltworks was overheard by no one. So she waited, she listened, she lifted her face defiantly and proudly against them. Her chin, her mouth, her eyes, all proclaimed an outraged innocence, and dared them to impugn her again.

Joshua Rind carried the day, and soon after they were all hurrying back to their homes, and none of them had time now to torment Martha further. But she was pushed as she left the church, she was spat at outside, and as she hurried back up the hill with her aunt and her cousins she heard hissing from the women even as they scattered to their homes. She did not bow her head nor lower her eyes. No, she strode up the hill with lifted head and lifted eyes, her cousin Sara by her side and her little Harry carried high on her breast, and despite the cold wind off the harbour she pulled the shawl off his back and displayed his little hump, covered only in a linen nightshirt, to all who cast their eyes upon him.

When they reached the house Maddy Rind was already flying from room to room as her daughters flung food and clothing into baskets and bags. She put Harry down in his crib – since they left the church he had been quiet, he had regained his customary composure and now watched these frantic preparations for departure with an expression of approval – and she ran upstairs, and in a few seconds packed into her canvas bag all they would need on the road, and God knows she had experience enough of those sorts of journeys, and of these sorts of departures! She hauled on her stout boots and pulled her old greatcoat about her shoulders.

She was coming downstairs when Joshua Rind hobbled in through the front door in a state of intense agitation. He fixed her with a gaze of such fury that she quailed, her step faltered on the stair and she stood there and quailed before his eyes. He was unable or unwilling to speak to her. His jaw was clamped tight shut and the colour was up in his cheeks, as it was in Martha's. His eyes burned with a terrible light. All he could say was, 'Damnable girl! Damnable girl!' – then off he went down the passage to the kitchen.

Martha followed him and found her aunt's party almost ready for departure. They would be thirteen, including Harry and herself, and a neighbour, Mary Coffin, and her children, who chose to travel with them. Joshua was talking rapidly to her aunt, a torrent of names, houses, instructions, advice. He pressed a purse into her hands, also a letter he had hastily scribbled to assure them all safe passage through the country. Then he told her to go, go, and turning to the room, said he wished them God speed but go, go, and as the women and children hurried out through the back door, and Martha lifted Harry from his crib and stowed him under her coat, he cast at her a last long look of direst reproach as he tapped his cane impatiently on the floorboards. He followed them out and locked the back door behind him. They had taken with them the muskets and pistols the men had left behind, and powder and shot as well. Sara had run into the meadow behind the barn to bridle the horses and bring them out on to the road, and even as they moved toward the gate they could see other women coming up the road with their children, pushing carts and barrows hastily filled with household belongings.

Then they were through the gate and on the road. They paused and stood a few seconds gazing out to sea. The two sloops were making full sail before a brisk westerly breeze, and the sight of them out on a strong-running sea, heeling in the following wind, would have struck Martha as a handsome scene, on a different day, in a different world. The fleeing women had several hours at the least before the soldiers could be landed, nonetheless Joshua Rind was waving his stick and crying out to them to go, go, so they turned their backs on the bay, and the port, whose streets were alive now with women and children all heavily laden and scurrying this way and that. The last Martha saw of the doctor he was descending the hill at as fast a pace as his gouty foot would allow.

The road climbed up around Black Brock then levelled off on the high ground above the town before plunging into the woods. Off they plodded, Maddy Rind in her swirling cloak and broad-brimmed hat glancing anxiously from one to another of her charges, and each one meeting her eye with a resolute expression as they laboured with their loads; and Sara, with a musket slung over her shoulder, bringing up the rear with the horses, three old slow animals left behind by the militia as unfit for service in the Revolution. Behind them other groups struggled up toward Black Brock, and here and there among them came a wagon hauled by some aged beast disturbed from pastoral retirement by the crisis. The day was clear, the wind sharp, and it had been decided in the kitchen between Maddy and the doctor that they would make for Cratwich, where the Rinds had friends, and try to reach it by nightfall; in the morning they would know more. Cratwich lay five miles off the Boston road, and they believed that the redcoats, if they pursued on foot, would not think to come there.

Slowly the caravan of women and children wound its way up the steep track that carried them round the side of Black Brock and out on to the high road. They were all accustomed to walking long distances and even the youngest had little difficulty keeping up with the pace set by Maddy Rind. The road was firm and dry underfoot, no rain having fallen for days, and all were comfortable with the loads they carried. Martha's Harry never complained despite being jostled about and switched from arm to arm, he maintained the composure he had shown ever since they left the church. Martha had had no chance to reflect on the events of the morning, but now as she settled into her stride she recalled with horror how the women had turned toward her like so many snarling animals, all of them certain beyond any doubt that she was responsible for the presence of the enemy offshore; and it was suddenly clear to Martha that whatever sort of a life she had hoped to make here in Cape Morrock for herself and her child, with the coming of the *Queen Charlotte* it was destroyed.

Not until two hours later, when they had come up round behind Black Brock on to the high road, could they again see the sea, and now of course from a much higher elevation; and what they saw at once filled them with the blackest foreboding. In the town below there was still movement in the streets, but most of the women who had elected to stay behind, those unable to travel, those who remained to care for them, those who simply preferred to stay in their homes, those women stood about in groups in front of the church and they too were gazing out to sea. The two sloops had by this time come broadside at the entrance to the harbour, a protective claw of jagged black rock with a wide opening between.

They had reefed all sail and dropped anchor, but as yet the women saw no sign of them letting down their boats to come ashore, and they turned to one another, asking why they did not, for surely their purpose was to occupy the town and prevent the escape of its people.

And then they had their answer. They saw a cloud of smoke appear midships below the gunwales of the sloop closer to the rocks, and a second later heard a distant booming sound that had the seagulls flapping off the water. A cannon had been fired. There was a commotion outside the church now, though the women on the road could hear nothing of it, but the doctor could be seen shepherding his people in. The cannon, had it been firing ball, had missed its mark; perhaps it was a warning shot, but to what purpose? If simply to terrify those who remained in the town, then it had surely succeeded. They saw other figures running toward the church, and even from a great height their panic was unmistakable.

It was no warning shot. That cannon was finding its range. A minute later another cloud of smoke, another boom – and they saw, and heard, a small explosion somewhere on Front Street, and seconds after that flames were shooting from the windows of a building not four doors down from Pierce's Tavern.

The town was filled with defenceless women and children and the British were bombarding it. Up on the high road they heard the crackle of musket fire but they knew the ships were far beyond their range. The enemy could take his time destroying New Morrock unopposed; and that is what he proceeded to do.

There was no question of continuing along the high road. Silently, their eyes fixed on the scene below, where the flames from the building on Front Street were spreading to its neighbours, they set down their bags and watched. It seemed a dream, the blazing building under the high blue sky, sparks and fragments carried upward on the breeze, and the two ships lying at anchor and rocking on their cables in the harbour mouth. Then more smoke, more booms, and an old house behind the saltworks had its roof stove in, and again they saw the flames come licking up. The British were firing mortar, and balls that came red hot out of the brazier, and the old wood houses round the harbour were going up like kindling.

Pierce's Tavern was on fire now. Where was Dan Pierce, where were the other men? Martha did not see them on the road; they had stayed behind to resist the enemy. Other women joined them on the road, and they stood together in silence. The ships had cannon the length of their gundecks and they were holding nothing back, now they had found their range. They were hitting other houses, higher in the town now, and the thought in all the women's minds, as yet unspoken, was that they were trying to hit the church. Did Joshua not realize this? Why did he keep his people in there? Did he think the House of God enjoyed divine protection from cannon and mortar? All at once the women began to cry out these questions to one another, but none of them had an answer, and it was unthinkable to go back down with death and fire raining from the sky. Only Martha was silent. She stood dumb, like a rock, gazing down, all colour drained from her face, all life gone from her eyes. The church bell was ringing wildly now.

At last there was a lull in the firing, the bell fell silent, the smoke was carried off by the wind and all was quiet; and into the sudden stillness emerged two women from the church. Then others began to come out, but even as they looked about them, some hurrying off toward their homes while others set off up the hill – the firing resumed.

None of those who saw it will forget what happened next. The church was hit, even as women and children came streaming out. They saw them fall. They heard the screams. For a while they could see nothing through the billowing smoke, then all at once they saw that the roof was on fire, and flaming boards and shingles were falling into the church below, where people were still trying to get out, those too sick or slow and those who were helping them. They could see nothing of Joshua, he was still inside when the roof fell in. The fire had caught on the steeple now, the flames were like living things and the blazing steeple was a beacon, or a weapon, rather, a fiery spear thrust at the eye of God!

Smoke now covered the town, and rising from it great showers of sparks and charred floating remnants of books and rags that swirled in the currents of the same wind that had pushed the ships across the bay and now fanned the fires they had brought upon the town. On the high road the women heard great distant crashes as roofs came down, as houses collapsed into the street. All of Front Street was ablaze now, the saltworks and the warehouse, the boatyard and the foundry, and back up the hill the church steeple burned high above the general conflagration. Nor was the devil's work finished yet, for there came now a series of explosions, great blasts of fiery debris flung high into the air with a violence that outdid all the other furies at work that day, and this was the distillery going up. On the edge of town a few scattered figures had got clear, they saw them running up the hill, others still down there they glimpsed through the smoke, and this Martha saw, a child with its clothing aflame running screaming along the street, and then collapsing, and writhing in a fiery heap on the hard ground.

How long did it go on? All day so it seemed; all eternity. There came a point when the cannons stopped firing but it meant nothing, the fire was all, the town was alight, the flames had surged up the hill, and the wind only dropped when it was too late to matter any more. Martha was silent throughout. She stood apart from her aunt and her cousins, stone-faced and rigid while they wept, watching the fire devour her home.

As dusk came on, and darkness descended, the women still watched from the high road. They could not turn their backs on the town so they waited, settling with their children by the roadside for the night, they waited until they could go back down and bury their dead. A blessed rain fell just after midnight, by which time the flames were guttering and dying; the rain extinguished the last of it, and in the moonlight black smoke billowed up in foul-smelling clouds. Few of the women slept. Martha still sat apart from the others, rocking Harry on her breast and staring out to sea with fixed unblinking eyes. The hours of darkness dragged by. Over the sound of the sea came now the wail of a child, now the sob of a woman, quickly stifled. At first light, when Sara came to her with food, Martha seemed not to hear her cousin begging her to eat, she merely pulled her greatcoat closer about herself and her infant, and withdrew deeper into her solitude.

Sara persisted however. For Harry's sake she must eat, she said, and this raised a response from Martha. Up came her head, she nodded, and Sara sank on to the ground beside her. In silence they ate. A mist had drifted in off the sea and partly obscured the horror below. The black smoky plumes of midnight were now little more than wispy grey fingers rising here and there into the dawn. In the harbour the two sloops rode gently on their cables, and the surface of the water all around them was scattered with blackened remnants floated high in the currents of yesterday's hot winds. Martha rose heavily to her feet, leaving Harry bundled on the ground fast asleep. Sara could think of nothing to say to comfort her cousin. Getting up and drawing close to her, she slipped an arm about her shoulder.

Martha seemed at last to awaken. 'It is me they have destroyed,' she whispered.

'No, do not say it,' said Sara, her voice hushed and urgent. 'After the war we will build it again.'

Martha did not appear to hear this, she was staring out to sea. 'It is my doing,' she said.

'How yours –?'

Martha was silent for a long time. She seemed to gasp for air. Her breast heaved, the tears stood out in her eyes. Then at last she turned to Sara, and taking her hands she poured it all out to her, poured out all the confused welter of emotion she felt for her father, and how he took to drink and lost his soul, yes, and she had had to flee from him, and then he had raped her – this of course Sara did not know, she cried out when she heard it – and she had conceived his child, he was not Adam's at all, and all this happened the night before she left England to escape him –

Sara was dismayed beyond words upon hearing of these things, but still she did not understand, what had it all to do with the British ships –?

So Martha told her, quieter now, how Captain Hawkins had promised her news of him.

'Of your father.'

'Yes.'

'And?'

He had made her tell him everything first.

'What is everything?' whispered the stricken Sara.

'Where the guns are, and the powder. Everything.'

A long silence here as the two girls gazed into one another's faces. Out to sea a misty radiance on the horizon announced the sunrise.

'What did he tell you about your father?' said Sara at last.

'That he is *dead*!' cried Martha. For a moment more they stared at one another, even as they became aware of movement and voices nearby, women rising to their feet and pointing at the harbour below. They turned to see a boat being lowered over the side of the *Queen Charlotte*, then soldiers clambering into the boat, followed by a stout figure in a powder-blue coat. Had anyone observed Martha Peake at that moment – and someone did, of course, Sara was watching her intently – she would have seen her body stiffen and her soul come rushing into her eyes, as she recognized Giles Hawkins; and that man seemed all at once to be the source of everything she had suffered, every betrayal she had endured – at his hands, at England's hands, indeed at *her father's* hands! – and all the rage in her heart, all the guilt, and bitterness, and grief that was in her, she could contain it no longer. She turned to Sara with wild eyes and there followed a brief tearful conversation during which Martha lifted up little Harry and pressed him on to her cousin, who took him, all the while pleading with her but to no avail. Then Martha seemed to lose patience, and seizing Sara's musket she set off rapidly down the hill, heedless of the cries of alarm from the women gathered on the road.

After several minutes the soldiers begin rowing across the harbour. The women watch in silence as the loaded boat moves toward the ruins of the town. It is still some way out from the wharf when from out of the mist appears a figure, a woman, her face and clothing smeared with ash and smoke. She crosses the dock and strides out along the wharf toward them, her open greatcoat flapping about her and her red hair flying free in the wind. Some astonishment in the English boat, and as Giles Hawkins rises to his feet he sees that the woman has a musket slung over her shoulder. The boat is drifting in toward the wharf now as the woman fails to heed the captain's shouted command to stop and lay down her weapon, and on she comes in a kind of trance.

Giles Hawkins's voice echoes over the water then fades away and a fraught silence settles on the harbour. Up beyond Black Brock the women and children gaze down as the redcoats in the boat level their muskets and Martha approaches the end of the wharf. The boat drifts in closer, oars feathered, over the lapping waters. Again the captain shouts to Martha to stop and still she does not hear him. She reaches the end of the wharf and without hesitation sets her legs apart as she has been taught to and brings the musket to her shoulder.

She fires at Giles Hawkins, and the report of the shot goes out clear across the harbour. The captain is hit, he goes down, there is blood on his coat, but even as he falls, and the boat rocks wildly, the redcoats get off a volley and half-a-dozen musket balls rip into Martha Peake's body. She drops where she stands and falls dead in a heap on the wharf.

39

Silence once more in the harbour, where the water is flat, and still, and greasy-grey, and the smoke from the muskets drifts in toward the town. The captain struggles up with the help of his sergeant, the wound seemingly a slight one, a flesh wound to the shoulder, he is not badly hurt, only winged. The boat drifts in and the silence deepens as the soldiers, having rapidly reloaded, kneel tense with levelled muskets, awaiting the attack that will surely come now; but it does not. The boat bumps against a piling and is tied up to the wharf. The captain lies groaning in the bow. His sergeant clambers up on to the wharf and looks about him, then gingerly touches Martha's body with his boot.

The sergeant leads his men through the misty ruins and is ignored by the ghostly darting figures of women searching for their dead. He does not interfere with them. He has his orders. He marches his men to Scup Head, where they find the *Lady Ann* riding at anchor in the cove, and they set her ablaze. They follow the track through the woods to the sawmill, but find it empty. It too they set ablaze. They then march to the Old Burying Ground to look for the arms and powder they believe to be buried there. They dig up several graves, but again find nothing, and return to the wharf. They are rowed back out across the harbour, and within the hour the two sloops have put to sea.

After they had gone, the women on the hill above Black Brock came down to load into carts those bodies not entirely devoured by the fires, having first wrapped them in blankets. They hauled them up to the Old Burying Ground, and gave them a funeral, of sorts. Maddy and Sara took responsibility for Martha. Only a few went into unmarked graves. It was in the course of this melancholy work that they discovered the graves desecrated by the redcoats.

Then the women went away and left the ruins of New Morrock

to the gull and the wolf and whatever other scavenger crept out of the woods at dusk and padded silently down the hill to sniff the ashes and carry off what it could find.

40

I awoke in my bed in Drogo Hall and for a moment or two I remembered nothing. I lay there blinking at the grey daylight sifting through the gaps where the great rotting curtains on the window had come away from the rail. Then all at once the events of the night came back to me and I sat up with a cry of alarm, the cry I believe I did not utter when that large cold hand clamped my shoulder in its iron grip. Whose hand was it? Mortal it was, of this I had no doubt, but what mortal? What had he done to me? And how had I got back to my bedroom, with no memory of what had happened in the meanwhile? My cry aroused Percy; and a minute later the key turned in the lock and in he came, rubbing his hands together and his little wizened face clouded with apparent concern, though I was not so blind as to miss the scorn that lay beneath.

I was sitting up in bed and shouting my questions at him before he could even cross the floor. His answers were far from satisfactory. It seems I had fainted in the cellars. They had found me down there, shivering and delirious. Fearing a recurrence of the marsh fever, they had somehow got me back upstairs and into bed, those two decrepit creatures, and after administering medicines had left me to sleep. How did I feel now?

With some heat I told the little man that I was not suffering from marsh fever, I had been attacked! Somebody had tracked me into the cellars, I cried, and crept up behind me with great stealth, and laid the chill hand of death on me! I had been supremely terrified, that was all, I was not *ill*! I demanded to know where my uncle was, and Percy told me he was in his sitting room. He did not know I was awake.

'Then tell him!' I shouted, and Percy, bowing, withdrew.

I climbed out of bed and confirmed that I indeed had no fever, nor any injury, although my shoulder throbbed and burned where the hand had gripped me. No, whatever violence my assailant had intended for me, something or someone had dissuaded him from it, and clearly I had had a very narrow escape. I was in no doubt that my uncle could throw light on these events and when, some minutes later, he appeared, shuffling forward in his old leather slippers, his brocade dressing gown shrouding his birdlike frame, and on his face that same expression of false concern I had earlier detected on Percy's face, I was already half-dressed, and in no mood for any of his footling nonsense.

'Somebody was down there,' I said, keeping my rage under control, determined to get to the bottom of the thing, 'and he intended to do me harm.'

'Oh no, dear boy,' he began.

'Oh yes, dear boy,' I said firmly. 'Oh yes indeed. Did you not hear him?'

He lifted his hands, palms upward, he lifted his eyes to the ceiling, he struck a comical pose of utter bewilderment and started to shake his head. This was precisely the sort of footling nonsense for which I had no patience.

'How could you not have heard him?' I cried. 'You heard me, did you not? What brought you down there, if you heard nothing?'

'Oh, we heard you, indeed we did, you made a deal of noise,' he said, 'but we heard nothing else.'

'What noise did I make?'

'Opening doors, stamping about and, I'm afraid to say it, jabbering like a monkey.'

'What about?'

'When we found you?'

'Yes, when you found me!'

'You were not yourself, dear boy. You were excited, oh, very excited. You were convinced Lord Drogo intended to murder you.'

At this I fell silent. I had spoken Drogo's name, had I? I will not pretend to you that the thought had not crossed my mind that Francis Drogo was still alive, though I had as yet to fathom what reason he could have for wishing to deceive the world as to the fact. Then what had caused me to speak his name when I was out of my mind with terror? Had I heard something, seen something, felt or smelt or perhaps *touched* something that raised him up from the recesses of my mind? Had I perhaps turned, had I stood face to face with the man, and fainted at the very shock of it, the memory at once wiped from consciousness it was so hideous?

By this time I was fully dressed and had no wish to linger in a cold damp bedroom. My uncle suggested I eat, but I did not want food, I wanted a good fire, and a large brandy, and a chance to *think*, I said, so he led me downstairs to his sitting room and there I sat gazing into the fire as the brandy did its work and my uncle for once held his peace.

I sank back at last into the armchair and rubbed my head. I no longer knew what to believe. Could I have been wrong? The hand on my shoulder – some creature, a small ape, perhaps, which years ago had escaped from Drogo's menagerie and lived like a troglodyte in those labyrinthine cellars – dropping on me from a high ledge – were there *apes* in the cellars, I wanted to know.

'Apes?' said my uncle. 'What kind of apes?'

I heaved a great sigh. Whatever he knew, he was not being frank with me, and I had no means of winkling it out of him. I must have more time.

'Tell me,' I said, 'what happened to Martha Peake.'

And that is how I learned of her death; and if it devastated me, to my astonishment it devastated my uncle William also, indeed he sobbed like a child when he reached the end. And this the man who had claimed indifference to the American adventure – whose cold eye was cast upon friend and foe alike –!

When news of the burning of New Morrock spread through the country, said my uncle, having brought his emotion under control, a rumour followed it that an English girl had betrayed the town to the enemy. And, it seems that on learning of this rumour, Silas Rind, encamped with the Continental Army in the hills above Boston – whom we would expect to be fiercest in his condemnation of Martha – instead issued a robust denial. He then, said William, put his considerable authority behind an effort to promote a different version of the story, one in which Martha played not the traitor but the patriot; and no ordinary patriot at that. Martha Peake, he made it known, was a heroine, and a martyr to the cause –

Silas responsible, I cried –? *Silas?* But Silas more than anyone would have known –

But my uncle would say no more about it then, and I was left to ponder the mystery of Silas Rind declaring Martha Peake a patriot and a martyr, she who had brought about the destruction of his town.

It was a long hard winter. How desperately they grieved for New Morrock. Maddy Rind was a broken woman. She had lost more than a home, she had lost a world. Joshua Rind was dead, crushed in the church when the roof fell in, along with many friends and neighbours of the Rinds. The men who had come back, Dan Pierce and the rest, they too had died in the fires. Their mourning was protracted through the long months they huddled in a farmhouse in Cratwich, with the great trees all around blocking out the sky, and the sun going down early, and nothing but darkness and candlelight in which to reflect on those they had lost.

Sara's grief was all for Martha. She often walked in the forest, before the snows came. She wondered at its great age, and its mystery, and remembered the many tales she had told Martha of the Indian tribes who lived deep in these woods; but her feelings were not aroused as they had been when, with Martha, she climbed to the top of Black Brock and there learned to see the great Atlantic through her cousin's eyes, and to love its stormy presence on their bleak New England shores. Ah, but Sara was young, the spirit was alive in her, and over the long dark months of the winter, confined in the ancient forest and grieving for her lost friend, she at last grew weary of her situation and decided that when the British left Boston, and it was possible to travel the roads once more, she would quit Cratwich and take her motherless nephew to find his father.

For she was Harry's mother now, and she did for him what Martha would have done, with the exception of the breast; with the result that despite everything, despite losing Martha, Harry was thriving. Already his character had announced itself in clear firm tones. They often rose from the table hungry, that winter, and Harry went short of food even with what Sara fed him from her own plate, but he never complained. And he displayed even then strong powers of concentration. A complex object could absorb his attention for hours, as he turned it over in his fingers, or put it between his lips and chewed it. He loved any sort of small machine. He made people smile, so serious he seemed, but when he became aware of being smiled at he would happily respond with a brief gurgling toothless grin, which at once faded as he resumed what Sara imagined to be the lofty thoughts going forward in that huge red dome of a head of his. As for his gibbous spine, it grew as his body grew, the skin lost its translucence, and the bones of his back became as hard and strong as the rest of his little skeleton.

They heard that winter that Captain Arnold was making an expedition to Quebec, his object to seize its walled fortress and assure American control of the St Lawrence River, which otherwise would serve the British in their attempt to seize the Hudson and split the colonies in two. Sara, like Martha, had been concerned at Adam joining the Ticonderoga expedition, and was still more agitated by this news, which involved greater danger and was being undertaken in the dead of winter; no season, I imagine, to be campaigning in the north woods!

But she had a blind faith that her brother would come back alive from Canada, and she intended to meet him when he reached Boston. She would comfort him in his loss, and present little Harry to him. Maddy Rind protested loudly when she heard this plan, but Sara was adamant. She urged her brothers and sisters for their mother's sake to be strong, for as Maddy's mind inevitably dwelled not only on what she had already lost, but on the prospect of losing Silas and Adam as well, she would need their support in the months to come. Sara then urged her mother to be strong for her children's sake, to teach them what a woman must suffer in this world, and how that suffering must be borne. And when they were all together in the evening, by the fire in the kitchen, and the weeping began, she urged them then to think of what Martha had given her life for; and she asked them to believe that it had not been given in vain, and to think how best they could follow her example and thus do honour to her memory and to their country both.

So they did not collapse into hopelessness and misery, they rallied; and later Maddy thanked Sara for what she had done, and apologized for failing properly to comfort her for her own loss.

Another farewell! Did war bring anything but farewells? It brought more farewells even than it brought deaths. The familiar scene, this time outside a tavern in Cratwich, one clear day in the early spring of 1776, horses harnessed to wagons and men with muskets on their shoulders, and rum, and much bravado, hearty laughter, oaths and promises, and a small crowd of women and children to see them off to war. Maddy Rind and her children watched the final preparations, the sergeant of militia testing the ropes on the wagons, counting his men, who had fallen in in ranks, each with the family musket slung on his shoulder. With them went Sara Rind and the infant Harry.

A tearful departure it was. Sara said goodbye to her mother, and then to her brothers and sisters, who had begun to laugh again with the coming of spring and the surge of hope that season arouses in young hearts; and this she took as her lesson, as she departed, that it was not an ending, that a new town would rise from the ashes of the old, first of a new nation. She said of the burning of New Morrock what she had said of Martha's death, that it must not have been for nothing. They would honour the town as they would honour Martha, as a sacrifice offered gladly for the cause.

Then there was kissing and embraces and yet more tears, and at last she mounted the horse she had been lent for the journey by her friends in Cratwich, with Harry strapped securely to her breast and their few possessions stowed in the saddlebags. She rode out of Cratwich with the soldiers, to the music of the fife and drum, the children running beside them, cheering them on.

★

After less than a day travelling south on the Boston road, Sara learned that over the winter the story of the burning of New Morrock had spread widely through all the colonies; and that Martha figured vividly in every account of the town's destruction. The shot she fired at the captain, and the death she suffered as a consequence, all this was common knowledge, but Sara was astonished to discover that not one person she talked to voiced the suspicion that the women of New Morrock had harboured, that is, that Martha Peake was responsible for the British bombardment of the town. Somehow, she did not know how – though my uncle, of course, was in no doubt as to how it had come about – an entirely new construction had been placed upon that event; and she realized that the story of Martha's death had become inspirational, that to a people staring into the teeth of defeat and ruin it lifted the spirit, it allowed them to glimpse a higher purpose for their suffering. Several times during the first days she was asked had she known the red-haired English girl from New Morrock, who alone and unaided had gone up against a company of redcoats; and understanding now the accepted version of events she soon had her listeners crying out with admiration for Martha's courage.

All along the road she saw signs that her homeland was at war, and that the British blockade of the coast was biting hard. It grew worse the closer she approached Boston. The country thereabouts had been depleted of men, crops, lumber, animals and machines, which had gone to serve the army laying siege to Boston. But the army was no longer at Boston, for after the departure of the British by sea Washington had marched south to New York to meet the enemy there.

She saw women and children out in the fields, but no longer was Massachusetts a peaceful and prosperous province of hard-working farmers in small towns of well-made houses. The land had been neglected, walls and fences and buildings were in disrepair, and the road was full of travellers like herself, shabby, weary folk pushed this way and that by the random currents of war.

But she saw no despair. She saw a people ragged and hungry,

grim-faced and burdened with cares, but they willingly gave what they could to their soldiers, and if they had nothing to spare from their larders and cellars they gave encouragement and gratitude, and Sara's rough companions told them they would surely drive the British out, had not Martha Peake shown them the way?

They came in by way of Charlestown Neck, where new building had begun on the site of the town burned down by the British during the battle at Bunker Hill. There Sara took her leave of the soldiers, who had warmed to this brave determined girl. She gave up her horse to a Cratwich man and boarded the ferry, burdened now with both Harry and their small stock of belongings.

She stepped off on the other side in Boston, and was soon directed to Foley's Tavern. And so, as the sun slipped down the sky, and twilight stole over the town, she set off to discover what news there was of her brother.

41

She wandered through the town for an hour searching for the tavern. The streets were not lit, and everywhere she saw the ravages of the recent occupation by the British. She saw the foundations and chimneys of houses that had been torn down for firewood, ruins that would have cast a melancholy chill over her soul had she not been so alive to the prospect of finding Adam. Shadowy figures shuffled past her clutching parcels and bundles, a few barrel staves for the fire, a coil of dirty hemp, a cabbage, a newspaper, a scrawny chicken for an empty pot. They passed taverns near the harbour in which Sara heard neither song nor laughter, but the sound of men arguing their politics; and churches silent as the grave. She heard moans of sickness, she heard a man shouting drunkenly from the window of a mean dark house down the end of an alley. She glimpsed crowded houses and crowded rooms, and everywhere she smelled waste and filth and rotting fish. She saw horses without flesh on their ribs, she saw starving dogs with their noses in the filth.

But she also saw handbills pasted on to walls, and even in the gloom their words were like fire.

O! YE THAT LOVE MANKIND! YE THAT DARE OPPOSE NOT ONLY THE TYRANNY BUT THE TYRANT, STAND FORTH! EVERY SPOT OF THE OLD WORLD IS OVERRUN WITH OPPRESSION. FREEDOM HATH BEEN HUNTED ROUND THE GLOBE. ASIA AND AFRICA HAVE LONG EXPELLED HER. EUROPE REGARDS HER AS A STRANGER AND ENGLAND HATH GIVEN HER WARNING TO DEPART. O! RECEIVE THE FUGITIVE AND PREPARE IN TIME AN ASYLUM FOR MANKIND — COMMON SENSE.

At last she found the street. Street, I say; four buildings only stood on the one side, five on the other, with large gaps between, like two great toothless mouths grinning at each other across a narrow stretch of broken cobbles. On the corner of the street was a tavern, and over the door hung the name Thomas Foley. Candlelight shone through the bubbled panes of the low small windows, voices could be heard from within. It was an old house and it had seen recent rough treatment. Empty window panes on the upper floors were patched with paper. Shingles in places had been torn off the wall, exposing the boards beneath. The top of the chimney had been shot away. The moon was above the houses now, and as Sara gazed at this damaged building, and saw its broken chimney and wavering roofline sharp against the moonlit sky, she asked herself could this truly be the house where her father had stayed when he came to Boston for business? But she could stand there no longer, for Harry was stirring in her arms, and announcing his hunger.

They came into a taproom lit by a few dim tallow candles and populated by a number of men sitting at a long table, others leaning against the wall close by, still others against the counter, all engaged in a loud conversation; that conversation ceasing abruptly, however, with the entrance of Sara and Harry. All faces were turned toward her. These were sober, frowning men, plainly dressed in black and brown, respectable, serious men; and she realized at once that she had nothing to fear from them, for she could imagine her father a member of this company. Only one man stood out from the rest, a shabby fellow with a hook nose and wild hair, his coat coming apart at the shoulder seams and his linen far from clean, and his hand upon a sheaf of papers on the table. He sat smoking a long clay pipe and staring at her from fierce, unblinking, red-rimmed eyes, and something in his manner told her that this was no Boston man, this was an Englishman.

Still they watched her. She stepped into the room, latching the door behind her, and approached the table. Setting her bag on the floor, and hitching Harry higher on her breast, she told them she was Sara Rind, eldest daughter of Silas Rind; she had lived in New

Morrock until the British burned it, and had come from Cratwich to find her brother.

She was right to think these men were her father's friends. At once several of them rose to their feet, a hubbub of talk broke forth, a chair was pulled out for her, and the man with the hook nose stared at her more intently still. In the midst of this welcome, feeling a great wave of relief sweeping over her as she sat down, and had a glass of wine poured for her, she saw one of the men slip away from the table and run up the staircase at the back of the room. Questions were coming at her from all sides at once, and in her bewilderment she could only look from one man to another. Then suddenly she heard a shout of pleasure, and turning, saw her brother come bounding down the staircase.

A second later Sara and Adam were in each other's arms, clinging together with Harry between them, as the men at the table murmured their satisfaction at this reunion.

Oh, but he had changed! Where was her boy? He was a man – more than a man, a soldier. There was no embracing for long with Harry at her breast, and Adam, after staring into his sister's face, shifted his eyes to the child. Sara lifted him high on her breast, she displayed him, and Adam and Harry gazed solemnly at one another as he took the little face between his fingers and turned it up to the dim glow of the candlelight. As he did so, as he examined Harry, Sara examined him; and yes, he had become a man, in the year he had been away he had grown up. It was in his eyes, first; gone, the languid dewy wondering look of the youth, in its place a brow knotted by weather and hardship and death – the death, above all, of Martha Peake.

It was in the mouth, the lips were set now, closed firm, the tiny lines about them etched with the effort of self-control called up repeatedly in the face of God knew what horrors. He was leaner and harder, his hair was cut short, there was a few days' growth of dark beard on his cheeks, and the fingers cupping Harry's face were strong and scarred. He lifted his eyes from Harry to Sara and grinned his horsey grin – and there he was, her Adam, still there within the man.

Now the other men were standing about them, peering gravely at little Harry, who peered gravely back at them. Harry was then introduced to the company, Adam becoming formal as he spoke the names, some of which would long be remembered in the annals of the struggle for independence, while others – those of men who would play parts of no less importance in these great events – history would forget; coming at the last to he of the hook nose and the blazing red-rimmed eyes, who rose to his feet and shuffled forward, as Adam told the infant boy that this man, *this* man, had so well caught the spirit of the American Revolution that Harry would dine out for a lifetime on it, when it was known he had shaken his hand.

That gnarly hand was now extended, and the fierce wild face of the Englishman peered into Harry's placid eyes; and Harry, for the first time in all the days of hard travelling he had endured, and to general amusement, burst into a howl of misery even as Adam introduced him to Mr Tom Paine.

A little later, after she had eaten, Adam took Sara to a room separate from the others where they could talk. She laid Harry in a drawer in the corner and at once he fell asleep. Two candles burned on a table with papers and pamphlets spread across it, a quill lying on a sheet in the middle. Bare floor-boards, bunches of drying herbs hanging from hooks in the old ceiling beams, and a shelf loaded with books and papers. A pair of boots by the door, and a peg above from which hung a muddy cloak and a battered hat. Adam flung himself into a chair.

'By Christ I am glad you are safe, Sara!' he cried, not for the first time that night.

'I came from Cratwich with the soldiers,' she said, wandering about the room. 'I could come to no harm with them.'

A snort at this, a manly snort, a snort that knew soldiers. He stood up and went to the chair to gaze some more at the sleeping Harry.

'He is exhausted,' he said.

'We have been on the road for days. The country is starving.'

Still he stood gazing at the sleeping boy.

'A handsome child,' he said. 'He looks well. He has the Peake spine.'

'Oh, he is well,' said Sara. 'He is strong as an ox, and as heavy.'

She sat down at the table. His back was still to her.

'He will need to be strong,' he murmured, and then, without turning: 'Not mine?'

It had to come, good that it came at once.

'No,' she said, 'not yours.'

They sat up late talking in the candlelight. Sara told her brother everything. Oh, she was happy he had become a man, he had seen so much of human nature since they were last together, she needed to explain little but the bare facts of the thing and he understood. In the last year he had seen strong men turn into animals under the hardships of campaigning against the British. He had seen brave men weeping like children after a musket ball had shattered a bone, or a bayonet had sheared their flesh, left them gazing in astonishment at a mangled limb or an opened belly with the guts spilling out. He knew the limits beyond which even the strongest could not go without the sacrifice of their humanity. He spoke of all this, saying that what he had learned in the north woods did not incline him to judge Martha harshly, nor her father either. Sara was strongly affected, and in a second her eyes were brimming with tears; and when he reached across the table and took her hands in his own, her heart heaved and the tears came streaming down. She took a little wine. She had come to the heart of the thing.

'So you will give him your name? He will be your son?'

He sat gazing at the table, and the wavering candle flame brought out the newmade clefts and knottings in his face and brow. For an eternity of seconds he sat like that, still as death. Then his head came up, his hands reached for hers once more, and she saw with a great leaping of the heart that he understood, that the answer was yes. Ah, her brother, her beloved brother – he understood. And understanding, accepted; and in that draughty ill-lit room in Foley's Tavern, as directly beneath them Mr Tom Paine, citizen of the world, drank brandy and talked on through the night – Harry's future as an American was assured.

Some months later, in the autumn of 1776, Sara met her father in that same room in Foley's Tavern. Sara knew the truth, of course, Martha had told her everything, but for the sake of little Harry she had determined that only Adam would know why Martha had done what she did. So she held her peace as Silas talked. He knew, he said, that Martha betrayed the town to the British, but he also knew that she was no enemy of the Revolution. Why then had she done it? Because, he said, she was seduced by Captain Hawkins. The Englishman slipped into her heart like a snake, he said, and like a snake he poisoned her, and so she gave up her secrets to him. And only when the town was in flames did she understand how he had repaid her. It drove her mad, said Silas, the Englishman's treachery, and so she took a musket and loaded it with powder and ball and went to the harbour to shoot down the man who had used her so ill.

Silas's own responsibility in this had not escaped him, though when Sara questioned him closely – asked him *why* he had sent Martha to Scup Head with Adam that day, and then thrust her into the captain's way, armed as she was with intelligence that had to stay hidden from the British – Silas was evasive. He shook his head. He muttered the Englishman's name. Ah, but she only winged him, he said, lifting his dark eyes to hers, and now she is a martyr of the Revolution. Sara began to speak, but he silenced her at once. He laid a hand flat on the table and stared into his daughter's face.

'And so she must remain,' he said. 'So she must remain.'

He then explained to Sara why she must speak of this to nobody, saying that *the Revolution required a martyr*. We need her, he said, we need her legend, which every day spreads further into the country, and wherever it spreads it rouses the people. With every new telling of it they love their country the more and the British the less; indeed, he said, their hatred of the British burns with a fierce heat when they think of what was done to New Morrock, and to Martha Peake; and that hatred will win the war, if we can sustain it. She is the Spirit of the Revolution, said Silas, and so she must remain. She destroyed the town, but she will make us a generous compensation, for the story of Martha Peake's courage on the wharf that day will be a rallying call when we are without bread or boots, and have little ammunition left, and Washington is leading us deeper into the back country, to keep us from being destroyed by the enemy on an open field. This war will not be won easy, he said, and we must have *gestures* to lift our spirit and drive our purpose forward. Sara, he said – and she found her father staring intently at her in the wavering candle flame – you see it does not matter that the legend is a lie?

Sara nodded. She knew all about lies now. Silas rose heavily to his feet. He paused at the door, then he went out, and she heard his footsteps on the stairs. She got up from the table and leaned over the sleeping Harry.

42

I slept late into the afternoon after my nightmare experience in the cellars, and by the time my uncle had finished describing the bombardment of New Morrock, and Martha's magnificent fatal gesture, the clock in the hall downstairs was chiming midnight. I had for some time been anticipating her end, but when it came I confess I was profoundly shocked, and sprang up from my chair with a shout of dismay. My uncle, as I have said, was no less distressed; and as I paced the room, pushing my hand through my hair, the tears came, yes, they came in floods, so real had she become to me; nor did he remain dry-eyed long.

'Shot down,' I whispered, 'in cold blood, by *Englishmen* –!'

William applied a large white handkerchief to his streaming face, murmuring: 'She fired on them first.'

'Ach, she stood no chance at all. And she did not kill him?'

The old man shook his head.

'Then let us hope the wound festered,' I said darkly. 'Let us hope it went bad, and he perished slowly, and in great agony.'

My uncle lifted an eyebrow but said nothing; and I think, for once – indeed, for the first time! – we two were in agreement.

Oh, I could not think of sleep, my mind was in turmoil! I drank more brandy, indeed I made free with the bottle, for the first time in my life I used the fiery liquor to still the turbulence that roiled and seethed within me. It had the effect, however, over the course of the next hour or so, not of stilling but of *inflaming*, rather, my passions, and I admit that I wept a good deal during that time, the memory of my own horrid ordeal lending heat and fire to my dawning horror as I tried to take hold of the fact of Martha's death. Oh, the mind could grasp it, it was the heart that rebelled, and time and again I rose from my chair and wandered about my uncle's room, crying – 'Why? Why?' – and finishing with my head against the wall, pummelling the panelling with my fist.

My uncle stayed with me throughout, and for once he allowed that better part of his nature to come forth; the doctor in him, that is, buried beneath the scaly skin of the cynic. He slowed me in my fervid consumption of his brandy, and allowed me to talk, and oh, my rebel heart overflowed that night, and William Tree for once proved himself a friend to his agitated nephew.

Came the moment at last when I was drained of emotion, weak and ready for sleep, as in the hall below the clock chimed out the melancholy hour of four. I murmured something to this effect, and rose up out of my chair, only to lurch sideways, and seize the mantelpiece so as not to fall down. I was not sober. I stood a moment, gripping the mantel with both hands, my head bowed and my eyes all damply red with brandy and spent passion, gazing unseeing at the ash and embers in the fireplace. I felt my uncle's hand on my arm.

'Come, Ambrose,' he said gently, 'I will take you up.'

I allowed him to do so. Slowly we ascended the old staircase, him holding the candle, myself clutching his arm. Our progress was halting and uncertain; more than once I had recourse to the banister, and leaned heavily upon it as my head spun and my stomach heaved. I was not accustomed to strong liquor in such quantity. At last we reached my door. I stumbled in, old William behind me, and as I flung myself on the bed he lit the candle on my nightstand. There I lay, panting and groaning, and he gazed down at me, the candle throwing up a trembling illumination such that his features seemed benign, and wise, and all-comprehending. I tried to raise myself, I lifted a hand, I wished to tell him that I loved him, but I had not the strength, and I fell back on my pillow even as he whispered his goodnight. I heard his shuffling slippers on the floorboards, and then the creaking of the door, and then – *the key turning in the lock.*

I sobered in an instant. No sound had ever chilled my heart as that sound did. I remembered then with a shock of dismay that when Percy had come to wake me earlier, he had first to unlock the door – and I struggled up from my bed, this one idea now suddenly athrob in my spinning brain, that I was locked in – I was a prisoner in Drogo Hall!

Oh, what a fool I was, to be deceived by old William Tree – he had not my welfare at heart, no, he had other plans for me – plans hatched, I could not doubt it now, in the malign brain of Francis Drogo, who had disturbed me even as I penetrated the secret places in the cellars of his house.

Unsteadily I stood up. My situation was grave indeed. What had I to fear? Perhaps the worst, perhaps that I would share the fate of Harry Peake and the countless others who had been butchered on Drogo's table. I paced the room, my step soon as firm and straight as ever, and my mind racing forward, burning with clarity and urgency and yes, no little fear, but they would not surprise me again! By the light of the candle I explored the room minutely, seeking some means of escape. There was none. The window would not yield, shut tight these fifty years, and the sashes warped and swollen with time and weather and neglect, and even if it could be opened it offered nothing but a sheer drop forty feet to a stone courtyard below, and no pipe, no ledge, no climbing ivy to allow a descent.

I slumped into my chair, despair beginning to announce itself at the outskirts of thought, but the mind still working, working rapidly for a means of release from a suddenly mortal predicament. And then an idea. The night before, descending into the cellars, I had of course taken the precaution of concealing about my person my pistol. I had had no chance to use it, my assailant having come silently at me from behind. But my uncle or his servant had undressed me – had he also disarmed me? The next moment I was across the room and fumbling at the inner pocket of the coat I had been wearing. The pistol was not there. A last possibility – I flung open the drawer of the nightstand – and opening the walnut box, there it lay, I saw the barrel gleaming faintly in the candlelight, I saw the glint of mother-of-pearl – and I lifted it to my lips, I pressed my lips to the cold grey metal; and then I ascertained that, yes, it was still primed and loaded with ball.

Little for it now but to wait, to wait and scheme. I dragged an armchair into the middle of the room, facing the door, and established myself with a blanket over my knees, and under the blanket the pistol. I had thrown off the effects of the brandy, I had dismissed for the present the figure of Martha Peake, wild-haired and maddened by betrayal as she strode down Rind's Wharf that day intending to kill Giles Hawkins, ay, and her father too, for what he had done to her, and England, for making him do it – to kill everything, in short, that twined about her ankles and kept her from the freedom that had seemed possible for herself and her child in America – no, my nerves were of steel now, and I possessed in addition the element of surprise. For whatever it was they planned for me – and I had begun to suspect that Drogo's researches were far from ended, and that a young body, quick with life, like my own, was a prize not to be passed up – whatever their plan, when they came for me they would not expect to find me alert and armed.

An hour passed, and I began to doze. Images rose in clusters in my mind, images of Martha, Martha dancing with her father in the garret in Cripplegate Street, Martha searching for her father in the horrid sinks and dens of the London docks, Martha taking ship for America . . . and I remembered then my mother talking about Martha Peake when I was a child, and her words at last came back to me, her story of the English girl who saved the Revolution –

It was then I heard the footsteps. I came awake with a start, every sense, every faculty trembling at the unmistakable sound of those same tramping footsteps I had heard some nights before. I brought the pistol out from under the blanket and cocked its hammer in my lap. On came the footsteps, yes, and stopped outside my door. I reached for the candle, which was almost burnt down, and with a silent breath I blew it out. In the darkness I turned the pistol toward the door.

Time then seemed to elongate, to stretch itself beyond its accustomed duration, a second an eternity as I anticipated the sound of the key catching in the lock. There it was. The key was turning. I lifted the pistol and pointed it at the middle of the door, at Drogo's black heart, ha! The key turned. The first creak of the hinges.

Another second, another eternity, but oh, the stealth of the intruder was no match for the cunning of the host within! In the blackness a thin bar of grey slid across the dusty floorboards as the door swung slowly open.

The pistol did not tremble, my grip was strong and unwavering, I held it straight before me in both hands. A few inches more, and then in the gloom of the half-opened door I had him in full view and I pulled the trigger, the pistol kicked up, I fired!

The night exploded with the discharge of the pistol! In the sudden smoky flare of light I saw the figure in the doorway stand for a moment as though stunned, and then crumple, his hand on his chest – he seemed almost to be bowing to me! – then his head fell forward, an arm was flung out, the hand groped for the doorframe and then slowly, slowly he fell forward into the room, white hair flapping about him as he went down. I was on my feet now, breathing fast, the sound of the gunshot still hammering in my ears, the room dark once more and thick with smoke and the acrid stink of burnt powder. Now my hand trembled, the pistol clattered to the floorboards, and from far off, from a distant passage, I heard the cry of an old man in distress.

I turned aside and was violently sick. I sank to my knees, clutching the arms of the chair, as I emptied my stomach of its foul contents, all swimming in brandy. I heaved, I retched, I gasped for air, as another and another convulsion racked my frame; and this is how they found me. I was not aware of the scurrying footsteps of my uncle and his servant, and I only turned when I heard William cry out with grief, and kneeling over my own stinking vomitus I turned to see the two old men, on their knees as I was, attending to the corpse of my enemy.

'It is over,' I muttered, spitting flecks and gobs of excreta from my lips.

My uncle stared at me, his face white and his eyes wide, and the ridiculous red nightcap askew on his wispy dome.

'You do not know what you have done,' he whispered.

'I have rid the world of a monster,' I said, and for an instant I felt a kind of peace in my soul. 'Drogo is no more.'

Silence in that trembling room, and then my uncle spoke.

'It is not Drogo you have murdered,' he said. 'He has been dead these fifteen years.'

I stared back at him, the peace of my soul dying like a shadow on water.

'It is Harry you have murdered,' he said. 'You have murdered Harry Peake.'

43

There is little left to tell. I did not murder Harry Peake, but I may as well have done. When the pistol kicked the shot went high, and tore a gouge in the panelling above the door. But Harry was old, and weakened by recurrent bouts of marsh fever, and he collapsed with the shock.

The morning after, as he lay gravely ill in his bed in the west wing, we sat in the kitchen, my uncle and I, drinking tea and talking about the past. Or rather, he talked, he told me how he had suffered this last half-century in the knowledge that it was he who had sent Martha to America, to her death; the circumstances of which he learned from Sara Rind, when the war was over. To her *death*, he moaned, and I the one who set it in train! You wonder why I would not speak of her time in America!

We were gentle with each other now, William and I. But you intended, I said, to save her from Harry.

Ay, the intention was good, he said; but the outcome was evil.

Was it evil, I murmured, for the republic –?

Damn the republic, that girl was worth a hundred republics!

Up came the old head, the rheumy eyes spat fire at me for a second or two; and then grew soft once more. Ambrose, Ambrose, he murmured, we will not quarrel any more. You also have produced an evil effect, which I know you did not intend.

He nodded. I nodded. No, we would not quarrel. We were the same. I asked him then what had happened to Harry after Martha took ship for Boston. Oh, we lured him in off the marsh, he said, we could not bear to listen to him any longer.

To listen to him?

To listen to his keening. That autumn they had heard him night after night, his heart and spirit broken, howling into the wind for his lost daughter. And nothing, said my uncle, nothing he had ever heard could express the sheer depths of misery and torment of that lonely howling in the night. But at last they succeeded in drawing him in, for Lord Drogo could not sleep, he barely touched food, so great was his own pain at the suffering of the poor wretch outside his walls. And what a pitiful sight he was, when once they had him in the house. They sat him in the kitchen, by the great fireplace, and he shivered and jabbered, his garments mere rags and so often soaked by the autumn rains that they would never dry; and his flesh all wasted off his great frame, which had preserved him only by virtue of its native constitutional strength.

At the mention of Harry's great frame I remembered my conviction that Lord Drogo had pursued him solely for the sake of his bones. I said this.

Ah no, said my uncle. He gazed at me sadly. Lord Drogo was no monster, he said. He did not care for glory, the applause of the world was nothing to him. No, he hated pain, and he gave his life to the mysteries of the human anatomy so that pain and sickness might be understood, and being understood, overcome. He wished only to bring Harry back to health, and allow him to resume writing the poetry that had made so strong an impression on his lordship when first he heard him in the Angel.

I pondered this. Lord Drogo as the benefactor of Harry Peake, as his *patron* – large structures were collapsing in my mind. And Harry allowed Lord Drogo to shelter him under his roof?

Harry was a sick man when we brought him in, said William. He had the marsh fever, it was raging in him, it would have killed any other man, and he was weak. Much of the time he did not understand where he was, nor what was happening to him. We put him to bed and we nursed him back to health. He was at Death's door; but Death would not let him in.

I was apprehensive of asking my uncle if I could visit Harry, but in the event I need not have been. Late that afternoon, as we sat together by the fire, Percy slipped in and whispered into my uncle's ear. I knew this concerned me, for William's eyes were upon me as Percy delivered his message.

'Percy has just come from Harry,' he said. 'He has asked if you will go to him.'

William accompanied me to the west wing. Our progress was slow, for he seemed to have aged another twenty years in the past twenty-four hours, and we paused several times on each staircase, and he clung to my arm as he shuffled along the dusty corridors of the old parts of the house. Much wheezing, and wherever a chair had been placed in a passage he would sit down for several minutes to gather his failing strength. At last we arrived at Harry's door. Percy had heard us coming, and now he opened the door and brought us in.

It was a large room with a southern exposure over the marsh, misty this day, the hills and woods indistinct in the far distance. I felt at once the warmth and comfort, intimacy even, peculiar to the room long occupied by this remarkable tenant, a man of simple tastes and bookish inclinations. There was a rug on the floor, a fire blazing in the wide hearth, a table beneath the window covered in papers, and one wall occupied by a massive glass-fronted bookcase. On the wall over the fireplace, and facing the bed, hung a portrait of a young woman who could only be Martha Peake, and painted by the same hand as 'The American Within'. All this I took in at a glance. My eye then came to rest on the great bed, piled high with bolsters, against which reclined the august figure of Harry Peake.

'Ambrose Tree,' he murmured, or lisped, rather, in the manner of old men who lack for teeth. 'Who taught you to fire a pistol?'

It took me a second to understand that this was a joke. Ah, he was benign!

'Come here by me,' he said.

There was a chair by the bed. I crossed the room and sat down, and Harry lifted a huge hand. I gave him my hand, and he grasped it, enclosed it, rather, swallowed it up in his own, and held it so firmly I did not believe he would ever let me go. He gazed at me for several moments before releasing me, and I held his eye. It was all there in his face, all I had seen in the portrait below, but faded and bloated by time, the starkness softened by a webbing of tiny lines, hatched and cross-hatched in the loose grey elephant skin that hung now from jowl and cheekbone and bagged about the mouth and beneath the chin. The great clefts were visible still in the gaunt structural joists of that massive face, but superimposed on every flap and wedge of baggy flesh the relentless crow's-foot markings of the years. The hair was white as snow now, pulled back from a peak high on his forehead and tied in a ponytail, and the large ears with their long droopy lobes flowered from the sides of his huge head, pale grey and translucent within. Oh, it was an atlas, Harry's face, and in it might be located every destination to which the human spirit ever travelled.

Thus did I regard him as I returned the gaze of those old dark eyes within which a flame yet burned, though weakly now. As for his spine, it was hidden in his heap of pillows, but in his posture, as he sat up in the bed, a bentness was evident, a stooping or hollowing of the frame. I told him at once and with some feeling how sorry I was to have shot my pistol at him.

He continued to gaze at me, a smile playing about his thin old lips, collapsed now upon their toothless gums. He waved away my apology with a majestic indifference.

'You have seen my Martha?' he whispered, indicating the painting.

I said I had.

'A strong likeness, do you think?'

My mouth hung open; I had been about to say I had never laid eyes on his daughter, she died before I was born, but I paused, I reflected that I *did* know her, had I not aroused her in my imagination and followed her from Cornwall to Cape Morrock, and been present at her death?

'A good likeness,' I said.

'Do you see her mother in her?'

'Indeed I do,' I said, and I did; wondering, which of us is the mad one here, him, to be asking this, or me to be answering?

'And do they still remember her?'

His wispy voice cracked a little as he said this. It had begun stronger, not strong as I imagined it when he strode about the taproom of a Cripplegate tavern and declaimed his ballad, but it lost more of that power with every succeeding question, and was now but a shadow of a whisper.

'She will not be forgotten,' I said, and I meant it. For his sake I would make her name live again as it had during the Revolution, for I could not tolerate the thought that all this suffering was for nothing.

'God bless,' whispered Harry, and sank back and closed his eyes. I found that he had taken my hand once more, and as he lay breathing deep with his eyes closed, his grip on me was as strong as it had been before. So I sat there, leaning forward, and the minutes passed. At last William silently approached the bed, extricated my fingers from Harry's grasp, and led me from the room.

In the hours after my visit Harry sank fast. Again I came to his bed, but he did not at first take my hand, nor did his eyes show the fire they had the day before, there was but an ember in them now, the faintest glow. When he spoke I could barely hear him, and I put my head close to his face.

Now his hand fell upon mine, and held it in a grip more steely even than before. I asked him to repeat what he had said, and he gasped it out with no small difficulty.

'We burn!'

'We burn?'

'We burn!'

And that was all.

44

The hours and days immediately after Harry's death are almost too painful for me to contemplate. What made my own remorse so intolerably poignant was observing the profound grief of both my uncle and his servant, Percy. They had loved the old poet dearly. For half-a-century they had sheltered him in Drogo Hall, far from the temptations of the London gin shops, and well beyond the reach of those of his countrymen who would taunt and abuse him for his physical deformity.

We buried him two days later. The minister had lived in the village for many years, and had known Lord Drogo well. He understood what his lordship had done for Harry, and he understood too, for William had explained it to him, the circumstances of Harry's death. I insisted of course on being a coffin bearer; and so, with nine strong men from the village, I helped carry him from the church to his final resting place, a grave he himself had selected, not far from the Vault of the Drogoes, and but a few feet from the tree beneath which he had committed his own great crime against Nature. I tossed earth on to the massive coffin, when it had been lowered into the ground, and made no attempt to stanch the flow of my tears. Nor was I alone in my grief, for when I looked up I saw that the old men gathered at the graveside, William, and Percy, and the minister, as well as several dozen men, women and children from the village, all were weeping as copiously as I was. During the long years of his seclusion in Drogo Hall Harry had been loved by all who knew him, and his gentle spirit was already missed.

After the funeral I returned to the house with my uncle. He had put it about that Harry Peake, after a short illness, had succumbed at last, in the weakness of age, to the marsh fever. Nor would Percy reveal the truth of the matter. The two old men continued deeply saddened by the tragedy, but in their sadness there was no anger directed toward me, nor even blame; they only wished that Harry had followed William's instruction, that he was not to show himself to me until Martha's story was at an end. I asked my uncle why he had given Harry this instruction, and he told me that if he were to answer that question he would have to tell me something of the years Harry had spent in Drogo Hall.

'Then tell me,' said I, 'for my presence is not required elsewhere.'

So my uncle began once more to talk, and although everything was changed now, it was as though this were a night like those which had preceded it, when we sat by the fire in his panelled study, the trolley clinking and clanking as Percy pushed it over to my uncle's elbow, and from the wall above the mantelpiece the proud features of Harry Peake gazed out across the wild windswept moors of his youth.

It was another picture of Harry Peake that William painted for me that night, and as he talked so did my own grief, and the remorse that came hard upon it, rise in waves within me, and I suffered the first and fiercest of the pangs that would harrow me in the months to come, indeed that harrow me to this very day. He described to me how they cleaned Harry up, Drogo and himself, how they burned his filthy rags of clothing, then bathed him, and shaved him, and cut his fingernails. They gave him new clothes, and hot food, and within a day he was already beginning to rally. Although his mind was still alienated, said my uncle, and he had no proper grasp of his own history or identity.

I was moved by this. The simple kindness of those two men, to a ragged lunatic in his last extremity – and Percy too, my uncle murmured, do not forget Percy, he it was who followed Harry in his mad wanderings, he who slowly won his trust and brought him in; Harry would doubtless have perished, but for Percy's vigilance. Percy's vigilance! – I was seeing my uncle's servant in a new light, as I was seeing everything in a new light. Oh, large structures were collapsing in my mind, but new structures were rising to take their place.

It was fortunate, said William, when we had refreshed ourselves, that Lord Drogo had recently started upon a course of study in the diseases of the mind, realizing, as no other anatomist of his day would do, that the mental faculty was in principle no different from the other faculties of the human integral, and no less subject to disorder; and that the investigation of such disorder was the royal road to an understanding of the structure and function of the mind.

He became a student of madness?

Among his many and various scientific pursuits, yes. And he undertook to effect a cure for Harry's madness, Harry's bodily ailments disappearing rapidly when he began to eat again, and had excreted the last of the gin that was in him. Lord Drogo believed that Harry's powers of mind were no less formidable than those of his body, and that they had only to be roused to their former vitality for the madness to dissipate like so much smoke in a closed room, after the windows are opened.

So he walked with Harry, and they talked, hour after hour they talked. After breakfast William would see them go off across the marsh together, and a strange sight they were too, Harry huge and bent, and still thin as a stick, Lord Drogo marching beside him, short and compact, and swinging a cane, each man in cloak and hat, two natural philosophers taking to the countryside. Only it was not natural philosophy they discussed, it was the wild imaginings of Harry's disordered mind, and these Lord Drogo listened to, and gently questioned, and day by day it became more apparent that Harry was recapturing his reason, which for so long had been fugitive.

I listened in rapt silence to these wonders.

In the fullness of time, said my uncle, Harry came to understand all that had transpired since the day he first walked away from Drogo Hall, and returned across the marsh to London with Lord Drogo's coin clinking in his pocket, and gave himself over to the gin. Oh, and the suffering he then endured! Harry Peake, said my uncle, had a large tumultuary heart, and his horror at his own actions knew no moderation. We had to watch him closely during this time, he said, for fear he would do harm to himself. Percy never slept, he was Harry's very shadow, for when Harry understood what he had done to his beloved Martha, how he had driven her from him with the violence of his suspicions, and then, at the last, attacked and ravished her in the graveyard – he wept like a child, he wept all one long night and all of the following day; and when his tears were dry he demanded the means to take ship for America, so that he could find Martha and make his peace with her; and he was cast into a deeper despair on learning that we were at war with the colonies, and that such a journey was impossible.

'Then I will join the king's army,' cried Harry, 'and once on American soil, I will desert the army and look for my lost girl.'

And he fully intended to do it.

But it was not to be. Lord Drogo persuaded Harry to wait until the hostilities had come to an end, which it was thought at the time would be a matter of months only, the Americans being regarded as poor soldiers, lacking in organization, money, materials of war, courage adequate to their purpose, and the will to persevere. Drogo was of course wrong in his estimate of the colonists' determination to be free, but he was not alone in this; and by the time they understood their mistake, said William, it was already too late, for news had come of Martha's death, and Harry sank into a more bleak despair than any they had yet seen.

Again I was seized up by my uncle's narrative, and again I had to be patient to know more; for soon after midnight he announced that the events of the past forty-eight hours had exhausted him, and he could talk no more. I did not protest, I made no attempt to detain him, I saw clearly the exhaustion in his pale drawn features; and having shaken his little bell, he went off to bed with the faithful Percy Clyte – whom I had so maligned in my imagination! – leaving me once more to pace the floor and ponder all he had told me.

The years passed, he said, when next we met, and Harry, having once more, and this time successfully, renounced all desire for strong drink, regained his full former powers of mind. He and Lord Drogo became boon companions, and until his lordship's death they would meet each evening for dinner and talk late into the night about their work; Lord Drogo being by this time well-embarked upon his researches into the diseases of the mind, while Harry had resumed his 'Ballad of Joseph Tresilian'. Martha's death was no longer for Harry the source of such acute distress as once it had been, the pain having mellowed, rather, to a gentle sorrow which never left him, and which aroused in all who met him sentiments of pity and affection.

He spoke often and wistfully of the son he had never met, but by this time he had become so rooted in Drogo Hall that he would never attempt the journey to the United States; unsure, also, of the reception he could expect from Harry Rind Peake, should he be able to find him.

Harry Rind Peake. As I run my eye over these pages today I am aware there is much to tell about that American original; but this is not the place, nor I the one to tell it. For I know nothing of Harry Rind Peake, and I prefer to know nothing; I would have him, rather, as I imagine him, bearing old Harry's spine. I never spoke to my uncle of my conviction that little Harry's spine was bent, nor of the joy I imagined Martha taking in this sign of a connection between the father she had left behind in England, and the son she had borne him in America; and certainly, I have no proof of it, no evidence with which to support my conviction. But I have something of far greater value. I have imagination. I have poetic intuition. I have the weight of symbolic necessity bearing down upon me. All of which tells me that Harry Peake's great back, the mark both of his shame and of his glory, was indeed copied in the body of his son. And to think of that giant constitution, in all its magnificent imperfection, being replicated in the new America – now that is sublimity incarnate.

So Harry Rind Peake is another story, and one day I might tell it, if I am strong enough, which I doubt.

And so we fetched up at my own arrival in Drogo Hall, a mere fortnight earlier, that fortnight seeming now an age. Harry by this time was an old man, of course – they were all old men – and contented himself sitting on a bench in the village and talking to whoever had the time to pass an idle hour with him. He had a particular fondness for children, and they seemed strangely drawn to the big humped wreckage who sat in the shade of an ancient oak, leaning on his stick, now and then producing from a pocket of his capacious coat an apple fresh picked in the orchards of Drogo Hall.

Into this placid household I had come, then, summoned by my uncle, who wished to introduce me to Harry, first, he said, by way of telling me the man's history, so that when he, William, died – and he knew, he said, that his time was drawing near – I would sustain the old poet in Drogo Hall, and not permit him to be disturbed in the westering of his days.

And so he had embarked upon the narrative; and I had questioned it, and doubted it, and reached my own wild conclusions about it; and Harry, aware of my presence in the house, and of my conversations each night with my uncle, had waited in an agony of impatience until the story was told, and he could meet this young man who was responding with such passionate sympathy to the events of his own early life, and to the later adventures of his daughter.

But alas, said William, poor Harry could not wait. He wanted to visit you at night, and tell you his own account of the story, which he did not trust me to narrate, for I had witnessed so little of it at first-hand. He followed you down to the cellars when you went in search of his bones. You did indeed faint, dear boy; and it was in the arms of Harry Peake that you were carried back to your chamber that night, and set down with infinite tenderness upon your bed.

At this I could restrain myself no longer, and burst forth in a flood of hot tears, the idea that Harry himself had lifted me like a child in his strong arms and carried me up from the cellars, and brought me safe to my own bed – it was too much for me, and I wept freely for some minutes. When I was finished I lifted my head and saw my uncle gazing at me in the firelight, his sad old eyes gleaming with a compassionate understanding, and at last I was able to tell him what I had intended to, the night I waited for Drogo to come to my room. I told him I loved him.

He nodded for some moments, he sighed, he reached for his little bell.

'It is over, Ambrose,' he said, 'and I am deathly tired.'

45

My uncle was almost done. He was exhausted, exhausted by the story he had told me, exhausted by the tragedy of Harry Peake's death, exhausted by life itself; and if, when first I came to Drogo Hall it appeared that he was not long for this world, he was closer than ever now to his end. I saw him reach for his bell, but I stayed his hand, and begged him to answer one question. Then I would never ask him to talk of these things again.

His old eyes rested briefly on me. He was too weak now to do anything but acquiesce, he did not have it in him to struggle with me any more. Very well, he said; and so I asked him, did it come out as Silas Rind predicted it would, did Martha Peake, through her legend, indeed save the Revolution?

The old man cocked his head to one side, he pursed his lips and expelled air, he gave a little shrug. It was late, a storm was blowing up out on the marsh, and gusts of wind came sweeping down the chimney and fanned the fire into brief surges of flame. Did she save the Revolution? Could any one person be said to have saved the Revolution? Another shrug. But by 1777, he said, the war was going badly for the Americans. The Year of the Gibbet, they called it – too many defeats, too many hangings, too much death. They were realizing the immensity of their presumption in challenging the armies of the British Empire, and many were losing faith, and drifting away, and those voices calling for a reconciliation with the crown were growing louder.

But I will tell you this, he said. In the years of struggle that followed Martha's death, as Washington led his ragged army the length of the island of Manhattan, and into New Jersey, and on into Pennsylvania, many of them without boots, without blankets, without anything but loyalty to their leader and faith in the cause, there were two items in every patriot soldier's pack that did more to keep him alive and marching than any pair of boots.

And what two items were those?

The first, said William, would be a dog-eared copy of *Common Sense*, which the soldiers read to one another over their campfires each night, many indeed having committed long passages to memory. And when their spirits faltered, when they lost the will to go on, even as they suffered through that bitterly cruel winter at Valley Forge, it was Tom Paine who kept alive their determination to drive the British from their shores and never again live under the dead hand of tyranny.

And the second item?

Ah, the second.

The old man smiled a soft sad smile I had never seen on his withered lips before. That would be a much-folded piece of paper, perhaps tucked into the pages of Mr Paine's pamphlet, an engraving which depicted Martha Peake on the wharf in New Morrock that famous day. For if *Common Sense* spoke to their minds, Martha spoke to their hearts. She came to represent for every patriot soldier the unspoken promise he had made to his country. Seeing her standing at the end of the wharf, a musket at her shoulder, as the hated redcoats fired on her, they felt the courage rise in them, they felt the compulsion to honour the sacrifice she had made. And in all the campaigns to come, no man ever forgot what Martha Peake had done for her country, nor did he forget his resolve to do no less. So of all the heroines of the Revolution – and to my astonishment my uncle seemed to know the story of every single one – Molly Pitcher, and Dicey Langston, Deborah Sampson and Experience Bozarth, and of course the cunning Mrs Murray of New York – in all this pantheon of heroic women, Martha Peake's fame burned the brightest.

Or so, at any rate – and here my uncle turned to me with a sly grin – I have been told.

A brief cackle, and then he fell silent. Somewhere in the house a shutter slammed against a wall, and a great gust of rain was flung at the window. His eyes closed, his breathing became slow and laboured. I allowed him a minute to compose himself. At last he opened his eyes, and his trembling fingers once more reached for his little bell.

46

Ah, but time ruins everything. All this was written long ago, and my memories of the strange few days I spent here with my uncle William have begun to fade and decay. The sense of a flowing continuum is lost, certain incidents emerge like mountain peaks to dominate the prospect, while others sink into glades of forgetfulness, and end their days in a dismal swamp of oblivion. I am the master of Drogo Hall now, and as I look back over the pages I wrote during those fraught days which culminated in Harry Peake's death I wonder that I am still sane. For at times, now, I glimpse a past that is no more than a catalogue of sacrifice and abomination and heroism and resolve and victory, and sunk in shadow are the lies and muddles and myriad random workings of chance in the thing, and to bring it all together in one coherent whole – why, the human mind is not up to it! And I am convinced that history can unhinge the brain, that a man might be *driven mad* by history –!

No, it is an effort to remember what actually happened, and I must struggle with the inclinations of my own heart lest I forget the truth. What is the truth? The truth is, that in death Martha Peake grew to a stature she never knew in life. The truth is, that the impact she had on her country of adoption, the America to which she came in the very birth pangs of its nationhood – that impact cannot be measured. But it could be argued that with her sacrifice Martha Peake *did* save the Revolution, and with it the republic.

I choose to believe it; and I revere her memory accordingly. Indeed, I have made her chamber my own, and often sit, as she once sat, in the deep window alcove, and gaze out over the marsh to the domes and steeples of the great toad smoking and stinking in the distance, I mean London. I watch the sun go down, I watch darkness fall, the lamps are lit, old Percy, faithful Percy, *eternal* Percy comes in with my tray and my medicines, and I sit at my table with my back to the fire and spread out my books and papers before me. The hours drift by, and close to dawn I retire to bed, and lie where Martha lay, beneath the high carved headboard where snakes and lizards and other strange creatures sport amid a vegetation that never flourished in English soil.

But before I slip into a restless doze, which is all I know of sleep these days, I gaze at the painting of Martha which hung once on her father's wall, and now is mine. And I see again those proud features, executed in the manner of a northern master, with *terra rossa* for the half-tones, and the underpainting in white lead – and her hair, of course, her glorious red hair – and I imagine her in this very room, her heart in a tumult of dread, and grief, and rage, and determination, as she prepares to take ship for America, and there meet her destiny.

It is all I have left of her. And so I haunt the chambers and passages of Drogo Hall, counting the days until I can sink into darkness with the others. And if Harry's spirit still wanders the Lambeth Marsh, as I believe it does, for I hear him at times when the wind is up, and the rain hammers at the windows, and the wild dogs howl – then I know that Martha rises from the Old Burying Ground, and ascends the great headlands of the cape, whence her spirit flies out to him across the North Atlantic, and they are, at last, and for ever, as one – ha!